D0629612

LUI
A View of Him

FWinterhalter

LUI

A VIEW OF HIM

BY

LOUISE COLET

TRANSLATED BY

MARILYN GADDIS ROSE

THE UNIVERSITY OF GEORGIA PRESS

ATHENS AND LONDON

Athens, Georgia 30602

Set in Linotron Bodoni Book
The paper in this book meets the guidelines for permanence and durability of the Committee on Production Guidelines for Book Longevity of the Council on Library Resources.

Printed in the United States of America

90 89 88 87 86 5 4 3 2 1

Library of Congress Cataloging in Publication Data

Colet, Louise, 1810–1876.
Lui, a view of him.

Translation of: Lui, roman contemporain.
Bibliography: p.
I. Title.
PQ2209.C6L813 1986 843′.7 86-1381
ISBN 0-8203-0859-5 (alk. paper)

The frontispiece is Winterhalter's sketch of Louise Colet, from the Musée de Versailles,

FOREWORD

ALBERT DE LINCEL, the "hero" in this novel, presumably falls in love with the heroine Stéphanie de Rostan. Yet after he has poured out his heart to her, entrusting her with his deepest secrets, he remarks, "You know, Marquise, it's a pity you don't have a slightly darker complexion and a slightly thinner figure. If you did, you could have put on men's clothing—which would have helped with the illusion—and we would have stayed the best of friends for life." Was Stéphanie left speechless? We don't know, for the remark ends the chapter. But what a strange thing to say to a woman you love! a woman whose luxuriant blond beauty should be a source of satisfaction—even if you are both in the early years of middle age.

In the novel this remark is a cue that Stéphanie may be romanticizing Albert's attraction to her. When she remembers a similarly curious remark by Léonce, the lover Albert expects to dislodge, her recollections are more consistent with the characterization. After she writes Léonce that Albert seems to be intent upon conquest, her lover replies that he would not stand in the way of such a great man. She is censorious: "What is the point of writing something like that to the woman you love?" As readers we could interpret these parallel instances of insensitivity as structural irony. We realize that Stéphanie can see Léonce for what he is but has chosen to have a blind spot for Albert.

But we should see in Albert's tactless remark more than structural irony. It is a cue that *Lui* is a novel based on identifiable persons and events. Louise Colet is an honest reporter, almost as thorough as her information permits, and she repeats even remarks which present her in a bad light. Albert is the Romantic poet and dramatist Alfred de Musset, and Stéphanie is Colet herself, a prolific professional writer, now remembered chiefly as the best-known mistress of Realist novelist Gustave Flaubert. With a slightly darker complexion and slightly thinner figure, Colet would have resembled the Romantic novelist George Sand (called Antonia Back), the most famous love of Musset's life. Léonce (no surname given) is Flaubert.

Colet was in fact a woman whose acclaim as a writer lasted only as long as her looks. Her beauty was overwhelming. Unfortunately, her talents as a creative writer were no match for her ambition. As a journalist, she was inspired with deeply felt and movingly expressed sympathies. She became a fearless champion of the oppressed, especially oppressed women. In life the men she loved did not show her the deference she considered her due. They were not notably subtle about being interested chiefly in her sensuous body and sensual temperament or—worse—her high-placed connections. The more she insisted on respect and reciprocal privileges, the more she exasperated these men. The double standard was entrenched, and, unlike George Sand, Colet did not have a genius to force an exception in her case. Hippolyte Colet, the man she married to escape her provincial environment, was a temperamental musician and confirmed womanizer. The eminent Eclectic philosopher Victor Cousin, the man she could have married once she was widowed, probably proposed to her at a time when she did not love him. Flaubert was not a man to marry anyone, certainly not a woman twelve years older whom he could use without marriage.

In retrospect, Albert's remark seems to typify her life: she was cast as second best, second choice, a woman to conquer and discard. Posterity should note that she was never subdued. She continually agitated for a better role. If she played the parts she got with poise and pluck, she was an unwilling understudy. She always wanted the lead, for she was confident that she had star quality. And she was probably right.

Colet was born Louise Révoil, at Aix on August 15, 1810. Her family was not unlike Stéphanie's, partly noble, partly bourgeois. (Indeed, through her sister who married into another branch, the family has remained prominent into recent years.) They were respectable, freethinking, and outwardly conventional.

The first setting for her dazzling beauty and derivative poems was Nîmes. On December 5, 1834, she married Hippolyte Colet, an Uzès native who had already escaped the stifling provincial milieu through his musical talent. Once he was named violin professor at the National Conservatory, he became a good catch, and at twenty-four Louise could not keep looking. They moved to Paris by the end of their first month of marriage.

With presence and aplomb she began making calls to place her poems. There is no doubt that her regal beauty and expressive voice helped. In 1836, her collection *Les Fleurs du Midi* brought her the lifelong friendship of the poet and songwriter Béranger, then a household word. Somehow, possibly through the offices of Marie d'Orléans, Louis-Philippe's daughter, she went on the government pension rolls in July 1837. She was on the rolls the rest of her life, although her actual income fluctuated with the changes of government, since she was never willing to make her published opinions kowtow to those of the current regime. When Marie died on January 6, 1839, the Académie Française set as the topic for its annual poetry prize the inauguration of the Musée de Versailles where Marie's statue of Jeanne d'Arc was the central display. This was an inspiring coincidence for Colet. Her poem on Jeanne d'Arc won. (It was dedicated to the now forgotten Népomucène Lemercier whose work marks a transition between

Neoclassicism and Romanticism.) The fifth woman medallist since the prize had been established in 1671, Colet stunned the crowd. She also stunned Victor Cousin, a leading intellectual light (and accomplished Don Juan), soon to become minister of public instruction. By December he was known to be her protector. She assiduously refused entreaties to use her influence with him, and she was so proud that he had to be covert to provide any support at all. (He did promptly have Hippolyte's salary raised.) But he held many strings and always pulled them for her. In June 1840, when a scandal sheet printed that Cousin was the cause of her pregnancy, her husband inserted denials in other papers, Cousin waited for the noise to subside, and Colet attacked the editor with a kitchen knife. This incident set the pattern her life would follow: her pugnaciousness and independence vis-à-vis the pusillanimity and surreptitiousness of the men in her life.

Head held high, she was proud of her daughter Henriette. Cousin accepted the paternity and provided for the child's support, although gossips were torn between attributing Henriette to Cousin and slandering Louise for adultery and attributing the child to Hippolyte and slandering the Colets for conniving fraud.

Writing remained her first priority. In 1843, she won the Académie Française prize for "La Monument de Molière," even though she was to grieve over the death of her infant son shortly thereafter. In 1844, she won George Sand's compliments on her translations from Italian and rebuffs of her efforts to have Sand for a friend.

On July 29, 1846, she met Flaubert in the studio of the popular Academy sculptor James Pradier, noted for his smooth pseudo-Greek creations. She was nearly thirty-six; Flaubert was twenty-four. The first phase of their liaison lasted until March 1848. During this period she was the established writer; he was the suppliant. The liaison came to a close when she became pregnant, by neither Flaubert nor Hippolyte, it would appear. The infant boy died shortly after birth in mid-June. The Colets soon separated.

She had to support herself and Henriette. One of her attempts to make money was disastrous. She had been the confidante of the famous beauty and hostess Madame de Récamier. After her death in 1849, Colet began publishing de Récamier's letters to novelist Benjamin Constant. She and *La Presse* editor Emile de Girardin were sued to stop publication. Although Colet was cleared of fraudulent possession, she had to stand damages. To add to the strains of her life, her husband returned because he was dying from tuberculosis and had nowhere else to go. He was right to rely on her sense of duty: she nursed him beyond the extent of her resources of money and energy. He died on April 21, 1851.

That summer Flaubert came back into her life. In the intervening three years he had lost his youthful good looks and had become more fanatical about his craft. He did not need Colet's efforts on his behalf, but he was pleased to have her bestir herself for his close friend Louis Bouilhet. The two men helped her revise and edit, and that service would comprise the sole "benefit" she received in exchange for her passionate love, psychic energy, and unstinting generosity. Thoroughly preoccupied with the composition of *Madame Bovary*, he felt no need to have amorous interludes very often. But he profited very directly from her letters and her presence. The reader of *Lui* never glimpses Léonce. Like Flaubert at Croisset, he is at his provincial home working on a novel. Nor does the reader receive details of Léonce's novel, but we know that Flaubert was working on *Madame Bovary*, a novel which exploits Colet as raw material.

Fortunately, Colet's writing was still remunerative and, thanks to the editing, better in quality. In 1852, the year of her friendship with Musset, she received the Académie Française prize for "La

Colonie de Mettray," on August 19, 1852. She dedicated the poem to Victor Hugo, then in exile. On August 24, 1854, she won the Académie Française prize for "L'Acropole d'Athènes," dedicated to Alfred de Vigny, Musset's and Hugo's closest rival in the Romantic pantheon.

This was the year when she turned down a trust fund from Cousin for their daughter and became intimately linked with Vigny. She was quite possibly driven to both imprudent expedients by her desperate desire to marry Flaubert. He and his friends considered the very notion absurd and presumptuous. Possibly, she could have kept him somewhat longer as a lover, but that would have meant accepting his categorization of her as a mere "habitude" (the French term for the female in a sexual routine). That was a sacrifice in self-respect she would not stoop to. Her subsequent behavior shows that she felt she had nothing more to lose. She put unflattering portraits of both Flaubert and Bouilhet in *Une Histoire de Soldat* (1856). When she read *Madame Bovary* the following year, she was horrified to see Emma give her lover Rodolphe a seal inscribed "Amor nel cor." Colet knew the motto came from the agate seal on the cigar holder she had given Flaubert. She published a poem "Amor nel cor" in *Le Monde Illustré* (January 27, 1859):

> C'était pour lui, pour lui qu'elle aimait comme un Dieu!
> Pour lui, dur au malheur, grossier envers la femme.
> Hélàs! elle était pauvre, elle donnait bien peu,
> Mais tout don est sacré quand il renferme une âme.
>
> Eh bien! dans un roman de commis voyageur
> Qui comme un air malsain nous soulève le coeur,
> Il a raillé ce don en une phrase plate,
> Mais il garde pourtant le beau cachet d'agate.

[It was for him, the him she loved like God!
For him, to women crude, to hardship rude.
Alas, the buyer was poor, her gift was small,
But any gift is dear, when it means all.

And now in prose intended for vulgar appeal
Which makes us heave and retch like a foul stench,
He ridiculed this gift with common lines,
However, he kept, let's note, the agate seal.]

In 1859 she decided to go to Italy where she was to be based for roughly nine years. In the first place, the political ferment of the risorgimento aroused her liberal-socialist enthusiasm for revolutionary causes. Further, respiratory problems made a warm climate seem desirable. A foreign correspondent, she interviewed leaders of the risorgimento. She toured the places she had described in *Lui*. She was nearly stoned in Ischia when local priests claimed her freethinking had brought cholera to Naples. In 1869, she covered the opening of the Suez Canal and went on to Istanbul. By this time her indignation at her own lack of freedom had become focused on the lot of women far more oppressed. When the Franco-Prussian War broke out, she made her way back to France via Budapest and Vienna. Although increasingly ill, she was shocked by the defeatism in some members of her former circles and was determined to rouse her compatriots. Her packed lectures to women audiences in the Faculty of Sciences auditorium in Marseilles were her last triumph, even though she later took to the barricades for the Commune uprising following the French defeat. The bronchitis she contracted soon after eventually catalyzed a series of illnesses that were ultimately fatal. She was never to be well again, nor even more than minimally comfortable. But she wrote and agitated tirelessly. Her bronchitis became chronic; she suffered anthrax, requiring surgery. After trying the climate at San Remo, she came back to Paris, where she died on March 9, 1876, after an attack of paralysis. Despite her last wishes, her daughter, by then married comfortably, gave her a religious interment.

Colet's life, like her novel, ended unhappily. Instead of being appreciated and comforted, she was obscure in her profession and alone in her pain. She was subject to slander even in death. But it was the life she chose by her principles as she saw them, and in the final analysis it was a courageous life.

OSTENSIBLY, *Lui: A View of Him* is just a fictionalized account of Colet's friendship with Musset in 1852. However, in hopes of being a lover instead of a friend, Albert de Lincel (Musset) tells Stéphanie de Rostan (Colet) the story of his liaison with Antonia Back (George Sand) which lasted from June 1833 to March 1835. He dwells especially on their stay in Venice from December 1833 to March 1834 when his physician Tiberio Piacentini (Pietro Pagello) became his rival. It was this interpolated narrative, roughly the inner half of the novel, which brought *Lui* its first readers. After Sand's *Elle et Lui* ("She and He") and Musset's brother Paul's *Lui et Elle* ("He and She"), readers went to Colet's novel for another fictionalized version of the liaison. "Lui" ("he" or "him") presumably referred to Musset.

Yet Albert's account, while intriguing in itself, is secondhand, and no more interesting than the firsthand frame narrative. This frame is the friendship itself, which Albert wants to change to a love affair, or even marriage. Stéphanie, however, is desperately in love with Léonce, the "lui" she loves, the "lui" who neglects her. Since this "lui," uppermost in Stéphanie's thoughts, is Léonce (Flaubert), readers in the subsequent 125 or so years have presumed that the title really referred to him. Actually, this French pronoun which can be emphatic subject, indirect object, or object of a preposition, refers to more than Musset and Flaubert. It makes a collective reference as well because the two narratives as a whole compose an implicit plot: the trials of being a professional woman writer in the man's world of mid-nineteenth-century France.

There are many men referred to in this novel, from those openly named like Hugo, Manzoni, and Byron, to those renamed like Duchemin, Delmart, and De Germiny (Villemain, Deschamps, Vigny, respectively). Some men are helpful; others try to help themselves. On the former a woman is dependent; from the latter she must be defended. "Lui" as a title thus becomes an umbrella pronoun covering the men who may not always thwart a woman's career fulfillment but must always be dealt with from a position of weakness. In short, *Lui* gives us a panorama of the French male intellectual; it is *A View of Him*.

Colet's friendship with Musset, which began sometime between his election to the Académie Française on February 12, 1852, and his reception there on May 27, was tumultuous, with both its tender and trying moments. Friendship or affair, it was short-lived. It was over perhaps by late August 1852 when Colet won the Académie's annual poetry contest for the fourth time; it was certainly over by November. The following year she published "La Servante" where she depicted a drunken lecherous poet whom many identified as Musset. If we are to believe the testimony of this novel, Musset might have been prepared to propose marriage at some point during their friendship. However, even by the logic of this testimony, the relationship could never have become an affair, much less a marriage, because Musset had been seeking a substitute for Sand since 1835, while Colet was still in love with Flaubert. Stéphanie, who is telling her story to Colet the novelist, concludes that after Albert died and Léonce left, she realized that she loved Albert dearly. However, it is clear during the novel that Stéphanie literally could not have stomached being Albert's mistress or wife, and it is equally clear that it was more the woman than the woman of letters who interested him.

Colet's novel, which went through three editions, is a far fuller account of the Musset-Sand liaison than Musset's *La Confession d'un enfant du siècle* ("Confession of a Child of the Century," 1836) or the narratives by Sand and Musset's brother Paul. While *Lui* purports to present Musset's side, it demonstrates a different picture than he intended. As Albert, he appears childish and irresponsible, irremediably faithless, trying the patience of Antonia who is a hardworking writer, self-sacrificing companion, and assiduous housekeeper. Not until both have returned to Paris does her behavior seem as egocentric and manipulative as his. Yet he believes his story will assure Stéphanie's surrender.

She would, however, be unlikely to surrender on the basis of such a narrative, for Antonia's ordeals—trying to meet deadlines, make ends meet, and look after a twenty-three year-old addicted to wasting time in dissipation—counterpoint her own. Stéphanie is a literary translator, a widow in straitened circumstances with a seven-year-old son to support and a debilitating estate suit to pursue. She must endure the hardship of enforced thrift and the neglect of an egocentric lover, a novelist who is married to his work and uses her, so we infer, as erotic relaxation every two months or so. It is not known whether Musset knew about Flaubert in 1852; Albert does not take Léonce's presence seriously, whether actual or eventual. When coincidences force Stéphanie into a choice between these two men, it is, she intimates, the wrong choice.

Today, we are far more aware of sexual roles and power plays, and hence unlikely to see here even a hypothetical possibility for right choices, if "right choices" mean "happy endings." Not only are the egos too strong and too ill-matched even to be complementary, but the main characters also have conflicting career goals and, above all, conflicting work habits. Albert works and plays by whim; Antonia puts herself on a strenuous regime. Stéphanie works on a schedule that accommodates Léonce; Léonce simply works, oblivious and indifferent to any sacrifice her accommodation might entail.

A wealth of subsequent biographical scholarship corroborates the characterizations here. There is no doubt that Colet's romanticized reporting gave this novel its initial public. Unfortunately for the fate of the novel and Colet's own reputation that was an initial advantage only. By the turn of the century, if not sooner, being known as a fictionalized novel-length feature story worked to the disadvantage of *Lui*.

As Flaubert's stature has grown in world literature, readers have tended to view Colet in terms of her passing usefulness to him and seem to have been indignant that she was not grateful for the role he gave her. After all, through his letters to her we see him working his way through *Madame Bovary*. It is understandable that scholars have often found *Lui* exasperating, for although it in no way damages Flaubert's reputation as a writer, it does show him to be unfeeling in a personal relationship. While the development of women's studies as an academic discipline has tended to revive Sand's work, both she and Musset have stayed at a relatively fixed place in the nineteenth-century French pantheon. That is, they are major figures in the canon, romantic figures in legend, but really seldom read firsthand outside French studies. Thus, the interest *Lui* aroused as a fictionalized feature story was soon eclipsed. Worse yet, the veneration justly accorded Flaubert as a master novelist has caused *Lui*, once classed as titillating gossip, to be classified as gratuitous and vicious and to be judged—not read—accordingly.

This extra-literary judgment has discouraged most readers, all of whom would be readers of French, most of whom would be scholars, and few of whom would have read *Lui* for a literary experience. (And since the novel has never been translated into English, there have been few other audiences possible.) Rather, such readers as the book has had have perused it in order to be thorough in their research: to discover another dimension to Flaubert, Musset, or Sand; perhaps to find an insight on a lesser prototype like Chopin, Liszt, Sainte-Beuve. From Flaubert scholarship, such readers might have hoped to catch a glimpse also of Béranger, Cousin, or Vigny. Such readers have expected biased reporting and uneven writing. They have skimmed the novel with note cards in hand, as if going through microfilm of old newspapers.

Although Colet herself has a large share of responsibility for this chain of events, we are now far enough removed from 1859 to read *Lui* for what it is: a credible and skillful counterpointing of the personal and professional dilemmas of two women of letters in the mid-nineteenth century. Stéphanie is basically conventional in outward behavior; setting a suitable moral example for her son is always her first priority. Antonia chooses to make her work her first priority, and the only time Stéphanie overtly criticizes her is when she witnesses Antonia setting a demoralizing example for her children. Neither woman, however, compromises herself for career advancement. *Lui,* in short, documents alternatives for literary career women and would do so even if there were no real-life prototypes.

We have seen that Colet dedicated her prize-winning poems to the exemplars of whatever type of Romanticism was most in vogue. If she had chosen to use the Romantic novelette as did Musset, Sand, and Musset's brother, she would have given her targets and critics far less cause to deplore her sensationalism and tastelessness. (Sand wrote Flaubert that the novel was a "chamber-pot excretion.") Nor would she have earned the exasperation of subsequent Flaubert admirers. Yet in the long run she would have given us only another, and possibly inferior, variation of these Romantic novelettes. By using the rhetoric of a Realist confession she could be complete, even exhaustive and detailed, in the Realist manner. Moreover, she could be herself, relying on firsthand experience, notes, aides-mémoire, and copies of letters she had written to Flaubert during her Musset interlude. As herself, she could be sincerely committed to both her explicit and implicit subjects: her friendship with Musset and the trials of being a professional woman writer. The off-stage choice Stéphanie makes between Albert and Léonce and her subsequent choice to live alone with her child are not unlike the choices Colet herself had to make (and not dissimilar to some of Sand's choices).

In short, life gave Colet both the material and structure of a Realist novel. Her life and loves were sufficiently similar to Sand's to set up a concentric counterpoint. Within the frame of Parisian restraint which often constrains the aristocratic widow Stéphanie, who is at heart more emancipated than she lets herself behave, we have the heady contrast of decaying Venice which is such a temptation to Albert and Antonia. In Venice their liaison is further contrasted by three other extramarital relationships: the Venetian diva and her playboy who plan to marry when no elderly relatives are alive to object; the Venetian ballerina and her long-suffering nobleman lover; and the Moroccan prostitute and her pimp. The overall effect of these couplings is to make us admire Stéphanie for deciding in the end to live austerely, devoting her moral and emotional energy solely to her son. Like the dramatis personae in a gothic novel, there are dark and light heroes, brunette Léonce and blond Alfred; dark and light heroines, brunette Antonia and blond Stéphanie. But as Stéphanie the narrator assures Colet the recorder, this is not fiction meant for a book; at least it is not Romantic fiction. The dark hero does not marry the blond heroine; nor does the blond hero marry either the brunette or blond heroine. Instead in cruel jest he says it is a pity the blond is not more like the brunette.

We may well wonder why Colet did not give Stéphanie a better role, since a novelist is only bound by the kind of credibility he or she establishes. Colet clearly felt bound to be as accurate as possible short of libel. There is very little in *Lui* which she invented completely.

She emended the account only by flattering improvements, "poetizations" as she puts it. In the embedded Sand-Musset romance, she makes all members of the Venetian triangle (Sand, Musset, Pagello) more honorable, consistent, and attractive. She closes the liaison after its second phase when Sand brings Musset her hair in a skull; in real life this was an effective ploy for another reconciliation. In the frame romance, the alterations serve the plot. For example, Stéphanie has a son (not a daughter) who can take initiatives that would be unseemly for his mother. Léonce is said to be robust and handsome, a fit object for Stéphanie's love, but by 1852 Flaubert had lost both his looks and health. Twice Albert picks up Stéphanie and runs, demonstrating his rage and impetuousness, but Colet herself was too Junoesque for Musset to have carried her.

Wherever in the novel it seems likely a reader would want to know whether the episode "really happened," I have footnoted the "facts." I have footnoted also character prototypes when they first appear in the novel. Some, however, I will mention here to indicate the spectrum of 19th-century French intellectuals who make an appearance in *Lui*. Although history has now reduced most of them to footnotes, at the time of the novel they were celebrities and well-known socialites.

Sometimes two persons appear in one character. For example, the German pianist Hess is both Liszt, a Hungarian, and Chopin, a

Pole. Stéphanie's devoted René Delmart is both Emile and Anthony Duchamps, distinguished Romantic translators; given his steadfast loyalty, Delmart probably also incorporates a bit of her protector Victor Cousin and her staunchest friend Béranger, the Romantic songwriter.

Usually Colet simply changes or omits a name. In the first category, the fictitious names have a sound similar to that of the real name. For example, Duchemin is François Villemain, Académie Française secretary, who presided at Colet's poetry award ceremonies. Albert's closest friend is Albert Nattier, in real life, playboy Alfred Tattet. Albert de Germiny is Alfred de Vigny and is identified as a "philosophical poet" for a further clue. Béranger figures also as a separate character Duverger, and Cousin is curiously absent altogether, although he had essayed a reconciliation during the year of the frame narrative. Critic Sainte-Beuve appears as Sainte-Rive. Albert's and Antonia's publisher Frémont is Sand's and Musset's François Buloz, editor of *La Revue des Deux Mondes*. The prototypes with omitted names can be identified by their contextual description, e.g., the "prince" is the Duke of Orléans, son of King Louis-Philippe; the "old marquise" is Madame de Récamier; Prince and Princess X are Emilio and Christina Belgiojoso, Italian revolutionaries living in France; Countess G. is Countess Guiccioli, Byron's beloved and a sometime mistress of Hippolyte Colet.

Even peripheral events may be alluded to, e.g., Stéphanie's lawsuit echoes Colet's against Récamier's heirs. Colet follows the chronology of her Musset friendship quite closely. We can tell that it occurs during the second phase of her liaison with Flaubert, from June 27, 1851, to June or July 1854. (Flaubert's last letter, dated March 6, 1855, informs her that he will never be in when she calls.) Finally, it can be assumed that she records accurately her passion and anxiety about Flaubert, her ambivalence toward Musset, her disappointment in not becoming a friend of Sand. Falling in love with Flaubert in summer 1846 was as fatal for her as falling in love with Sand had been for Musset. After the fact, it can be asserted that she was bound to sympathize with Musset since his love affair, as she records and interprets it, paralleled her own. Together, however, each longed for someone else.

Translator's Note

IT SHOULD BE REMEMBERED that translating *Lui* this long after its publication inevitably means that the translator, too, originally went to it for research purposes. I did. Allusions in Flaubert scholarship had prepared me for a sloppily written exposé. My first lesson, taught me by the task of translating, was to learn to respect the text—to read it directly and not through critics.

By twentieth-century standards it is candid but discreet. Further, while no *Madame Bovary* in stylistic and substantive richness (and we should never forget that without Colet, Flaubert's characterization would not be as rich as it is), *Lui* is readable and unpretentious. It is an adroit example of an authentic memoir presented as a novel that purports to be a memoir. If it were as self-consciously artful as *Madame Bovary,* it would be false.

Lui does have alterations in tone and register. After all, as Albert says to Stéphanie upon reading the introduction to her first translation, "Le style, c'est la femme." Colet's style here is a mood indicator. Sometimes she is so rhetorical as to seem bombastic; sometimes so casual as to seem breezy. I had to resist an almost overwhelming temptation to unify the style of her diction. Except for her padded sonnets, which I have trimmed to lyrics, I did not try to improve Colet. I believe she wrote what she meant to say. The printer, however, did not always print her text. There are a few instances where mistakes have to be corrected, for example, the moralist Chamfort is misspelled Champfort.

Respecting a text does not require duplicating it. Colet herself was attentive to readers and was somewhat traditional in taste. (She once said that she couldn't love Musset because his "rhymes" weren't "rich" enough.) She knew English and would have wanted, I believe, to be rendered in an idiom a reader would recognize as educated and correct but alternating between the formal and colloquial. She would have wanted the prevailing taste accommodated. For example, this was necessary in Chapter IV when Stéphanie says that Duchemin "avait les allures d'un Tartuffe grotesque." I believe the cognate (usually a false cognate) "allure" or "charm" is what is meant and that it is redundant to specify that Tartuffe is grotesque. (Of course, Tartuffe, grotesque in essence, can be given a suave and subtle characterization, but repertory does not invariably do so, and this is not a moment where Colet is making fine dramaturgical distinctions.)

It should not be forgotten that she is frequently quoting, paraphrasing, or writing from notes. Her passages from Léonce's letters are directly from Flaubert; some episodes are from copies she made of her letters to him. Her narratives from Musset, who entertains her with stories, are his but in a transition stage between reminiscence and fictionalizing. What we have is polished Flaubert and rough Musset. She distinguishes between voices, and I have tried to follow her cues closely.

Overall, my resulting choices are cued by my translation of the title as "A View of Him," rather than "Musset as I Knew Him" or "The Man Himself (Flaubert)." I interpret this novel as a subtle class action against the French male intellectual of the mid-nineteenth century as waged by a woman who would probably have found the present wave of women's liberation far more congenial. I hope my choices make her novel contemporary for the mid-nineteenth century and timely for the late twentieth century.

Works Consulted (A Partial Listing)

Banquart, M. -C., ed. *Louis Bouilhet, Lettres à Louise Colet*. Paris: PUF, 1973.

Barnes, Julian. *Flaubert's Parrot*. New York: Alfred Knopf, 1985.

Bart, Benjamin. *Flaubert*. Syracuse: Syracuse University Press, 1967.

Berry, Joseph. *Infamous Woman*. Garden City, N.J.: Doubleday, 1977.

Colet, Louise. *Lui: Roman contemporain*. Paris: Michel Lévy Frères, 1864; Geneva: Slatkine reprint, 1973. The Library of Congress lists two editions by Librairie Nouvelle in 1859 and one by Calmann-Lévy in 1860.

Enfield, D. E. *A Lady of the Salons*. New York: Charles Scribner's Sons, 1923.

Flaubert, Gustave. *Correspondance I*. Edited by Jean Bruneau. Paris: Gallimard, 1973.

———. *The Letters of Gustave Flaubert, 1830–1857*. Translated by Francis Steegmuller. Cambridge, Mass.: Harvard University Press, Belknap Press, 1980.

———. *The Letters of Gustave Flaubert, 1857–1880*. Translated by Francis Steegmuller. Cambridge, Mass.: Harvard University Press, Belknap Press, 1982.

Freilich, Hélène. *Les Amants de Mantes*. Paris: SFELT, 1935.

Gann, Gilbert. *Alfred de Musset, sa jeunesse et la nôtre*. Paris: Librairie Académique Perrin, 1970.

Gastinel, Pierre. *Le Romantisme d'Alfred de Musset*. 1933. Reprint. Osnabrück: Otto Zeller, 1978.

Haldane, Charlotte. *Alfred*. New York: Roy Publishers, 1960.

Jackson, Joseph F. *Louise Colet et ses amis littéraires*. New Haven, Conn.: Yale University Press, 1937.

Jacobs, Alphonse, ed. *Gustave Flaubert–George Sand Correspondance*. Paris: Flammarion, 1981.

Lainey, Yves. *Musset ou la difficulté d'aimer*. Paris: Société d'enseignement supérieur, 1978.

Lescure, Mathurin de. *Eux et Elles*. Paris: Poulet-Malassis et Debroise, 1860; Geneva: Slatkine reprints, 1973.

Mestral Combremont, J. de. *La Belle Madame Colet*. Lausanne: Payot et Cie, 1913.

Musset, Alfred de. *La Confession d'un enfant du siècle*. Edited by Maurice Allem. Paris: Ed. Garnier Frères, 1960.

______. *Confession of a Child of the Century*. Translated by Robert Arnot. New York: Current Literature Publishing Co., 1950.

______. *Oeuvres complètes, I* (poésie). Edited by Maurice Allem. Paris: Gallimard Pléiade, 1957.

______. *Oeuvres complètes en prose*. Edited by Maurice Allem. Paris: Gallimard Pléiade, 1951.

______. *Poésies complètes*. Edited by Maurice Allem. Paris: Gallimard Pléiade, 1939.

______. *Théâtre complet*. Edited by Maurice Allem. Paris: Gallimard Pléiade, 1934.

Musset, Paul de. *Biographie d'Alfred de Musset*. Paris: Alphonse Lemerre, 1876.

______. *He and She*. Translated by Ernest Tristan and G. F. Monkshood. New York: Brentano, n.d.

______. *Lui et Elle*. Paris: Charpentier, 1871.

Poli, Annarosa. *L'Italie dans la vie et dans l'oeuvre de George Sand*. Paris: Armand Colin, 1960.

Pommier, Jean. *Autour du drame de Venise*. Paris: Nizet, 1958.

Pirotte, Huguette. *George Sand*. Paris: Gembloux, 1980.

Sand, George. *Elle et Lui*. Paris: Michel Lévy Frères, 1869.

______. *Oeuvres autobiographiques*. Edited by Georges Lubin. Paris: Gallimard, 1970.

______. *She and He*. Translated by George Brunham Ives. Chicago: Academy Press, 1977.

Séché, Léon. *Alfred de Musset*. Paris: Mercure de France, 1907.

Winegarten, Renée. *The Double Life of George Sand*. New York: Basic Books, Inc., 1978.

AUTHOR'S PREFACE

"False modesty is the ultimate refinement of vanity. It keeps the vain man from appearing so; indeed, it earns him esteem for the virtue which is the exact opposite of the vice forming his character. You say one must be modest, that the well-born ask for nothing better. Well, then, try to see that men don't trample those who give in through modesty or break those who bend."

This is La Bruyère.[1] Since people have tried to use this book to break me, I will hold my head high; I will pick up the gauntlet they have thrown.

I left Paris the day after the first edition of this novel came out. Four editions followed without my having the possibility of seeing proofs again or writing a short preface to warn the reader against the newspaper attacks. They were numerous and fierce. Although two novels of the type I was being criticized for had preceded mine, the "responsible" press, as they say, mobilized a crusade, concentrating their indignation and exorcism on me. "Don't read this book," the most established critic advised fashionable women, "Don't read this immoral work!" thus applying to me the arrogant epithet which Rousseau put at the beginning of *The New Heloise*. Another critic treated me as if I were half Madam Cottin and half Mogador;[2] a third called me a pagan longing for the

1. Jean de la Bruyère (1645–96) was a French moralist.

2. Madame Cottin (Sophie Risteau, 1770–1807) wrote sentimental and religious novels. Céleste Venard Mogador (Countess of Chabrillan, 1824–1906) was an actress and novelist whose works tended toward the sensational.

Priapean orgies of yore. The most temperate considered me a creature led astray by imprudence and doubt, someone who ought to return posthaste to a life regulated by human decency and devout penance.

"When some people read a work, they extract things which they haven't understood and which they alter still more by what they bring to it, and these elements, corrupted and disfigured and which are nothing but their own thoughts and impressions, they expose to censure."

That's La Bruyère again characterizing book critics in his deft, deep way. Yes, indeed, he has said it perfectly: the work, "corrupted and disfigured by what they bring to it," is exposed just that way to blind public censure, deliberately deceived by treacherous critics. It is the latter, who, in all fairness, ought to be condemned as violators and falsifiers of thought, which is the most sacred of all human attributes.

So what was my crime? I couldn't be accused of denigrating the powerful personalities whom they were pleased to recognize in my book. I had left their grandeur somewhat beclouded but intact, and, out of respect, I had poeticized and ennobled the secondary personages clustered around them. That is why I endowed with irresistible appeal the chance lover who distracted my heroine for a while. Now, if Venetian gossip which I reported in *L'Italie des Italiens* is to be believed, poor Dr. Tiberio was extremely homely.[3] Looks have lost their luster in modern society, entirely too contemptuous of the physical, and our Neo-Christian women make a point of extolling homeliness—to redeem their fall, always a consequence, they claim, of two souls uniting, rather than two perishable bodies lusting. Classical antiquity was both more natural

3. When Colet queried, Pietro Pagello (the model for Tiberio Piacentini) was overweight and balding, but he was a handsome, cultivated womanizer when Sand met him and a stately old gentleman when he died in 1898.

and sophisticated in matters of love. The power of pulchritude was acknowledged to be so great that it sufficed to justify the love of goddesses for simple shepherds and patricians for slaves. Did I diminish my heroine in giving her Grecian taste? To take up here only the general question of the magnetic attraction of beauty, isn't it obvious that the women who hold out for this physical ideal and make it one of the exclusive conditions of love are chaster by nature and hence less easy to seduce? Men's physical beauty has now become as rare as their moral beauty has always been, and women who require it before surrendering to love's spell have fewer opportunities for succumbing than the ancient goddesses and patricians. But whatever the case, this book was declared immoral and its author contemptible. From such calumnious judgments, however casually pronounced, can come a writer's ruin and despair. But what difference does that immolation make to the frivolous judges of an ephemeral tribunal?

I remember that I was in Venice in the large gallery of the Academy of Fine Arts where Titian's "Assumption of the Virgin" is hung. Seated in front of that painting, I was simply enthralled by that admirable grouping of stricken apostles. On their uplifted faces we see sorrow and fear. They stretch out their arms imploringly to the Holy Mother, who from one moment to the next will disappear into Heaven. What gestures! What heartrending and suppliant poses! We can hear these souls beseech and pray. Their eyes, lips, gestures, muscles compose a single invocation. "Stay with us," the apostles are saying to Mary. "Your Son has gone, leaving us His Doctrine and His Mother. But our spirits bend with the breezes of earth. Oh stay to guide us, visible and palpable creatrix of the Divine Redeemer!"

And so we too weep and lament when love, the human ideal, leaves us. I was studying attentively each expressive, living face in that magnificent painting when the *cameriere* of my hotel came in to hand me an overdue packet of newspapers and letters that he knew I was awaiting impatiently.

I skimmed through the newspapers where I found the gracious remarks just alluded to. Then I opened a letter with the seal of the Ministry of Public Instruction and there I read that my literary pension of the past twenty years had just been suspended.[4] The seeds of the critics had borne early, poisoned fruit. Our ministers, unlike Monsieur Cavour, don't have time to read novels.[5] They had taken the yellow journalists at their word. I was a dangerous Eumenide who should be punished as soon as possible. Another letter informed me that the director of a large newspaper had decided not to publish the novel he had accepted because of all the unsavory publicity aroused by the last one.

Thus I was struck from every side. But by one of those strokes of providence which pour balm on a poet's wounds, I received those repeated blows while I was in the midst of all those immortal figures, in communion with masterpieces, linked to genius. The faces looked at me pensively: some compassionately, others proudly; all were serene and steadfast. They filled me with their dignity and calm. Outside was Venice enslaved, in mourning but bearing her chains proudly as she waited for her deliverance. Still, floating on the lagoon, she was smiling sadly at her radiant and beautiful azure sky.

I left the gallery of the great masters of the Venetian School. I took a gondola and had myself taken to the Lido. Absorbed in the splendor and quiet of the day, my heart was already lighter, barely a faint black spot remained.

"But why," I asked myself, luxuriating in the brilliance and

4. Colet's pension was reduced from a onetime high of two thousand francs per annum to eight hundred francs by December 1859.

5. Camillo Benso Cavour (1810–61) was the first prime minister during the unification of Italy in the mid-nineteenth century.

solitude, "do painters or artists need the same daily bread as the common man? This inexorable necessity continually plunges them back into the troubled currents they would like to escape and casts a shadow on their enjoyment of nature and beauty."

Several days later I left for Milan. My novel, denigrated by the French press, had aroused curiosity. It made friends for me in Italian society which did not care about our coteries. It was after having read this book that Cavour wanted to meet me. Massimo d'Azeglio and Giorgini, both sons-in-law of the illustrious Manzoni, read it themselves and had the incorruptible author of *I Promessi Sposi* read it, too.[6] I myself would never have dared present him this narrative of stormy passion. Here is that virtuous poet's opinion:

"From a Christian point of view," he told me, "I couldn't approve of your protagonists' feverish and exclusive preoccupation with earthly happiness which always eludes us. From a human point of view I found in this book sincere psychology, noble emotions within a courageous satire of modern society."

There is another compliment which I would like to repeat here, although not from anyone famous, because this person has the most upright and moral heart I know. When I returned from Italy, I stopped for a few days in the Midi with an aged relative on my mother's side. As we were chatting one morning in his vast library filled with masterpieces of classical and modern literature, I saw my poor novel, so berated by the Paris press, on one of the shelves—and luxuriously bound.

"What's this?" I asked that benevolent old man. "This wretched book found favor with you?"

"My dear child," he replied, "you have written there a bold and truthful work which the unnatural and unhealthy minds of the time

6. Alessandro Manzoni (1785–1873) authored the masterpiece *I Promessi Sposi*.

will never forgive. That's why poisoned clouds have burst upon you. Secure virtue doesn't get carried away like this. You have irritated all the hypocrites who are the law-givers of our morality today. Their hypocrisies are the simulacra of love and talent, political and religious conviction. The rough, staunch words of a true believer, thrown into that pandemonium of insecure consciences, will always be treated as seditious and impious. But there are still, thank God, a few honest, secluded souls who don't confuse the yapping of official morality with the immutable voice of eternal morality. Such souls will absolve you as I do."

Oh, La Bruyère, Montaigne, Molière, Diderot, Voltaire! high priests of the imperishable religion of justice and truth, and you, Balzac, their glorious brother, you the bold exposer of cowardly contemporary passions hiding their leprosy beneath a puritanical mask! Oh, proud, free spirits who have never accepted the timorous compromises of regimented writers. Perhaps my pride leads me astray, but it seems to me that if you were alive, you would ratify the judgment of that serene recluse, and applauding my unbending spirit which is impervious to fear, you would say to those who have insulted me, "Let that soul sing in peace. She still believes in beauty, freedom, and love!"

LOUISE COLET

August 1863

CHAPTER I

"YOU'RE A WRITER," Marquise Stéphanie de Rostan said to me one evening. "As a writer, you should avoid the pathos of love and forbear sermonizing. Don't use the language of metaphysics and mysticism to discuss this simple, natural feeling, this powerful and distinctive attraction which brings human beings together and makes them one." (The Marquise has one of those rare, incisive eighteenth-century minds that seems to have leapt over the intervening years directly to our own times. Now intellects look for their way; leaders of conscience look for their moral code; and writers look for their style.) "If heroines in modern novels are so boring," she continued, "and, in my opinion, so immoral, it's because apropos of love, they discuss God or motherhood and obscure by such completely extraneous concepts that beautiful flame of youth which no longer kindles a single heart or lends its hues to a single narrative. Since Rousseau's Julie and Lamartine's Elvire,[1] all women have more or less preached apropos of love, sometimes philosophy, sometimes religion, sometimes socialism, and to such an extent that love has been smothered by these sublime—or pretentious—aspirations which are only incidentally in its purview."

"To make sure I understand you, Marquise," I replied. "Would you kindly define love for me?"

1. Julie is the title character in *Julie, ou la nouvelle Héloïse* by Jean-Jacques Rousseau (1712–78), French-Swiss moralist. "Elvire" was the name Alphonse Lamartine (1790–1869), Romantic poet and Liberal politician, gave to his beloved Julie Charles.

"Define love? Do you imagine that anyone can? If I tried, I'd be as ridiculous as the women I'm criticizing. I will not do so. But I've felt it in my heart, in my mind, in my senses, and I assure you that it bears little resemblance either to the descriptions written about it or to most women's hypocritical confessions. Very few women dare to be frank on the subject. They're afraid people will consider them immoral, and I believe—and I trust you'll excuse my pride—that only the most honest and honorable will tell the truth on this subject. Love is no disgrace. Love is not remorse or mourning. It can bring that anguish when it ends, but at the time it is felt and shared, it is the expansion of the whole being, the joy and moral tone of the heart."

"So you don't regret having loved," I asked, "despite the despair and emptiness love brought you?"

"I would like to be able to love again," she countered heatedly, "if a new, consuming passion could obliterate the ashes of my burnt-out passion. But since that is impossible and since we have no faculty for rejuvenation or oblivion, I am content to savor the memory of what I once felt. Because desiring only complete satisfaction, I would always reject the "almost" in love. But I haven't gotten so numb and mystical at forty that I repent the shining hours of my youth. They are still my finest hours despite the distress and tears, and, as you put it so well, the despair and emptiness they left behind. Doesn't the navigator propelled by fate into the glaciers of Greenland remember fondly some balmy, blooming beach in Cuba or the Antilles?"

"Oh, Marquise," I exclaimed, "you really ought to tell me your story, or, rather, your feelings!"

"It would be painful to talk about myself," she replied. "I've recovered my serenity, and I don't want to lose it again. And you as my friend wouldn't want to make sparks fly from the cold ashes or tears spurt from the polished rock I now tread calmly. But I am willing to talk to you about *him,* that famous friend you knew, whose story consumes society, about whom so many false stories are being written. And in telling you how we met, how he loved me, how I have stayed loyal to him after his death, I can let you find in my account of our friendship what that great poet meant by love and what I said to him about love with a frankness that a more intimate bond would perhaps have hindered but which in our fraternal and spiritual relationship could be expressed without restraint."

It was in the garden of her lovely mansion on Rue de Bourgogne on a beautiful May evening that the Marquise de Rostan was telling me this. We were seated by the white marble basin which was in the center of the garden. A flowering Judas spread its first tender red branches above our heads. The sky was calm and clear, the air so mild that it lulled us like a blessed philter. The Marquise's still-slender figure combined with the fluid lines of her white neck and her beautiful head and face crowned with thick golden blond hair burst forth, if I may put it that way, above the innumerable pleats of her panniered violet gown. The delicate folds of the silken material fell gracefully around her. Her upright back rested arched against the wrought iron armchair, while her small hands were clasped around her crossed knees. In this pose of Pradier's Sappho, her loose flowing sleeves let her perfectly modelled and dazzling white arms be glimpsed to the elbow.[2] The warm breath of that magnificent spring evening had brought a pearly rose to her cheeks. She was a ravishing sight, and I said to myself, "She would still inspire adoration."

She seemed to read my mind, for she suddenly exclaimed, "It is better not to be loved than to be ill-loved or half-loved. For a fiery temperament like mine, hesitation and insecurity are worse

2. James Pradier (1792–1852), a French sculptor, introduced Colet and Flaubert.

than despair. I owe to my cultivated peace of mind my love of nature and the sense of well-being a beautiful evening like this can give.

"Let's not discuss me any more; let's talk about him. It was on a day like today that he died two years ago. I don't like to have those dear ashes disturbed so soon, and I would have preferred that his be left in peace a few years more. But there are glorious ashes which send forth their own Phoenix. Their brilliance attracts attention. Moreover, envy is as likely to attack the dead as the living, and sometimes love still holds a grievance and does violence to them. This is when friendship owes them the truth, that eternal justice."

CHAPTER II

BEFORE TELLING YOU how we met and how we became close friends, let me tell you how he whirled past me in a waltz in 1836. That brief apparition of a young genius gliding by, nodding his graceful blond head, has always stayed with me, a sharply etched picture in my memory. It was at the Arsenal in that salon where wit and poetry filled every Sunday evening. In those days women, those of high society, at any rate, loved writers of genius and sought them out. Unlike today, it simply wasn't permissible to have read nothing, admired nothing, felt nothing great and beautiful, loved nothing illustrious. A woman would have blushed to enclose her life in the ample folds of a gown and to force her pretty diamond-covered head to incessant, degrading calculations of bankrupting luxury. In those days we had less costly outfits but more sentiments in the heart and more ideas in the head. We made flirtatious advances to men of wit and letters. Princes and princesses set the example.

So it was a privilege, even for a young marquise, to be received at the Arsenal's informal Sunday evenings. Our great poets read their verses; our celebrated composers played their music; then, to end the evening, there was dancing to piano music for the girls and young married women.[1]

I had been married scarcely two months when I went to the Arsenal for the first time. My husband, who was strange and jealous, forced me to go out in long sleeves and high necklines. I obeyed, for I was quite indifferent then to anything which wasn't a matter for heart or mind. That evening I was wearing a black velvet dress which imprisoned me to the base of the neck. My hair, parted in the back, fell in long thick ringlets on each side of my covered shoulders. Tendrils of white convolvuli encircled my chignon and floated down my back. This coiffure would have been elegant on bare shoulders, but heaped upon a black velvet bodice, it was odd, to say the least. When I entered the Arsenal salon, the readings and music were over. At the piano a girl was playing the opening bars of a waltz. A lot of people looked me over because except for the master of the house, who had known my father, I didn't know anyone. A young man receiving compliments from several women,[2] darted over to ask me to waltz.

I told him I never waltzed.

He bowed, turned on his heels, and I saw him float by, dancing, a minute later. He had in his arms a young brunette who was the muse of the moment in that salon.

1. The Arsenal Library was the scene of the first Romantic coterie. The host was Charles Nodier (1780–1844). Musset's partner was probably Marie Nodier-Ménessier.

2. In 1836, Musset published *La Confession d'un enfant du siècle* and was in the midst of his *Nuits*.

"Why did you refuse a waltz with Albert de Lincel?" my host asked.

"What! Was that he? De Lincel himself?" I cried. "He's the person I so much wanted to meet!"

"The very man, he's dancing with my daughter right now."

I began to study the dancer. He was slender, of average height. He was dressed with extreme care, even a touch of the dandy. He was wearing a bronze-green frock coat with metal buttons. A gold chain fluttered on his brown silk waistcoat. His pleated batiste shirt was fastened with two onyx buttons. His narrow black satin cravat, pulled in at the neck like a jet carcanet, emphasized the matte finish of his complexion. His spotless white gloves outlined his delicate hands. But it was especially the arrangement of his beautiful blond hair which showed the care he took in his appearance. Like Lord Byron he knew how to use a natural crown to give noble grace to his inspired brow. Innumerable blond ringlets waved over the temples and clustered like grapes down to the nape. Whenever the rapid circling of the waltz brought him beneath the chandelier, I was struck by the variegated shades in his hair. The first bands, caressing the forehead were golden blond, the next were amber, and the most abundant, clustering on the top of his head, were graduated from blond to brown. When I met him again later, he still had this beautiful, unusual hair pattern which he kept until his death. Unlike most blond men who often have red sideburns, his were chestnut. His eyes were almost black. All this gave his physiognomy more vigor and fire. He had a perfect Grecian nose, and his mouth, which then had fresh contours, showed white teeth when he smiled. His traits as a whole conveyed aristocratic distinction which was heightened by the sparkle of his eyes and the ideal curve of his forehead. It was genius bearing the stamp of race. While he waltzed with his head thrown back, I could see his face in all its handsomeness. Twice the pauses in the waltz put him only a few steps from the chair where I was seated. The first time, he looked at me and I heard him say to his partner, "Is that blond lady who is so conscientiously muffled in her black velvet some Englishwoman, a Quaker perhaps?"

"You're very mistaken," the young woman answered.

The second time his partner said with a nod in my direction, "I assure you she's a girl from the South, and why are you so surprised she's blond? You've lived in Venice and seen the Titian types in flesh and blood."

He looked almost sadly at her.

She continued, "Of course, it's true that in those days you had eyes only for brunettes!"

"Just like today," he replied with an admiring smile for the brunette in his arms. But it seemed to me that a cloud had passed across his face.

When the waltz ended, he took his hat and left the salon.

CHAPTER III

MANY YEARS ROLLED BY after that evening at the Arsenal. I lost my husband, and a disastrous lawsuit temporarily deprived me of my entire fortune. This very house where I was born, where my grandfather and my mother had lived, was put up for sale and while we waited for a buyer, it was rented completely furnished to a wealthy family. Trusting to an intuition, in all respects true, that this house would become my property again some day, I didn't want to leave it. So for a place of my own, I had rented to myself a little apartment on the fifth floor which was reached by the back stairs. Among its five rooms were two which had formerly served my grandfather as study and laboratory when he conducted chemistry experiments with the great Lavoisier.[1] The windows of my humble dwelling opened on this garden where I had played as a child. If you raise your head, you will see those windows smiling beneath the roof. The crests of the trees sheltering us now brush against them with their branches.

There I surrounded myself with some cherished keepsakes, some furniture and family portraits which had escaped the inventory. I kept in my service a former kitchen maid named Marguerite, a kind, old peasant whom I had brought from Picardy and who was devoted to me.

By now I had an income of only two thousand francs. After the fortune I was used to, it was almost destitution, but I possessed two opulent splendors which towered over all the vulgar, petty constraints—radiating upon them like a sun beaming upon the moors. I had a magnificent child, a seven-year-old son who spread laughter and life around me, and I had a deep love in my heart, blind as hope and strong as faith. I expected everything from this love, and I believed in it the way the faithful believe in God! You can imagine how much energy I drew from it to live in what the world called poverty and how much indifference I felt for anything not bearing on that happiness or on my maternal joy. However, the man I loved was a kind of myth for my friends. He was seen at my place only at rare intervals. He lived at some distance in the country, working on a great book like a fanatic in a cult of art, he said. I was the confidante of this unknown genius. I received his letters every day, and every two months when a part of his task was completed, I became once more his fond reward,

1. Laurent de Lavoisier (1743–94) was one of the founders of modern chemistry.

his shimmering sensuality, the passing frenzy of his heart, which, strange to say, opened and closed to these powerful sensations at will.

I had been overwhelmed by so much disillusionment during the dreary years of my marriage. I had lived until thirty in such gloomy isolation that in the beginning this love affair consumed me entirely and seemed to me the feast of life I had so vainly longed for.

I was coming out of the night. This flame stunned and blinded me. It had first shone on me like a forbidden happiness when I was still bound. When I was free, I rushed headlong towards it as if to the hearth of all warmth and light. Narrating this story compels me to touch that image, in ashes now, and give it substance. I shall do so discreetly because if it is sinister to call forth the dead from the tomb, it is even more so to call forth the dead from the living.

I found in that love an atmosphere of ethereal exaltation which made me savor only the joys which flowed from it. Receiving his letters every day when I awoke, writing to him every evening, spinning in the vortex of his ideas, whirling them around me, plunging into them until I was dizzy, such was my life.

He seemed so indifferent, both for others and for himself, to anything that wasn't the abstraction of art and beauty, that, given the distance we lived from each other, he acquired a special grandeur and prestige. How would someone like him, who esteemed only the ideas of things, have noticed my straitened circumstances?

However, even for the illuminati and cultists of love there are positivist moments when the earth and its necessities exert their claim. I was recalled to reality by my son, by that dear child who formed the natural and true half of my life. In order to give him better food, nicer clothes, and all those maternal indulgences, I looked for something to do which could be a small monthly increment to our meager resources. I had received serious instruction from my mother, and progressively my taste, which was extremely bent on reading, helped me acquire for myself an extensive education. My grandfather, after the agitations of a political life that bridged the Revolution, found teaching me a little Latin and some Greek poetry one of the pleasures of his old age. He would remind me with a smile that the women in the courts of Francis I and Louis XIV had remained free of pedantry yet beautiful and attractive while knowing as well as a man the languages of Sophocles and Virgil.

Later I learned Italian and English easily. How I congratulated myself when I became poor that I could find in these matters of the mind an unexpected resource.

At that time foreign novels were very popular with the reading public. I translated two of them. An editor accepted them and paid me six hundred francs. It was one of the greatest and proudest moments in my life when I felt those bank notes rustling in my hands. That day I rented an open carriage to give my son an outing in the Bois de Boulogne, as I once used to drive him in my own carriage while his nurse seated opposite from me held him wrapped in his embroidered blankets.

The evening of that memorable day I had in a few friends who had remained faithful. The guests included three of our great poets and several famous writers. I laughed when I said to them that to some extent I had joined their ranks since straitened circumstances forced me to write and since, encouraged by the result of my first translations, I would henceforth ask for their support with editors. Each replied in turn—and they were telling the truth—that by unhappy accident they were on bad terms with the fashionable dealer who published foreign novels.

"But now that I think about it," René Delmart,[2] one of the three poets, added suddenly, "we have friends who have made Frémont's fortune.[3] They should be able to get through the thick skull of that autocrat of the book business. They would be extremely happy, Marquise, to speak to him on your behalf."

"That sounds fine," I said to René, whom I'd loved like a brother for ten years. "Well, whom did you have in mind?"

"I'll be seeing Albert de Lincel tomorrow, and I am sure that he will be at your disposition."

"Albert de Lincel!" I cried, remembering that I hadn't set eyes on him since that evening at the Arsenal.

"Albert de Lincel?" everyone else present exclaimed in unison.

"What makes you suggest him?" put in Albert de Germiny, the philosophical poet.[4] "That madcap is going to fall in love with the Marquise and take our place in her heart; we have to make do with friendship anyway."

"Indeed," I laughed, "your prophecy might come true. Albert de Lincel has remained one of the sharpest pictures in my mind. One evening he glided in front of me like a phantom. That was over twelve years ago. I haven't seen him since that evening. But I've read everything he's written, and I know it all by heart. Just look over there where I keep my favorite books. His are there, and I open them every day. I'm attracted and delighted by his keen inspiration and his clear, precise style, which can be eloquent

2. René Delmart is based on the brothers Emile and Antony Deschamps (1791–1871, 1800–1869), loyal friends and men of letters and, like Stéphanie, translators.

3. Frémont is François Buloz (1803–77), founding editor of *La Revue des Deux Mondes*.

4. Albert de Germiny, or Alfred de Vigny (1797–1863), was said to be a very dear friend of Colet after the break with Flaubert.

without being diffuse and ardent without being pompous. It seems to me that in French literature de Lincel has no predecessor. His verve and his humor, like summer sunbursts, stand out against the mists. His passion has sudden, unexpected, superb flashes which I should like to call Olympian, like the sacred arrows the gods used to rain upon mortals. You can almost hear the vibrating bow of Diana the huntress through the elegance and grace attending his grandeur. Like all original and trenchant geniuses de Lincel has inspired and will inspire dreadful imitators. It is so easy to confuse familiarity with irony and cynicism with restless passion. To come back to the author himself, if Buffon's immortal aphorism 'Le style, c'est l'homme' is true—and I'm convinced it is—then I am sure that de Lincel bears in his person the seduction of his work. But, thank heavens, I'm no longer vulnerable. Vertigo doesn't attack people who are happy, and as I have told you, dear friends, I am happy."

"Even if you weren't happy or merely believed in an illusion," said my old friend Duverger,[5] the patriotic poet, "I doubt that de Lincel holds any danger for you. His life of amorous adventures over the past fifteen years has made him a mere shadow of his former self. He is no longer the handsome dancer you saw waltz past one evening. His wasted body could not inspire love now. He's a sick, bizarre spirit who continually goes back on his word. In a benevolent mood he would promise to speak to his editor Frémont about you, and he would forget it an hour later. I think it would be more dependable to have an old pedant like Duchemin recommend you.[6] He's a serious man, a select mind, as the pro-government newspapers say, and a former university rector. He's Frémont's official patron and could ask him to do anything."

5. Duverger is Pierre-Jean de Béranger (1780–1857), noted as a lyricist.

6. Duchemin, or François Villemain (1790–1870), served as the minister of public instruction from 1839 to 1844.

"But so important a person would not ever put himself out for me."

"Write to him, Marquise," replied old Duverger slyly, "I'm sure he'll come running. He's said to still be very gallant."

"Gallant beneath his pedantic exterior. Oh, you are a crafty poet," I replied. "You're always joking."

"Ah well, my dear child, you forget when you talk to me like that, that I am extremely ugly, but that doesn't keep me from having a heart." And Duverger gave me one of those melancholy looks which sometimes gave his cheerful face such a heartrending expression.

"I share Duverger's opinion," continued Albert de Germiny. "Write to the learned Duchemin. Considering himself a patron of letters is one of his little vanities, and he will make it a point of honor to prove it to you, while de Lincel might affect a disdain which would hurt your feelings."

"You're wrong," said René Delmart who had been silent up to then. "Albert has remained kind and good-hearted." And turning to me, he added, "I'll vouch for him, Marquise."

"He still does you the honor of seeing you, even though you're a poet, too, my dear René," continued de Germiny.

"I go to see him when I know he is sick and sad, and he always receives me like a friend."

"He does? then why does he avoid the rest of us?" replied de Germiny. "We all loved him like a glorious young brother whom we awarded all the prizes without being jealous. Weren't we good, steadfast friends from his first appearance on the scene? Didn't we acclaim his genius with warmth and sincerity? Didn't we spoil him with our heartfelt admiration? Well, he suddenly left us as if he were embarrassed to be in our company. He has affected for contemporary poets a kind of aristocratic disdain that Byron never had for Wordsworth and Shelley."

"You're mistaken," cried good-hearted René. "He has rendered homage to Lamartine publicly, and when he speaks of the great lyricist in exile, he proclaims him the master of us all in the science of versification."[7]

"None of which keeps him from preferring the company of rich bankers and a few English debauchees—castoffs of the famous Regent's Club—to ours," Duverger laughed sardonically. "How can he make his closest friend that Albert Nattier whose latest rakish exploit was shaving off his sleeping mistress's beautiful hair after a night of love—because he suspected her of infidelity![8] What a blackguard! How can he treat as friends that Lord Rilburn and his brother Lord Melbourg? Their debauchery shocked London. Today they flaunt their millions and their premature decrepitude on the streets of Paris. I feel sorry for de Lincel," Duverger continued, "but I agree with de Germiny that he would have done better to stick with us."

"Oh, if you judge him by political or moral standards, he is lost," kind René replied. "But for God's sake make an effort to remember your own youthful impetuousness and poetic fantasies, and then you will be more just towards him. Remember especially his very volatile temperament. He tries out all experiences, all emotions. He imagines that he will find a new, unknown poetry there, and I would dare to say that he has often been able to extract from his very immoderation cries of pain and love that are more heartrending and sublime and hence more instructive for the soul than all the morality of honest works composed in tranquility. You are surprised that he occasionally accepts as companions in pleasure the idle rich of ill fame! But their fortune for him is the stage where he sees them preen and strut, and their orgies are a show he treats himself

7. Musset published *Lettre à Lamartine* in 1836. Hugo is the poet in exile.

8. Albert Nattier is Alfred Tattet (1809–56), nouveau-riche playboy, art lover, loyal friend of Musset.

to. There he imbibes bold, poignant, fantastic images, and he was the first to introduce them into French literature. From these nocturnal feasts of debauchery, like so many black corridors hollowed in a mine, he has extracted sparkling precious stones. He is more a spectator than an accomplice in this turpitude of the rich. If his body sometimes capitulates, his mind is on the alert, even if he is unaware of it. He controls this contrived intoxication, regurgitates it, stigmatizes it, and extracts definitive masterly tableaux. You should be wary of believing that these men, whom you call his companions in pleasure, possess him. Albert has a genius which escapes any influence. For a long time he was the friend of a young prince, but who among us would ever have considered him a courtier? How can you hold his charming, enthusiastic disposition against him? His poetic inspiration always soars above his youthful follies. It ennobles them, removes their slime, so to speak, and changes them into beams of light. They're like bursts of flame hovering over a swamp!"

"You're a loyal friend," de Germiny cried, "and it's a pleasure, René, to be defended and praised by you, but in the end you will agree that being a poet is a sacred trust, and that it's a shame to see Albert accept as Amphitryons rich parvenus and drunken lords."

"All the more shameful since there aren't any truly great lords these days; no more in England than France," continued Duverger, "and the people who deck themselves with such a title haven't much in common with those who used to bear one. Good God, lords and gentlemen, I would say to them, if you're going to ape their exterior, try also to have the wit of a Bolingbroke, Horace Walpole, Gramont, Francis I, Henri IV or Maréchal de Richelieu![9] You can risk being a poetry-loving debauchee only at that price!"

"We've moved quite a ways from our point of departure in this

9. These leaders were all competent in the arts.

conversation, my dear masters," I laughed. "Let's see. My dear René, since you are both a friend of Albert de Lincel and an acquaintance of the scholarly Duchemin, which one should I write for a recommendation?"

"Write first to the pedant," René replied. "Like Duverger, I think Duchemin will be flattered and treat you to a personal visit. But if you don't like him, I'll answer for Albert."

CHAPTER IV

As soon as my friends had left, I wrote a few lines to Duchemin to request his good offices with Frémont. I didn't mind doing it. When you're in love, your own pride doesn't matter very much. The joy I hid in my heart made everything I did carefree and happy—the way merry songs cheer the workman.

After that short note, I wrote my daily confession to the man I loved. I did this every evening. Chateaubriand has said, "If I believed happiness was to be found somewhere, I would look for it in habit." As it was, I found in writing him all my thoughts both a deep happiness and a kind of protective moral well-being. I would not have wanted to commit any unworthy act during the day because in the evening, rather than lie or confess my lapse, the pen would have fallen from my hands. Those were the purest and proudest days of my life when my spirit embraced to the fullest the rays of beauty and goodness.

As soon as I finished my letter, I would lift the white curtains of the little bed where my son was sleeping. I would place a lingering kiss on his smiling brow and try to go to sleep myself. That evening I stayed awake a long time, involuntarily thinking over everything my friends had said about Albert de Lincel. I was grateful to René Delmart for having defended him. I respected René as much as I liked him, so I kept telling myself that since he always spoke truthfully, he couldn't have lied about Albert.

René has one of the noblest and rarest minds of our times, and if his literary fame has not risen to the height of his talent, this is due the very beauty of his character which owes its originality to his absolute integrity and to his demi-god indifference to any activity promoting a writer's renown. He came into prominence suddenly during the Restoration in a constellation of great lyric poets. After a trip to Italy, he published an imitation of the *Inferno* where he skillfully infused his lines with all the precision and grandeur of Dante's epic. He did also a series of tableaux, masterly essays on Italian manners, landscapes, and art. An illness afflicting his nerves closed both his heart and lips for some time. His friends announced that his brain was affected, as if mental faculties could not rest or move in mute dreams. He soon returned to real life, but with a mind larger and stronger. From that interruption of human commerce he derives his lofty contempt of all that goads men's vanity and ambition. He alone among his contemporaries has never longed for a decoration, an academic chair, newspaper feature stories or salon panegyrics. Duverger has some of the same disdain, but he has courted popularity. René has never flattered anyone, not even his friends. He loves them and serves them.

When I was happy, I saw him twice a month. When grief overwhelmed me and death nearly claimed me, he was the only person who came every day to comfort me, to distract me with the ironic yet ennobling verve of the true sage who calls on infinity to help heal our limited miseries. He never mocked sorrow, but he mocked those who cause it, from persecutors of nations to oppressors of women. He had a gift for belittling and vulgarizing mean creatures. In this way he stripped them of their power and prestige, making them appear to their victims in their ugliness and inferiority. He made women like us amazed that we ever loved or feared such men.

So I was thinking that if this proud, generous soul had defended Albert, the latter certainly had retained much of his early grandeur and sensibility. I felt that my very keen desire to know him—which I had always had—was growing, and in order for that opportunity to arise, I almost hoped that Duchemin would refuse me his support.

But the next afternoon I received from that important personage the most gallantly phrased reply to the effect that he would lay his paltry influence at my feet and that he would make every effort to come that very evening after dinner to receive his orders.

I remember that day was bitterly cold and seemed still colder because of the gloomy rain. As a cold-natured Creole, I had an enormous fire in the study where I was working, surrounded by my books and my cherished keepsakes.

Duchemin arrived much later than he had said he would, so late that my son, who had fallen asleep in my lap, had just been carried off to bed by Marguerite when the scholar arrived. Thus he found me alone, next to the flaming hearth, my head illuminated by a lamp with an opal shade.

I have never seen anyone bend his torso so low as that pedant did when he bowed to me. His bow was a series of disjointed inflections where the head and back each struggled to get the better of the other. His forehead, wan and shining like a skull, crowned, or rather bristling, with short, gray hair, was traversed by floating wrinkles when his mouth tried to smile. Duchemin's toadies, the young prigs he has trained and the hack journalists, have repeated ad nauseum that he has the wit, smile, and expression of Voltaire. As for his wit, this important personage's writings can refute this monstrous hyperbole by themselves. As for his smile, when he blinked and squinted his piercing little eyes, it always seemed like a smirk to me. The cutting, ironic smile and wide, open expression of Madame de Châtelet's lover were of a different stamp.[1]

I wanted to rise to receive him, but he checked that impulse by curving towards me like a hoop and seizing my hand, which he kissed. "My dear Marquise, I'm at your feet," he repeated soulfully, "I'm at your feet."

I drew back and prevailed upon him to take a seat, and after thanking him for replying to my request so promptly, I explained to him, quickly and curtly, how he could help me.

"Oh, you poor woman," he replied theatrically. "Are you thinking about this sorry trade of letters? My dear, do you want to write and stain with ink that lovely hand just meant to be kissed? You want to poach on our preserves? Oh, believe me, love is worth more than fame!"

While he was babbling these banalities, I looked him over with a contempt which must have disconcerted him. "I thought, Monsieur, that I had explained my purpose better in my note. I have no pretensions to creating literature, but only to making translations from English, German, and Italian. As for fame, I have no more pretension to it than to talent. Necessity forces such work upon me."

"Oh, you beautiful angel," he replied in tones of a precentor singing a choral response. He seized my hand and squeezed my arm through my full sleeve. "Necessity! What an ugly word you utter. You, whom I've seen brilliant and adored in all our salons, is it possible that you would be exposed to hardship, necessity?"

1. Colet is referring of course to Voltaire (1694–1778), French moralist, poet, and dramatist, and to his hostess and mistress at Cirey in the independent duchy of Lorraine.

"Don't feel sorry for me," I laughed as I disengaged my arm from his sticky, hairy paw. "I've never been happier."

"Oh, it is not you I feel sorry for, heroic woman," he continued with the same pious intonation, "but these so-called great poets in your circle, who call themselves your friends, who have the good fortune, perhaps, to be more than that" (with these words his squinting eyes sparkled) "and," he added, "who have never found a way to help you with the burdens of life." Without giving me time to reply and judging from the expression on my face that his familiar pity displeased me, he began speaking with arrogance and disdain about all the great contemporary poets. Pedants and critics don't like poets. They imagine themselves superior. They really don't understand poets, but they sing their praises when posterity has crowned them. They analyze poets to tear them apart. However, they are nothing without poets. They appropriate the poets' beauty and borrow some creative breath for their own sterile criticism. Without the poets' genius, their own wit would be nil. Their own verve springs from envy.

After hateful and jealous generalities, Duchemin concentrated his blows on three or four poets whom he knew were my friends. He was especially brutal with Albert de Germiny, whose long youth and good health exasperated an ugly man like himself.

"Now there's a happy man, for he is said to please you. Yet how can it be that this man who has a fortune, leaves you a prey to *necessity*?" and he stressed the word I had used.

"What are you saying" I cried angrily. "Do you think I beg alms from my friends?"

"Don't you understand that it is they alone whom I accuse," he resumed, making a move to seize once more the hand I had pulled away. "If ever I had the good fortune of being loved, even tolerated, by you, you would have my fortune and my life at your disposition." And in uttering these words the old fool knelt at my feet. He held the folds of my gown between his knees like a vice, and taking a greasy billfold out of an inner pocket of his suit jacket, he opened it, drawing several bank notes halfway out. "Let a friend do something," he said holding the bank notes out toward me, "and give a little love to a man you've set on fire!"

He was as alluring as Tartuffe. For a moment I thought my hilarity would overcome my contempt. But my indignation was stronger. With the back of my left hand I struck out at the billfold which fell to the edge of the hearth, and with my other I pushed the wavering old windbag so roughly that he rolled over backwards on the rug. His first concern was not to get up but to reach out his bony hand for the gaping wallet which was touching live coals and could have burst into flame. I confess I would have been ecstatic to see those insulting bills go up in flames.

I invent nothing in this scene.

Only an old man of sixty-six would act like that. Pedants especially. As soon as they sniff a tête-à-tête with a fashionable woman, they rush to put a white necktie on top of a dirty shirt. Their greasy hair straggles over the collar of their frayed suit. Their hands are half washed. And in such a state they dare kneel at some elegant woman's feet, if that woman is not defended by a discouraging entourage or a fortune. Poverty provokes such men and pushes them to temptation and profanation. Since in their ugliness, they have laid a hand only on poor girls who sell themselves, they imagine that with a full purse they will prevail over all revulsion of the flesh and pride of the soul. What a joy it is to humiliate them!

When Duchemin had gotten his billfold back in his hands and gotten himself on his feet, I pushed him towards the door and shut it.

He never forgave me for that scene. He became my enemy and

prevented his editor Frémont from publishing any of my translations.

Scarcely had he gotten out than I was overcome with hysterical laughter. In my mind's eye I saw him again in that buffoon's pose. I was laughing so loud that my old servant came in to warn me that I would wake my son. In those days I had such hilarious moods. And I told about them the same as my sad moods, and all I saw and felt, to the Léonce I loved so much. His name just escaped me. I had to mention it to keep this story from being confusing. But I can never say it without painful hesitation. It burns my throat and leaves a profoundly bitter aftertaste.

I immediately wrote up for him the strange scene that had just occurred. He had formerly seen Duchemin during a tour the great man had made in the provinces, and I imagined his sardonic surprise picturing the pedant at my feet—offering love and cash! However, when I got to that point in the narrative, at that final instance of cynicism and hope, I couldn't keep from a few poignant reflections on a woman's lot, so that my letter which began lightheartedly ended on a somber and bitter note. My observations were general, but a truly tender and loving heart would have discerned transports of love and devotion.

In Léonce's reply, I found only—and I was somewhat surprised—a curious and very erudite enumeration of all the debauched and lascivious old men whom poets have ridiculed from antiquity to the present. He cited the old men in Aristophanes, Plautus, Terence, Shakespeare, and Molière. He even found a scene from Chinese drama to illustrate the amorous confusions of a graybeard. His letter was ingenious and amusing. I saw in it only one more proof of his fascinating intellect. Later when my eyes were no longer sealed, this mind so lacking in soul seemed devoid of grandeur to me. A loving heart has a cataract and cannot see.

When René Delmart visited me next and I related my scene with Duchemin, he took it seriously even while making light of the pedant. "My dear, dear Marquise," he said, clasping my hands affectionately, "do you want me to teach that man a lesson?"

"Heavens, no!" I exclaimed. "That would make him feel too important."

"You're right," he replied, "because it is well known that he acts that way with every woman."

"If love to him is a monomania," I laughed, "it deserves respect, like practicing a religion, like fanaticism."

"Maybe so," he answered, "but Duchemin is mean-spirited. He will hurt you."

"Let's rush to counteract him," I rejoined, "by calling on the good offices of Albert de Lincel."

"Unfortunately he is ill," René said. "He must stay in by his fire and won't be able to pay a call for several days."

"But my dear René, why couldn't we go see him?"

"That's true. That's the simplest procedure. He'll be touched, and perhaps we will have distracted him—even if only for an hour—from the anxieties of his genius."

CHAPTER V

THE FOLLOWING AFTERNOON René came by in a carriage to take me to see Albert de Lincel. He lived near Place Vendôme on the second floor of the house where he was to die. We crossed the small oak-panelled anteroom where he had hung a painting of the Venetian School. It was a life-size nude Venus reclining in folds of purple drapery. This beautiful figure was so highly modelled that she seemed real when you passed her.

We found Albert in a small salon which he used as his study. An entire back wall was filled with oak book shelves. Two pencil portraits, of Mademoiselle Rachel and Madame Malibran, were placed on either side.[1] Large armchairs, a piano, a desk of violet ebony, and a clock topped with a classical bronze statue completed the furnishings. Albert was partially stretched out on a violet leather settee. When he saw us come in, he rose abruptly, like an automaton, as if a spring had set up him upright. I couldn't hide my dismay; it kept me from speaking to him at first. What a change had taken place since the evening I had seen him at the Arsenal! His body had perhaps more distinction for being thinner, and the mortal pallor of his face increased the spiritual in his expression. But, my God, how ravaged! His wan, shining cheekbones jutted out. His cavernous eyes shone with a strange light. His lips were almost white. His tense smile revealed his damaged teeth. Oh, it was no longer the fresh, gay smile sparkling with youth and love! It was as if the bitterness in his soul had burned his mouth with corrosive acids. Only his forehead had stayed pure, smooth and unwrinkled. The night before René had alerted him to our visit. He had dressed with the extreme care that was typical of him. A black redingote of extremely fine weave closely fit his arched torso.

I was overwhelmed by what I saw. René meanwhile explained what I would like him to do for me.

"Oh, I'd love to," he said. "I'll write to Frémont this very evening to drop by to see me."

1. Rachel (Elisa Félix, 1820–58) was an actress specializing in classical repertory. Maria Felicia Garcia Malibran (1808–36) was a mezzo-soprano and contralto versatile enough to do dramatic soprano roles.

I thanked him, adding that it was really indiscreet for someone who didn't know him to trouble him like this.

"Oh, you are no stranger to me. I know a great deal about you from my friend René, and I am extremely happy to make your acquaintance directly because you are very good to look at." And he kept his large, deep eyes on me for some time.

"But it would seem," I said, lowering my eyes beneath the intensity of his gaze, "that you didn't recognize me."

"Recognize you?" he repeated.

"Yes, indeed, we saw each other first on a Sunday evening at the Arsenal, years ago. You took me for a Quaker that evening."

"What? That was you? Oh, yes, yes, you had long blond curls rippling over a black velvet bodice. You see, I've remembered everything. You refused to waltz with me, and that was a mistake on your part, Marquise, because, really, we might have fallen in love."

"How you go on," René said. "Are you never going to change, Albert? Can you never set eyes on a woman without bringing up love?"

"Well, what do you think you should talk to them about?" laughed Albert. "Our friend doesn't look like a bluestocking, and I don't suppose that heavy doses of metaphysics and socialism would be to her taste."

"What makes you think that love will be?" René shot back.

"What you're saying sounds like a jealous lover. I could smell that a mile away," rejoined Albert, laughing even harder.

"I have only friends," I interjected.

"What that implies," said Albert, "is a secret love affair. Are you happy?"

"More than I've ever been."

"Ah," he sighed, "you say that with a sparkle in your eyes which makes you even more beautiful."

"I don't want to mislead you," I said, trying to change the subject. "I'm a bit of a bluestocking myself. Not only did I translate an English novel, but I added a short preface to introduce the author who is unknown in France."

"Oh ho! Let's see," he said. *"Le style, c'est la femme!"*

And picking up the book where I had written a complimentary dedication, Albert skimmed through the preface I'd written.

"Good," he murmured as he read, "the style is natural and concise. There's elegance, and here and there a spark of sensitivity. Your mind must be rigorous and decisive; your heart, frank and honest."

"You can pass judgment later," I replied, "for I hope we'll see each other again."

"Sooner than you think and sooner than you wish, perhaps," he answered taking my hand.

We were getting ready to leave when Albert's mother was announced.

She was tall, still slender, her face proud and aristocratic. Her son looked very much like her, but his traits were a shade more intellectual and finely chiseled. Albert greeted his mother with a kiss, and his cheeks glowed with pleasure at the sight of her. He had a very strong affection for his family. In the midst of his sad and stormy life, he had kept the cult of the family. He always spoke of his mother with respect and emotion. It's true throughout time: only the mean and mediocre fail to love their mothers. Those with passion in their hearts or minds feel they absorbed it in their mother's womb.

Albert introduced me to his mother, telling her who I was. We exchanged a few pleasantries. Then I rose to leave. Albert shook René's hand, kissed mine, and said, "Au revoir!"

CHAPTER VI

THAT VERY EVENING I wrote up my visit to Albert de Lincel for Léonce. He replied right away with what I would call burning curiosity. He would be charmed, he said, to get to know through me one of the persons who had interested him more than anyone else. He asked me for every imaginable detail on Albert and urged me to see him as often as possible. Thus I was quite naturally disposed to accept Albert's sympathy without any reservation or misgiving. I had found him cheerful and friendly. I liked the simple style of his genius which he offered me without that solemnity and pomp to which all famous men consider themselves more or less bound at a first meeting.

The day after I called on Albert, we had one of those brilliant winter days, so rare in Paris. The sky was a vivid blue. The sparrows flew back and forth in the sunlight on the bare treetops and occasionally ventured as far up as the balustrade of the high window where I was sitting, leaning on my elbows. I was like the sparrows, breathing in the warm, refreshing air of that Italian day while I watched my son running as he played ball on the same paths where we are seated now. Every day the porter who was fond of us let him into the garden which once belonged to me.

I watched my child's happy romping. He greeted me with his squeals, and if I looked somewhere else, he called up, forcing me to look down at him. In front of me were the tile roofs and bell towers of a section of Faubourg Saint-Germain. The noise of carriages and voices came up as far as my window. The sounds and sights prevented me from hearing my doorbell ring. Abruptly I felt a hand pulling on the pleats of my gown. It was my old servant telling me with her usual fat happy face, "Madame, there's a gentleman to see you."

I turned around and found myself face to face with Albert de Lincel.

He was paler than the day before and so out of breath that he looked ready to collapse. I took him by the hand and made him sit down. He fell prostrate into an armchair.

"You see," he said, "I lost no time repaying your call."

"How good of you," I replied, "to have come so soon and climbed so high."

"It's true that it's a bit high up, Marquise, but it's to your credit not to have left your house and to have had the courage to live under the roof. I see a good omen in this. The day will come when, once again, you will own the entire building."

"Poets are prophets," I laughed. "What you say will bring me good luck, and I shall win my suit. In the meantime, see what a good view I have." I led him over to the window, then, turning around, I added, "Besides, I have my dearest possessions here, and I in no way miss my large second-floor apartment."

He began then to study three portraits which separated the bookcase units covering the walls. The first was my mother's, a large watercolor with muted tones which perfectly rendered the gentle distinction of her features. Next was my grandfather's; his face was severe, almost glowering; his wide mouth and compressed lips had a bitter expression, while his sparkling eyes and calm forehead made the upper part of his face look extremely serene. The pure lines and sober coloring of this painting were reminiscent of David. His hair, brushed in pigeon wings, was frosted with powder. His barbel blue jacket of a Republican cut had two broad, pointed revers; so did his white Robespierre waistcoat. Between these revers was the puffed knot of the mouseline cravat wound in deep folds around his neck. The overall effect was in marked contrast with the pallor and gravity of his bearing.

The third portrait, a magnificent Petitot miniature, showed my great-uncle, a Knight of Malta.[1] His proud, young head was crowned with a long thick wig, the kind worn at the end of Louis XIV's reign. His neck rested in a white cravat with majestic pleats. His beautifully burnished steel cuirass had a relief pattern of gold filigree and blue enamel. A purple mantle fell from his left shoulder.

After examining these portraits, Albert leafed through some of my books. He was struck by an edition of Volney's works as well as by a book of Condorcet, which these authors had given my grandfather.[2] On seeing their signatures, he said, "Do you realize, Marquise, that in some respects we come from the same milieu? My father was an intimate of those famous men Bonaparte called ideologues. Many a time my father used to talk to me about his friends, the great philosophers, as he called them, and after his death, I found their letters among his papers."

While we were chatting, his voice was so strained and his malaise so obvious, that I interrupted, "It wasn't very hospitable of me not to have offered you some sugar water after you climbed five flights."

And taking a glass, sprinkled with gold stars (which I usually used myself), I held out to him a glassful of sugar water.

He burst out laughing like a child.

"My dear Marquise, do you think this insipid drink will give me back my strength?"

"Would you like for me to add some orange-blossom extract?"

"It's getting better and better," he cried, laughing more heartily.

1. Jean Petitot (1607–91) was a French-Swiss portrait enamellist.

2. Constantin de Volney (1757–1820) was a historical writer. Antoine Caritat, Marquis de Condorcet (1743–94), was a mathematician and a Reign of Terror victim.

"Oh, now that I think about it," I said, "I've some excellent Spanish chocolate. It could be made quickly. Do let me have some made for you. I wouldn't dare suggest tea or coffee. They would be too stimulating."

"Don't go to so much trouble, Marquise. Simply have me brought a generous glass of wine."

Born and bred in the Midi, I had never touched wine—like most women from warm climates. I had put my son on the same regime, and since my bankruptcy, I had given up my cellar. I told all this to Albert—adding that my servant was the only one in the house who drank.

"All right," he replied gaily, "Kitchen wine, let it be, but believe me, Marquise, you should have your son drink some, too, if you don't want him to grow up lymphatic and sickly."

I rang for Marguerite who soon brought a big black bottle and a glass. Albert drank half the bottle, and as he drank, his complexion took on color, and his eyes, new vitality.

"Ah," he said, touching the bottle, "this and those kind long rays of sunlight greeting me from your window, give me vigor and cheer. Now, Marquise, I will be able to walk, talk, even write, for a long time."

"The wine really does you good," I remarked, still astonished.

"I've been slandered on my alleged abuse of it," he replied. "But if ever, Marquise, you were dying or desperate, you would see what strength the body can find in it; what enchantment and oblivion, the mind can extract."

"How horrible," I laughed. "I won't sully my lips with that bitter-tasting liquid. Speak to me instead of the perfume of lemons and oranges. I still remember that when the big-footed wine-dressers used to crush the harvest at my father's château, I was so frightened by the smell of the vats that I used to go far off to some high place to breathe the wind of heaven."

"With the sun gilding and burnishing your hair, you must have made an extraordinarily beautiful Erigone," he responded gallantly. "Believe me, your disdain of the beverage which all peoples have called divine, has something affected and mannered about it. It's beneath you."

"But I assure you: I'm not affecting anything. With me it's an instinct of revulsion. And I promise you that the day when that repugnance stops, I'll try to drink with you."

"Oh, what a good woman you are! You won't believe what they say about me, will you? that I drink to stupefaction? that I throw myself headfirst into drunken oblivion? It's not true. I have my eyes open. I know what I do and what I want when I sometimes go under. Dear Marquise, if ever your heart is broken, don't look at a common man when he's drunk, singing and laughing in his wretchedness. That in itself would intoxicate you, and make you want to imitate him."

"That's a blind, material expedient," I countered. "Can't a person lose himself in love, devotion, patriotism, or the pursuit of fame?"

"I've tried everything, and oblivion is there alone," he answered, tapping the bottle with the back of his delicate, tapered fingers. "But I get drunk only when I suffer too much and the imperious desire to forget life makes me envy death."

Everything he said about the benefit of intoxication to which he was accused of being addicted made me feel uncomfortable. I didn't even understand the genuine strength that wine lent his failing health and that had imperceptibly become a necessity for him. Later when my sick chest bent and weakened my body, formerly so robust, when I was short of breath walking and had trouble breathing, and my hands were thin and limp, then I was constrained to approach to my lips this beverage which had repulsed me for so long. Imperceptibly it brought back my strength, and if he had still been alive, my great, beloved poet, I would have asked him to celebrate in my honor the slopes of Médoc, as Anacreon had once sung the wines of Crete and Chios.

"You love poetry, Marquise," Albert continued, "and in order to have you appreciate the poetry in wine I would like to quote all the fine lines that the great poets of antiquity and the genuine modern poets have sung in its honor. You may be sure that they have all loved it because you can only write poetically about what you love. But I'm getting pedantic and forgetting to tell you that I saw Frémont this morning, or rather I hesitate to tell you because I don't have good news for you."

"I can guess. Your editor refuses my translations."

"He refused them in a tone of voice which made me suspect a prior decision that could even put me on bad terms with him."

"I see Duchemin's revenge in that," I told him. "He forestalled your efforts on my behalf and has prejudiced him against me. I have no quarrel with your publisher, but I do with that dreadful satyr."

"Moreover, Marquise, I shall find you another editor."

"Thank you," I replied, holding out my hand, "but let me enjoy your first visit without wearying you with this matter."

At that moment a little hand scratched at the door of my study and gently pushed it open. It was my son. Since he hadn't seen me at the window, he had gotten bored with his game and come to find me. Children always want a companion or spectator in their amusements. It's a foretaste of human vanity and sympathy.

"Oh, I figured you had a visitor," my son said, kissing me. "But I don't know this gentleman," he added, glancing at Albert.

"Do you want to know me and maybe love me a little?" Albert asked, pulling the boy over to him.

"Yes, I like your looks."

"You're being honored," I said to Albert, "because this terrible child can hardly bear some of your fellow writers who are friends of mine."

"I like René because he is good for you and because he hugs me," replied the child, "but the others talk only about themselves and send me away when they're here."

"And what do you like about me?" Albert asked.

"Because your face is so pale and sad that you remind me of my father when he was about to die." And with that, the child sat on Albert's knee and gave him a kiss.

"Since you like me a little, won't you ask your mother not to refuse us a nice treat?"

"What treat?" my son asked.

"You see this pretty card?" Albert replied, pulling a pink cardboard square out of his pocket. "It will open all the gardens and galleries of the zoo at the Jardin des Plantes. I have a carriage below, and if your mother would be good enough to get in with us, we can be there in fifteen minutes."

"Oh, mama dearest, don't refuse," my child said, throwing his arms around me. "How much fun it would be to see all those ferocious animals who scare me!"

"And with this good sunshine all the gorgeous birds will be in fine feather," Albert added.

"Oh, let's leave right away," cried my son, jumping up and down.

"Don't deprive him of such a great treat," said Albert smiling kindly.

"I want to go, I want to go. Say 'yes'," my son kept repeating, pulling on my skirt.

"I can see. I'll have to obey," I laughed, "but you must agree, Monsieur de Lincel, that we're proceeding a bit fast down the road to friendship."

"Oh, I should much prefer a different destination," said Albert, kissing my hand, "because I feel disposed, Marquise, to fall in love with you."

"In that case, I'm not going out," I replied, "for you frighten me." And I acted as if I would untie the bow of the hat I had just put on.

"I want to go. I want to go," my son kept repeating.

"See the beautiful sunshine urging us on," Albert added. "Come on, my dear Marquise, let's hurry. I write; so do you. There, our common ground is established."

And so saying, he opened the door, and we left. My son gleefully went ahead. In order to go down the stairway Albert supported himself sometimes on the child's sturdy shoulder, sometimes on his curly blond head. I followed behind Albert, watching him sadly.

We climbed into the carriage, Albert by my side, my son facing us. The sun beamed through the carriage windows, making it as warm as a hothouse.

"Well, I feel really good," Albert said to me. "It's been a long time since I've felt such a respite from pain. People slander me, Marquise, when they credit me with unbridled passion. I assure you that it would have taken very little to make me happy. Like now, I desire nothing more: this brilliant day makes me warm; your beautiful child gives me his attention; you yourself are so charming to see and so good to hear. It all seems to me like supreme happiness."

"I am really delighted to hear you say so," I replied with friendship in my heart. "You can expect to return to a calm, normal life because what you are calling happiness at this moment is easy to find."

"Why don't you simply tell me I've found it?"

"I'm not sure I really understand," I said, pulling back the hand he was trying to take.

"Come now, Marquise," he retorted almost angrily, "you're as much a coquette as the rest of them, and I'm an incurable maniac who can't be around any woman whatsoever without my old bruised heart acting up."

As he said this, his lips curled bitterly and contemptuously, and he had said "any woman whatsoever" in a tone that really hurt my feelings.

My son interjected in his pearly voice, "Are you going to fight in such a short time? You'd do better to look at that church over there. See how beautiful it is, reflected in the water. It's right next to us."

The carriage going along the Quays had just passed Notre-Dame. Its large nave with strong, finely carved buttresses stood out against the azure sky like a large ship on a blue sea.

"Perhaps your son will be an artist," Albert turned to me. "He's just been struck by a truly beautiful sight which neither of us thought to notice." And as he spoke, he had the driver stop, lowered the window on the left and said "Take a look."

We leaned out the window on my side. For a few moments we contemplated the cathedral, a majestic vessel suspended in the air. The trees on that square, which today replaces the dilapidated archbishop's residence, spread their leafless branches around the gothic steeple.

"This is a charming spot on summer evenings," Albert said, "when the trees are green and you go up the Seine lounging in a boat. It makes you think of Esmeralda fleeing the sack of Notre-Dame and seeing the grandeur and beauty of the dark church in the starlight. Oh what pages of description that poet gave us! What a sublime painter Victor is, besides being our greatest lyric poet!"[3]

(One of Albert's most attractive traits was the homage he paid to genius.)

While we were admiring the church so beautifully displayed

3. Victor Hugo (1802–85) was in exile during the time of the frame narration.

behind us, my son had gotten on his knees on the seat, had lowered the front glass to pull the coachman's jacket. "Let's get going! Come on! We'll get there too late to see the animals!"

The carriage started moving again, and we were at the entrance of the Jardin des Plantes very shortly.

A crowd of children were going in with their mothers or maids, fathers or tutors. Most were stopping first at the little stand for cakes, oranges, barley sugar, and sweet drinks on either side of the outside grill. The ladies vending hawked their wares to the children, "Come get your supplies, my fine young gentlemen, my beautiful young ladies!"

Albert said to my son, "We must get our supply of brioches for the bears, giraffes, and elephants, too." And he began to fill up my son's pockets and hat with pastries and candies. "You can, of course, taste them and lick your chops first."

And as if to follow suit, Albert got a glass of absinthe which he gulped down.

"Oh, my dear poet," I cried, "how can you do this?"

"Marquise," he replied airily, "I'm giving myself legs to accompany you through the galleries, down the paths, into the hothouses, and you would have shown your good heart and unprejudiced mind by not noticing."

"But it's only because I'm afraid it will hurt you."

"If you try to wean opium smokers too fast, they'll drop dead," he retorted.

While he was speaking a slight flush spread over his cheeks, coloring his frightening pallor. His eyes were bright. The pure air of day enlivened his face, and the breeze from the tall trees stirred the blond ringlets on his inspired forehead. At that moment he was very handsome, and his youth seemed to have come back again.

"I used to walk here often with Cuvier," he resumed.[4] "I'll show you soon where he stayed. His treatise on the formation of the globe made me dream of a poem where the characters would have been the race preceding our own. You can imagine what fantasy one could let loose dealing with creatures in an era before history!"

"Oh, please, do write that poem," I said. "It's been such a long time since you've written anything."

"Write again? What would be the use?" he burst out laughing.

"But it would be a noble distraction."

"I don't think so. Look, I prefer the fun your son is having right now throwing cakes to the bears."

And, moving over to the child, he took a cake from the boy's hat and began throwing pieces to the heavy panting beasts.

After having regaled the bears, my son wanted to visit the monkeys. But noticing my great revulsion for their foul gambols and human grimaces, he abruptly said to Albert, who was laughing at my discomfort, "Let's leave. Mama is scared."

He mistook my disgust for fright.

"Let's go see some beasts which are more noble and more genuine," I said to Albert. "I can't help it. Monkeys seem to me like some crude sketch for man."

We went into the circular building housing the reindeer, antelopes, giraffes, and elephants. Albert became quite gleeful, a child again himself, seeing the glee of my son when an elephant raised up in his trunk the cakes his little hand had held out. Then came the turn of the giraffes who lowered their long flexible, undulating necks down to my boy, soliciting his attention with looks from their large, gentle eyes, sticking out their black tongues to receive their share of the feast. One of the custodians put my son on the back of a

4. Georges Cuvier (1769–1832) founded comparative anatomy.

magnificent reindeer, who immediately shot around the enormous pillar supporting the edifice with elegant, rapid movements. The child was wild with laughter. The custodian held him on firmly, following the animal around the track. There was no risk in the game, so I rejoined Albert who called me over to point out a beautiful, svelte antelope who seemed to be looking at us.

"See what an interest she takes in us. Wouldn't you say she was thinking and that she is speaking in her own way when she undulates her head? How lively and piercing her eyes are! In my opinion, Marquise, they look like yours."

"But hers are black," I said.

"And yours are dark blue, which produces the same expression in the glance."

Then he began to stroke the antelope, kissing it on the forehead and neck, saying while the lovely animal looked at him with wide-open eyes, "Perhaps you contain the soul of a woman. I'll never forget, my beauty, how you looked at me today!"

The custodian who had gotten my son down, informed us that it was feeding time for the wild animals. We went into the gallery where tigers, lions, and panthers were enclosed. We could hear their terrifying roars from the outside. An acrid, wild odor filled this overly warm gallery. You felt nauseous and almost suffocated as soon as you entered. Albert's pallor changed suddenly to scarlet, and his eyes glittered with a strange fire.

This heavy, unhealthy air went to his head and gave him a kind of vertigo. At first I didn't pay attention, concerned as I was to get my son to move away from the bars of the cage and to contemplate from a distance the magnificent pose of two tigers, peacefully stretched out, until bounding in a sudden ferocious swoop at the stumps of raw meat they had just been thrown. Albert followed us silently from a distance. He seemed to hear and see nothing, apparently absorbed in an inner vision.

I had stopped in front of the cage of a colossal Sahara lion, recently shipped from our African colonies. The superb beast reclined majestically, his head resting on his two front paws which hid their curved claws beneath long red hair. His round eyes observed us without hostility. He rose slowly as if to make us welcome. He shook his massive golden mane against the bars. It was so brilliant and silky that it made you want to touch it involuntarily.

A few tufts extended through the bars, and forgetting my admonitions to my son, I automatically put up my hand. The lion let out an impressive roar. My child shrieked in terror, and Albert, who had rushed over, seized my ungloved hand and bore it to his lips, kissing it frantically.

"You wretch!" he shouted, frightening and hysterical. "Do you want to die? Do you want me to see you there in bloody pieces, your head opened, your hair pulled off your skull, nothing but a formless, ugly thing, like disintegrated corpses in a cemetery?"

While shouting, he seized me in his arms, and, weak as he was, carried me, running outside the gallery. My son followed us, still shrieking. The custodians watched us in amazement, thinking I had fainted. Once we were in a neighboring room where less ferocious animals were kept, I freed myself from Albert's grasp and sat down on a bench. My son jumped in my lap and threw his arms around me, kissing and crying.

"See here, I'm not hurt in the least," I said to him. Then, turning to Albert, still visibly distraught, "But, heavens, what is the matter? You frightened me more than the lion."

He looked at me without speaking and with a fixity which disturbed me. Suddenly he grabbed my son roughly by the shoulder and pulled him away from me.

"Let's leave," he said, taking my arm. "You can tell that this display of affection makes me ill."

I acted as if I hadn't heard him.

My son said, "You're mean. I don't like you anymore."

But soon we reached the thoroughfare of the large aviaries. Turtle doves, parrots, guinea hens, and herons were preening their lustrous feathers in the sunshine. Peacocks, spreading their tails, filled the air with their screeches of complacent pride. The chattering parakeets seemed to be making fun of them. The ostriches shook their long wings like fans so that the sharp light filtering through the bare branches of the trees projected lacy shadows on the sand. Gradually the cheerful serenity of the day took hold of us again and effaced the memory of what had just occurred.

"Let's make up," Albert said, holding out his hand to my son. "I'm going to take you to the Cedar to eat some sugar cones."

So we made a stop beneath the centenarian tree planted by Jussieu and touched by the hand of Linnaeus.[5]

But soon the nursemaids' babbling, the commotion of the children, and the cries of the lady hawking sugar cones wearied Albert and got on his nerves.

"Let's go sit in the greenhouse," he said. "We'll have it to ourselves since it is closed to the public."

I didn't want to refuse. It would have looked as if I were afraid, and as a matter of fact, I wasn't afraid of anything. My safeguard was my love affair, far away but always with me.

We entered a large square hothouse, completely filled with tropical plants and flowers. I experienced almost infinite well-being inhaling that warm fragrant air. We sat down facing a clear pool from which rose a white marble naiad. Her feet were ca-

5. Antoine de Jussieu (1686–1758) was a director of the Jardin des Plantes from 1708 until the end of his career. Any tree he planted would have been 100 years old when Musset and Colet visited this zoo in 1852. Carolus Linnaeus (1707–78), a Swedish botanist, was a friend of Jussieu.

ressed by water lilies floating on the surface of the water while her neck and hair unfurled in the shade of large-leafed banana trees and flowering magnolias.

"Isn't this beautiful?" my son was saying, carried away by the sight of strange plants that were completely new to him. "Doesn't it smell good? I would sleep as well on that warm moss bank as in my own bed," he added, stretching out at the edge of the pool. "But I'm hungry and I gave all my cakes to the animals."

Albert went over to speak to the man who had let us in, and I heard him say, "Take my carriage. You can get there faster."

He returned to sit down next to me while my son, stretched out on the grass and at first silent and still, had fallen asleep.

"Aren't you tired?" I asked Albert, who had become extremely pale again.

"A question for a mother or sister," he reported, teasing. "Be a little less good and a little more tender, Marquise."

"Goodness and tenderness are not mutually exclusive," I told him. "See it rather as motherly love."

"Well, here we are again, enmeshed in motherhood and sisterhood. It's the current jargon of fashionable women. It serves as decent coquetry when they do not want to understand or when they have stopped loving you."

"By that hypothesis such jargon is useless to me, even alien. After all, our acquaintance is too recent for me to have thought either of tightening or loosening our ties."

"At least you're frank, and I prefer frankness to circumlocutions. So if you were never to see me again, you would have no regrets?"

"I certainly would," I answered. "You're not the kind of man whom one forgets."

"Thank you," he said, squeezing my hand. "That will do for now. Let's talk about something else, and not spoil these words.

The more I look at you," he added, "the more I find you have eyes like that antelope. If I could manage it, I would take that charming beast home with me to replace my dog who barks and whom I don't like anymore. Wouldn't she be graceful lying there next to your son, nestling against him as you did a little while ago when you put me in such a foul mood. One moment I feared for you with the lion. The next moment I wanted to be the lion myself, carry you off in my claws and devour you."

"These trees and liana weaving a jungle around us must inspire these carnivorous ideas," I laughed. "Let's try to be serious. For example, tell me the names of all these plants."

"Do you take me for some professor at the Jardin des Plantes?" he teased. "Monsieur Humboldt, whom I accompanied here a year ago, did indeed tell me the names ending in *us* of all those interlaced trees.[6] But I've retained two or three at most. I preferred to immerse myself in the essence of the inspired disquisitions of that genial savant. They were so novel and imagistic. What's marvelous in the great German geniuses is the breadth and diversity of their talents. They partake of the universal soul, and sometimes you'd say they absorb it. That's how Goethe assimilates science and refurbishes it with his genius, while a scientist like Humboldt adorns his knowledge with grandeur borrowed from poetry.

"In France we stay immured in our separate aptitudes. A scholar is a pedant; a poet, an ignoramus; our musicians and painters, illiterates. Germany seems to have inherited the synthesizing intelligence of Greece, which wanted genius to embrace all human knowledge. Monsieur Humboldt has a mind which shows itself in all subjects, with that divine facility which characterized the demigods of antiquity. I shall never in my entire life

6. Alexander von Humboldt (1769–1859) was a German botanist.

forget the eloquence and wit he expressed in this very place where we are sitting. Did you ever hear him, Marquise?"

"I met him in Gérard's salon," I replied.[7] "There's a painter with an incisive mind; his conversation is worth more than his painting. Monsieur Humboldt took a liking to me one evening and wrote on a large vellum sheet an unpublished passage from his *Cosmos*, to which he added a gracious dedication. That's where I met Balzac also.[8] Do you like him? What do you think of him?"

"Oh that man was a great force. His genius was reliably indicated by his massive, powerful bull's neck. His creations are sometimes so abundant and overgrown that they smother themselves. One would like to make their lines stand out better by pruning here and there, but perhaps that would spoil them, just as we would spoil the interlaced trees shading us now if we tried to trim them. The beautiful, luminous and always noble in the classical sense of the term, is hardly suited for anything except poetry in my opinion. Prose has rhythms which are less restricted and more familiar. It blends with everything and takes every liberty. In prose we have the failure of taste which is the supreme refinement of genius. Balzac's taste doesn't always seem very pure to me. Nor do his characters, especially his women of high society, always seem true to me. He exaggerates nature and sometimes pads it. The deep ocean has a viscuous scum; molten metals produce dross."

While we were chatting in this vein, the man Albert had sent off somewhere came back into the greenhouse, holding a silver tray laden with ices, candied fruits, cakes, and a flagon of rum.

My son woke up at the tinkling of the platter as it went past. He ran over to us licking his chops over these goodies. I thanked

7. François Gérard (1770–1837) was a historical painter.

8. Honoré de Balzac (1798–1850) would have just died.

Albert for his thoughtfulness and urged him to taste the sherbets and fruits.

"Eating is often an intolerable burden for me," he explained. "When I have dined the night before, I am never sure of being able to have a meal the next day. Let me renew my strength as I see fit without worrying about my regime." While talking he drank two small glasses of rum. I didn't dare say anything to him, but I was afraid that his head would get inflamed again.

"The air in this conservatory is making me tired," I said, getting up. "Let's go back out into the cold, tonic garden air."

"But we are fine here," protested Albert.

"This time, my mother is wrong," my son added. "She's keeping you from drinking and me from eating."

"You're both children!" I said, taking them each by the hand and dragging them to the door. We crossed the garden rapidly. My son began running ahead of us. I barely leaned on Albert's arm because he was almost staggering. He stopped speaking to me and fell back into his black mood. However, when we climbed back into the carriage, his gaiety suddenly returned. He proposed crossing the Pont d'Austerlitz, to take a turn around the Arsenal, no longer host to poets, and then taking us home by the boulevards, Rue Royale and the Pont de la Chambre, "Or what would be even better," he added, "go have dinner in some cabaret on the Champs-Elysées. Say 'yes,' Marquise, we must do it; I want to, and it will be fun." He used that capricious, juvenile insistence which was one of his charms.

"On that score, I refuse, I rebel. If you are really intent upon having dinner with me, it will be at home with us."

"I accept," he said, "but on the condition that some other time I will be the Amphitryon."

"What would our friend René say if he saw us passing the day together like this?"

"My word, that's a good idea," Albert replied, "what if we went over to his Auteuil retreat to get the good fellow to eat with us?"

"What are you saying? If you did that you'd be driving us all the way to Versailles. How you go on, poet of mine."

"I go by inspiration and instinct. I follow my heart which impels me forward. Marquise, do you have some lover waiting for you this evening to make you want to go home so soon?"

"You can tell I don't since I'm asking you for dinner."

"So then, you're really free this evening?"

"As free as work and poverty."

"That generally means slavery," he rejoined.

"No," I said, "the world hardly notices anyone except the idle rich. It leaves the rest of us completely at liberty in sadness and solitude."

"If you were utterly and completely free," he repeated. "That would be fine, but, bah, you're fooling me."

I no longer knew how to answer him, but we took up word games good-naturedly enough until we reached home. When I reached the bottom of my staircase, I raced ahead to send my old Marguerite out to get a chicken and some Bordeaux. Albert and my son followed more slowly. When they came in, I had already taken off my hat, put away my shawl, and knotted a white apron around my waist. I was getting ready to help with dinner.

"You can go rest in my study," I said to Albert, "and browse in my books and albums. If you want to do something really nice, make me one of your clever ink sketches, like the Sahara lion who frightened you so much."

"Never," he replied. "You want me to take note of my moments of anguish, so that I can express them objectively. I'm staying in here with you, and I'm going to help you cook dinner."

The idea made me laugh.

"Oh, you think I don't know anything about it. Well, what's your order? What dish are you going to make?"

"Something sweet," I answered, "a dessert of pears in meringue, and since you insist, you can beat the egg whites."

"That's fine. I'm ready."

He had grabbed a tea towel and jauntily tied it through the tails of his black jacket.

"Let me at least give you an elegant vessel worthy of a poet." I handed him a real Sevres china bowl which had belonged to my mother and an ivory fork, and so there he was at the window, beating the whites which beneath the blows of his nervous hand soon rose in snowy heaps. I had to give my son something to do, too. I grabbed some gorgeous pears from the étagère and put him to peeling them. In a few moments, my dessert was assembled, and when Marguerite returned, all she had to do was put it on the fire.

Then Albert and my son helped me set the table.

"All this brings back my student days," Albert said. "I haven't felt so happy in ages, and although I've almost stopped eating, I feel ravenous this evening."

However, when we sat down at the table, he ate only a little bit of white meat and tasted my pears in meringue only to be polite. To my great surprise, he drank only water mixed with red wine. Since he saw me so worried about his health, he doubled his efforts to be gay and lively to show me he felt marvelous. After dinner he and my son played like two schoolboys. However, the child, worn out by a day spent outdoors, began to fall asleep around ten o'clock, and Marguerite carried him off to bed. I remained alone with Albert, feeling a little tired myself. I was sitting motionless in a large armchair while Albert, sitting opposite me at a corner of the fireplace, rolled a cigarette I'd given him permission to smoke.

We weren't talking and little by little I almost forgot he was there. Another image took his place, surging before me young, smiling, beloved. Without thinking I bent toward the table I used to write on every evening. I picked up a pen and touched the folder of stationery. It was the hour when I always wrote to Léonce, and the habit of my heart was so imperious that even in the theater or at a party—although I almost never went out anymore—when the hour for my daily letter rolled around, I felt keenly frustrated if I couldn't write.

"You have something you want to do, and I'm in your way," Albert said. He had noticed my distraction and had followed all my movements.

His voice made me start, reminding me of his presence. I blushed so openly that he continued as if he had found me out, "You're thinking about someone who isn't here."

"I'm a little tired from this long day, good as it's been," I said, not replying directly.

"Which is my cue to withdraw," he retorted without getting up. "Oh, Marquise, you don't know where you're sending me."

"To sleep soundly, I hope."

"Soundly . . . you talk like a coquette because at your age, you can't still be naive. If you want me to stay calm, let me stay here two or three hours. How does that get in your way?"

He was so pale and distraught that I didn't have the heart to cross him. Then despite my secret preoccupation, I felt the great charm of his company.

"If you think it would do you good," I said, "stay a little while longer."

As he thanked me, he took my hand and kept it in his.

We were lighted by a lamp whose pale gleams were muted by a pink shade. The full moon seemed suspended just outside my window—sending its brilliant beams through the panes. No noise from the outside reached us. A large fire was burning in the fireplace. He was still holding my hand, but he kept so very still that if his eyes hadn't been wide open, I could have thought he was asleep. I didn't dare move for fear of making him say something untoward. I was very uncomfortable in the silence we were keeping, but I no longer knew how to break it. Finally I brought myself to tell him that I hoped he would come back some evening when I was entertaining Duverger, Albert de Germiny, and René.

"Of course," he replied, "if you let me come all the other evenings when you are alone. Otherwise, no." And he shook my hand, repeating, "Don't you see? I don't want to suffer anymore."

"What a tortured soul you must have," I told him, "to speak this way to me the second day you've seen me. I think I've been friendly and open with you. I will not add 'sisterly' since this word makes you angry."

"And sisterliness itself still less," he retorted.

He was sitting on the throw rug at my feet and still held my hand. He went on, "If only you would let me stay here forgetting the time, my head on your knees, not saying a word, not asking for anything more of you, but certain that one day I could ask everything of you, certain then of being your favorite, the one you wait for; that before me, you had only friends; that I can fill the empty place; and that in the end you will love me even though I am no more than the shadow of myself, a creature whom the past has submerged."

I got up at once, in so doing pushing away his head and hands.

"You're going too fast," I said, "you're changing the gentle joys I'm savoring in getting to know you. You are disturbing friendship. You want a place for yourself in my heart. You already have in my admiration a special place, a choice place, nearly an exclusive place. And that explains the charm your mind has over mine, but for that other attraction which overwhelms, staggers, stuns, I . . ."

"Don't go on, Marquise. I understand. You feel that attraction for someone else. But how does it happen that he isn't here? and I am? Ah, I've got it. Perhaps he's waiting peacefully in your bedroom until I've given you the full spectacle of my soul."

After saying all this in a very cutting voice, he lit a cigarette, picked up his hat, and bowing almost ceremoniously, got ready to leave.

"I can't imagine," I said, "what kind of interpretation you will give what I'm going to do now, but follow me." And with that I picked up a candlestick and took him into the bedroom where my son was sleeping.

"Here is the person who watches over me and waits for me," I said, indicating the child's bed.

"Well, then, love me and save me from the life I'm leading," he cried, seizing my arm and clutching it. "Perhaps there is still time for you to make me well!"

"Let's leave it on that word," I replied. "Yes, I want to make you well, see you, hear you, strengthen your resolve, but please do not have any more of these outbursts which I cannot respond to and which would separate us. That would be painful for me."

"I'd be a fool," he jeered moving away from me. "You're not built like some mystic. If your lover isn't in this bedroom, he is certainly in that dressing room."

With a gesture I pointed to the exit. "Good evening, Monsieur de Lincel."

"Good night, Marquise. I will go divert myself in turn. I'll sup with some beauty who will spare me metaphysics."

I couldn't think of anything to reply. Anything moralistic would have been unfeeling and superfluous. Any denial would have been hypocritical. He had guessed that I loved someone else. Near or far, this someone existed and possessed me entirely. I walked silently behind him, lighting his way to the outside door. There I held out my hand.

"No," he pushed me away, "because within the hour I will be enlaced by common hands."

He tore down the stairs, singing a sarcastic ditty. I heard him slam the carriage door with a bang.

I was petrified for a few moments. "But what could I do for him?" I asked myself. "Nothing," replied the voice of inflexible logic, "since you don't love him with passion. At this very moment he is rushing off to some cabaret. Besides, to save him, you would have to open your arms and say 'Stay here; it will be better.'"

When I could get settled back down in my study and could take up my pen to write Léonce, his dear, cherished image, magnified by his solitary surroundings, quickly dispersed Albert's agitated image with a tranquil glance. Léonce didn't have these anxieties, these childish fits. Love illuminated him without burning him. Love was the lamp of his nocturnal labor, the reward for his completed task. Now that is real love, I told myself: strong, radiant, sure of itself, continuing unchanged, at a distance from the beloved!

This is how in the excess of love, I blasphemed love itself; love that is demanding, bizarre, anguished, headstrong, such as Albert had felt in his youth, love whose echo was reawakening in him. Can love be calm, resigned, free from desire? Impetuous only a few days a year and relegated the rest of the time to a compartment in the brain? Oh poor Albert, in your apparent madness, you were the man who loved, you who were inspired by life! The other man, away out there, far from me, in his laboring pride and eternal self-analysis, he didn't love at all. Love for him was only the subject for a disquisition, a dead letter!

CHAPTER VII

I SPENT part of the night writing up that strange day for Léonce. He replied very quickly to tell me that I had gotten too alarmed by a sick man's overexcited and nervous disposition. It would be a rather splendid task, well worth my dedication, to try to make that great troubled mind well again—if it were still possible. Despite the immense love he had for me, he didn't see that he had the right to stand between Albert's desires and my attraction to him, if I should ever begin to love him. The happiness of a man of Albert's caliber imposed every sacrifice, but, he added, he doubted whether such happiness was still possible. He considered Albert's ruined body and collapsing genius like those marvelous monuments of antiquity which can only move us now by their fragments.

This section of Léonce's letter made me very sad. What is the point of writing something like that to the woman you love? It's true that his closing expressed only tenderness. He said I was his life, his conscience, the treasured reward for his labor. He got carried away whenever he thought about our next meeting. The end of his letter erased the impression of the beginning, and I no longer found in what he said about Albert anything but an exaggerated but generous cult of genius. If it wasn't quite the language of a lover, at least it was that of a truly great philosophical mind.

Léonce's letter reached me the evening of the day following our visit to the Jardin des Plantes. All day I had worried about Albert coming back, and in the evening when any likely hour for his visit had passed, I really felt relieved that he hadn't appeared. I read, I translated a few pages, and I wrote to Léonce again. I resumed the routine of my love affair. That night my sleep was as sound as it had been fitful the day before. When I awoke, Marguerite handed me a little packet containing a book. It was one of Albert's with the following note:

> My dear Marquise,
>
> Beauzonet has bound this book, making it less unworthy of being opened by your beautiful hands. Will you permit its author to come pay a visit with René? It is very cold this spring, and I tell myself that it would be very cozy by your fire.
>
> Please accept, my dear Marquise, my very best wishes.

I decided neither to answer nor thank him until I'd consulted Léonce. But that very evening as I was getting ready to write him, my old Marguerite ushered in Albert.

"Do you have any idea where I've been?" he asked. "Don't hold it against me for coming alone. I spent five or six hours trying to find René. I decided to eat dinner at a cabaret in Auteuil to wait for him and come to your place together. But in the end I lost patience. So here I am. Receive me, my dear Marquise, as if our friend were here, too."

"I can't imagine anything nicer," I told him, "and I am counting on good René's influence to inspire in you a little of the friendship he has for me." I added quickly, "You see I have your beautiful book by my side. I'm delighted with it!"

"I gave one like it to my sister," he replied, "and when I was sending it to her this morning, I thought of you."

Everything he said that evening seemed meant to erase the painful impression his nervous ardor could have caused. His manners were exquisite, but I was sad to see his weakness and paleness continually worsen. His eyes themselves, which on the preceding days had lit up his face with sparkle and life, seemed to have been extinguished. He bent toward the fire in the fireplace as if he wanted to extract life from it.

"Some people say it's a sign of approaching death when our mind obstinately dwells on childhood memories. I don't know whether this omen will come true for me, but it is certain that for some time now, my thoughts keep turning to family tableaux and *collège* scenes which once thrilled my heart. I see my classmates again; our games, our studies come alive for me. I see especially those who have died: some in war, some in duels, several from consumption. Among them all, the most endearing, the most intelligent, and the most sadly missed is that young prince, my friend whom destiny floored with a single blow.[1] How many enchanting hours we spent together in the bare, dreary courtyards of the school. We were called 'inseparable.' During class when we couldn't talk to each other, we still found a way to write each other our ideas and projects for the days off. Often he came to my aid for the Greek translations, and I in turn helped him compose French verses. Would you look, my dear Marquise, what frank and wholehearted camaraderie is revealed in these little notes signed by the son of a king!"

As he spoke, he pulled from his pocket a deep envelope which contained a great many strips of notebook paper, which had originally been folded into tiny squares to be passed from hand to hand under the study tables. That way the pupils could transmit these short missives from prince to poet from one end of the room to the other.

1. The young prince is Ferdinand-Philippe, Duke of Orléans (1810–42) who attended Henri IV, and served with the army in Belgium in 1832 and in Algeria in 1835, 1839, and 1840. He died when his carriage overturned in Neuilly.

I was touched to read some of these little bits of paper, yellow with age. They have stayed in my memory.

"If your mommy will let you," wrote the prince, "come to Neuilly next Sunday, and we'll have a really good time. We can go boating and have refreshments with my sisters."

On another strip I read, "Tell me if this line has enough syllables. I think I have a hiatus. I'll always be a bad versifier."

On another there was "I'm desperate. I'm restricted to Neuilly for a week. There's no way to have refreshments at Neuilly. Mommy couldn't get my father to forgive me. His Highness, alas, is unbending. But perhaps you and the others could still go without me!"

Still another: "I would really like to escape. My word, if I weren't such an 'important personage,' I would risk it. But where would I go? Here's my idea: Could you have me at your mother's? We could have a good time without going out."

While I read, Albert was murmuring, "What an attractive and gracious disposition he had! What a catastrophe his death was! What a derisive blow for any legitimate hope! He carried into his tomb a part of my energy and will. If he were alive, I would consider myself bound in life to something more steadfast and noble. Shortly after his death, his poor wife, who was aware of our friendship, sent me the portrait which you probably noticed in my apartment."

"Let me thank you," I said, "for bringing those tender emotions to life for me. Notes like these are worth many a love letter."

"Oh," he replied reproachfully, "now you have pronounced the burning word that I was trying to keep myself from uttering. You're the insensitive lamp, and I'm the anxious moth who rushes into the consuming flame."

"Yours is a poet's heart; it's attractive and dear."

"A heart like René's? Less attractive perhaps? Like de Germiny's or Duverger's? That puts me in your circle of friends. This is quite consoling for my vanity, but quite insufficient for my aspirations."

"However, a moment ago, you seemed peaceful, almost happy."

"Of course, for two days I haven't had anything to drink and almost nothing to eat. I am very calm."

I couldn't think of anything to reply. I watched his gentle, pale face which looked heartsick at that very instant. An involuntary tear escaped from each eye, and he saw them rolling down my cheeks.

"Ah, how I should like to drink them," he said. "Thank you, my dear Marquise, please forgive me. I am becoming as stupid as a mediocre elegy, and you are going to hold me in contempt. It was hardly worthwhile paying you a call if I don't have wit enough to distract you a little. Come now, let it not be said that Albert de Lincel made the Marquise de Rostan depressed. Let me tell you a few anecdotes which are rushing back pell-mell.

"Among my memories of adolescence, there is one which always makes me chuckle. When I began to scribble (a sorry exercise which makes us examine our joys and pains without respite, bruising them and ourselves and burdening them to the point that our dreams spoil reality), I used to read my poems and prose pieces to my family. My father, a Neoclassic with a very clear philosophical mind which was never confused by the mists of modern metaphysics, used to wonder where I picked up my manner of tormented raillery where anguish pierced through the sarcasm and frivolity was as painful as a hair shirt. My style disoriented him as much as my ideas. I didn't use the pure crisp verses and calm, limpid sentences of the French writers of the two preceding centuries. What I did was a mélange of English humor and sallies in the *rhétoriqueur* manner of Mathurin Régnier.[2] One of my maternal

2. Mathurin Régnier (1573–1613) was a satiric poet.

great-uncles had written essays and verses without any concern for a public or fame. My father, as a Neoclassic, was somewhat contemptuous of these unpublished pages which, in his opinion, were ungrammatical whimsies. I had discovered them in an old cabinet and read them eagerly, finding them to my taste. They really charmed me with their originality and flair, so completely devoid of banality. I immersed myself in this unknown genius and assimilated his free, tempestuous manner. That's what happens when you start writing very young; while thinking I was writing like myself, I was to some extent the reflection of that earlier mind. One evening when I was reading to a group of relatives, my father began pacing up and down in the room, showing from time to time his surprise and displeasure at what he called the new literature. I was betraying the masters, he cried, where was I digging up my style and my ideas? Who was my source? Suddenly he stopped in front of my mother who was smiling as she listened, and said with comic rage, 'Madame, whom does this child take after? He resembles me in no way whatsoever. He's the bastard of his great-uncle!'

"My mother burst out laughing, and the rest of us joined in, my father first and foremost, although he kept repeating with flamboyant gestures, 'Bad seed! Bad school!'"

The longer Albert spoke, the more animated his face became, the more his eyes sparkled. I admired the mobility and charm of his genius.

He continued, "You were amazed the other day at my ability to beat egg whites. You should know, Marquise, that for eight days of my life I turned myself into a cook."

"Let me guess. Cooking for love."

"There you go again pronouncing the cabalistic word," he retorted. "But this time I'll keep going without pausing over it. Back when I frequented the Latin Quarter, before I knew love completely (a sad store of wisdom), I had tried love in all the forms caprice can give it. One evening at the Bal de la Chaumière, I met a ravishing grisette. Don't laugh. The grisette has vanished today. They've all become lorettes.[3] My grisette was a kind of plebeian Diana Vernon, timid as a titmouse and very proud of her gentility.[4] She was looked after by a great big fellow, a medical student whose awkwardness and stupid expression were a sharp contrast to her pretty, piquant grace.

"'How in the devil can you love him?' I asked as we were dancing—and while her sweetheart looked daggers at us. 'Why don't you let me replace your grotesque boyfriend immediately?'

"'Of course, you're obviously a better catch than he is,' she replied, looking me over from head to toe with her wide-open eyes, which hardly flattered my pretentions to being well turned out, but she added seriously, 'He has good qualities.'

"I answered with one of those gross expressions one uses with a grisette. She didn't seem to understand it.

"'Oh, if you only knew,' she continued, 'how well he keeps house. He helps me make my bed, sweep, iron my clothes, and he does the cooking all by himself.' She added appreciatively, 'This lets me save my hands and rest and enjoy dinner.'

"'If that's all that stands in my way,' I said, 'I promise to be an excellent cook.'

"'You're joking,' she replied, 'you're a dandy, a beau, a nobleman who's never scraped a carrot or made a stew.'

"'That's right,' I shot back, 'but I excel in some complicated dishes that I've watched being made in my father's kitchen. If you ever tasted them, you'd rave.'

"A few days later when I had conquered her hesitation, I got

3. A grisette was presumably a shopgirl or factory worker available for a temporary liaison. A lorette (the term dates from the turn of the century) made being kept her occupation. The Bal de la Chaumière was a popular dance hall.

4. Diana Vernon is the heroine of Scott's *Rob Roy*.

interested in the game and kept my word. For eight days I served her chicken fricassee, filet of sole, cutlets à la Soubise, rum omelettes, and a heap of other dishes which delighted her in their diversity. She prepared the basic ingredients wearing gloves. I lit the stove, mixed ingredients, butter, shortening, etc., I kept those pots and pans hopping. I wouldn't swear, Marquise, that my sauces were always orthodox. I must often have gotten recipes confused, as will happen, if you try to practice from the memory of a theory. But my grisette didn't inspect that closely. And when we would sit down to eat, she would say as she savored the concoctions I served her, 'My word, you're right. You're much better than he is. He only knew how to fix steak and potatoes and kidneys in sour wine.'"

I laughed heartily at his tales, "How thoughtful and kind you are this evening," I said to Albert, "Please tell me another one. You tell them beautifully."

"That's what I should have done the first day and not worn you out with the impulses of my heart," he replied. "But I follow my instincts, going where the devil takes me."

He was right, of course, and that's what gave him his distinctive charm. He didn't have the typical eccentricity of writers and poets, almost always posing. He lived as his fancy dictated—without plans for success, without systematically pursuing fame. His feelings and his conversations were, like his life, poetic and unpredictable. He had, indeed, all the attributes of a man in love: a breathtaking imagination, a child's disdain for anything stable or the passing of time, a denigration of fame, an indifference to public opinion, and an absolute obliviousness to anything that didn't bear on his desire of the moment or the object of his affections.

He went on, "If I hadn't been checked by an involuntary emotion, perhaps I would have proceeded with you (and I confess that I momentarily thought about it), following the methods of my friend Prince X, that handsome foreigner who used to sing better than any of the tenors in our theaters and who had the face and form of a Greek statue."

"I've met him," I replied, "and his manner with women interests me less than your stories. But why are you making this digression?"

"Because I don't know how to be didactic and monotonous like some formal speechmaker, and if you don't let go of the bridle around my neck, I'm going to stop talking."

"All right, go ahead and say what you wish."

"I am quite tempted to use that permission and tell you point-blank that I love you. Prince X wouldn't have failed to do so, and he would have accompanied his words with action."

"Not to mention being thrown out," I retorted.

"He claims, on the contrary, that all doors close tenderly and discreetly behind him. It was his custom to say that with all women, especially elegiac types, you should always do just the opposite of elegizing. I suspect he learned that secret from his wife, who could have demonstrated it to him in some bold experiment before she wrote those books on dogma and went off to Asia to amuse herself with Arabs.[5] Now there was a woman," he continued, "who was surely created to give her lovers the devil of a hard time. I was once in her velvet paws for a week, and I still bear the scratches on my imagination. I won't say in my heart, for her claws didn't go that deep."

"It's about time. Here's a story with a sting to it. I'm all ears," I encouraged.

"I had gone to see her at Versailles where she had rented a very

5. Princess Christina Trivulzio (1808–71) was the wife of Prince Emilio Barbiano de Belgiojoso. The princess, an important personage in Musset's love life after Sand, was a noted anti-Austrian patriot, writer, and newspaper publisher. Scrawny or slender, depending upon the viewer's taste, her physiognomy and physique are reflected in Zéphira, the première danseuse of La Fenice, later in this work.

beautiful mansion near the park. My heart was empty. The princess' beauty was too meager to please me more than half-way. But her large, ecstatic eyes and her provocative remarks, abruptly interspersed with disquisitions on the other world, made me persist. One evening we were out strolling in the park. She asked me to recite some love poems. The lines recited, I wanted to put them into action. She got away from me and ran off nimbly and quickly through the paths and labyrinths. I pursued her, but at a turn around a quince tree, my foot twisted. I wanted to get up and keep running, but it was impossible. I had sprained my ankle. Groaning, I dragged myself to a bench. She heard me and came back. She was suddenly affectionate, caressing, almost passionate, and seemed disposed to grant me what she had so haughtily refused me a few minutes earlier. That's because she saw me dependent upon her, and she's one of those women who want above all to feel that a man is under their control, either by moral inferiority, or physical weakness, or even by some lapse they are privy to. The idea of being able to do almost all they want with a soul or body sends them into rapture. After having overwhelmed me with tender caresses to which the very sharp pain in my foot rendered me almost oblivious, she helped me stretch out on the lawn and ran back to the house to get her servants. Two lackeys came out with a large armchair which they used to transport me back to the house. She had me put in a room opening on the garden, next to the large salon on the first floor. I was put to bed. The doctor came to look at my leg and prescribed immobility for several days. I submitted to his orders unhesitatingly because it was impossible for me to move my foot without horrible pain.

"Thus I had become an involuntary guest and the princess' plaything. I was like one of those bulls in the ring, when he has darts in his side, defenseless against the pricks and goads of the toreador. She could torture me at her convenience; take her time, choose her hour; go away, come back, play with my nerves like a clavichord. I assure you that she didn't let any opportunity slip by. If a hare has nothing to do but sleep in his nest, a playboy, kept bedfast by injury in the home of a society woman, has no other distraction but falling in love. In my idleness I imagined that I loved the princess a great deal more than I actually did, and when she would come over to my bed to offer a sherbet or smooth my covers, I thought I was burning with passion. In those days she had quite a few in her court, and her two favorites were two quite different types. One man was a political personality, tall, dignified, cold; the other was a little pianist, a pretty boy, lively and self-confident, kind of like her cocker spaniel.[6] Each took his turn very assiduously, and I, her leading admirer at the time, saw myself condemned by my sprained ankle to watch her stroll off in the garden with the diplomat and disappear from view along the dark paths. Or I would hear her in the salon trilling duets with the pianist. When I would reproach her with my jealousy, she would say that she took an interest in European affairs or wanted to improve her singing. But how could I think that she preferred such men to me. I was her dear, young, handsome poet! And when she would say that, she had such fetching fondling ways that I was inclined to believe her. I was so eager to believe what she said. However, you mustn't imagine, Marquise, that this woman had ever inspired the most miniscule tenderness. It was more like some kind of exasperation attracting me to her. I did not have good intentions.

"One morning when she had been more provocative than usual, sharing the breakfast served to me in bed, she suddenly

6. Because of her political interests, the princess cultivated politicians. The dignified personality could be Colet's longtime protector Victor Cousin (1792–1867). The pianist may combine Franz Liszt (1811–86) and Frédéric Chopin (1810–49) who were both close to Princess Belgiojoso.

snatched back the hand which I begged her to leave in mine, and wanted to leave on the pretext of taking a singing lesson. And, in fact, I heard the pianist warming up on some preludes. I would have sent him to the devil, but I was chained to patience and had to see the princess disappear laughing—escaping, getting the better of me. She didn't even close the door to my room; only the portieres of the salon fell behind her. She was well aware that this was enough of a barrier. The essential thing was that I couldn't see anything. What difference did my suspicions make since I was forbidden to get up to check for fear of delaying my recovery by a month. She was counting too much on my caution. I don't know what vapors of rage went to my head when I heard them trilling burning and passionate notes in the air. I threw off my covers like a madman. I undid the bandage on my injured leg, and I was off limping the distance which separated my bed from the door of the salon. I lifted the tapestry portieres and appeared like a ghost to the two singers. At that moment the princess was resting her lips on the cheek of the pianist who was looking at her in a pose right out of an English engraving, while repeating most properly the amorous refrain of their duet. The Princess gave a start of fright in seeing me. My presence wounded her pride, but she straightened up instantly and burst out laughing,

" 'I knew you were there. I saw you and wanted to test you.'

" 'Well, Princess, the test is over,' I replied in the same tone. 'I've had enough of your hospitality, and I'm bored at your house. All this music keeps me from resting. If Monsieur, who is acting like the man of the house, would be kind enough to ring for a servant, I'd like to be dressed, put in a carriage, and driven to Paris.'

"The pianist bit his lips, but he had to obey an injured man in a nightshirt who was suffering so much that he had to drop down on a sofa. The princess tried her kindliest manner to retain me, but in vain. I gave her people enormous tips to pay for the expense I'd caused her. As her berlin was leaving to drive me back, she cried out with a confident smile and an assured tone of voice, 'You'll be back!'

"That was ten years ago, and I've never once dreamed of going back to see her again."

"Is this passion some women have for pianists some kind of obsession for making an effect?" I asked Albert. "Following the princess's example, Countess de Vernoult has become infatuated with one of the clavichord heroes, and to enhance her passion by scandal—since the object alone could never enhance it—she carried off this 'god of art and inspiration,' as she puts it. She has linked the vanity of her young lover to her female pride loving on the rebound. There is still a third woman, more celebrated and intelligent than the other two, who nevertheless wanted to drag one of these brainless virtuosos around on a leash. Instrumentalists are to the writer and creative artist what a piece played by an organ grinder is to the eternal voice of the sea."[7]

"Well, why don't you go on and name the third woman since you've named the other two?" Albert asked, rising and watching me closely. "Do you think her phantom will make me ill or her name frighten me?"

"I don't know," I replied, "but I'm sorry that the allusion slipped out."

"That's a mistake on your part," he countered. "Sooner or later we'll have to talk about Antonia Back, whose image may be standing between us. Do you see her? Do you know her? Do you like her? Come now, Marquise, answer frankly without fear of offending me."

7. Countess de Vernoult, or Marie d'Agout (writer "Daniel Stern," 1803–76), was the sometime liaison of Liszt. The third woman, of course, is Sand, and her pianist is Chopin.

"I barely know her. It's been years since I've seen her. I admire her talent, her incessant lifelong industry, and I believe in her kindness which several people have spoken to me about."

"Yes," Albert replied, "she is extremely kind to people who don't love her, just as she appears to be a great genius to people who aren't writers themselves. In love, she lacks tact; in art, conciseness. When did you see her? What did she say to you? Tell me what you know about her," he pursued with burning curiosity. "I'll tell you about her myself some day."

"I met her for the first time two years after that evening at the Arsenal where I saw you. Her name, which filled the newspapers from 1830 on, had reached me resounding and glowing in the remote château where I lived with my mother before my marriage. You cannot imagine how passionately they followed her ringing renown in the provinces. Each new work Antonia Back published caused acrimonious discussion in my circle—sometimes degenerating into dispute. The majority said terrible things about the author, but a few enlightened minds, including my mother, who had superior intelligence and was both tolerant and philosophical, admired Antonia and defended her as you would defend an article of faith. My mother had passed her sympathy on to me, and I was very impatient to see Antonia when I settled in Paris after my marriage.

"Probably you've met Baron Alibert, Louis XVII's sardonic and skeptical physician?[8] He's told me a quantity of pointed anecdotes which I'll regale you with some day. At his place I used to see often an old marquise of Faubourg Saint-Germain.[9] She had been a celebrated beauty and to the scandal of her family had married a very handsome Italian, the last love of her life. She had gotten him

8. Baron Alibert's son was a good friend of Colet's.

9. Madame de Récamier (1777–1849) was a celebrated beauty and confidante of Constant and Chateaubriand.

a title and then a job in the diplomatic corps. Because of her marriage, she was somewhat isolated from her own set, especially the women, so she had formed her own salon where artists and men of letters could mix with former ministers of Charles IX and a few foreign ambassadors. The ex-marquise was on good terms with the most famous women artists of the day. She could count on Malibran's sister, the English tragic actress Smithson (Berlioz's first wife), and Madame Dorval; and at the time I met her, she called Antonia Back 'sister dear.'[10] Antonia's friends had become her friends. What she did or thought was only as inspired by the person she called 'The Great French Sybil.'

"Knowing how much I wanted to meet Antonia, the old marquise invited me to an evening party the former was to attend. Antonia, who was the main feature of that reception, arrived very late. In order to temper the impatience of the guests, we entertained ourselves with music while we waited. In those days I had a rather nice contralto voice, somewhat indifferently trained, but pleasing enough in certain songs. The old marquise asked me to sing. I demurred. She insisted and said, 'When she comes, you'll sing for her.' Almost immediately Antonia entered, leaning on the arm of the fat philosopher Ledoux whom she called her Jean-Jacques Rousseau. She was followed by young Horace, whom in her admiring phantasmagoria she had nicknamed her young Shakespeare. Horace was a rather handsome escort; his bold, quick glance seemed to double in intensity in coming from the sole eye lighting his male countenance. He was the author of an extravagant drama recently successfully staged at a boulevard theater, and this had

10. The sister of Maria Malibran (1808–36) was Pauline Viardot-Garcia (1821–1910), also a singer. Harriet Smithson, a Shakespearean actress, married composer and conductor Hector Berlioz (1803–69) in 1833. They had been separated for some time when she died in 1854. Actress Marie Dorval (1798–1849) was one of Sand's dearest friends.

won him the hyperbolical nickname which Antonia had bestowed in all seriousness.[11]

"What has always shocked me in that woman of genius is her almost total lack of critical acumen. They say that if she irrevocably annihilates her lovers, you still have to agree that she always begins by exalting her friends beyond measure. It's certainly true that she wanted to make a Plato out of the nebulous, chimerical Ledoux, that she wanted to make a Mirabeau out of a lawyer of limited eloquence, and she incautiously perched one of our modern painters above Michelangelo.[12]

"When Antonia entered the salon of the old marquise, everyone rose to greet her, almost to acclaim her. I was so moved to see her face to face, that I couldn't study her objectively. What struck me as soon as I looked at her was the beauty and splendor of her expressive eyes. Large and dark, they seemed to dart internal flames, and when that would happen, her whole face would light up. Her thick, black hair curved in smooth bands on her forehead, and cut short on the nape, was curled in two large chignons. The rest of her face impressed me as somewhat ill-featured. Her nose was too large, her cheeks sagged. Her mouth revealed long teeth, and her neck was prematurely lined. For some time, she had given

11. Ledoux could be Saint-Simonian Pierre Leroux (1797–1871). The description of the dramatist fits Alexandre Dumas the elder (1802–70), since his *Henri III et sa cour* (1829) and *Antony* (1831) were resounding successes. However, Hugo's *Ruy Blas* was the only memorable success in 1838.

12. Orator, lawyer, radical politician, Louis Chrysotome Michel, called Michel de Bourges (1796–1853), handled Sand's separation proceedings with Casimir Dudevant. De Bourges, whom she called Evérard, was probably far more important in Sand's life romantically and spiritually than Musset. If the "painter" is a reference to Sand's blackguard, bankrupting, sculptor son-in-law Jean-Baptiste-Auguste Clésinger (1814–1883), praise would have been incautious. Sand and her daughter met Clésinger when they sat for their busts in January 1847.

up men's clothing. That evening she was wearing a very simple gray silk gown. Her body struck me as too small for the head, and her waist was hardly indented, of a piece with her shoulders and hips. I think wearing men's clothing had hurt her shape. Her ungloved hand was exquisite. She waved it like a natural scepter and extended it to the guests she knew. The old marquise introduced me and insisted then and there that I sing.

"I had composed an unpretentious song on the death of Léopold Robert.[13] Encouraged and supported by Antonia's gaze, I decided to recite it. My voice trembled, and my emotion was so strong that at the last couplet I nearly fainted. Antonia came over to me and said as she looked me over, 'Madame, you have the arms and shoulders of a Greek statue.'

"There was something strange in such a remark, uttered point-blank. It was as if in complimenting the woman, she wanted to denigrate the artist. But since I had no pretentions to fame, I wasn't hurt, and I was effusive in my enthusiasm for her genius.

"'You'll deride it some day,' she said and turned on her heels.

"The emotion I had felt while singing caught up with me suddenly, making me queasy. My head was on fire, and I felt as if my temples were clamped by an iron ring. I was obliged to go breathe some fresher air in a bedroom which was connected to the large salon on one side and on the other to the smaller salon where the old marquise generally received. Byron's friend, beautiful Countess G——, who was a guest at the party, came with me.[14] I had known her for several years. She had given me details on that noble poet—who loved her—which made him live again for me in his veritable grandeur. When judged by her feelings, Byron was no longer that bizarre, haughty creature grimacing beneath

13. Léopold Robert was a painter who committed suicide in 1836.

14. Teresa Guiccioli, Marquise de Boissy, allegedly Hippolyte Colet's mistress in 1838, was Byron's mistress from 1819 to 1823.

the pen of biographers and journalists. He was kind, generous, and proud. As a final sign of his genius, he abandoned without fanfare his life and fortune for the cause of freedom.

"The amiable, poetic countess had me half-recline on a sofa in the bedroom, and standing close to me, sent short, rapid, regular puffs of her refreshing breath across my burning forehead. The cool, pure air gliding through her pearly teeth penetrated all the pores of my brain through some kind of magnetism. In a few minutes I felt much better.

"While I was still resting, Antonia passed through, escorted by her Jean-Jacques Rousseau and her Shakespeare. The old marquise followed after. Antonia was saying, 'My dear, I'm extraordinarily bored here with all your starched friends looking at me as if I were a strange beast. Let me go into your little salon for some air and a smoke.'

" 'Would you like to have some ices and tea brought in?' asked the marquise.

" 'I'd rather have some oysters,' Antonia replied, 'that's all I'm in the mood for.'

" 'I feel very hungry, too,' the philosopher added.

" 'And I'd happily keep them company,' the young dramatist chimed in.

"Soon I heard them eating supper in the small salon. They smoked while they ate. The bedroom door remained half-open, and gradually the smoke from the cigars mixed with the odor of the dishes penetrated and filled the room. Feeling my migraine coming back, I decided to leave.

"I didn't see Antonia again for eight years. The old marquise lived in a very beautiful apartment on the same square as Antonia. One day when I arrived, she was getting ready to visit her famous friend. She got me to go with her, assuring me that Antonia would be delighted to see me again. We found the great sibyl still in bed in a huge room. Men's and women's clothing was scattered about, and her children were playing on the rug. The pale pianist, who was her lover at the time, was stretched out on a sofa. He looked exhausted. He had coughed a great deal during the night, she told us, and she hadn't been able to sleep. While chatting, she smoked cigarettes which she took from a small Algerian pouch on top of the night stand. She stopped smoking only long enough to offer some tisane to the musician with whom she used the familiar 'tu.'[15]

"Such loose manners in front of her children shocked me deeply. You shouldn't disturb the purity and ignorance of childhood by such familiarity with mature passions.

"I haven't laid eyes on her since."

While I had been speaking, Albert had remained standing, leaning against the mantelpiece, motionless and mute. You would have called him a statue of memory. His attention seemed less to follow me in my narrative than it folded back upon itself, calling up, no doubt, scenes from the past. His gaze hadn't rested on me once.

Only my silence seemed to remind him of my presence. He took my hand, "The Antonia I loved was not the woman you met. She was beautiful indeed with a strange charm, provocative and fascinating."

"You loved her deeply," I said.

"Yes, and anxiously. But let's not talk anymore about it. This is enough for now. There are phantoms which shouldn't be brought back to life in the evening, because they will hover obstinately around the head of the bed. Marquise, unwittingly, you have prepared for me one of those nights which are the explanations of my days. When my visions rise and threaten me, I have to chase them away in drink and debauchery."

15. The "pale pianist" is Chopin, of course.

"Oh, let my friendship chase them away, instead," I implored, forcing him to sit down by my side, but he remained inert and distracted, and that evening it was he who wanted to leave.

CHAPTER VIII

TWO DAYS went by without a sign of Albert. I was going to send over to find out how he was, when, to my great surprise, he turned up at my place around noon. I was still in a dressing gown and was eating lunch with my son.

"Oh, I know I'm coming to call too early," he said, "but I couldn't resist the invitation of this brilliant sunshine flooding Paris. It pushed me outdoors at an hour when I hardly ever go out. I got in a carriage, and here I am, Marquise, ready to carry you and your son off on a long excursion."

My son rushed over to kiss him by way of a thank-you.

"But have you had lunch?" I asked.

"No," he replied, "but I'll have it with you right now, if you agree to come with me."

"I shan't agree sight unseen. Where are we going?"

"To Saint-Germain. You know I owe you a dinner. You have promised to accept, and a woman as decisive and clear in her feelings and opinions always keeps her word."

"Couldn't we go out for a drive and then come back here for dinner? I'd prefer that."

"But it's precisely in the evening when the forest of Saint-Germain is so lovely to ride through," Albert argued. "I will tell you the story of a fabulous hunting party. Please, Marquise, if you refuse, you're going to make me feel fatuous. I'll think you're afraid of me."

"Don't make him unhappy," my son pleaded, hanging on my neck. "He's so nice."

How could I refuse them? Living in isolation as I did, I sometimes felt an imperious desire to get out, take a drive, pay a call, be a part of the bustle outside, anything that would tear me away, jar me out of my absorption in my love affair. Albert was offering his company like a loving brother, an intelligent companion with an exciting mind. I was both too charmed by his genius and too sure of my own heart to be formal and reserved with him. When his mood wasn't exacerbated by drunkenness or memories of his sorrow, he combined the kindness and grace of a poetic heart with the accomplished manners of a man of the world.

"All right, I accept," I said.

"And take my word for it, Marquise, you shouldn't take the trouble to dress. Just put a black taffeta wrapper over your dressing gown. Sweep your hair up under a hat, and let's go."

"Yes, hurry," said my son, "While you're getting ready, I'll have Albert eat lunch."

I left the table smiling. When I returned a few minutes later, Albert had eaten two eggs and drunk a cup of black coffee. He was less pale than usual. His deep, light eyes were clear, free from the clouds of the preceding days. I was overjoyed to see that he was going down the stairs with less difficulty.

We found at my door a calèche with two horses. I exclaimed at such unnecessary luxury just to go to the train.

Albert informed me, "This carriage is going to take us all the way to Saint-Germain. I would never get in a common railway car with you. It would make a stroll or a chat out of the question."

"He's right, as usual," my son said. "We're much better off alone by ourselves in this nice carriage."

We crossed Paris quickly and soon were out among open fields where spring was just beginning to stir. There were buds on the trees, and the wheat fields were turning green. Flocks of sparrows cavorted from branch to furrow with a whir of wings and sharp happy cries. In the distance the sun lit every uneven line in the terrain. There wasn't a fleck of gray in the blue sky. Nor a pebble or puddle on the smooth highway. The coach flew, for the driver kept the two fine horses at a lively gallop. We breathed in a tonic air that revitalized our shut-in Parisian lungs.

My son enjoyed all the changing scenes along the road: landscapes, other travelers, farms, barking dogs running after us, roosters crowing and swelling their red combs. Everything made him squeal with pleasure. We left him to his glee and stayed quiet ourselves, Albert and I, at the back of the calèche.

Albert knew how to bring into his conversation the marvelous variety found in his writings. From a profound and gripping thought that opened horizons onto infinity, he would pass suddenly to a caustic, acerbic sally, as quick as the ancient javelins whose precision Homer described for us. Then would come somber and melancholy ideas which drowned the heart in an English fog, just as suddenly lit by beams of naive and silly childlike gaiety, railing by its momentum the burden of sorrow and experience.

"Let's laugh, feel and taste the passing hours," he would cry at such moments. "Why should we darken them with memories?"

With an intelligence of the caliber of Albert's, boredom was impossible. Even during his days of delirium and distress, when he made your heart sad, he never made your mind weary.

In his company the road from Paris to Saint-Germain seemed so short and animated to me, that whenever I've gone by train since, the trip has always seemed slow and monotonous.

The carriage, going at a walk, crossed the vast terrace of the château where you have the superb panorama much too often admired and described, but its beauty always seems new when you look at it. We entered the forest avenues without making a stop, and we went down the oldest lanes every which way. The tall trees where a few budding leaves barely fluttered let the pure light of day in through their branches. The carriage rolled silently over the sand. It was a lulling moment, gentle and regular. I don't know whether Albert felt its influence, but all at once he became silent. I assumed that his thoughts were serene since his expression remained calm.

"Are you getting drowsy?" I asked. "Why have you stopped talking?"

"At this moment," he replied, "I am watching one of Louis XIV's ostentatious hunting parties file by. The young king with haughty mien passed by surrounded by the important lords of his court. The trumpets sounded; the huntsmen and packs were set off into the distance; the ladies from the queen's household followed in open carriages. Amongst them, Louise de la Vallière appeared before me wearing a pale grey gown with flounces held by knots of pearls, like her portrait in the gallery at Versailles. Her long blond hair floated in the breeze and clustered on her cheeks which were flushed crimson by the heat. Wait, we've reached a crossroads where the royal party made a stop. Shall we rest here, too?"

"Oh, yes," my son cried, "let's get down from the carriage. I want to see what's hanging from that large tree, run around in the woods a little and have something to eat, if I can, for I feel very hungry."

He said that with a child's naive presumption, never recognizing any obstacle to his desires.

"Here's something to staunch your hunger," Albert said, taking some fruit and candy out of a pocket in the vehicle.

"Are you a magician?" the child asked.

"Not in the least. But I'm treating you the way Louis XIV

treated Mademoiselle de la Vallière, and I want to fulfill your every wish."

We had gotten down out of the carriage, and my son, crunching on pears and pralines, amused himself looking over the ex-votos and little altar, attached to the trunk of a large oak. Soon he was off racing down the paths nearby.

Albert and I sat down on the lawn and basked in the healing warmth of the day.

"So it was here," Albert resumed, "that the hunting party stopped. Mademoiselle de la Vallière, breathlesss with emotion, followed the king's gaze with her tender blue eyes. Overwhelmed both by the August day and the love overflowing her heart, she exuded a languor which doubled her charm. She sat down at the foot of one of these trees, as if exhausted. The king approached her and asked with a loving smile, 'What is your wish?'

" 'Oh sire,' she replied with childish grace, 'at this moment, a sherbet would be a sensual and royal treat.'

"The king gave the order, two huntsmen rode off at full speed and soon returned from the chateau with sherbets and syrups on ice.

"A short while ago, right where you're sitting, I thought I saw Louise de la Vallière holding in her dainty hands a small crystal goblet filled with strawberry ice, her reddened lips delightedly melting the rosy snow and her eyes saying 'Thank you.'

"Well, did you know, Marquise, that the sherbet savored in just that way later caused that beguiling sinner's death?"

"And why is that?"

"When she had become Sister Louise de la Miséricorde, Mademoiselle de la Vallière, who wore a hair shirt and did penance for her love affair, remembered suddenly as she was crossing the cloister on a scorching day, the ineffable sensation of that sherbet she had savored on just such a day in the forest of Saint-Germain.

She asked herself how she would be able to expiate that sensuality. So, kneeling at a tomb, she made a vow never to approach a drop of fresh water to her lips again. She underwent the trial heroically, and death came swiftly. Who wouldn't be touched by that last act in the life of the famous mistress who became a saint? Centuries hence, when time has left its trace on this story, it will be transformed, you can be sure, into a pious and touching legend."

After Albert had ended his story, I got up, took his arm, and we went off down the lanes looking for my son.

"Let's get back in the carriage," Albert advised, when we had found the child. "We can take advantage of the last hours of daylight to visit some of the more distant crossroads in the forest."

Soon we were deep into some of the darker lanes where the leaves of the huge trees must keep out the day in summer. These lanes crisscross on rough escarpments cut by ravines.

"We must come back to see these gorges when the brambles and vines are intertwined," Albert continued. "In the meantime we shall drive through them again this evening so you can see the strange effect of these tall tree skeletons in the moonlight."

Night was beginning to fall when we reached the house of a game warden who kept a cabaret. We ate quickly and gaily. Albert drank a bottle of wine and had my son drink some. This plunged the boy into deep sleep almost instantly. I placed him on the front seat of the carriage, and he didn't wake up until we got to Paris. I had never seen a more beautiful night come on in the Paris sky, so often overcast. You could count the constellations in the heavens. Thousands of stars in the Milky Way formed a procession for the luminous full moon.

While the stars lit us from above, the large lanterns Albert had lighted on the coach, projected zones of light on the road.

"It was on a September night as pure as this," Albert began, "that I followed a huge torchlight hunt through this forest. My friend the prince was the leader. He had brought together all his friends from his childhood and youth, including those who loved him in school and followed him in war. There were thirty of us assembled in hunting costumes on the Arab mounts the prince had assigned us. The part of the forest we were to cover was illuminated, and the huntsmen preceded us with torches. The distant avenues in the lights looked like some kind of fantasy, and those centenary trees assumed forbidding shapes in such unusual lighting. It looked like an enchanted forest.

"The air resounded with joyous fanfares alternating with choruses from *Der Freischütz* and *Robert le Diable*.[1] Echoes prolonged their melodies indefinitely. That nocturnal music seemed to partake of the immensity of the forest and the starry sky. Suddenly two stags were let loose. They bounded into a thicket where their antlers were silhouetted against the backdrop of light, and they sped off running with all the speed expected of their slender legs. The frightened eyes of these noble beasts glowed like carbuncles, and each looked at us out of the corner of his eye with the tender expression of a woman. The hunting horns clamored more loudly, and our horses ran more quickly. Soon the two stags were tracked into a crossroad formed by gigantic trees, which we circled as if it had been a fort, our guns against our cheeks in aim position, and our hunting knives gleaming at our belt. The hallali rang out, and the two victims were immolated. I remember one dying stag resting his wide-eyed gaze on me as he died. I saw his tears spurt out, and I shuddered with sympathy. That poor beast's gaze reminded me of that of a young woman I had watched die. The torch-bearers surrounded the enclosure where the two stags had fallen on their

1. *Der Freischütz* (1821) by Carl Weber (1786–1826) and *Robert le Diable* (1831) by Giacomo Meyerbeer (1790–1864) are Romantic operas with forest settings.

flanks. You'd have thought them varlets of the Middle Ages, coming ahead of armed knights. The master of the hunt proceeded with the dismemberment of the poor beasts which were still warm. The quarry was taken care of on the spot, and the dogs, enraged by running and waiting, were set loose on these strips of bleeding flesh. One hundred red, acerated tongues came out like so many darts and snapped up fragments of vertebrae and intestines. The huntsmen stirred them up with their cries. The fanfares, their clamor, and the wavering of the torches against the dark forest made these famished dogs seem like a pack out of hell. When they had lapped up the last drop of blood, the signal for departure was given, and we resumed our unbridled ride through the magic avenues. Soon we came out on the illuminated terrace where the music of several regiments saluted our passage. We were carried away, it seemed, by the double magic of sound and light. We reached the portal of the château. There we dismounted and after a few minutes were led into an ancient armory where a sumptuous banquet was spread on a huge table. The supper was so gay that it made us believe in eternal youth. Our noisy voices shook the walls of the old château until dawn."

As Albert was speaking, I wondered whether he really had taken part in that nocturnal hunt or whether it was a vision in his mind. I still wonder. But does it matter whether it was a memory or a dream? It was enchanting to listen to while the calèche carried us rapidly back to Paris.

My son was sleeping peacefully in front of us, and from his purity and the mild night, Albert seemed to imbibe a state of complete peacefulness. No more bitter words, no more reversals of passion. You would have thought the poet's soul was floating serenely through the calm of nature.

When we reached my door, Albert kissed my forehead, murmuring, "Until tomorrow."

How could I tell him not to come? How could I abandon the hope of raising up that genius and seeing it soar again?

CHAPTER IX

I HAD MET Albert de Lincel at the end of winter. Spring had come quickly with fine days at first, as so often happens in Paris.

A woman is especially susceptible to this rapid transition from one season to the next. To go from the icy chills of winter to a warm temperature, to feel in yourself the sap of the trees and plants budding and blooming when you are near the man you love, you yourself blossom in intoxication and pride. But in solitude, this overabundance of being is transformed into suffering and torture. What can you do with a heart that is full to bursting? What is the purpose served by the sudden flushes coloring your cheeks? The sharper flames darting from your eyes? What is the good of feeling stronger and looking better if there is no beloved to enjoy your beauty and energy?

Léonce had promised to visit in the spring, but now he wrote me that finishing the first part of the great book he was working on would chain him to his lonely desk for another month. I should feel sorry for him, he said, since a powerful abstraction was like religion, like martyrdom, and he owed himself to it entirely. After the harsh labor was completed, just like the devout believer who has paradise for his reward, he would savor all the more intensely the immense joy of love.

These letters caused me pain and irritation. Such quietude, real or feigned, seemed cruel to me. Sometimes I even saw in it the negation of love. But then my despair would be so great that in order to keep on believing I would cling to his words, tender, occasionally passionate, which concealed from me the cold, unshakable priority of that heart of steel. He would reply to my cries of pain with cries of passion. He was suffering more than I, he claimed, but suffering was grandeur in itself. He delighted in comparing himself to the Desert Fathers, consumed with desire but immolating their heart and flesh for the jealous god of Thabor. For him Art was the jealous god which can be possessed and assimilated only when you dedicate yourself entirely to him in solitude.

I was broken by his obstinacy, and sometimes I simply gave up trying to express my anguish, but then my letters emitted such dejection that he would become alarmed. Then he would advise me to seek distractions, to see my friends more often, to work at attracting Albert who should be cured at any price.

How often I used to cry reading these stoical letters! How often when midnight struck and I could hear around me only my son breathing in his sleep and the treetops rustling in the winds of the night, I would stand in front of my mirror, letting down my hair before tying it up to sleep. Then how often I would be seized by an overwhelming desire to see him! I wanted to go to him, surprise him in his nocturnal labor, throw my arms around him, and say to him between sobs, "Let's not be separated again. Old age will come quickly. Death will follow. Why spend in tears of anticipation these brief, happy days, so soon passed, when body and soul celebrate their prime? Oh, if you don't spend your youth when you're in love, you're like the miser who dies of hunger next to his treasure or like the invalid who knows the secrets that can save him but prefers to die."

While the man to whom I had given my life left me prey to all the anxieties of love, Albert, who found in my company a tranquilizing distraction, gradually fell into the habit of coming to see me every day. Sometimes his visits calmed me down. Sometimes they made me nervous. My heart was obsessed by its secret torment.

Well, what did a man I couldn't love matter to me? I wasn't waiting for him. I wanted youth, handsomeness, strength. I wanted the man whom banal passions had not damaged, whose lofty severity held me in his sway. Albert, love's sickly, frail, broken and withered remains, interested me like a brother and touched me like a child. But as for being the complement of my own being, my master, he was not, not then, and probably never would have been. In our basic natures we shared too many sensitive fibers, too much parity of ideas and imagination. Like and like make brethren, but the tormented union of lovers requires opposites.

I am going to risk a complete confession. Sometimes in the despair Léonce reduced me to, I almost wished that Albert would inspire a more romantic attraction, that my heart would beat faster hearing him come in, that I would feel near him a turmoil that could lead to infidelity. He always succeeded in distracting me with his wit, but he never alleviated my distress. Sometimes I was brusque and unreasonable with him, and since he was determined to be with me, he redoubled his kind and imaginative efforts to entertain me for a few hours.

My son had become very fond of him. Whenever Albert came in, he would throw his arms around him. Sometimes he would say to me, "Mommy, you're treating him very badly. He's so pale and looks so sick you just have to love him. I like him much better myself than that tall dark-haired man who comes here every two months and doesn't even look at me."

When I learned that Léonce's arrival would be postponed, I fell into such a state of depression that for more than eight days I refused to go out altogether. Albert reproached me for what he called my distrust. Wasn't I sure by now that he really was a friend? He came nearly every day to spend an hour or two with me. We read together. He gave me advice on style for my translations, taught me to write poetry, and urged me to try my hand at it. When he wanted to leave, my son would hold him back. Then he would agree to eat dinner with us. He ate hardly anything and drank only water. He seemed to have given up looking for intoxication and oblivion in drink.

My heart was touched by this metamorphosis, and putting my own troubles behind me, I felt I owed this renascent genius some words of affection and encouragement. "You know," I said to him one evening, "you should try something big. At this moment your genius is secure in its strength. You can act with authority, certain of being listened to by the young intelligentsia, like soldiers on a battlefield harking to the bugle. Why don't you put your magnificent genius to the service of some great cause, proclaim the proud principles which were the faith of your father and my grandfather? Don't immure your intelligence further in the pursuit of happiness and aspirations of the self." While I was speaking, Albert listened in that attentive pose which Philippe de Champagne has given to his elegant portrait of La Bruyère, which belongs to Monsieur de Monmerqué.[1] He had the same penetrating glance, the same gently mocking refinement in his smile, the same lofty, pensive brow. I was struck by the resemblance, but a flash from the satiric depths of his eyes stopped me short.

He was both sad and ironic: "Marquise, you have just treated me

1. Philippe de Champagne (1602–74) was a Flemish Neoclassical painter. Moralist Jean de Bruyère (1645–96) was quoted in the preface. Louis-Jean-Nicholas Monmerqué (1780–1860) was a judge, man of letters, and book collector.

to a little exhortation worthy of Madame de Staël; this Geneva morality doesn't become a *philosophe*'s granddaughter like you.[2] But are we of the same mold as our forefathers, and could we put on their convictions like an article of clothing? And, besides, what use would their convictions be to us? And whom could we find to share them? You can no more improvise a public to suit your intelligence than believers for your faith. Our era is as insensitive to a poet's genius as the desert is to a traveler's weariness. Some poet has said, Marquise, 'We live on dregs as if the end of the world had come, only instead of despair, we have only insensitivity. Even love is treated today like fame and religion. It's an old illusion. So where has the soul of the world taken refuge?' Just look around you, Marquise, you will look in vain for grandeur. Republicans, monarchists, priests, and philosophers, none have convictions any more. They fly a flag that is meant to bedazzle, like the scarlet cape the toreador flourishes in the ring, but the flag is no longer buoyed by the breath of great beliefs. All these men bereft of belief march in a torpor, impelled solely by their mean lusts. Is it worth the trouble to try to awaken and lead such a herd? I didn't always think this way. I began with hope and faith. I believed in patriotism, and I composed a war song against the foreigner. I believed in liberty, and I composed a drama against a modern Brutus. I believed in love, and I scattered in my verses my ecstasy and pain. All that was thrown to the winds by an indifferent crowd which enjoyed only my wit and sarcasm. After having scaled all the heights, I climbed down in disgust. What does a large audience mean to me now, if it is uninformed? Light is dispersed at the expense of its intensity."

He continued, "The bourgeois reign of Louis-Philippe has made us a nation of pompous, unfeeling bourgeois who no longer under-

2. Madame de Stäel, or Germaine Necker (1766–1817), was a role model for Madame de Récamier and Colet. The *philosophes* were her rationalist predecessors.

stand anything about poetry, and as if they feared that one day the youth would take over, they corrupt it throughout the country. They keep the youth out of great public works. They close to youth careers of the mind. They deny youth access to political careers. The high functions of the state are monopolized by old codgers like Duchemin who hide their immorality and calculation beneath their pedantry. You'd think they were specters preparing to dry out the heart of France which the enthusiastic efforts of the young perhaps could have brought back to life. Look around to see where these young men have gone. You'll find them at the Stock Exchange, running after loose women, or in tobacco dives! As for the men in their forties like me who have felt, believed, loved, and suffered, all like me have stopped, discouraged, for they have lost hope."

I was struck by the truth of what he said, but wanting to attach him to some glorious illusion, I replied, "Well, at least, stay with your art. The artist can rise and shine in the midst of the ruins of a dead race. He is the flame which dominates the crater when everything else is cinders and ashes. Write, if you cannot act. Write your doubts, your anguish. Write for art, your poet's fantasies. Don't let it be said that your instrument is broken like your convictions."

"I shall try, Marquise," he said, kissing my hand with a smile. "But do note that you want to make an instrumentalist out of me. Still, if you wanted to love me the way those three women loved their pianists?"

"I love you better than that," I replied. "I love you with a sincere affection that will outlive death."

His glance was long, deep, and tender. Then he left.

CHAPTER X

THE NEXT DAY I had a visit from René who had been away from Paris for a while. He found me pale and sad. He came in as I was standing at my window to breathe in the spring fragrances rising from the garden.

"How good and beautiful this happy new season is," I exclaimed. "How I'd like to break my chains and leave for the land of my dreams!"

"So why don't you go to the country?" he asked. "This sedentary life is doing you harm."

"You're forgetting my poverty."

"But you could get out a little. I know that for several days you haven't wanted to leave your apartment."

"The quivering plenitude of nature makes me feel ill. I'm alone too much, my good René." And in spite of myself I began to talk to him about Léonce.

René shook his head. "That man is really strange to sacrifice the joys of life to some kind of abstraction."

"This sacrifice has its grandeur," I insisted, "and when we see each other again, that will show in our happiness; it will be all the more intense and complete."

"Sometimes your philosophical mind amazes me," René replied. "Because your soul is so credulous it is simply made for martyrdom. Léonce has told you that once his task is completed, he will belong to you. Well, I'm afraid that once his work is finished, even if it is formless and vulgar, he will belong to it. A passion for the abstract, pushed to excess, atrophies the heart."

René's remarks made me feel vaguely panicked about my love affair.

"If my sick brother wasn't expecting me at Versailles, I would force you to get out this very day," René went on. "When I get back, I'll come by, and we'll go take your son out to breathe the air in the Bois de Boulogne. In the meantime, go out with Albert a bit. You're doing him a world of good. He's not the same man since he met you." And shaking my hand warmly, René left, repeating, "Take heart."

It was one of those hot, enervating days which stir up a storm inside a southerner's system. First you feel weighted down, then your pulse beats more quickly, then hot flashes rise to the brain. The mind wanders while your blood boils, like a vine carried on the crest of a torrent. The soul is uprooted. Will and resistance are annihilated by these formidable forces of nature. False and cold are the moralists who have never taken into account the influence of the atmosphere, a glance that touches, a breath that penetrates.

Struck down by this ineffable malady, I was idle and listless until evening, dreaming of the hours of love I had enjoyed, hours I couldn't bring back. The inflamed memories of passion spoil all other happy moments in life. My son's innocent caresses got on my nerves. I had unfulfillable desires for someone's crushing embraces. After dinner I sent my child to play in the garden so that I could be alone with my amorous fantasies.

I stayed motionless in my big armchair without looking out the window at my son's games, even though he called me from time to time. For two hours he ran and skirmished with some little friends in the neighborhood. When he climbed back upstairs, he was so worn out that he fell asleep immediately. Marguerite carried him to bed, and I remained alone at the open window, bathed in the mild moon light, inhaling, intoxicated, the acacia perfume wafting up to me.

A ring at the door made me start, jarring me out of my ecstatic immobility. I rushed to the door, shouting inwardly, "Perhaps it's Léonce!"

There are times when destiny ought to grant such overwhelming wishes!

It was Albert, looking radiant and inspired, which made him seem younger to me.

"I've obeyed. I've been working. I've begun something whimsical, just a trifle on Madame de Pompadour. But it is an act of good faith, and as such, an act of a man. I'll read it to you tomorrow. In the meantime, I've come for my reward."

"Speak," I said somewhat weary and uninterested.

"Let's go out for a drive beneath the stars. See how beautiful the night is. It invites us to go out."

"My son's in bed, and I don't like to go out without him."

"Well, what difference does it make whether that child tags along or not?" Albert exclaimed, losing patience with my lack of enthusiasm. "Is your virtue a matter of partition walls, like that bourgeois heroine in the last play at the Comédie française? Remember, she said to her good-natured procurer of a husband, who was offering hospitality to his head clerk, whom the lady secretly loved, 'What? you're going to let him sleep here this evening?' That seemed more indecent to me, I'll swear, than all the grossness in Molière."

"I think I have proved to you," I replied, "that I don't fear being alone with you at all."

"Oh, that's only because there's no electricity between us, as you let me know one evening," he retorted bitterly. "Otherwise, you would have already felt the truth of those two lines from an old Corneille comedy:

> Lise, if we were destined by the fates,
> Human vows will make us mates.[1]

1. Lise, lorsque le ciel nous créa l'un pour l'autre,
Vois-tu, c'est un accord bientôt fait que le nôtre.

"No more declamations needed," I said. "Let's go."

We went down the stairs without talking, and I took a seat by his side in the coupe which had just brought him over to see me.

He took my hand, keeping it in his, "You're kindness itself."

I didn't answer. After the sensations of the day, the contact with his quivering fingers disturbed me.

"What power you have over me," he began. "I hadn't worked for a year. Your voice stirred me. You spoke of fame, a mute echo to my ears, and the echo came to life. My entire soul vibrated as soon as you willed it. I have just written for eight hours without a break. You see that you could bring about my rebirth, if you loved me. What a beautiful life, Marquise, to give one's days to art, and one's nights to love!"

I listened to him, heartsick. Why, I was thinking, doesn't Léonce have ideas like that? Why doesn't he find inspiration by my side? And why does he look for it in a solitude which cruelly separates us?

"Oh, my dear, dear Stéphanie (it was the first time he had called me by my name), if for lack of the true and complete love I wanted in my youth, I've looked for its approximation among women in high society, its desperate simulacrum among beautiful courtesans, it's because what is considered my instability and immorality could well be, believe me, the endless, painful pursuit of love. With a woman like you, I could become myself again, happy, confident, proud. The drunken bestiality for which I'm criticized and of which I am occasionally ashamed, is the blind I have to have before throwing myself in the arms of certain women. Once I'm stunned, I no longer blush for them or me. Do you imagine that cold sober I could love flesh that has no soul attached? Please, Stéphanie, love me a little, and let me weep upon your heart and grow young again!"

"Oh, I'm the one who's weeping," I said, pushing away the arms which were trying to clasp me fast.

At that moment, the carriage which was going up the Champs-Elysées went through a patch of moonlight. He saw my face covered with tears.

"My God, what's wrong?" he asked, bending his face toward mine. His hair brushed my forehead.

I recoiled with a start, and my emotions which had been repressed all day broke out in convulsive sobs.

"What's on your mind? What's in your heart? What do you feel for me?" he implored, "For heaven's sake, speak to me!"

"You have moved me. You are tender and kind," I replied, "but I must insist that you not ask me any questions, so we can enjoy this beautiful balmy evening undisturbed."

As if he were afraid of losing the hope my involuntary tears had given him, he made his heart keep still. His charming, mobile mind seemed only bent on cheering me up. By now we had reached an avenue in the Bois de Boulogne; its dark, high vault unrolled before us.

"Let's get down," he said. "The air will do you good, and we can chat as we walk, less cramped and disturbed than in the carriage."

I obeyed. I wanted to drink in the night air. I thought it would deliver me from the burning obsessions of the day.

I barely needed his arm for support, as we glided like two shadows down the dark, deep lane. We came to a kind of small clearing where there was a stone cross. This was a celebrated site for duels. Albert had me sit down at the foot of the cross and sat down by my side. The moonlight fell on his forehead. The twinkling stars played in the moving treetops, stirring in the night wind. The freshness made me feel calm all over.

"How nice it is here," I commented, thinking only of the peacefulness I felt.

"I know of no spectacle more impressive and beautiful than a starry night," he said. "During the day, the firmament seems deserted and empty. But on a clear night, once again it is populated and animated like an unbounded City of God. Some claim that the discoveries of modern science have eliminated the imagination. On the contrary, I think that science in its enlarged state has enlarged the Milky Ways of poetry. If the earth seems narrow and limited to our view now that we believe in innumerable worlds floating over our heads, what a terrain for our imagination we get from this endless evolution going on in infinity. But in this same infinity, they say, we lose God's personhood. It escapes, dispersed to those myriad infinitesimal beings which are too numerous to matter to Him. Well, what does quantity matter to infinity? God embraces everything in an easy grasp, and we feel His power more when we think Him Master of these untold thousands of unnamed spheres than merely the petty possessor of our known and thoroughly explored universe."

While he was speaking, Albert had risen, standing on one of the steps of the pedestal of the cross. He gestured towards the beautiful stars, his inspired brow caressed by their glimmers. Lit from above this way, his face was superb. His figure, somewhat frail and small, seemed to touch the sky. In my eyes he took on the proportions and prestige of genius.

"Please go on, do go on," I said, looking at him ecstatically.

But suddenly he shot a bitter, sarcastic glance at me.

"You're a prude, a marble statue," he shouted. "You pluck me like an instrument instead of loving me." And seizing me with a burst of strength, weak as he was, he began to run down the dark lane, repeating in leaden tones, "You have to love me, you have to love me."

Soon, apparently exhausted, he put me down at the foot of a tree.

"Oh, don't be afraid of me," he begged softly. "See, I'm at your feet, and I never get on my knees unless I'm offering my heart."

There was something so tender in his submission that I was affected by it. He stayed there, trembling in front of me like some poor child, a great tormented poet like him, an implacable cynic conquered by passion.

For a moment I was proud and excited.

"It's really true, you do love me," I said, bending my astonished face toward him. Then I felt his lips racing frenetically over my forehead, eyes, mouth. I wrenched myself violently away and dashed down the first lane I saw. When I reached the carriage, I curled up inside. Just for a moment I considered leaving without him. But my whole soul revolted against this cruel temptation which my blind passion for Léonce suggested. Could I leave him alone there in the night, exposed to a long walk, sick as he was, tender, loving, still seeking in passion the life that was getting away from him? Had he made me so afraid that I had that cowardly impulse? But did I love him? Alas, I loved only love, and at the moment love was the other he . . .

In the meantime, he was running after me like a madman. When he got back to the carriage, he jumped in and started shaking my arms in rage, repeating convulsively, "So, you don't want to love me?"

The carriage had resumed its course down the deserted avenues. A cloud drifting across the moon plunged us in darkness. I could no longer see Albert's face, but I suddenly felt his tears falling on my hands. It was his turn to weep. I felt an irresistible impulse of tenderness: "Oh, please don't cry. I wish I could love you."

"I realize you're making an effort, and that's what's making me heartsick," he replied. "Whatever you say, I know what I lack to attract you, and you feel it yourself, without admitting it to yourself. At least you're not a hypocritical coquette. No, you follow the leanings of your strong, forceful disposition. Oh, one thing is certain. Love has its imperious physical laws which modern societies neglect entirely too much. I am too weak, too frail, and too decrepit for someone as beautiful and robust as you. If I had the same soul in a powerful body and the same brain in a skull covered with black hair, would you love me? For you, I'm a ghost who dreams of life. Oh, you're right. A pale, sickly Hamlet would never bring Venus de Milo to life." And while he was speaking he lurched over into a corner of the carriage and stayed there crestfallen.

Perhaps what he said was true, but that completely material appraisal of love made me ashamed of myself. I felt warm and supportive toward that proud, despairing mind, and taking his head in my hands, I placed my burning lips on his brow. At that moment I forgot his aging features. It was neither the tumult of blood nor the cry of passion; it was the spiritual appeal of genius. He on the other hand interpreted it as an ecstatic shudder of the flesh and clasped me to his chest with such abandon that I nearly felt rapture. No one but Léonce had ever embraced me like that. Giddy and dazed, I had a fleeting sensation that he was Léonce. But the moon reappeared to light up Albert's face.

"But you're not he," I cried, pushing him away. "I only love him, him alone!"

He didn't try to grab me again. He became gloomy and silent. I was increasingly uneasy, but I didn't dare break the silence.

However, as we were approaching my place, he said in a voice so calm it surprised me, "My dear Marquise, it is true that I am not the ideal man, the 'him' your heart and imagination desire. I am no longer the man I used to be, 'he' who knew how to love and care. But I am not any longer the degraded and evil creature who's been described to you either. Because I understand now. You would love me if I hadn't been slandered. Your resistance, your tears, your loving impulse a while ago, all this indicates to me that you would love me if you didn't have misgivings about me. Well, Marquise, you will love me when you've heard me out!"

He begged me to let him come up. He wanted to tell me his sad and painful story that very evening.

"But don't you see?" I started, "someone else . . ."

"Shhh, shhh," he interrupted. "Don't say anything that can't be taken back until you've listened to me. We'll do it tomorrow then since you're so unbending."

I stayed at the threshold listening to the carriage driving off. I reproached myself for being harsh. I was unhappy with myself and exasperated with Léonce. At that moment Albert seemed to be the best of the three.

A letter from Léonce which I found on my table when I went in changed my train of thought. He was going to move up his visit, he said. He would be with me within two weeks. Oh, it was truly he; I loved him alone. And all night long he appeared in my dreams in all his beauty, youth, and strength.

CHAPTER XI

THE NEXT DAY is one of the most vivid memories of my life. I have not forgotten a single detail.

Around noon I courageously set to work to let this salutary discipline banish any lax thought or unhealthy distraction. Marguerite, who recognized the useful results of my translating novels, had taken my son on a walk to give me a few hours' peace. I was hoping that Albert, somewhat wounded by the way we had parted the night before, either would not come or would come late. He arrived around two o'clock. In my white peignoir I was just barely dressed. My hair was carelessly piled up on top of my head with random curls falling here and there on my neck and forehead. From this casual disarray and from the fresh ink on the sheets of paper scattered over my work table, Albert realized that I wasn't expecting him but was working.

I had never seen him so pale and unstrung. His distraught features alarmed me.

"How calm you are," he smiled sardonically. "How beautiful and fresh! It's easy to see that you slept the sleep of virtue and indifference. I passed the night enraged. I didn't believe I still had so much youth and desire left in my heart. I was tempted to come back to tell you 'if you're going to love me, do it right now!' But I supposed you would stand on ceremony and that your door would be closed to me. And yet for a moment last night you loved me! For one minute! Whatever happens, don't forget that! If you say 'no,' Marquise, your conscience will cry out that you lie."

"On the contrary," I replied to calm his increasing agitation, "I deny none of my feelings for you, none of my words, none of the impulses of my heart."

"Then, it's all right," he continued. "I feel it. I know it. In the end you will love me. That's what held me back, you know, when I wanted to indulge in every kind of inebriation. When I left you last night, I was tempted to go forget you in somebody else's arms because you are making me suffer, and I don't want to suffer any more. You can certainly see that life is getting away from me. But instead of stupefying myself, I remembered your lips on my forehead. I still feel them, and I didn't profane that kiss. It's a promise, a bond. It's a presage that you will be mine. Something still separates us. I've ransacked my mind over it for a long time, and I think I've found it. Now I'm going to stir the ashes of the dead with you. I'm going to reopen for you the scar of my bleeding heart. I'm going to tell you about my love affair with Antonia Back."

He had to make a real effort to pronounce her name. Then getting up, he paced nervously from one end of my study to the other and continued:

"Stéphanie, you admire this woman. You like her, and her image is standing between us. You believe that goodness and grandeur are on her side because she has walked through life practicing charity, making converts, working patiently to rehabilitate her feelings by her doctrines. While I for my part, broken and mortally wounded, blown by all the winds of despair, have deserted the ideal and accepted debauchery for my consolation. In many people's eyes I personify degraded egotism. Nothing generous or useful directs my life any longer—as if a soldier who lost both arms in a cannon blast could still carry a rifle! She, on the other hand, has seized in her vigorous, decisive hands the flag of socialism, a hollow, resounding word which allows great elasticity in its moral code. She has made partisans among the utopians, both in the university and in the general public. She excites the young whom I can merely amuse. Even those who oppose her concede that the incessant—and often nefarious—work of her mind is a kind of a moral atonement of her life. She loves public demonstrations and manifestos, a dramatization of what she calls her humanitarian beliefs and her faith in progress. This is the modern jargon for what used to be called perfectionism. Such ideas in a different form and in due moderation are not alien to me. I share the opinion of the contemporary poet who said, 'Perfection is no more made for us than immensity. We should not look for it anywhere, nor ask for it in anything, not in love, not in beauty, not in virtue. But we must love perfection to be as virtuous, handsome, and happy as a man can be.'

"The crowd," he went on, "is excited only by exaggeration and overemphasis. I don't aspire to please this common public. I've already told you I disdain it. I'm not really known and loved except by a few friends who know what I've suffered in my painful search for love, which is also a search for the ideal. Where the masses have seen only a personal passion, you will see, I hope, the manifestation of my soul, and therein, the human soul. Do not imagine that in the narrative I'm going to give you I intend to diminish or denigrate Antonia, as others will perhaps do someday to avenge me. No indeed, I shall speak to you about her with tenderness and justice, but with inexorable truthfulness, and when you have heard me out, you will love me."

Despite my acute curiosity regarding this story, I felt that fairness obliged me to say, "But I swear to you that it is not my knowledge of Antonia which stands between us. The obstacle to love lies elsewhere."

"I know, I know," he replied. "I've guessed, and I've said it already: I am sickly and decrepit, but once you love me, you won't notice anymore. It will be like last night in the shadows when my soul attracted your entire being. Besides I shall become so young and gay again in loving you that in the end my imperfections will charm you as well. That's the way I was when I loved Antonia."

While he was saying this, he sat down on a cushion at my feet, and resting his chin on the palm of his hand, prepared to resume his story. I got up and moving directly opposite him, forced myself to interrupt him, "But suppose I love somebody else . . ."

"Bah!" he cut me off. "That's impossible. If you loved somebody else, I would have already met him here, and I know you live the life of a saint. What kind of fantasy lover would he be, for heaven's sake, whom no one ever sees, who abandons you to solitude, who exposes you to all the temptations of loneliness and leaves the field free to the desires of your friends? I'm not afraid of a phantom! You are a romantic woman, and in your pride you would be satisfied with *him*, the imaginary ideal man. But last night, resting on my heart, didn't you see it was some chimera? Well, I am here. I am reality, not dream. Why do you resist me? You are too spirited to continue this struggle. Oh, my dearest, let's trust in nature and not keep deceiving ourselves!"

I sat back down, touched by his blind persistence. But I felt so impassive as I faced him that I fully realized that he had in no way convinced me.

"I'm listening," I said. "Tell me about your romance that made the whole world talk."

THE WORLD, he retorted, never sees behind appearances. I was twenty-five, and some fast and felicitous literary successes had brought me public attention and, more sought-after, the acclaim of those salons which at that time made a writer's reputation. In addition, my father's name had quite naturally given me entrée into that exquisite milieu, so attractive on its surface, which eventually develops delicacy of heart and mind. The women in high society were delectable. Several showed me their favor and loved me as they know how, from the tip of the lips to the brink of the heart. Their life of ease and elegance is so filled with charming novelties that a lover has hardly more place in it than any other caprice. I loved them with due deference with all the powers of my youth and imagination. Their fickleness and empty egotism made me indignant. I was unjust and untutored. Loving me wouldn't have changed their basic nature. For their part, these frivolous affairs came undone without damage; but in my heart I felt an ironic rage that I transformed into sentimental satires on Spanish duchesses and countesses who were so many French aristocrats.

Following the example of Don Juan, nothing could stay the impetuousness of my desires, and I thought I had a heart for loving the whole earth. Like Alexander, I longed for other worlds for my amorous conquests. I sought out the intimacy of grisettes, in hopes they would have more heart and passion than society women. I found them more natural, with a certain rectitude and often a touching kindness. But between them and me there were too many discordant notes which shocked my susceptibility as a gentleman and poet. They would suddenly utter vulgarities which sometimes made me burst out laughing and other times made me lose patience. Their minds revealed such an abyss of ignorance, so that aside from naive and tender remarks, they never said anything worth being remembered. Their thoughts in no way matched mine, except in those moments in which our senses brought us together. Society women are hardly less ignorant, but they can supplement their vacuousness with jargon that gives the illusion of intelligence, and they conceal what they lack beneath an exquisite exterior.

This was about the time I became a close friend of Albert Nattier, who was very much sought-after socially because of his large fortune and amiable disposition. He was neither a writer nor an artist, but he loved anything that had to do with wit and art. The publication of my first books attracted him to me. He showed me a very steadfast friendship which nothing changed and which lasts to this day. Albert Nattier loved me as his mental luxury. I was as necessary to his intellectuality and idealism as were his mistresses and horses to his habits of dissipation. He loved me simply and wholeheartedly. Why would I have rejected his sympathy? I've been reproached for preferring his friendship to that of contemporary poets. What has always kept me at somewhat of a distance from these men of genius is certainly not envy, as I've proved by praising them in my works and applauding them in public. But almost all of these men of letters, René excepted, are too much concerned with making an impression, sometimes by conventional morality and rectitude, sometimes in wanting to be politicians, and by showing contempt for the very profession which has made them great. You know the cry of desperation I addressed to one of the most famous?[1] Well, that lamentation of a bleeding heart remains unanswered. All of which will perhaps not prevent that great lyric poet from one day pronouncing a heart-rending elegy at my grave!

I like minds that are generous and unpretentious, moved by our passions and pain without thinking about how to link us to their ambition or system.

Albert Nattier pleased me from the outset by his nonchalance, the openness of his life, and his indifference to opinion. Since he could see I was disgusted with society women and grisettes, he introduced me to the world of actresses and courtesans who were eating up his fortune. For a short while I was dazzled because these women truly make a science of luxury and a certain poetic

1. This is "Lettre à M. de Lamartine" (1836). Alphonse de Lamartine (1790–1869) promised a response to this appreciation of his "Méditations," but he had to be prompted by Paul de Musset to include Alfred in the second series of his *Cours familiers de littérature*.

appearance. They are ravishingly adaptable, possessing the genuine gesture and gaze of the sentiments they are intent upon acting out, and when they don't talk too much, they are more seductive than the others where the senses and imagination are concerned. Unfortunately, even in my most futile liaisons, I have always wanted to reach the soul, to analyze the being in depth. You can imagine what disgust I soon conceived for these women who almost always keep their mother with them, making her a servant or a go-between! Later, when despair sent me back into their arms, I could only seek and receive their caresses after getting drunk.

I was beginning to tire of my amorous developments in these diverse spheres of society when I met Antonia Back one evening at a small gathering of artists where I'd gone because I was curious to see her. For a year or two, there had been a lot of talk about her, and each work she published was a smashing success. I had noticed in her books some very fine pages which revealed a real writer, something rare and nearly unfindable in a woman. I especially liked her descriptions of nature. There she is truly great and unsurpassable. I have less admiration for her heroes and heroines. Her characterizations are often contrived, falsely philosophical and pretentiously overdrawn in sentiments. Their imperturbable paradoxes and arguments exasperate me, although she clothes them with eloquence and with a style that is always limpid, in its very diffuseness. Such as she was, this woman promised to be a glorious, curious exception, inevitably attractive to me. I knew, of course, that her way of life was strange and unfettered by any prejudice. I promised myself a thousand novel experiences. Before we love with our heart, we already love with our imagination. On the subject of her beauty, I had collected a myriad of contradictory opinions. Some found her irresistibly beautiful. For others, all she had was very large, expressive eyes. Most of the time—and rather unbecomingly—they said, she wore men's clothes or fantasy costumes. The day I saw her for the first time, she was dressed as a woman, somewhat in the Turkish style because she wore a loose, gold-embroidered vest over her dress. Her petite figure moved gracefully in the ample folds of that garment. Her hands, whose perfect beauty struck you, emerged white and delicate from the sleeves. On one wrist she wore a gold Egyptian bracelet. She held out her hand to me when I approached, and it seemed so small to me that I pressed it in amazement. I didn't analyze her face at all. At that time it still had the velvety matte of youth. The sparkle of her magnificent eyes and the shadow of her thick black hair made her look so perceptive and inspired that my blood and soul were overwhelmed. She spoke seldom and to the point. Her brow and gaze seemed to contain infinity.

She seemed pleased by my attention and began to speak to me apart. She didn't much care for my light, satirical verse, she said, but she predicted some very great things from my talent. Her first words were bits of advice. She's always enjoyed preaching a little. It was the natural tendency of her mind which by now has gotten somewhat ponderous as a result. What she found charming in me, she added, were my polished manners and good breeding.

At that time she was surrounded by men friends, one of whom, everyone claimed, was her lover to some extent.[2] All were men of some worth and rather good writers, but totally vulgar in appearance, speech, and bearing. With her they affected a familiarity which she encouraged when she was feeling nonchalant and bored but which sometimes revolted her natural pride and distinction. Her grandmother had aristocratic manners, and she knew how to act in a more proper milieu. So, a man's politeness

2. This could be an allusion to dependable François Rollinat, the prototype of Trenmore in *Lélia*.

she always took for heartfelt deference, and she was touched, given the completely free life she was leading.

As we parted, she invited me to go see her. I went running the very next day. I already felt that I loved her. At the end of three days we belonged to each other. Never, never, never have I experienced love that was so beautiful, ardent, and complete. I felt exalted, delirious, the joy of a child, a nearly maternal softness of soul mixed with the strength of a lion. I had generous and arrogant impulses. I clasped all creation in my arms. I was twenty times the poet I was before. There is no doubt that this immense capacity for loving had been latent. She was merely the spark that made it burst into life. It was my youth running over. But the spark came from her. Before her no woman had produced that bedazzlement, that intoxication. I am indebted to her for knowing love other than in dream, and I bless her for it. I bless her for it still after all these years. I bless her despite the anguish that followed. What does it matter that our love has disappeared, was it any less real? Doesn't everything die? Both our feelings and our bodies? Haven't all the vows and kisses exchanged by all those generations before us been dispersed? We come and go, and time carries us away. But in those lost depths where our soul is drowned, as soon as it seizes the spark of love again, it regains warmth and light. When we're ready to die, we still stir those burning embers. It's the shroud in which we wish to sleep, for we feel it contains what our life really was."

He paused and went on.

"Loving Antonia made me proud to love. She was beautiful, and her mind was equal to mine. People think it shows good taste in our era of gross manners to jeer at intelligent women—between two cigars and a couple pitchers of beer, as we go out for an evening with loose girls. Byron called some pedantic Englishwomen "bluestockings," so "bas-bleus" has passed into French at the service of mean columnists of minor newspapers. I've made fun of mediocre women authors myself. But whenever a woman is endowed with a truly natural, that is, involuntary and sacred, genius, whether this genius is revealed in works or only in speech, as is the case with most intelligent women who carry their secret to their death, well, this genius attracts a poet like a kindred spirit. Only with such women does one enjoy the double and complete voluptuousness of soul and sense.

It's especially after experience with society women, grisettes, and courtesans that you are inebriated by these noble love affairs where the mind takes part. You feel as if you're flying; even in each other's arms you don't touch ground. You blend sublime cries with the tears and laughter of sensual pleasure. You exchange during these brief, fixed hours all the aspirations of infinity. All this is so true, that when a woman like this crosses a man's life, she burns a furrow of fire: the heart is consumed, but the genius bursts forth.

Vittoria Colonna made Michelangelo; Madame d'Houdetot, Rousseau; Madame du Châtelet, Voltaire; Madame de Staël, Benjamin Constant; to cite some examples at random. A poet has said, and it expresses my most heartfelt conviction, "There is no people on earth which having considered woman either as man's companion and consolation or as the sacred instrument of his life, has failed to worship her in these forms."

Therefore, it is quite true that superior women attract us in spite of ourselves and attach us with a stronger bond. To deny it would be puerile and false or a confession of inferiority. But with such women the inevitable struggles in love increase. They spring from every contact, for even if the two persons are of equal worth, their aspirations and sensations can be very different. In such a union, the joys are extreme, but so are the heartbreaks. Having chosen them above all others, we ask these women for the impossible: ideal love. They in turn read us, analyze us, treat us as a peer. As soon as some conflict arises, our brutal male pride, accustomed to domination, is riled by their temerity. In the raptures of passion parity is admitted, happily exalted and proclaimed because a woman's value doubles the man's power. In any other situation, such a woman is denied, insulted, rejected as a shackle to our freedom. It costs us to have to contend with their intelligence. Ordinary women give in to us and flatter us in everything that springs from the mind. They apply their natural intuition and finesse only to enthrall us or deceive us—without contradicting us and with the passiveness of a slave.

God is my witness that with Antonia I didn't begin the struggle. I loved her marvelous faculties without dreaming of directing her or challenging her, even when she wounded me with her ideas. I hate the pedagogical profession. Not especially capable of taking care of myself, I consider myself unqualified to give advice to anyone. People I love, I like as they are. I don't flatter myself: I'm not a greater master than Nature. Nature made us as she meant to; we can change ourselves only slightly and slowly through reflection and suffering.

From the first day Antonia presumed to change me. I was four or five years younger, and that, joined to her tendency to protect and preach, brought out maternal mannerisms which spoiled the romance for me. In her moments of most intense tenderness, she would call me her "child." That expression would either check my ardor or elicit some sarcastic remark which made her angry. Then she would purse her lips, assume her most serious manner, and begin some discourse on morality. She said I must pay attention, for her age, experience with passion, and meditations in solitude justified her authority over me. I was a product, she added, of a world where nothing was sacred, where they wanted to continue the ancien régime without taking heed of our glorious revolution and the new era it opened. What I had written adequately testified to the frivolity of my doctrines. It was time to think of being useful to the cause of the future, as she herself was doing. She would love me twice as much if I followed her in that path where the greatest minds of the times were encouraging her. Then she would name some of her friends, nebulous, mediocre writers whom she treated like sublime philosophers. I would stifle mild yawns as I listened. But as soon as I looked at her, the flame in her eyes went straight to my heart. I would raise her in my arms, cover her with kisses, and say, "Let's make love! That's worth more than your long disquisitions. Or if you want to talk, tell me about nature, describe some beautiful landscape for me. That's when you are truly inspired, beautiful above and beyond all the others. But your philosophizing bores me. I know what you're going to say. For me it's old hat, and your friends can't rejuvenate it, rant as they may. The Encyclopedists wore out my father. They, at least, were original minds."

When I talked that way to her, she would become cold and silent. If we were alone, I could eventually break the silence by some lighthearted caress, some cajoling gesture inspired by my youth and love. But if one of her pedantic friends happened by during our metaphysical discussions, she called upon him as witness to my inferior soul and her self-imposed obligation to convert me. Then I would light a cigar and go out to escape such a tendentious colloquium. Nevertheless, she loved me because of my youth and the raptures she inspired in me. But I don't think I ever made her feel the supreme thrill that I owed to her. Where the senses were concerned, she was more curious than ardent or lascivious. Because of this I sometimes found her wanton even when she was frigid. When I was swept away by passion, she was frightened, as if by some secret force, and she was very often disoriented by my poetic temperament. In those days, my dear Marquise, that temperament, now dormant from illness and disappointment, was always with me. It took various forms, but it never deserted me. It broke out in sexual ecstasy, idle conversation, and work. I was always the same person, that is, a poet, a sensitive and incandescent creature, continually vibrating and bursting into flame.

Antonia, on the other hand, was intelligent and passionate only from time to time. She would lay down her exaltation with her pen. Then, she would either go completely inert or else she would launch into interminable arguments on what she called human dignity. She was all of a piece. I felt that my complex nature escaped her and that she must almost have a secret contempt for me. Later, when I saw her praise two worker poets, apparently in good faith, I wondered if she had really understood the literary qualities in my work.

But, I repeat, such spiritual dissonances, which showed up from the very first, in no way diminished my burning love for her, and it was only when one of her tedious friends became the third party in our discussions that I showed some impatience with her. One day when she acted as cold and ceremonious as a nun, I blurted out, "My dear, one can certainly tell that you spent your childhood in a convent. You have kept the manners of a Beguine; it will be hard for your intellect and your escapades to rid you of them."

Her most adulatory friend replied that I used the language of a libertine and that I would never appreciate the grandeur of Antonia's love and sacrifice. I would have liked to throw that fellow out the window, for Antonia's "comrades," as she called them, hurt my happiness with their vulgarity. I hated to see them interrupt our beautiful moments together whenever they pleased.

Antonia reproached me for my continuous agitation and what she called the fever of my love.

One day I said to her, "Let's leave Paris where we're getting too much attention. People are already discussing our liaison. Soon everyone will know about it. The scandal sheets will regale the idle reader with it. Let's not let our hearts be food for gossip. On autumn days like these the country is lovely, and the deep woods are marvelous. Let's go. You can choose the spot for our solitude."

Her reaction was frank and enthusiastic. While kissing me, she replied that I had had a happy idea which we should put into operation the very next day.

Since she grew up in the country, she has always loved open spaces. She identifies with them, gets her inspiration there, and becomes greater and better as a result.

We decided to go settle in at Fontainebleau without delay. We got ready very quickly, and without telling a soul, fled Paris like two schoolboys playing hooky.

A hired carriage took us as far as the forest entrance. There we stopped at the gamekeeper's cottage where we rented a spotlessly clean room whose window was shaded by huge trees. When we awoke each morning, we were exhilarated by the tonic air, the woodsy fragrance, the changing masses of colored leaves. Antonia, brisk and quick, helped the gamekeeper's wife prepare our lunch. Then we took off on excursions through the forest. Each day we explored some new part of that immense expanse of old, old trees. Antonia was wearing men's clothing again—not for effect, but to facilitate walking. She wore a blue wool tunic, belted tightly at her waist by a black leather belt. I never saw her more beautiful than in that simple costume. Sometimes when the exercise made her velvety cheeks crimson, when her large, intelligent black eyes rested enraptured on some feature of the landscape, when her curly hair billowed around her head like the wings of a bird, I rushed over to her and made her stop by taking one of her silky locks in my teeth and closing my lips tightly. Then I would pull her to me and force her into my arms.

O beds of perfumed heather, rays of sunlight filtering through the trees, singing birds, faint breezes rustling in the leaves, distant hunters and woodcutters who made the forest hum, evening stars taking us by surprise in the cleavage of moss-covered rocks, bright, smiling moon who showed me her beauty—you know if I loved her!

We were so enchanted by our new discoveries in those immense woods which seemed to belong to us that we decided to penetrate further by spending an entire day and night inside them, sleeping on a bed of leaves. We set out one extremely warm morning with our knapsacks of provisions slung over our shoulders. Antonia had never been so gay. She bounded along the difficult paths like a doe. I could scarcely keep up with her dashing about. Sometimes she projected notes of her pearly voice making it re-echo to infinity. Sometimes she struck up some country song from her province. Then she collected all the plants and wild flowers she came across. She told me their names and properties. When she lived in the country, she had studied botany at a very practical level and knew in depth the ingenious science of Linnaeus and Jussieu, that she poeticized in her own words. I watched and listened, enraptured. She had become once more loving, simple, kind, truly great. She harmonized with the immensity of nature. We made a stop near a spring surging from the base of a boulder. We sat down on some soft grass to take our morning meal. I served her and brought her water to drink in the cup of my hands. When lunch was over, I insisted she take an hour's nap to rest her pretty feet, which had run so nimbly. I held her against my heart, rocking her gently until she finally fell asleep. It was ecstasy watching over her, supporting her head on my folded knee. I was also a little tired from our long walk, but too keyed up by my happiness to fall asleep. I followed the palpitation of her long black lashes on her bright cheeks, the movement of her breast, and the fleeting smiles of her dream. I told myself, "She's still caressing my image, without knowing it." When she awoke, she threw her arms around me, thanking me for taking care of her. We resumed our hike, exchanging stories of our childhood. Often we stopped to take in the changing aspects of the majestic forest. Towards evening we reached the center of the gigantic, craggy rock formation which had been our destination. These enormous boulders, covered with moss and vegetation are simultaneously magnificent and sinister. They seemed to have been broken apart by some earthquake long ago. Some hardy plants had taken root in their fractured surfaces. Large oaks climbed out of their entrails. In some places a trickle of water gurgled and bubbled around their base. There were uncanny contrasts of strength and grace. I said to Antonia, "Like you, where genius and beauty are combined."

I wanted to climb up to the top of one of the highest rocks, and I shouted to her to follow. But she, who up to now had been clearly indefatigable, asked me to let her stay where she was, sitting on a heap of dead leaves. Her strength failed her, she said, she would wait for me there on the leaves which would make a soft bed for the night. I chided her on her fatigue and kept climbing, still repeating, "Follow me, follow me. You must see what I see. The horizon is splendid. Come on, come on, how can anyone in love get tired?"

Twilight was giving way to night. Some stars were coming out, and a pale sliver of moon stood out over the green crests. In front of me the last purple bands of the setting sun ribboned out in lines of flame. They projected their fiery lights on my head. Antonia told me later that I seemed to be walking through fire and that my blond hair shone like the tail of a comet.

"Hurry up! I want you to! I'm waiting!" I cried, still carried away by the spectacle which grew broader the higher I climbed.

In all directions, everywhere, to the furthest horizon stretched the green forest spangled with the red and yellow shades of autumn. It seemed as vast as the sky which covered it. I had reached the uppermost point of the boulder where I found an oval cavity, a kind of partial grotto forming almost an alcove tufted with black moss. "I've found a nest for the night," I called down. "Come join me. I insist!" And I sat motionless on the edge of this recess as I watched her come up. She had gotten up grudgingly and was climbing slowly, one step at a time, the steep rock I had climbed so quickly. From time to time she would stop, look around her, take a few more steps and sit down as if exhausted. My voice was a stimulus. I wished I could lift her up to me with one breath, and yet I didn't go down toward her. I was thinking to myself that if I joined her, she wouldn't want to climb anymore but would force me to go back down with her. I thought this spot I'd just discovered would be such a good place for us, so far away from everything that I was less concerned with her fatigue than the enchantment I wanted her to share. By dragging herself step by step, she reached the next-to-last plateau. Then I bent over for her to clasp my arms and pulled her up to me. I crushed her to my chest and holding her head tilted back so that her beautiful eyes were facing the firmament, I said to her, "Look, see how peaceful, how private, how quiet! What marvelous oblivion for everything except ourselves!"

Not a breath of air ruffled that imposing calm. Not a noise could be heard. The earth seemed to immobilize in going to sleep. The night was getting blacker and the stars brighter. Antonia was very pale and shivering in my arms.

"I'm very tired," she said, "and I think I'm taking cold."

"I'll put you to bed in our shelter," I responded. "I'll cover you with my coat, and while you rest, you can gaze on the double expanse of forest and sky."

I carried her as gently as a mother carries a sleeping child into the hollow cushioned with moss. But she had barely stretched out when she cried, "Oh, I'm afraid here. It's as if you put me in a bier covered with a black pall!"

"Afraid?" I retorted. "Afraid, when I'm clasping you in my arms, when I love you? Would you be afraid to die with me, too? Well, if God were listening, *I* would be willing for this night to be our last. Here, next to you, ending our lives, going to sleep, radiant, young, content, loving and beloved before old age had sent its chill through our souls, before boredom or infidelity had blighted our romance, before society had separated us. Oh, what do you say to that, dearly beloved, do you want this day to be our last? Shall we jump from this rock, heart to heart, so closely entwined that we can't be separated in the tomb?"

In this vein, mad with love and drunk with infinity, I was showering her with caresses and tears. I raised her in my arms and embraced her so hard, still walking to the edge of the precipice that she shrieked from fright. She struggled frantically to free herself from my arms, kicking and flaying, repulsing me with a kind of hatred. She managed to free herself.

"I don't want to die!" she said, and without listening to my pleas, she let herself slide to the foot of the rock. I tore after her, and when I reached her, I knelt before her, seeking her forgiveness for the terror my love had caused her.

A love so great and true that for an instant I had dreamed of perpetuating it by death!

"Extravagances like these are criminal," she said rather harshly, "and love such as you understand it is self-absorption and egoism that God will punish. Right now we are living like perverse children, with no check to our actions, no moral code, glutting our sensations and forgetting suffering humanity. We're even forgetting the work which is our duty and justification. Starting tomorrow, I am going to change this way of life and return to reason."

"Oh cold and frigid woman," I cried. "Are you like every other woman when she's not in love or has fallen out of love? Women always say the same thing, deck themselves out in morality. Passions are always immolated for virtue. We men are flagellated without pity with an abstraction or a bitter penance, making us seem impious if we resist. I remember a young countess who broke with me on the pretext that I didn't go to church and she couldn't keep a lover who didn't believe in the same God she did. Another on the day her husband was named a peer of France, declared that at that lofty level, she could no longer risk the scandal of our affair. A third who had abandoned her children to throw herself in my arms, felt overcome with remorse one fine morning and left me—for another lover. A fourth found that my courting could get in the way of the marriage of a younger sister of whom she was jealous."

"That's enough," Antonia interrupted angrily. "You're not going to parade that entire aggregation of mistresses in front of me? Do you think I'm unaware of that mob?"

"At least I was in love," I snapped back. "What about you? I'm not *your* first lover. What did you feel, since passion terrifies you? Did some kind of instinct of self-torture goad your morbid curiosity?"

While I was talking, she had begun to walk fast, trying to find the forest path we had taken to get there. I followed her like an automaton. My strength was broken. My heart had lost its spring.

When I caught up with her, I forced her to take my arm. "Antonia, dear, let's stop this pointless quarrel. This morning we started out so happy and loving. Did we need only a few hours to change happiness into bitterness, rapture into recrimination, caress into injury? No, we couldn't have been the ones speaking. It was some evil forest spirit whose solitude we must have disturbed. Stop. You're really too tired to go on. See what a good place we would have under those trees which form that dark arch. I'm going to gather some moss and leaves to make you a bed."

I wanted to kiss her and lead her to the place I had in mind, but she resisted me softly but firmly, "I don't want to sleep here. I would be afraid."

"Afraid of what?" I cried. "Afraid of me who would die a thousand deaths to watch and defend you! Oh, if you say that, you don't love me anymore!"

"Albert, take yourself in hand," she said in the same even tone. "Am I leaving you behind? Aren't we going back together to the same house to rest? Why hold it against me if it's all making me a little bit afraid—the boundless woods, the sky clouding over, and the wind beginning to roar in the branches like a wild beast? After all, I'm a woman," she added, as if confessing a pretense of weakness. Pressing against me, she continued, "Come on, walk faster, and we'll soon be in our little nest."

"We have a three-hour walk," I replied. "The night is getting completely black. No more stars, No more moon. How will we get our bearings? See the heavy cloud moving over there? It looks as if a storm is going to break out."

"Well, it will be fine. We'll put it in a book later."

"Then you're not afraid anymore. So, let's stay here. Look, there's an abandoned woodcutter's hut we can use for a shelter."

"No, I want to sleep in my bed and get to work tomorrow. That's all there is to it."

"Oh, yes," I jeered, "work at regular, fixed hours like dressmakers or farmhands who do the same number of stitches or furrows every day. My poor Antonia, you forget that we poets are a bit like the lilies of the field. We toil and spin as the spirit moves us. God's eye is on us, and we work under Him, not harnessed to some human mechanism. Look at that tall ash whose upper branches touch the sky. Was it regularly pruned and trimmed by human hands as it grew? No, it spread out by itself and climbed freely through space. Its sublime vegetation was helped only by the sun and stars. Let's be free like that tree, feeling and loving. And one day our work will be all the more beautiful for it."

She didn't answer but kept walking, pulling me along.

However, large raindrops were falling like hail on the thick leaves overhead. We could hear some claps of thunder in the distance. A storm was threatening and would soak us.

"Let's go faster," Antonia kept repeating like a sentinel giving orders in the vanguard.

Day was breaking wan and gray when we reached the gamekeeper's cottage. My God, what a homecoming! Our shoes were torn, our hands and feet were bleeding, our clothing soaked and covered with mud. We looked like a convoy of wounded soldiers who only that very morning had set out full of resolve to fight and conquer!

They lit a blazing fire for us. Antonia, thoroughly worn-out, went to bed and slept for a long time.

I myself was shivering as I watched her sleep. My teeth were chattering, and my head was on fire. During my feverish insomnia I went through the entire forest excusion in my mind. I saw again the woodcutter's hut where she hadn't wanted to stop, and I said to myself, "But the night could have been so beautiful and tender."

And to think that when she reported on this night to her friends, she claimed that I had been mad for several hours, mad enough to make her fear for her life. O you pitiful poets! Your souls athirst for infinity in love. Will you never be understood?

After eight hours of sleep, Antonia woke up. She was frightened by my livid and pinched face. Seeing me seated on the edge of the bed, she cried, "Didn't you get some sleep?"

"No, I watched you," I answered. "You were very beautiful and quite calm. I got my rest watching you."

"But you have a fever," she said, taking my burning hands in hers. "You must stay in bed. What a selfish person I must have been to sleep while you were getting sick."

She got up quickly and wrapped me in warm covers. She made me herb tea and lavished me with care, all in her calm, silent, tender manner. She was for me, as she was instinctively for everyone, an excellent woman, inexhaustibly devoted and kind. But as for a passionate sensitivity, that special, exquisite inspiration which divines hidden wounds, that sensitivity which is to the heart what genius is to the mind, I doubt that she ever understood it.

Eventually the magnetism of her gentle, deep gaze put me to sleep. My fever fell the following night. Two days later I was on my feet again.

At the same time she was nursing me, Antonia had repacked our modest baggage, payed our host, and gotten everything ready for our departure.

"We'll be back in Paris in one hour," she informed me with a laugh as I was getting dressed.

"What? So soon? weren't we fine in this dear little hideaway? What's wrong? I can guess. You want to leave me." I wound my arms around her as if holding her back, binding her.

"You'll always be childish and suspicious," she said. "We're going because absolute isolation is bad for both of us, but I'm not leaving you."

"I know. We're returning to Paris to find your friends who bore me and society which spies on us."

"No, if you like, we can travel. We will go to Italy. We'll be just as alone there, but we shall have as companions and escorts monuments and vestiges of great civilizations, all those things which fire the mind, vitalize talent and rescue them from the mists of solitude and the subtleties of passion. Here we're a little too much like two prisoners of love condemned to a forest cell."

Without dwelling on those last words, I kissed her rapturously. She wasn't going to leave me, and we would visit together that land which has remained the ideal patria of poets and artists: Italy!

CHAPTER XII

When I announced this trip to my family and friends, I met with very stiff opposition. My family was distressed, and my friends railed at the absolute sway Antonia had gotten over me. There is nothing more nefarious for a serious love affair than your fellow womanizers. They analyze the woman you love. They judge her mercilessly and begrudge her the hours stolen from their company. They are intent upon proving that she is neither better nor better-looking than women who are much less demanding. They maintain that it is absurd to go into seclusion and forget your friends for a romance that will end sooner or later anyway. Then, if we admit them into this seclusion to prove that our mistress is superior to all other women and that far from trying to separate us from our old friends, she is anxious to treat them like brothers, if, I say, we let them into our life, we inevitably run two risks. Either our friends try to charm her themselves or they try to separate us by flippant references to her beauty and mind, and they diminish our idol by their very indifference.

I had seen Albert Nattier no more than once or twice since my liaison with Antonia began. When I informed him that we were going to Italy together, he protested like all the rest, "You couldn't even live together peacefully at Fontainebleau for more than a week. What is it going to be like during a long trip where everything will be a source of contention between your two artists' souls—stops at the inns, weariness on the road, landscapes, monuments, paintings, beautiful Italian women? Besides," he added with a naiveté which made me laugh, "we run the risk of running into each other in Italy because I'm leaving for Naples in a week in the company of a woman I love a little bit more than any I've met up to now, without going so far as to say I have any great passion for her."

"Good grief," I remonstrated in turn, "doesn't the prospect of boredom and annoyance in an extended tête-à-tête with that woman alarm you?"

"No," he replied, "because she's a singer used to such adventures, and I can leave her at the first way-station if I get bored with her."

"And what about me?" I parried.

"Well, yes, you could, if you wanted to, do the same thing with Antonia."

Albert Nattier's assumption made my cheeks burn and my heart pound. I would have cheerfully picked a fight with my friend at the insulting idea that I could treat Antonia like that. Even the hypothesis of a breakup overwhelmed me so much I was ready to faint. Oh, how I loved her!

In spite of everything and everyone, happy and giddy, oblivious of the rest of the world, we left one evening in a post chaise. As soon as we had left the outskirts of Paris, I kissed Antonia passionately and said, "Finally you're all mine. We are going on an enchanted voyage, without anyone seeing us, truly free, our beings intermingled. We shall be inebriated with the delights of life in the country of sunshine, poetry, and love! All our tenderness will be renewed. Do you see that bright star rising opposite us, over there? It represents the hope of our beautiful future."

I was laughing and talking at the same time, entwining her little hand in mine. I was singing happy refrains. And I urged on the postilion, crying "Faster, faster."

We are right to celebrate hope. It is the finest part of happiness. As soon as it is transformed into reality, it loses some of its charm and infinity, and always bruises us somewhere.

When we reached Marseilles, we weren't tired, taking the incidents of the road good-naturedly as food for our curiosity and fascination. We rented the best cabin of a boat leaving for Genoa and set out on the Mediterranean. The first hour of the crossing was dazzling. Seated side by side on the bridge, we watched the boundless blue waves, polished like enormous turquoises, striated by the golden blades of the sun. A few sailing vessels here and there were moving out to the high sea or returning to the port. Imperceptibly the waves were growing bigger. I suddenly felt sick. Sky and sea merged in my disturbed vision. I saw nothing but a crushing mass which seemed to weigh on my chest. Seasickness overcame my admiration. Antonia, more resilient, didn't succumb to the debilitating influence. She had me lie down under a canopy where I could get enough fresh air but where I was sheltered from the harsh, burning light. Throughout the crossing, she took care of me, sensibly and tenderly. Thanks to her I escaped the more degrading aspects of that unsavory disposition. I was a little embarrassed to be weaker than she, but I was grateful for the support she gave me.

As soon as we saw land and Genoa displayed her marble palaces like an amphitheater, I got my strength back. I gulped down two glasses of Spanish wine. I could stand upright in the bridge, and I revived in the wind which was blowing stronger. We disembarked in the midst of a populace which always seems to be on a holiday, intoxicated by its sun, flowers, and melodious language.

Once on the quay of the port, I took Antonia's arm in mine, pressing it ardently. "Now, my beauty, it is my turn to care for you.

As your guide, Madame, I shall presume to do the honors of Italy."

We stayed in one of the best hotels.

After we had dressed elegantly and eaten heartily, I informed Antonia that our carriage was waiting. I had rented an antique berlin with impressive fittings in which we were very comfortable. When the servants of the inn saw us leave, they sang praises to the blooming good looks of the *giovani sposi francesi*.

We were driven to the promenade of the Acquazola. It was the end of September, but the evening was as warm as an August evening in Paris.

The Acquazola is a charming esplanade where you see a sliver of the sea, the mountains, the valleys, an entire smiling countryside, fragrant and flower-covered, red, white, and green houses with balconies, jalousies, and facades painted with frescoes. It is in this setting amidst pungent shurbs and plants and along shaded walkways where Genoese women parade on summer evenings, in their costume of true fantasy. Parisian fashion has extended its sway over the entire world. It has invaded Turkey and Persia and is making inroads in China. In Genoa it dominates during the winter. But as soon as the fine days come, the women there put away their little Parisian capes and hats and replace them with the *pezzotto*. This is a long white muslin scarf, starched and transparent. Beneath this veil the Genoese woman, naturally beautiful, appears even more beautiful. The *pezzotto* allows every imaginable fantasy or caprice in coiffures. You see rolls and twists that are whimsical yet extremely graceful. The black hair is braided and arranged into various forms of baskets which anchor the *pezzotto*. It falls, curving around the shoulders, and undulates over the arms in ample, harmonious folds that bear comparison to ancient Greek statuary. This national veil is worn by all women without distinction of rank or age. Mothers and daughters, patricians, bourgeoises and peasants, all appear beneath the *pezzotto*. Their figure is outlined through its white film while their face is framed by it. They are most likely to wear it on feast days to church and on promenades.

Antonia and I were thrilled at the sight of all these women gliding softly under the dark trees like white shadows. We had dismounted, and we strolled arm in arm through the splendid shade trees of the Acquazola. Women selling flowers passed by, laughing, pushing their large bouquets of tuberoses, acacias, roses, and carnations under our nose. Their fragrances were overwhelming. I filled Antonia's lap with flowers, for we had by then found a seat on a sheltered bench near a pool where refreshing fountains sprayed the air. Vendors of sherbets and candied fruit passed by with their loaded trays. The sea breezes stirred the supple branches overhead. It was Sunday. A military band played medleys in which we recognized themes from the greatest Italian masters. Everything was part of the enchantment in our hearts. O ineffable, tender Genoese nights, can't you return?

Anything is an excuse for celebrating when love is kind. You belong to the gods during that ardent phase of life. You think your body's immortal. After short nights, filled more with bliss than sleep, we would go out every morning to visit some famous garden. Then we would go out into the countryside. We admired the beauty of the light and its magical effect on the mountain crests, making them sometimes look like masses of iridescent opal. During the heat of the day we would wander through the huge marble palaces, enraptured, studying the paintings and statues in the vestibules, salons, and galleries. What grandiose luxury there was in those decorations!

I said to Antonia, "If I were rich, I would give you one of these magnificent palaces. I would bring in a select ensemble of musicians and conceal them in some distant room to inspire you with harmony while you worked. Whenever you finished one of your works, I would want the world to shower praise on you. So I would convene everyone who understands, applauds, or practices art to unparalleled festivities. I would display you to the bedazzled disciples of beauty as the queen of my heart wearing a velvet gown with an ermine-trimmed train and golden chains. You would greet them with a nod of your inspired head, wearing above your brow some enormous gem of the Orient, less sparkling, however, than your eyes."

When I went on like that, Antonia would put her arms around me and say with tender simplicity, "My poor Albert, you put me on a pedestal. I only popularize art and feeling. You're the genius!"

Sometimes I thought she was right, that she could reach beauty only by deliberate and slow reflection, while I had either an intuition or a sudden shock. When we looked at some masterpiece together, the dominant qualities would escape her at first. Then she would make a reasoned analysis, a little vague and sometimes paradoxical. I myself would either say nothing or just a word or two. But I believe I expressed exactly the artist's thought and feeling and the effect his work was to create. When we went to the opera in the evening, the music also would arouse very divergent impressions. True cries of passion from individual characters never struck her. She was most moved by religious choral music and choruses expressing group sentiments. It seemed as if she needed a mass rallying of souls before her own could be stirred. In her own works, what I am noting here is even more obvious. She has a mobile mind, enamoured with universal sympathy, which can expand infinitely in charity, love, utopia, but which is lacking a sense of the individual and of the passionate.

It was especially in our love affair where the dissimilarity of our two natures was most jarring and obvious. Even in our most completely happy hours, I never felt she was entirely mine. She didn't seem in the least desirous of possessing me, as I was of her. Her emotions were general, rarely circumstantial and focused on me. I would say to myself, "Anyone else would please her just as much. I'm in no way as indispensable to her heart as she is to mine."

She was a creature of predilection who seemed to have been created by a breath of Spinozan pantheism, while I was strictly the incarnation of an absolute spirit, a human personality reflecting the personality of a distinct god.

When such a reflection hit me like a light or spun around my weary brain, I didn't make any inference critical of her. Rather, I would doubt myself. I'd think, "She's better than you are, fairer and stronger. Superior personalities have more intense sensations and more energetic geniuses. But they always crush someone around them, and you could well be only a cruel, tyrannical child piercing less bountifully the mysteries of humanity. She is kind, attentive, compassionate for anyone who suffers. Like Rubens' 'Charity' who seems to hold on her robust lap and against her innumerable breasts the wretched of the earth, she would like to dry with a single breath all the misery and tears. Her forbearance and tenderness are sublimely expansive. What does your limited and exclusive love matter to that immense love? Concentrate on her the warming fire of your heart, but let her spread her beneficent rays over all."

That's how my conscience, or rather my bias, reasoned on her behalf, and such theoretical justice was easy for me. But in every minute of practical living, my reasoning was destroyed by my senses. She and I almost never expressed by the same words thoughts which should have been identical.

When we happened upon some poor person, both of us instinctively reached for our purse to give him alms. Sometimes, depending on the degree and aspect of the wretchedness, my eyes would fill with tears. I wasn't harsh; I've never lacked heart. But Antonia expressed her emotion by dogmatic explosions censuring wealth and espousing the absolute necessity to put an end to human inequality. At first I listened to her with interest, then with distraction, and finally with a wounding boredom that she sensed. She treated me as a puerile mind and spoiled by quarrelling the new impressions which could have superceded the impression made by our encounter with the beggar.

Everything lively and inspired in me would then cry out in revolt against the pressure exerted by that ponderous mind. Like a lizard imprisoned under a bell jar, escaping to wiggle in the sun, I began to run about the countryside or in the streets, acting like a schoolboy playing hooky just to have a chance to think as I pleased.[1]

CHAPTER XIII

We began to get a little tired of Genoa, so we left at the beginning of October. We stopped at Leghorn and made a detour for a visit to Pisa. Byron said that Pisa with its Leaning Tower and cathedral like Saint Sophia makes one think of a city in the Near East. We spent eight days in Florence and then crossed the Apennines to go to Ferrara. I won't give you a description of all these cities. Our life together was just like Genoa, sometimes enraptured with each other, sometimes dumbfounded, but happy all the same. I loved her sweet and serious company, and I felt that from then on she would be indispensable to me. Our funds, which we had pooled, were being depleted by such attractive excursions. Antonia, to whom I had given complete control of our expenses, warned me that it was time to think about planting our tent and getting down to work. I

1. This is a highly romanticized account of the stay in Genoa. It was a nightmare for Sand, bedfast with diarrhea, while Musset pursued loose women, especially the prototype of Négra, the Moroccan dancer in the Venice interlude.

had put off doing anything with the notes I had taken at Genoa, Florence and Pisa. Even while travelling I had made sketchy outlines for several works. I felt in the mood to start writing them. The rapid conception of a subject gives us the illusion of having the sustained inspiration necessary to bring it to life. However, there is quite an abyss between having the first idea for a book and giving birth to it!

So I replied that like her I was consumed with the desire to work, and that all we had to do was choose the place where we'd settle in.

Venice seemed to us a city of silence and contemplation, ideal for the writer and poet. It offered the inspiration of great memories and the revitalizing relaxation of excursions on the sea. Byron had written his most beautiful poems there. I thought that on the banks of those lagoons, I would breathe in the spirit of that immortal poet.

We rented three rooms in an old palace near the Grand Canal.[1] The largest, which we used as a sitting room and study, looked out on the lagoons, while the others, adjoining bedrooms, got their daylight from one of those rather filthy alleys so common in Venice. Antonia, who could be an excellent housekeeper when she wanted to, made our somewhat delapidated dwelling comfortable. She had rugs put down on the floors and heavy drapes hung over the doors and windows. She even got the smoking fireplaces fixed. While our winter nest was being prepared, we toured Venice: the Schiavoni Quay, the Piazzetta, St. Mark's Cathedral, the Doge's palace, the prison of Leads, all those monuments already described a thousand times over. Every morning we took a boat excursion. One day we went to the Island of Armenians. We vis-

1. Their luxurious apartment was in the Hotel Danieli, where the Schiavoni Quay merges with the Grand Canal. It was on the second floor. Later Pagello found them a cheaper flat.

ited the convent and its famous library. I was struck by the ease with which a young religious, about my size, wore his rough serge cassock, its deep pleats held in at the waist by a cord. I asked him to have one made like it for me, and as soon as it was delivered, it became my dressing gown. Antonia pretended that I was a charmer in my monk's costume, and I, in turn, found her even more beautiful when she put on every morning the black velvet dogaressa gown that I had had copied from the portrait of some illustrious Venetian woman. When we went out, we put on our simple French clothing so that we wouldn't attract attention. Only any time I took Antonia to the Opera, I insisted that she wear flowers or jewels in her magnificent hair. Her beauty was noticed. People found out who we were, and the French consul, for whom I had letters of introduction and whose father had known mine, paid us a call, offering his services during our stay in Venice.[2]

With dignity Antonia courteously declined his gracious offer. She explained that we had to work. We had been able to take time seeing monuments and enjoying ourselves during our first days of getting settled. But now that our curiosity was satisfied, we would be going out very seldom.

"You're making a mistake to run away from the people seeking your company," the consul replied. "You would have found appealing distractions in Venetian society and curious subjects of study."

Antonia did not answer, and her face immediately assumed such a forbidding expression, almost discourteous, that I had to be twice as amiable with our visitor. When he left, I thanked him for his kindness, adding that I would come to see him soon and that it would be a pleasure to have his company and that of the Venetian nobles he had mentioned.

2. The French consul is Samuel Silvestre de Sacy (1801–79).

As soon as we were alone again, Antonia burst out in reproaches, accusing me of being frivolous and making plans for dissipation. Now that our lodging was arranged, the hour had come, she told me, for going into seclusion and getting down to work. We were going to run out of money, and we should make it a point of honor never to borrow from a friend.

Everything she said was perfectly reasonable, but I found her language a little too didactic. Since I joked about it, she was cross when she went into her room, closing herself in and not coming out until suppertime.

I called to her several times in vain, begging her to come out and be with me. She replied that she was working and asked me to leave her alone.

I tried to imitate her and write a few pages of one of those books germinating in my thoughts, but it was futile. I've never been able to work unless I'm in the mood. I can't do it on order or by regimen whether prescribed by myself or somebody else. I couldn't find a single sentence. So, exasperated by both my lack of inspiration and Antonia's decision, I went out for a stroll on St. Mark's Square. I sat down at the front of a café; I smoked, ate some sherbet and drank curaçao. I spent two marvelous hours there just watching the continuous pageant of passersby and groups. It was a new, diverting spectacle, accustomed as I was to seeing the uniformity and monotony of the Parisian population whose costume is not the least picturesque and whose physical type, let's be frank, has none of the beauty and strength of the southern races. Besides the handsome Italian natives, there were the Levantines with long velvety eyes and wide pantaloons. Then there were the Illyrians with their free and barbarous charm. Maltese who looked sly and sullen. Presumptuous Portuguese draped in their destitution as they used to wear their wealth when they owned the world. Melancholy Spaniards whose haughty, piercing eyes endowed their gloomy faces with life. All these men passed back and forth, some clothed luxuriously, smoking pipes with amber stems, strolling idly. Others were in rags. Turks and Arabs put out their stalls in the open wind; there paste and glass sparkled, aromatic pastilles sent up their fumes, pyramids of dates and pistachios stood in heaps. Most of the men were tattered vagabonds, carrying goods, doing errands, sleeping in the sun; among them were a few blacks, their backs bent beneath their heavy burdens. Women crossing the Piazza presented the same diversity of types and costumes. There was a Venetian noblewoman in French dress gliding under the galleries with her lackey. Some beautiful veiled Greeks were entering a shop selling sumptuous fabrics. A few Tyrolean peasant women in their picturesque costume were looking at the St. Mark facade, dazzled. An acrobat with a faded face but proud of her spangled smock stretched a worn mat on the ground and began a rapid dance, her castanets clicking. Another poor girl in a saffron-colored dress, wearing a kind of green turban, accompanied her on the drum. This girl was as gold as an orange and solicited our attention with her velvety eyes and long black lashes. She must have been a stray, cast ashore at Venice by some Moroccan vessel. Her voice and gestures prodded a very small African, who looked like a wastrel, to hold out his greasy fez to the café loiterers. Nearby a poor child, barely nubile, made monkeys go through a dance. Still another, smiling like a cherubim, was singing a barcarolle while gracefully accompanying herself on a viola d'amore.

I was so enthralled by every detail of that fantastic gathering on St. Mark's Square that I would happily have spent the night there because it's especially toward evening that this section of Venice becomes crowded, coming to life as the theater of pleasure for the entire city. When I heard the clock strike eight, I remembered that Antonia would be holding supper for me. I went back to our lodgings a little embarrassed, like a schoolboy who's afraid of being scolded.

I found Antonia radiant. She was just getting ready to sit down and asked sarcastically if I'd gotten any work done. I confessed I'd been loafing.

My mind was filled with images. I had felt and observed. All that found a place in my poems and prose eventually, but at that precise moment, I had not written a line, while Antonia had filled twenty pages with her firm, compact handwriting. She had a good appetite. I watched her but said nothing.

When I tried to kiss her during dessert, she said that she was going to take an hour off, smoking at the window, and then would go back to work.

"We'd be better off," I replied, "if we took a gondola ride or got some fresh air on the Piazzetta."

"Go ahead, if you want to," she said, "but I've put myself on my honor not to allow myself any diversion until I've sent a manuscript to my publisher."

This kind of language from a woman humiliated me a little. I felt she was usurping my place.

I leaned on my elbows at the window, too. We could see a section of the Grand Canal and the Schiavoni Quay. While smoking the cigarettes that she handed me silently, I ran my fingers through her fine hair. She remained impassive, watching the black gondolas file past.

"However, it would really be nice," I resumed, "to stretch out in one of those gondolas and go out into the Grand Lagoon. We wouldn't have to stay long, if you don't want to, but, please, let's go out for a little while."

"Don't tempt me," she replied. "My thoughts are relaxing under the influence of the tobacco aroma and the motion of the passing boats. Soon my mind, like a good horse who's had her oats, will gallop over the paper."

After she said that, her gaze appeared lost in space. She seemed to forget I was there.

Not being able to get a glance or a word out of her, I took my hat and went out. Rather automatically I headed for Theater La Fenice.[3] I entered and stood by a column. The consul, who had visited us in the morning, saw me and came over to take me to his box. I found there two young Venetians: one very rich, the other very handsome. One's mistress was the most popular dancer; the other's, the most acclaimed prima donna. They proposed taking me backstage to visit these ladies. I followed, and the consul came too, saying he would be able to vouch for me to Antonia.

I begged him under my breath to keep still and not bandy about my beloved's name. Just hearing her dear name made me feel remorseful, and I was ready to desert those gentlemen. False shame restrained me, and then a little curiosity led me on. We found the first lady of dance and the first lady of song in an elegant little salon which served as the dancer's dressing room. She was stretched out on her black velvet divan in a coquettish, tempting pose which she must have worked on for a long time in front of her mirror. Her right leg was raised level with her left thigh where her dainty right foot was resting. She was lightly veiled in a tunic of rose gauze scattered with silver stars which left bare her arms, shoulders, and somewhat thin chest. Her neck was perfectly modelled, and her very small head was pretty and provocative. She wore a crescent of enormous diamonds in the middle of her forehead. The iridescent gems made her black hair

3. This early eighteenth-century theater, which saw the premieres of *Rigoletto* and *La Traviata*, is still in use. It is on the same tongue of land as St. Mark's Square.

sparkle. She held out her hand to the rich Venetian who introduced me, and I immediately became the object of all her flirtatious maneuvers. The prima donna was more sedate. She was wearing a kind of white peplum bordered in purple and held on her broad and muscular shoulders by ruby clasps. Beneath the folds of her Greek drapery could be discerned a beautiful large bosom. Her superb neck was straight as a column. Her face had the regular features and pensive expression of the muse Polymnia. She held out her hand cordially and told me she loved poets.[4] The dancer, wanting to do her amiability one better, immediately invited me to have supper at her lover's home when the performance was over. She called me *caro amico* and laughingly exclaimed that for her a refusal would be the same as an insult.

I resisted on the pretext of a migraine and left this attractive company a bit abruptly. The dancer called after me "A rivederla." The consul made me promise to go with him soon to visit the singer, who wanted to set one of my songs to music.

I left the theater in a state, wondering why I was by myself, why Antonia wasn't there to smile at me lovingly, to protect me from desiring any other woman, from even having the possibility of looking at another woman because when she was with me, I had eyes only for her. I threw myself despondently into a gondola and had myself driven around for two hours. It was after midnight when I returned. Antonia was still up. There was a rim of light from her lamp around the door separating her room from mine. Her door was locked. I made some noise bumping into furniture, in hopes she would speak to me. Exasperated, I decided to call her.

4. The prima donna bears similarities to Guiditta Pasta née Negri (1798–1865). Her combined soprano and contralto range and timbre was further enhanced by her intelligent and sensitive dramatizations. Bellini created *Norma* for her. Note that the Moroccan dancer will be called Mlle. Négra.

"What do you want of me" she asked sweetly.

"Why is this door shut? Let me in!"

"No, no, no," she laughed, "you would divert me from my duty, and I want to work for three more hours."

Seeing the futility of persistence, I went to bed hoping to sleep. But I was gripped by feverish agitation which chased away sleep and left only dreams. The little silver of light piercing her door was direct and sharp. Sometimes it seemed like an ironic smile jeering at me. Other times it was like a fine blade whittling my flesh here and there. This malevolent ray stung my eyes which it kept from closing and burned my forehead like a bandage of fire.

Finally, around three o'clock Antonia's lamp went out, and the hypnotic ray vanished.

"Open up now," I called.

"Go to sleep," she answered. "I'm going to sleep so I can get back to work tomorrow."

I didn't say anything else to her. I bit my covers in rage, and feeling that I couldn't conquer my insomnia, I decided to get up to try to write. My overexcited brain was at that moment in a creative mood, which is always painful for me, a kind of explosion of bitterness and love. I heard Antonia's regular breathing. She had fallen asleep at once, and I heard her breathing until daybreak while my inflamed thoughts rushed over the paper like a hurricane. I finally fell back into my chair in exhausted slumber. Antonia found me when she came in to say that lunch was ready. She realized that I had been working. She must have been touched, for I woke up in her arms.

She was saying, "So you spent the night writing? Oh, that's more than I can do myself."

She forced me to lie down and had lunch served at my bedside. The meal was rather gay. Seeing her in a good humor, I at once asked her to give up her idea of complete seclusion and go out with me on some excursion that very day.

She replied that she never went back on a resolution, that to distract her from her work would be making her risk never finishing it, and that I certainly knew the compelling necessity behind her speed.

"Imitate me," she advised, "and afterwards we'll have some vacation days."

"You well know," I replied, "that I can work only in spurts. What will happen to me in this solitude in which you let me suffer?"

"Are you sick?" she asked. "If you are, I'll stay with you. I'll sit and sew by your bedside."

"All I need is a Sister of Charity," I snapped irritably.

"All right. This is just idle anxiety. Good-bye till suppertime."

And ignoring my outstretched arms, she locked herself in her room again.

Lunch had revived me. An hour's siesta had made me feel like myself again. I got up and while choosing a nice outfit to wear, I hummed a few lines of the barcarolle I was to take to the prima donna. I opened my window. The sky was brilliant, the temperature mild and warm. It was the end of November, and I thought about the gray, chill atmosphere that would be enveloping Paris at that hour and the still blacker mist descending on London. I said that youth there had cause for despondency, but that beneath the blue Venetian sky, it was self-deception. Shaking off my silly melancholy the way you throw off a heavy garment, I went out, making my cane whistle as I cut through the air. As I crossed the hall, I saw the door to Antonia's room ajar. She called out without raising her head, without even laying down her pen, "Have a good time!"

"I'll do my best!"

Her words had provoked my response, which I in no way meant

as a defiance. I was back in shape, gay with the gaiety of a beautiful day, pleased with having done some work. I reflected that it would be silly for us to torture each other, that Antonia was a heroic woman and that her courageous work revealed her pride. It was impossible for me to imitate her in all respects, but I, too, would work on my own schedule, after I returned and after I had absorbed outdoors the fresh air and inspiration my fancy needed.

Before getting in a gondola to go to the consul's I wanted to cross St. Mark's Square. In front of the cafe where I had been sitting the day before, I found the little Moroccan saltimbank who played the drum. She was wearing the same ragged green and yellow dress that made her such a pitiful sight. She must have remembered that I had given her some coins, for as soon as she saw me, she fastened her sad and pensive eyes on me. Her eyes looked like Antonia's when she was feeling tender. Those eyes, whose expression I loved followed me with such fixity that they finally exerted some kind of fascination over me. Although the poor child was rather homely, her copper complexion, her white teeth, and her remarkably deep and gentle gaze kept her from looking common.

I was studying her, wondering how she would end, and this mysterious obsession might have held me until nightfall if one of my acquaintances of the night before hadn't crossed the Square. It was the handsome Venetian lover of the prima donna.

He asked me if I would like to climb in his gondola to go see his mistress. I replied that it was precisely what I had in mind but that I was intending to visit the French consul first.

"Fine, let's go to His Lordship's together and then go on to the diva's."

I followed him, and after we had settled down in reclining positions, complimented him on his mistress's beauty.

"Stella is just as kind as she is beautiful," he replied simply. "I loved her just hearing her sing, and she loved me just seeing me listen. Later, she told me in her language full of imagery, that this had to happen since we both wore our souls on our faces. She chose me, although I have almost no fortune, over princes who offered her millions. 'Anything worth having,' she often tells me, 'cannot be bought: love, genius, and beauty are divine gifts which even the richest cannot purchase.' "

"You can read those proud convictions on her face," I replied.

"She is at home with everything that has to do with art," he continued. "She composes music, writes Italian poems, and draws from memory the places and persons who have impressed her."

"Do you really love her?"

"So much so that I shall marry her the day an old uncle makes me his heir. In the meantime I am forced to leave her to the theater."

"It seems to me that the première danseuse is completely different from your beautiful friend, am I right?"

"The dancer Zéphira," he answered, "has neither brain nor heart. But she is very mean and controls the impresario while leading poor Count Luigi around by the nose. My dear Stella treats her very carefully to avoid trouble at the theater."

Chatting in this vein, we reached the French consulate. The consul had gone out, so the gondola resumed its course through the labyrinth of canals and soon deposited us in front of the palace where the prima donna lived.

We found Stella at the piano, rehearsing a role she was to play the next day for the first time. When she saw her lover, even before greeting me, she threw her arms around his neck in that openhearted way of Italian woman; it has always moved me. Then turning to me, she held out her hand, she said, "It was very kind of you, Signor, to have come to see me. Do you have your couplets with you? I'm counting on them," she added immediately, "for I feel in the mood to write good music."

"They're in here," I said, touching my forehead. "Just give me pen and paper." And forthwith I wrote down one of my Spanish songs.

The prima donna spoke French very well, and while skimming my lines, she hummed them to a tentative melody.

"I've got it!" she exclaimed. "*Amico caro,* take the French signor into the gallery for cigars and coffee, and come back in an hour. The song will be ready."

We obeyed, and as we withdrew, I heard her powerful voice make my lines soar in a melody she was improvising. "Let's listen where she can't see us," I suggested.

The melodic line she had found and which she continually modified as she repeated it was truly inspired. It enhanced my lines, giving the words a more spiritual sense. Everytime I hear beautiful music, it seems to me that poetry is as cold and colorless beside it as reason is to passion.

While she was singing, her lover murmured, "Doesn't she put her soul in her voice?"

I was thinking about Antonia, and I wished she could have shared the pleasure that fine voice was giving us.

We were soon joined by the cantatrice. She reported that she had found the right melody and was ready to have me hear it. "But," she added, friendly and gracious, "if you would be so kind, Signor, as to stay for supper with us, I shall be in better voice, and you'll like *our* song better."

Her lover insisted that I stay.

"It's impossible; I'm expected at home."

"Oh, I understand, it's your sweetheart, *una amica,*" the good-hearted woman interjected. "Well, let's go get her. I love people in love."

It seemed like a good idea to me. I thought Antonia would be touched by the sight of those two beautiful young people in love and that she would consent to spend the evening with us. But once we were in front of the house where we were living, I didn't dare bring in my new friends before warning Antonia. I asked them to wait.

I found Antonia at the table.

"I thought you weren't coming back for supper," she said.

"I've come to whisk you away," I laughed, kissing her to break the ice. I told her quickly what was up.

She replied with haughty astonishment that I was going astray. She would certainly not go out like that, running after adventure. "Go have a good time," she added. "I've got a job to do, and I'm staying." At that moment she seemed as sententious and harsh as a teacher scolding an affectionate child.

"So stay!" I shot back and turned on my heels.

I had to lie to the prima donna, telling her that I had found my sweetheart indisposed. At that, she offered to take care of her and entreated me not to leave her.

I replied that Antonia was resting and a few hours alone would do her good.

"In that case, you'll have supper with us?" Stella asked.

"Yes, that will be an honor," I replied, sitting back down in the gondola which resumed its course. At the angle of a canal, it crossed the gondola of the première danseuse Zéphira who jumped up when she saw us.

"I knew it!" she shouted. "The French signor is paying court to Stella!"

"Come to my aid, Zéphira," the cantatrice's lover parried gaily. "Without you, I'm lost." And seeing her ready to jump into our gondola, he gallantly held out his hand.

"And where are you going like this?" the dancer asked.

"Back home to eat," Stella answered.

"I'll go along," Zéphira said. "Luigi bores me. He is ugly and jealous. I'd like to have him eat his heart out waiting for me. I'm not dancing this evening, Signor Francese, so after supper I can take you riding in the moonlight. It would be inhuman for the two of us to disturb Stella and her sweetheart's tête-à-tête."

The dancer's company spoiled things a bit for me. Involuntarily I was depressed by Antonia's obstinacy. In my frame of mind that mindless girl's flirtatiousness got on my nerves like sour wine. I stretched out at the back of the gondola, and on the pretext that I must surely have a headache which needed soothing, Zéphira came back to sit with me. She agitated her spangled fan rapidly over my hair and forehead. Her beauty was piquant and didn't lack charm. How could I get offended and tell her I found her unattractive? Stella, reading my mind, called to me in English, which the dancer didn't understand, "Please, bear with her, for my sake. She would be capable of having me hooted and booed tomorrow evening."

"What did she tell you?" the dancer asked suspiciously.

"That I'm falling in love, and Count Luigi will kill me."

At that she smiled graciously at me and continued to fan me, while running her fingers through my hair. I uttered a few flirtatious remarks, and, once launched into that fiction, had to play the role of the amorous admirer.

Supper was extremely high-spirited. Zéphira emptied a huge flagon of Spanish wine and forced me to keep up with her.

When we went into the drawing room and Stella sat down at the piano to let me hear our barcarolle, Zéphira, a bit unsteady on her feet, sank down into an ottoman and almost immediately went to sleep.

So deeply, in fact, that none of our bravos and applause after each couplet Stella sang disturbed her deep sleep. I was able to escape by myself, despite the vow she had extracted in striking glasses that I would take her home at midnight.

CHAPTER XIV

THE FRESH NIGHT AIR immediately dispersed the burning vapors running through my brain from the supper and wine, the dancer's overtures, and Stella's impassioned singing. I suddenly felt gloomy and depressed just as if I'd been abandoned in a large foreign city.

In the wavering light of gondola lanterns, Venice floated before me, black and silent. It looked like an immense coffin lighted by tapers. It seemed to me that my heart was being enshrouded and that it would never again be reborn to life and love. I began to weep for myself as you would weep for someone beloved who has just died. Why was I feeling this premonitory mourning? What was causing this omen?

I was ashamed of my weakness and making a strenuous effort to grasp once more the happiness I felt was getting away from me, I resolved to break the ice around Antonia's heart that very hour and throw myself passionately into her arms.

"After all," I said to myself, "I carry my own destiny. Let us try to love valiantly. I shall persuade her and bind her to me. Why should I feel this terror of misfortune which I can conjure away on the strength of my love? Leave me? Forget me? How could she? Who would ever give her what she loses when she loses me? This pride of love substantiates its excess and contains its truth because few creatures here below burn with this life-consuming flame. Such passion is as rare as genius."

I came back in without a sound and felt my way in the dark to Antonia's door on the hall. The head of her bed was next to this door. The door was closed. By pressing my ear against it I could tell she was sleeping. I didn't dare wake her. I went to the kitchen where our maid was waiting up for me, snoring, her head resting on the table. She lifted up her head at my voice.

"Is Madame ill?" I asked.

"No, Monsieur, but she is very tired. Madame wrote all day long. At midnight she couldn't write another line and went to bed. It would be kind of Monsieur to let her sleep."

I made no comment to that woman but with the same feelings of a mother who is afraid of disturbing her child's sleep, I tiptoed into my room, undressed, put on my monk's robe and began to work. While I wrote, tears rose from my heart to my eyes and from time to time rolled down upon the page. I could still show you the pages they stained. I didn't put down my pen until daybreak. Around noon I was awakened by Antonia's voice as she leaned over my bed. I sat up instantly and embraced her passionately to remove her indifference and possess her forever.

"This is enough suffering! Enough obliviousness! How frigid and foolish you've been! Don't you realize that love is the only happiness?" I covered her with kisses and hugged her so fiercely that she squealed, pretending I was hurting her. Then she began laughing drily, not rejecting my caresses but not returning them either. Her large eyes, studying me intently, were not the least bit tender.

"What gives you the right to make fun of me and look at me like that?" I let go of her.

"It's just that I see you're a child who will never understand mature love."

"Please!" I said irritably. "No sermons on how to love. All I know is that I love you. What do I have to do to prove it?"

"What's the point of telling you? You won't do it!"

"Tell me anyway."

"You shouldn't run around cafés and theaters. You should accept the discipline of a regimen. Stay here when I'm working. Work yourself. And before allowing ourselves love and its distractions, we should wait until our double task is accomplished."

"What you suggest would be possible," I replied, "if heaven had created us both absolutely alike. But we differ by nature and aspiration. What sets you aflame puts my fire out. What makes you soar makes me plummet. Does the galloping horse have the right to begrudge the bird its flight because it moves by different means? Why do you want to restrain and humiliate me? So long as I act, that is, produce on my schedule and according to my abilities, what difference does it make to you? Let's leave ourselves free. Besides if you could make me follow in your footsteps, I would be only a schoolboy or a slave, and then you would be contemptuous and stop loving me!"

"I would love an honest man who didn't think he would diminish his genius by quickly completing a useful work which would help replenish our funds."

"Be patient. I'll get to it. But I've told you already. I'm unable to turn out a set amount of verse and prose at a set hour every day, like a weaver at his loom."

"No," she jeered, "the gentleman-poet requires prodigal behavior and frivolous distractions for inspiration."

With this she left me like a preacher coming down from his pulpit after the sermon.

I confess I would have cheerfully sent her to the devil. She was beginning to make me feel trapped in the apartment. The bad side of daily intimacy in a love affair is that it soon engenders all the cares and chains of marriage. We men should see our mistress at her place and at her convenience and never make an appearance before her loving eyes except in good health and a gala mood and when her heart and lips desire us. Not wishing to expose myself to another of her sermons—this would have brought on a still worse quarrel—I left her to lunch alone and went to a restaurant on St. Mark's Square to have some fried fish and a chocolate. I had only two louis left in my pocket. I broke one to pay for lunch and buy some cigars. While I was smoking under the arcades, I espied the little African of the day before. She wasn't accompanying on her drum the dancer in a spangled skirt. The silent instrument was by her side while, poorly clad in a brown Indian print, she sat in the sun to mend her yellow tunic with gold paillettes. It was pitiful to see the rags which made up her shabby covering and the cheap garb she was mending so carefully, probably her only adornment. I stopped to watch her, and although I was placed at an angle almost directly behind her under an arch, something seemed to alert her that I was there. She turned her head, fastened her eyes on me and wouldn't take them off. I was going to move away to escape from this strange creature when suddenly I had the feeling her glance contained a prayer. I reached down in my pocket, took out my last louis and said in Italian, "Something to buy you a dress."

"Oh, thank you, Signor, thank you," she replied, joining her little brown hands and raising them toward me like a sign of benediction.

I moved away quickly to flee her gratitude and entered the Doge's Palace. I went there almost every day to admire the paintings and ceilings of the Venetian school. By dint of studying them, I managed to bring to life those allegorical and historical personages, those beautiful faces of women who have lived and loved and seem to live and love still, since art has preserved them from death. The fabulous gods, the heroes and especially the smiling women immortals opened my imagination to the limitless fields of fantasy. Sometimes it was the warlike pose which suddenly reanimated for me the Homeric melee of ancient battle. Sometimes it was a detail of a costume, a fold of garment, which made my thoughts wander from the brocade gowns of the patrician ladies to the peplums of the young Greeks following the Panathenaea.

On that day I forgot myself for hours in the company of all ages and all civilizations. Towards evening I remembered that I had promised to go to the theater to hear Stella in her new role. I also thought I ought to eat without going back to the apartment. I didn't want to think about Antonia, but I felt her presence at the bottom of my heart like a painful, natural weight. I ate quickly at the same restaurant where I had lunched in the morning, and as I left by recrossing St. Mark's Square, lighted now by street lamps, I saw in a circle of light the little drum girl wearing a red tunic with silver paillettes. In her black braids little coral bells tinkled and jingled. She was almost beautiful in that costume which made her proud and poised. Instead of accompanying the acrobat of the day before, she herself was doing the dancing and doing so with nimbleness and style. She was using castanets which clicked in rhythm. The moment she saw me, she stopped her dance, leaving her spectators in suspense, to flounce her beautiful dress and shout that she owed it to me.

I replied that she danced like an angel. I had a sudden impulse. "Would you like to be engaged at the theater?"

"Jesu Maria!" she was ecstatic at the idea.

"You'd really like that?"

"Oh, yes, even if I were the very lowliest figurant in the chorus, I'd have enough to live on and be respected."

The last part made me laugh, "Do you think those ladies get much respect?"

"It's in my own house that I would be respected," she explained. "My master treats me badly, and he's no more married me than he has any of the other girls, although he promised to. But if I earned only two or three sequins a month at the theater, he would marry me, and I'd certainly kick out the others in a hurry." Then she told me how she and five or six other little dancers and acrobats of the Piazzetta and St. Mark's Square made up a kind of harem for the robust Algerian merchant who sold aromatic pastilles. "But I'm his first woman," she said proudly, "he brought me from there while he picked up the others off the streets in Venice."

"And are you faithful to him?" I was still laughing.

"Yes, when poverty and rage aren't too much for me, but, Signor, the theater! The theater! That would make me a good, kind woman who loves her children."

I have always noticed that the most fallen woman dreams of her rehabilitation.

As I left, I promised to see what I could do to help her. I bought a large bouquet with my last ecu and went to the opera. I took my seat in the consul's box. But I had hardly gotten settled when the prima donna's lover entered to see me. He was obviously upset.

"Ah, Monsieur, Zéphira's rage knows no bounds. She claims that Stella put a powder in the wine yesterday evening to make her silly and drive you away. She is swearing vengeance, and I'm convinced she'll actually organize a faction against my dear Stella. Please, before the curtain goes up, go into Zéphira's box and try to placate her. Offer this very bouquet, meant, I imagine, for my sweetheart. You will spare Stella hoots and catcalls that all the flowers in Venice could not smother."

I obeyed the young Venetian, and willing to play the role, I gaily entered Zéphira's box. She turned crimson when she saw me, and to get rid of her lover Count Luigi, ordered him to go get her some candied orange peels. As soon as we were alone, she demanded point blank why I had abandoned her the night before.

"You were sleeping so soundly and gracefully I thought you looked like a goddess on Olympus. I felt unworthy of you, mere mortal that I am, and I respectfully withdrew, trembling to receive your orders."

I knew that such elevated, somewhat bombastic praise always pleased courtesans.

Zéphira simpered, not without shrewdness, "But now you're here without my having called you."

"Do you want me to leave?" I asked submissively.

"No, because I was expecting you." She added lower, "and desiring you. That lovely bouquet is for Stella, I suppose?"

"You can tell it isn't since I've brought it here."

She seized it, kissing it wildly and shrieking, "Oh, what beautiful myrtles!"

I hadn't noticed that the bouquet was made up of myrtles and white carnations. Count Luigi was coming back in as she was saying, "Be backstage at Stella's dressing room during the intermission."

"I trust you're going to applaud her and treat her as a fellow artist," I replied in a normal tone of voice.

"Have no fear. I'm going to shower bouquets on her, but," she added under her breath, "I'm keeping this one."

I left on the pretext that the consul was waiting for me.

"In a little while," she said as I went out.

"Yes, just after Stella's triumph," I answered.

From the first act, the prima donna's success was immense. They acclaimed her in the Italian style, with sonnets and coronets raining on her head. Zéphira kept her word. She cheered her, clapping her hands and throwing flowers. At each intermission she went to congratulate her and embrace her in her dressing room. She always found me there, and this made her still more tender and expansive for her friend. She wanted to improvise on the spot a party that evening at Count Luigi's to celebrate Stella's triumph.

And as she insisted that her friend persuade me to come along,

Stella countered, "Only you will be able to make the French signor join us."

I replied that I could not dispute Zéphira's hold over me but that a sickly aged relative was expecting me and that I wouldn't be free for several days.

At these words Zéphira sprang at me as if she were going to claw me with her pretty fingernails. She cried that she perfectly well realized that what I was saying was a pretext and that I didn't want to love her or see her.

Gallantly I replied that my sole desire was to spend my life near her and that to bind us together from this evening on I was going to ask a favor of her. Then I spoke to her about the little Moroccan dancer and her theatrical ambitions. Since I assured her that the African was not beautiful, she promised to recommend her that very evening to the impresario who would be taking her back in his gondola.

"I do it on one condition," she added, "that you will come to the party I'm giving in three days."

"No, in one week," I parried, "for the uncle I'm looking after is very sick. In a week he will be cured, you will have arranged the debut of this poor little dancer, and I will be all yours, my beautiful Zéphira."

She stamped with one leg while extending the other at a right angle. I clasped the tip of that foot in its nacarat satin. Then, not wanting to hear anything more, I set off through the backstage labyrinth.

Under the peristyle of the theater I found the French consul. He said he was waiting for me because he was having that very evening a *media-noche* for a few distinguished Venetians and foreigners. I would enjoy their company, he said, and they would be happy to meet me. "There will be no women," he added, "so you can come without making your beautiful friend angry."

I followed along. Just as well, I was thinking. What's the use of returning home before daybreak since Antonia's door would be closed anyway?

Some twenty men were already in the consul's drawing room when we arrived. Some were seated at card tables. Others, standing in small groups, were discussing music or politics. Several were smoking, their elbows resting on the balconies of the open windows. The Consul introduced me to his friends. We exchanged a few pleasantries. Then I sat down at a gaming table, mechanically giving in to some instinct to forget myself. As I was shuffling the cards, I remembered that I didn't even have a franc on me. I called the consul over and said, "You carried me off from the theater without giving me a chance to go home. I realize that I don't have my wallet."

He handed me fifty louis.

I gamble only when the occasion arises. By that I mean the game must come to me; I never go to it. But if I meet by chance, like that evening, at a card table, a rich, passionate partner, calm on the surface, showing no excitement when he wins, not raising an eyebrow when he loses, that spurs me on. Then I play as I work: feverishly, nervously, relentlessly, voluptuously. That evening getting absorbed in the game appealed to me. It made me forget even Antonia. Besides, I was playing with a happy streak of luck and skillful moves which seemed almost magic. Around two o'clock in the morning when a servant informed the consul that the meal would be served, I had won one hundred louis from the Venetian nobleman opposite. I told him I'd give him his turn to get even when we got up from the table. He replied lightheartedly that after the Cyprus wine we would think only of going to sleep. But if I would do him the honor of visiting his art gallery some evening, he would be happy to resume the game.

There were about thirty of us at the splendidly set table. Although there were no women present, they were the first topic of conversation. Love always enters where there's a party. When an affair isn't in progress, it's remembered. A few young men regaled us with their most recent conquests. But two painters and a poet among the guests soon raised the conversation to art, that ideal love of great souls. One of them asserted, "For us, art is a question of patriotism. What would modern Italy be without poetry, painting, and music? Our glory is the Renaissance and its dispersed geniuses who have kept the echo alive to this day. If Italy still lives and still keeps her name in the world, she doesn't owe it to nationhood but to some great men she produced to protest her annihilation."

"Art enervates us. It lulls our pride with superficial glory," countered a Venetian nobleman, a friend of Count Confalonieri, with some bitterness.[1] "Our history also, the role Rome played in antiquity, rises to our heads. It's a deceptive intoxication which leads to inertia. Misfortune comes to peoples who live only on the memory of their past grandeur. They soon lose the active life of nations and disintegrate in oblivion. Remember Byron's advice in the last lines of "Ode on Venice":

> Still, still, for ever
> Better, though each man's life-blood were a river,
> That it should flow and overflow, than creep
> Through thousand lazy channels in our veins,
> Damm'd like the dull canal with locks and chains,
> And moving, as a sick man in his sleep,
> Three paces and then faltering:—better be
> Where the extinguish'd Spartans still are free,
> In their proud charnel of Thermopylae,

1. Federico Confalonieri (1785–1846), a Lombardy separatist, headed a Carbonarist offshoot. He spent 1835 through 1837 in the United States.

Than stagnate in our marsh,—or o'er the deep
Fly, and one current to the ocean add,
One spirit to the souls our fathers had,
One freeman more, America, to thee!

"That's despairing of our future too soon!" shouted a young Carbonaro, who had just escaped from proscription. "I've secretly taken the pulse of Italy, and I assure you that she is alive. She's in no way like Greece, whom Byron compared to a sickly girl, just deceased. No! Italy will rise in force like one of those beautiful Amazons in *Jerusalem Delivered,* but France must treat her like a sister, not an enemy."[2]

And turning to me, he asked, "You, Monsieur, are a friend of the young prince destined to govern France. Do you think he will be as intelligent, generous, and liberal as he's said to be?"

"I give you my word," I replied, raising my voice, "that nothing noble will be alien to him and that nothing great will be alien to his reign. I ask you, gentlemen, to join in this toast to him and thereby join France and Italy. Tomorrow I shall write him, conveying your good wishes."

The consul was the first to raise his glass, and we all drank to that beloved prince who was to live so short a time.

But despite the vivacity of the conversation which changed subject from one moment to the next, we were all beginning to go numb from the assortment of wines, the savor of the dishes, and the hours stolen from sleep. The conversation became less general, and soon each of us was chatting only with his dinner partner. On my left was an amiable scholar of fifty who had the best library in Venice, where rare, unpublished documents and re-

2. Carbonari belonged to an anti-French revolutionary organization recruited from nobility, officialdom, and army officer corps. The speaker is alluding to Tasso's masterpiece of 1575.

cords of the public and private lives of celebrated Venetians were stored.

"In browsing through them," my interlocutor said, "you will see our doges, magistrates, generals, artists, adventurers, and courtesans come to life."

I promised him to take up his attractive offer at the first opportunity.

Although the brocade drapes at the windows had been hermetically sealed, every time one of the lackeys serving opened the doors, a broad band of light beamed upon us. It came from the terrace where daybreak was brilliant. Soon rays of sunlight broke through the opaque, white line. Several guests, yawning slightly, said it was time to retire. We all rose, and regained, with some staggering, the waiting gondolas.

When I got back to my room, I confess the only thing on my mind was getting to sleep, without worrying about Antonia. But I was surprised to see the door between our two rooms open. I rushed in terrified, was she sick, had she gone out, left altogether perhaps?

I found her unperturbed, writing at her work table. She had just gotten up and resumed working. Her face looked rested. Her black hair, barely tied up out of the way, escaped in curls on her temples. Her eyes shone with the flame of inspiration—or perhaps focused fury. The drawstring on her dressing gown was loose, so her arms, neck, and part of her shoulders were bare. She seemed so beautiful, so admirable in that pose of solitary endeavor that I was compelled by some irresistible attraction to kneel by her side and kiss her. She put up with it, but she didn't respond. She looked disapproving and cold.

"I supposed in finding the door open that peace reigned again," I said, "but now I find you like a block of ice."

"I left the door open so I could give you advice. Your features are ravaged. Your pallor is frightening. You will not be able to withstand this life of dissipation, perhaps even debauchery. Then you surely lack money. I have to ask myself who is taking you in and feeding you when you pass your days and nights out. It's one of two things: either you are getting into debt, which is madness beneath a humble artist. Or other people are paying for you, which is humiliation beneath a gentleman. I beg of you, Albert, give up this way of life. I won't ask you to do it for love of me because your behavior proves you don't love me, but out of respect for human dignity. If I stop being your mistress, Albert, I will always be a mother to you, and I've had to speak to you as I would speak to my son."

"Good heavens," I burst out laughing, "I've listened to you without interrupting, and you in turn would be so good as to give me five minutes of your attention, you can see that in your little maternal discourse, not very tender and still less charitable, you have most gratuitously accused me of indelicacy, dissipation, even debauchery." I then gave her a true, detailed account of how I had spent my day and night.

"If you had been willing to accompany me," I continued, "you would not have lost your time entirely, seeing and hearing the beautiful prima donna. She would have furnished you a character type of the woman artist for one of your novels: simple, loving, impressive. She would be a very sympathetic figure, I assure you, provided you didn't try to embellish her by adding humanitarian aspirations to her natural gifts!" I opened my mouth very wide at these last words and yawned involuntarily.

"Good grief, go to bed!" Antonia snapped.

"I have only two more sentences," I continued, "and then I'll go take a long nap. My night passed at the consul's in the company of Venetian noblemen taught me more about Venice and its history than many an hour of solitary reading. The old comparison is still true, my dear. The poet is like a bee, flitting from flower to flower, savoring the nectars to compose his honey. I have therefore enriched my mind, as you might have enriched yours, during those hours so idle in appearance. And as a final argument in favor of the 'reasonable' way I lead my life, here are 100 louis that a happy accident let me win last night, handily and opportunely, from an opulent Venetian. Take half of it for your expenses, since you so often reproach me for leaving you without funds." And I lined up fifty louis on one of her manuscript pages. She shook the page angrily, sending the coins to the parquet.

"Gambling—that was all you lacked. It won't be long before you divide your time between the gambling dives and the little African acrobat."

"She has your expression in her eyes, Antonia. That's why I like her," I replied from the threshold of the door between our rooms. "Come now, my dear, rock me in your arms or spare me your sermons which fall on the deaf ears of a man falling asleep."

"May God save you. I can't," she retorted, as if she were closing a sermon.

Judging from that appeal to Divine intervention (entirely too frequent among Romantic writers, I might add), that she wouldn't allow me the least little kiss, I closed my door and went to bed.

My sleep was long and refreshing. Antonia, who in the end always goes back to being a kindhearted woman, made sure the house was quiet so that no sudden noise would wake me.

I didn't get up until one o'clock, and I was delighted to see that she had held lunch for me in our sitting room overlooking the Schiavoni Quay.

I didn't look at her, however, for I was afraid of being excited by her beauty which always held new charms for me, and anxious to avoid any quarrel and not to put her in a worse mood, I told her, rather offhandedly, all the interesting and curious things I had learned from the consul's guests. She appeared to be listening with interest, and when she saw me getting ready to leave, she asked, "Will you be coming back for supper?"

"Yes," I answered, "if afterwards you'll agree to go on a little outing. We could go to St. Nicholas of the Lido."

"You're still at it," she snorted impatiently. "You can't wait until I've got this big weight off my mind?"

"I'll wait as long as you like," I replied, affecting an indifference which I hoped would pique her jealousy and revive her love.

But that wasn't to be. She resumed her impassive expression as I left. When I climbed into the gondola, I saw her calmly smoking at the window.

I felt that I had stupidly lost face. I wondered what good I got out of my youth and imagination if they were powerless over the will of that stubborn woman. I promised myself that at least I wouldn't give her complacent pride the spectacle of my agitation, and I swore I would lock up my anguish beneath the double dignity of calm and silence. But when the heart achieves such restraint, what happens to love?

Completely lost in my own feelings, I hadn't remembered to cross St. Mark's Square to give the poor little dancer my card with Zéphira's address written on it. I was annoyed by my absent-mindedness and retraced my steps. I found the brown girl at her usual place, wearing, as the night before, her new dress with an even more coquettish hairdo. She had studded her thick black hair with large, fragrant red carnations.

"Go remind Zéphira the dancer," I said as I held out the card, "that I won't see her until the day you perform at La Fenice. Until then, as she will recall, I have to stay with a sick relative."

"And what about me, Signor, won't I see you either?" the African girl asked, looking at me strangely.

"Neither one of you," I replied crossly, trying to get rid of these two fixated women.

"If that's the way it is, honorable Signor, let me accompany you a few moments in your gondola. Now, thanks to your generosity, I am clean and pretty. I have something to tell you."

"Well, I don't want to hear it," I answered, throwing a louis in her face as I disappeared under the arcades. As I turned my head at one of the angles of the square, I saw her crying.

I began to curse women in general, their bizarre influence, so harrassing and continually detrimental to a man's peace of mind. In this mood, I rejoined my gondola, stretched out completely, and asked the gondoliers to take me out into the open sea and make a tour around Fort San Andrea. The waves rocked me gently, the black gondola tent enclosed me like the curtains of a bed. The faces of the women I had just rejected passed before my eyes. I held out my arms, so unnerved to clasp only emptiness, that, given Antonia's absence, if either the little acrobat or Zéphira had offered herself at that moment, I don't know what would have happened to my faithfulness. A lurch from the waves brought me back to my senses. I tore open the blinds of the gondola. Broad daylight and sea air both took hold of me. We had reached the south bank of the Lido. A sheet of blue Adriatic waves unrolled before me. I inhaled the revitalizing air from the open sea as deeply as I could. I disembarked, and wanting to explore the sandy beaches alone, I instructed my two gondoliers to wait for me on the opposite bank.

I walked at random. Sometimes I sank in sand up to my shins, and I thought about Lord Byron trying to ride a spirited horse over such unstable ground. I saw again the great English poet, his inspired brow crowned with silken curls, his eyes bursting with genius, his mouth as pensive and charming as that of a dreaming girl in love, his sculptural neck almost always bared by a loose tie. This superb head molded by ideal beauty which I had seen living again in Thorwaldsen's magnificent bust, seemed to be watching me during my solitary walk.[3] I thought of his long-lasting ennui which a glorious death cut short. To me he always seemed weary of life and uncertain of love. I took this invisible companion's arm and said, "Console me. The malady which struck you has attacked me, and I find nothing either within or without to appease my soul! If Antonia were to love me to the full extent of my infinite desires, I would still feel a torment of unknown cause."

And Byron's shade replied, "That's your poet's heart lamenting. The knowledge of all that was, the sight of human passion and misery, the perception of impenetrably mysterious infinity, the sentiment of unseizable fleeting beauty, the dazzle of fame whose nothingness you can measure. This is quite enough to make up the crushing burden which breaks your soul night and day. O my brother, you are suffering from the disease of thought, and this illness is incurable. Look at that vessel gliding over the calm sea. It is heading toward the Orient where it will hail in passing my beloved Greece. The sailors were sad saying good-bye a little while ago. There were even tears rolling down their swarthy cheeks. But now they're crossing the open sea. The sun is shining. A good wind fills their sails. The crossing will be fast and fine, so why be downhearted? Don't you hear their happy refrains echoing over the waves? They are singing as they were weeping this morning. They respond to the naive animalism of their sensations. But suppose you, a creature dominated by spirit, should try to embark as a passenger on that ship. Vainly the skies would greet you, the waves cradle you, for you will always, always feel the reflections of your own sorrow, ricocheted into infinity by the

3. For Colet's long note on Byron, printed in the original text as a footnote on four pages, see the author's note at the end of the chapter—*Trans*.

immemorial sorrows of the earth. Remember Leibniz called the poet's soul the mirror of the world. So live without self-pity and without hope of cure."

The voice died in me or around me, for I wouldn't dare swear that it had not really spoken to me.

I went into the Jewish cemetery and sat down in the shade of some tall bushes. In studying these tombs which the intolerance of old Venice had pushed outside its walls, I thought about the contempt and proscription which had for so long struck down the great Jewish race, even in death. Beautiful, tenacious, intelligent throughout so many centuries of persecution, it has kept itself separate and strong. Its hereditary patience has triumphed over obstacles and humiliations. Today its sons reign, the equal of Christians, many through the genius of arts and letters, an even greater number through industry, the new power of modern times. Their wealth lets them sit at the side of kings and associates them with the destiny of all peoples. Who would ever dare turn their backs on them? Where are the persecuted Shylocks and their persecutors now? What happens to our hatreds and injustices? What happens to our beliefs? The convictions and certainties of nations and individuals grow, decompose, and disappear throughout the troubled course of history. Those who know little vegetate in peace. Those who know much, who encompass this annihilated past with a backward glance, take fright. They can see that what has been is no longer, and they wonder what will come. What remains of the symbols and passions of vanquished ages? A single feeling: love! which many people are beginning to deny. Already we mock love as once we mocked faith and royalty before we destroyed them. Sarcasm is the weapon which dislodges the crown prior to the decapitating blade.

While seated in the Jewish cemetery, assailed by these

thoughts, I had in front of me the peaceful sea where several boats were gliding by. I turned my back on Venice where the setting sun would spread its hues of crimson fire. I heard my two gondoliers, profiting from the leisure I'd given them, singing barcarolles. Their voices, amplified by space, rose in wonderful intonations.

Somewhat tired from walking through the sand, I headed for a Lido cabaret, noted for its Samos wine. The owner, who was beginning to gray, told me Lord Byron often used to sit at the table I'd chosen in the grape arbor.

"I was young then," he added, "and every day I would follow His Lordship's horse on foot. When I could see that the beast and its rider were worn out, I would offer my place to His Lordship to rest. Sometimes he would eat dinner here. Wouldn't the French signor like to do so, too?"

How could I resist a man who used such a great name to recommend him? My walk along the seashore had left me famished. The peacefulness of the place was tempting. Under the arbor I ordered a dorado that had just been caught, a polenta, and some of the famous Samos wine. I'm not sure I really had Greek wine, but the name alone entranced me. I love those euphonic names from Homer's language. They abound in Venice. You would think that the waves and the breeze from the Pirean Sea had rolled them into the Adriatic.

This generous wine, the solitude of the beach, and the refreshing evening air gave me a sense of calm and well-being. When I climbed back into the gondola to return to Venice, I wasn't the same man I'd been in the morning. I opened the blinds of the boat to watch the poetic city stand out in front of me against the red depths of the setting sun. The cupolas of St. Mark's rose into the luminous sky. I disembarked opposite the Bridge of Sighs, and I stayed there until nightfall, looking from one view to the next and repeating in English the first stanza of the fourth Canto of *Childe Harold:*

I stood in Venice on the Bridge of Sighs,
A palace and a prison on each hand;
I saw from out the wave her structures rise
As from the stroke of the enchanter's wand:
A thousand years their cloudy wings expand
Around me, and a dying Glory smiles
O'er the far times, when many a subject land
Look'd to the wingèd Lion's marble piles,
Where Venice sate in state, throned on her hundred isles!

She looks a sea Cybele, fresh from ocean,
Rising with her tiara of proud towers

Absorbed as I was both by Venice, bathed in floods of light, and the lulling harmonies of the great poet's lines, I didn't notice steps coming up to me. Suddenly a dress brushed me. I turned my head and saw the little Moroccan dancer. I must have looked furious, for the poor girl trembled and joined her hands beseechingly, "Please forgive me, Signor, but Signora Zéphira sent me."

"Well, what does she want now?" I snapped impatiently.

"She told me, when I gave her your card, that if you didn't go to see her this very day, she wouldn't arrange my debut. She claims that you must choose me a stage name, for my Arab name is too long and too hard to remember."

"All right, go tell Mademoiselle Zéphira that you should be called Mademoiselle Négra; it fits your face." And with that I turned away, crossing the courtyard of the Doge's Palace, then into St. Mark's Square, filled with people strolling.

Just as nature and solitude pacify me and bring out my soul, a laughing, bustling city crowd and happy couples excite and agitate me, luring me to seek pleasure. When that happens, I'm no longer a poet, but quivering, eager flesh which wants its share of universal life.

However, having made up my mind to stay under the tranquilizing influence of my excursion around the Lido, I tore through the Square without looking to right or left and returned as quickly as possible to get down to work.

I saw Antonia, pensive, looking out our living room windows. I went into my room without attempting to speak to her and sat down at the table where I had been writing. I noticed on my scattered sheets a large envelope with the seal of the consulate. The seal had been broken, but I wasn't surprised, for I saw "urgent" written above the address. Antonia could have thought we were receiving letters from France. I found in the envelope the following note from the consul: "This idiotic Zéphira, who doesn't know your address, has just sent me these two letters one after the other. I wouldn't have consented to serve as an intermediary in her correspondence, if she hadn't assured me that it concerned some good deed that you were planning together."

I was exasperated to read the dancer's two letters (they hadn't been opened). In the first, dated "morning," she said, "This little streetwalker is less ugly than you pretended, and I suspect you are looking after her *con amore*. Never mind, I'll keep my word, since you love me, *carissimo*. Come to my place as soon as you can, for I'm alone under the pretext of taking a siesta. We need to get together to baptize the little blackamoor with a Christian name."

The second letter, written less than two hours earlier, had this message: "If you don't come to ride in my gondola this very evening, I'll send your little tramp back to dance on St. Mark's

Square and the Piazzetta. I'm willing to oblige you, but you mustn't be an ingrate."

I answered immediately, "A Frenchman is not led around on a leash like an Italian. I told you I would see you the evening of Mademoiselle Négra's debut. The next day I shall attend the party you are to give at Count Luigi's. Until then I shall remain your most humble—and distant—servant."

After writing this note, which I placed unsealed next to Zéphira's, I began rereading the pages I'd done the evening before. Suddenly the door to Antonia's room opened, and I saw the woman I loved above all else smiling slyly.

"I broke the seal on the Consul's letter only because I thought it would contain some important news from France. But you see that my curiosity stopped there. I don't want to know anything about your affairs with these sluts."

"Well, I want you to know about them," I shot back, pushing towards her both Zéphira's letters and my answer.

Undoubtedly somewhat curious, she read them and said, "So, what does this prove? You pay court to Mademoiselle Zéphira when it suits you, and you have a soft spot in your heart for Mademoiselle Négra."

"If you say so," I replied, determined not to get into an argument.

When she saw me pick up my pen and resume writing, she came over, "Albert, dear, won't you let me talk to you like a sister?"

"Yesterday you were my mother; today you're my sister."

"I am always a woman who loves you," she added, kissing me lightly on the forehead. "Be patient for a few more days, and you'll have my complete attention."

"Oh you're an exasperating woman and an immodest mystic. You don't understand anything about love," I was shouting. I tried to clasp her to my chest. But she freed herself and unconcerned about the sorry state she was leaving me in, she shut herself in her room.

I worked all night, conquering my sadness and my desire.

*Author's note: A woman [Teresa Guiccioli] who was for Byron what Beatrice was for Dante and Vittoria Colonna for Michaelangelo, that is, inspiration and love, wrote me when I was in London three years ago, "Go to Sydenham to see the bust Thorwaldsen made of the handsomest man who ever lived. Thorwaldsen was an artist of genius. So, although Byron's beauty was of so elevated a nature that neither brush nor chisel could ever seize it, since as a manifestation of his great genius and beautiful soul, his beauty was almost supernatural, still this eminent sculptor has interpreted it better than anyone else and was able to infuse the marble with a spark of that captivating handsomeness. As for that other bust, the one by Bertolini, don't even look at it. It was an embarrassment for the sculptor, a man of talent but without any sense of the ideal. You remember what Shakespeare says in *Hamlet:* 'He was to this as Hyperion—to a satyr'."

The same heart who had written these lines, was outraged when Mr. Trelawney in his recent book on Lord Byron, [E.J. Trelawney (1792–1881) *The Last Days of Shelley and Byron,* 1858] published in London, claimed that having wanted to see Byron once more and happening to be alone in the mortuary chamber, he raised the pall and discovered that the poet had the bust of Apollo and the twisted legs of a satyr.

La Revue des Deux Mondes and *La Presse* discussed this book, and that prompted the woman who had known Lord Byron in all the brilliance of his glorious youth and beauty to write me the following letter which forcefully and persuasively refutes Mr. Trelawney's fantastic invention.

"What can I say? What words can I use to express what I feel when I read such things, especially when I see people of good faith and decency accept such lies—regretfully—but accepting them all the same? You must believe that never was God so lavish in giving one of his creatures so many gifts as to Lord Byron. But never, alas, have men been so intent upon disputing these gifts one by one. Not being able to rise to him, they have tried to bring him down to them. They have spared him only where he was absolutely untouchable. Not being able to deny his great genius, obliged to recognize his intellectual superiority, they have attacked his moral being. Forced to confess that his beauty was nearly divine, they have invented fables to make people believe that there were mysterious flaws in his person that put him outside humanity. In this fine exercise of their wit and ingenuity, they have found food for their vanity and, often, their cupidity. Fortunately those who can refute this calumny are still alive and will not fail to reestablish the truth of the matter.

"I heard about Mr. Trelawney's absurd invention. Perhaps he was afraid he'd be forgotten about and wanted to remind the world of his existence once more by an odious lie about Lord Byron, a lie that would be ridiculous if it weren't revolting. I was in England when this splendid work came out, and I can tell you that it made the public thoroughly indignant. Mr. Trelawney has enjoyed a well-merited reputation throughout his life—a tissue of extravagances, to put it as kindly as possible—for *never telling the truth*.

"Lord Byron, for whom Mr. Trelawney was never a friend, simply an acquaintance of the former's final days in Italy, had invited the latter to join him in Greece where he could be useful during the insurrection. Byron used to make fun of Trelawney, knowing that he wanted to be the very picture of Byron's Corsair. However, as Byron put it, Conrad did one thing *more* and one thing *less* than Trelawney—he washed his hands, and he did not lie.

"On board the ship taking him to Greece, he often joked about

Trelawney's lying, and these remarks were published after his death. This explains Trelawney's hostility, but he waited until after the death of Byron's loyal valet Fletcher to take his revenge.

"But there are too many arguments and too many witnesses against Trelawney for him to prove his odious lie. If Lord Byron was born with such deformed legs, how could that have remained unknown until his death? Although angelic by his perfections, he didn't fall from the sky fully grown and clothed, nor arrive a stranger from foreign lands. He had nurses and maids who have been questioned. They have told all they knew about him, and they have always declared that as a child he had one of his feet misshapen from a fall shortly after his birth. He had been treated by doctors at Nottingham, London, and Dulwich with the sole aim of rehabilitating his foot and finally after the treatment of Dr. Glenine, he was able to recover sufficiently to wear an ordinary shoe. The elated child announced this happy event to his maid in a letter which has been kept as a testimony of his good heart. And besides that, didn't he go to boarding schools in Aberdeen, Dulwich, and Harrow before going to Cambridge? Could he live in the midst of children of his own age and every age, living with them, sharing his life, and manage to conceal his deformity with special clothing? And his former school friends, most of whom are still living, would they have hushed up the physical flaws of a comrade? Physical deformities make such an impression in childhood. Would they have waited for Mr. Trelawney's revelations, cowardly if true, odious since false, to say that Lord Byron not only had a defective foot as the result of an accident, but monstrous legs since birth? And if he had this deformity, could he possibly have distinguished himself among his friends as superior in physical skills, as was the case, and later distinguish himself in all sports without ever revealing more than a scarcely perceptible defect in one foot which detracted neither from his grace nor agility? Didn't he always ride horseback with remarkable elegance? Wasn't he the best swimmer of his time? Didn't he find all games of dexterity easy? And, if I may say so, did he always love platonically? Didn't he marry? And in all these different circumstances could he hide such deformities as those lent him by Mr. Trelawney? Let us add one more material proof: his body was embalmed by doctors Milligen, Bruno, and Meyer, and these gentlemen have said that Lord Byron's physique was perfect except for one foot.

"There is a charming portrait of Lord Byron as a child, painted by Finden who shows him standing and playing with a bow and arrow. In this picture his legs are as pretty as the rest of him. But if I wanted to enumerate all the proofs refuting Mr. Trelawney's lie, I'd never finish. As for Lord Byron's melancholy, it has been, to say the least, very much exaggerated. He was habitually serene and gay in the last years of his life. Whenever he suffered from a few moments of melancholy, it certainly wasn't because of some imperfection of his body whose beauty, as with his other qualities, made him so privileged a creature that he could only thank heaven. Rather, this melancholy stemmed from his poetic temperament, so sensitive and loving; from the loss of friends and persons dear to him; from the loss also of some youthful illusions, and later from the ingratitude, calumny, from all the low and hypocritical passions conjured up against him to punish him for his superiority. It can be attributed also to the weight of the great problems of human existence which affect great souls more than ordinary minds.

"But during the last years of his life when a more philosophical spirit and more religious tendencies than ordinarily believed, which he wasn't even yet confessing to himself, were beginning to act upon him, his soul became more and more serene, and everyone who saw him then is agreed that he was habitually gay, lively, and charming."

CHAPTER XV

THE FOLLOWING DAYS slipped by without a disturbing incident. I rarely saw Antonia, and I made it a matter of pride to appear carefree and cheerful. I spent my time wandering around Venice. Every morning I left either before or after lunch, depending on when I woke up. Sometimes I visited a monument, sometimes I took a ride out to the open sea, sometimes I shut myself up in a museum or in the library of the rich Venetian I had met at the consul's. I often had dinner or supper at a restaurant. I avoided eating with Antonia because in those generally intimate hours of a meal taken together, she exasperated me either by sarcasm or indifference. I shunned the sight of other women also. I scarcely glanced at the beautiful Venetian women leaning on their balconies or trying to catch my eye through the blinds at their windows. I didn't want to betray my love even by a fleeting temptation.

I kept my mind working at a breathless pace. While walking I imagined the outlines of works, I constructed dramatic effects, I composed lines of poetry, and when I returned at midnight, I made myself write until I collapsed with fatigue. Then I threw myself on my bed, sometimes with my clothes still on. I was still worn out when I woke up. I would shake off my nausea and depression and start out again on my Venetian vagabondage.

One day it was St. Mark's Cathedral that held my attention. I stopped first in front of its portico to study the famous bronze horses which victory drove to Paris and which my father had so often cited as one of the trophies of our glory. Seeing the horses was enough to let me imagine the whole Empire. In my mind's eye I could see Napoleon, like an ancient hero, holding these Greek chargers by the mane. But as I went further into the basilica, the figure of another emperor, this time from the Middle Ages, rose before me. The mosaics, the marbles, the gold and gems of the resplendent altars glowed in the taper light. Pope Alexander, sheltered like a god by a dazzling canopy, was seated on the threshold of the church, surrounded by his cardinals, the patriarchs of Aquilea, the bishops and archbishops of Lombardy, all in scarlet pontifical robes to await Frederick of Barbarossa, whom six Venetian galleys had brought from Chioggia to the Lido. The doge, surrounded by a splendid cortege, escorted the emperor. They disembarked together at the quay of the Piazzetta and went to the front of St. Mark's. There, the Latin chronicler says that Barbarossa removed his imperial mantle and prostrated himself at the feet of the pope. The latter, moved at the sight, raised the emperor, blessed and kissed him, and immediately the entire assemblage began to intone Psalm 86 "Domine, Deus salutis." Then Frederick Barbarossa took Pope Alexander by the hand and led him into the church.

However, while the pope was intoning mass, the emperor removed his imperial mantle for a second time and officiated as the verger-bearer at the head of the laity in the choir. After the gospel was read, the pope preached with the emperor seated at the foot of the pulpit. Next came the singing of the credo. Barbarossa did his oblation, then kissed Alexander's slipper. When the mass was over, the emperor once more led the pope by the hand to his white horse. He held the stirrups for him and led the horse by the bridle to the edge of the lagoon.

In those days the papacy represented intellect and freedom. An old, infirm, unarmed man tamed a powerful and feared potentate. Might bowed to mind. Today we go as we please, having nothing more to believe or revere.

Another day I toured the Arsenal Museum, reanimating the arms and forces enchained there with the vanquished glory of Venice. On nice evenings I loved to climb to the top of Campanile which joins St. Mark's Square to the Piazzetta. In front of me was the marble column crowned with the crouching winged lion and on the matching column the holy protector of Venice. The city unfurled at my feet, surrounded by a band of darkening, becalmed waves. There Byron's lines came back to me once more, and I repeated them to fix the moving tableau in my memory:

The moon is up, and yet it is not night—
Sunset divides the sky with her, a sea
Of glory streams along the Alpine height
Of blue Friuli's mountains; Heaven is free
From clouds, but of all colours seems to be
Melted to one vast Iris of the West,
Where the Day joins the past Eternity;
While, on the other hand, meek Dian's crest
Floats through the azure air, an island of the blest!

A single star is at her side, and reigns
With her o'er half the lovely heaven; but still
Yon sunny sea heaves brightly, and remains
Roll'd o'er the peak of the far Rhaetian hill,
As Day and Night contending were, until
Nature reclaim'd her order: gently flows
The deep-dyed Brenta, where their hues instil
The odorous purple of a new-born rose,
Which streams upon her stream, and glass'd within it glows,

Fill'd with the face of heaven, which, from afar,
Comes down upon the waters; all its hues,
From the rich sunset to the rising star,
Their magical variety diffuse.
And now they change; a paler shadow strews
Its mantle o'er the mountains; parting day
Dies like the dolphin, whom each pang imbues
With a new colour as it gasps away,
The last still loveliest, till—'tis gone—and all is gray.

That's how I was living, plunged into all the intoxication possible from imagination and poetry.

Antonia, probably made spiteful by my apparent calm, continued imperturbably with her work.

The dancer Zéphira seemed to have given in to my will and no longer importuned me with reminders. I had overcome my desire and turmoil by the very excess of my agitation. You know what they say, "You have to work at wisdom; you have to take pains to be reasonable, but to be foolish, just let yourself go."

CHAPTER XVI

ONE MORNING while I was lunching with Antonia, the prima donna's lover was announced. I was eager to receive him, and I begged Antonia to stay for our conversation. He complained that I had forgotten him. His dear Stella was surprised not to see me, but she understood that I couldn't leave the Signora, he added, turning to Antonia; if his friend had been so bold, she would have come herself to invite both of us to go hear some music at her house.

Antonia replied graciously that she was most eager to meet the famous singer who was the talk of Venice and would like to do so within a few days. But at the moment she could not take a minute from her work.

Stella's lover, then addressing me, informed me that the poor little dancer I had given alms to was making her debut at La Fenice that very evening. She had gone to humbly beseech Stella to persuade me to go to the theater.

"I'll go," I said.

Antonia threw me a sardonic glance.

"That's not all," continued the Venetian, "Zéphira, who's been very kindhearted for your protégée, is giving a masquerade ball at Count Luigi's as soon as the performance is over. She hopes you will be present. All the young and idle rich men in Venice will be there. As for the women, I do not promise you they'll be either patrician or honest. I must confess that the women you'll meet are hardly fit for my dear Stella's company. But the politics of the theater force her, you know, to be careful with Zéphira. Besides, everyone will be wearing a mask, so you can stay incognito. This means," he turned to Antonia, "if Madame were tempted to accompany you, she could see, without risk of recognition, one of our legendary Venetian fêtes, so rare nowadays in our sorrowing city."

I agreed with our visitor and urged Antonia to treat herself to this distraction.

The Venetian added with a laugh that her dear presence would protect me against all temptation.

Antonia retorted that she left me perfectly free to disport with such ladies. She failed to comprehend slave love, a feeling so elevated should have its strength only in the soul's moral code. And with that pretentious maxim, she rose, bowing to Stella's lover, and left us.

"She is very beautiful," the Venetian said, "but her eyes are terrifying."

Determined to stupefy myself and forget that inflexible woman, I asked the amiable young man what costume he was planning to wear.

"Stella has had a 16th-century Venetian nobleman's costume made for me. What costume do you have in mind?"

"I think I'll go as a Knight of Malta."

"Very good. That's a good omen, since you want to keep the vow which that disguise will impose," he laughed.

We left together. First we went to a costumier, then we went to the prima donna's where I had decided to spend the end of the day calming my nerves in the music and harmony which the two happy lovers shared with everyone around them.

We had hardly arrived when a shrill voice calling for Stella announced a visit from Zéphira. I had just time enough to hide behind a tapestry portiere.

"Well, is he going to come to the theater? Will he come to my party?" the dancer shouted from the other end of the gallery.

"Yes, *bellissima,*" the prima donna answered. "He promised my sweetheart."

"Do you think this proud phantom will keep his word?" Zéphira continued.

"There's no doubt about it," interjected the Venetian, "since he and I both left the costumier at the same time."

"Ah, *bravissimo,*" cried the dancer, "but you should have brought him here."

"No," replied Stella shrewdly. "He must see you at your dazzling best. You've been too agitated the past few days. You've gotten pale and thin. Take a friend's advice. Go home, take a bath, and nap until this evening. The roses of your complexion will return, and you will be irresistible."

"Am I as ugly as all that?" the dancer simpered, going up to look at herself in a mirror. "You're right. I look like a ghost. It would be better if the French signor didn't see me in this state."

I took a look by peeking through the curtain hiding me at the other end of the gallery. She looked pale and worn. Since her black taffeta coat was open, I could see how thin she was.

"You're a true friend," she said, kissing Stella good-bye. "I'm going to sleep until it's time to go out."

A few minutes later we heard the oar of the gondola taking her away.

"We are free," shouted the prima donna sitting down at the piano. And while her lover and I smoked cigarettes, she sang us some of her most dramatic roles and then a few piquant Venetian barcarolles. She was tired of singing before we were tired of listening.

At her command a servant brought in a huge wicker basket filled with the most beautiful flowers. They made the entire gallery fragrant. With her own hands, Stella artistically composed bouquets and braided a coronet of roses, carnations, Spanish jasmine, myrtles, and pomegranate blossoms.

I guessed what she was doing and smiled at her kindness. "Do you want to make that child go mad with happiness?"

"You must keep in mind that this may well be the sole celebration in her life. Tomorrow they may hoot and whistle. So this evening her friends must provide her as much happiness as they can, so she'll have the memory to fall back on later."

When she had completed her fragrant task, Stella left us for a few minutes to get ready. She almost always wore flowing gowns which were ravishing on her statuesque Greek figure. That day she was wearing a gown of Indian muslin, caught at the shoulders by antique cameos. Three circlets of gold, joined at the nape of her neck, confined her curly black hair. Her lover beamed at her. I myself, albeit calm, was so charmed by the sight of such perfect beauty that I said to myself, "She's a muse who doesn't know it, an intellect without arrogance, calmly inspired and confident."

The gondola taking us to the theater carried also the cargo of flowers for the little African.

We found Zéphira already ensconced in the prima donna's box. She was so bedecked with dazzling jewelry that she shone as brightly as the chandeliers which made the auditorium as bright as day. Her bosom and neck, somewhat on the thin side, were hidden by a large Byzantine necklace in diamonds, emeralds, and rubies. Her hair was becomingly dressed with a snood of matching gems. Her silver gauze tunic, studded with red ranunculi was the object of everyone's attention. With the help of rouge, her piquant beauty was very alluring that evening.

Stella complimented her on her outfit.

"But you're not saying a word," she said, taking my hand and shaking it in rhythm.

"One doesn't speak to goddesses—or to stars," I replied. "One remains bedazzled, overwhelmed. That's what happens to Hindus in their pagodas, when you hold up to their eyes the golden, jeweled images of the incarnations of their gods."

"I can see," she retorted, "that you are making light of me and that you think my outfit is too showy. Have patience, later this evening I'll have a costume which is quite the opposite."

The orchestra was starting the overture. We heard Venetian carnival airs, and soon everyone was watching the stage instead of Zéphira. When curtain went up, we saw a stage set imitating a Moorish courtyard with arcaded galleries and white marble basins sprinkled with orange blossoms and reflecting rose-laurels. The Fenice director, accomplished impresario that he was, had commissioned a ballet for the debut of Mademoiselle Négra, a pearl buried in the byways of Venice and discovered one fine day by a French poet who had brought her talents to light. That's how the city newspapers and theater posters had been announcing her for the past week, linking me to her presumed virtuosity but without naming me, thank heavens.

The ballet designed to show off Négra's grace hadn't required much imagination from the choreographer. It was the same old story of the blasé pasha wanting to revamp his harem and having a slave merchant parade his female merchandise. When the curtain went up, the fat pasha was seated on his cushions, smoking a long amber pipe and examining through tobacco smoke the beauties fluttering about to please him. He scowled disdainfully at the first four dancers, balancing on tiptoes, pirouetting and preening, keeping their eyes on his face. But suddenly Négra appeared. She glided in front of the pasha without stopping and as if horrified by his corpulence. With a contemptuous gesture, she seemed to say to him, "I belong to myself!" This pantomine, which, however, wasn't in keeping with the spirit of the ballet, was welcomed by enthusiastic applause. It's true that Négra's beauty was so new and strange that it took hold of the senses like magic. She was like one of those rare southern wines, liquid beams of sunlight, that go to the head with the first sip. I hadn't imagined that the little dancer from the streets could have affected me like that. She was wearing two tunics. The gilded top tunic was tiger-striped and tightly moulded to her slender figure. It was worn over a longer red tunic embroidered with paste gems. Her slightly heaving breasts set aquiver the three rows of sequins bordering the neckline. Her small, perfectly modelled arms wore ruby-eyed serpent bracelets at each wrist. I had never seen more darling hands or more slender, better-formed fingers. Her neck undulated like a flamingo. Her burnished skin had the lustrous glow of flamingo plumage as well as the crimsoned tone and polish of beautiful pink seashells. It was especially her bare legs, entwined with gilt laces and illuminated by ramp lights that made one think of flamingos and seashells. But one almost forgot the morbidezza of the body when one looked at her expressive face and burning eyes. Her black hair was pulled back and threaded with sultani coins which were tied to a large opal in the middle of her forehead. She danced and seemed to be transformed by a precipitous and spirited routine which forced the orchestra to speed up its tempo. Then her head sent sparks. Her eyes, teeth, and quivering nostrils seemed to send out rays. Everything harmonized in her dance. The fire in her eyes quivered through her body, into her feet which vibrated on their toes, into her arms reaching out for voluptuous satisfaction. Her dance was intoxicating. There was something in it which couldn't have been learned; it was in her blood.

Like all other spectators, I was caught up in the contagious passion she projected. It is true that her gaze embraced me, her smile called to me, her arms reached out to clasp me across space. As soon as she came on stage, her eyes found me, never to leave me. I felt lured, carried away in her arms, pressed against her breast. I was that woman's master in no uncertain terms, the favored sultan she wanted to fascinate. She knew how to conquer through her own will and love. I didn't belong to myself anymore. I twisted and turned with her, enlacing and enlaced, like Goethe's Walpurgis Night.

The most fiery dancing would have seemed cold after that African dance. It wasn't lasciviousness but ardor. Instead of the quivers of pleasure and gaiety, it was sober, untamed frenzy, intoxication that kills. This incandescent dance was to Italian and French dancing what Dido was to a Roman matron or Othello to Gonzalvo of Cordova. I could imagine her one of those girls of the Sahara who proves her love by putting out burning coals on her flesh. Her every gesture and movement emitted some kind of ambiant fluid that filled the auditorium. The audience seemed possessed by the fiery demon that was shaking this young body. There were ecstatic cries and moans, kisses thrown in the air, frank words only said in a whisper. Flowers were falling at Négra's feet. But she saw nothing, continuing to dance out her dream, if I may put it that way. Suddenly sharing the crowd's intoxication, I began shouting out her name. I seized the coronets and bouquets Stella had prepared and began throwing them one at a time. The first bouquet struck her heart. She clasped it with a kiss and with a graceful movement rested her cheek against it like a child on a pillow. The entire audience applauded that gesture. Flowers were growing in heaps around her like a poetic shroud. At first she pushed them away and kept on dancing. But imperceptibly, as if overcome with lassitude or giving in to some voluptuous ecstasy, she collected all the scattered bouquets, moving around the stage with aerial steps, and made herself a little bed, and there she gracefully stretched out, her face looking into mine. On that tableau the curtain fell.

In the libretto she was supposed to lie down at the pasha's feet, but that forgotten supernumerary had actually fallen asleep on his cushions.

Négra's new passionate admirers went running backstage to congratulate her. I went, too, followed by Stella, her lover, and Zéphira, strangled with rage. She was looking daggers at me, and from time to time she threatened me with her clenched fist.

We found Négra half fainted in an armchair. The fat Arab merchant she had told me about was using a fan of peacock feathers to give her some air, all the while repeating to the impresario, "Signor, my fortune is made." He drew back obsequiously when he saw us come in.

Négra, whether she had espied me or merely felt my presence, came back to life at once. She threw herself at my feet, seized my hands, covering them with kisses and saying for everyone to hear: "This is my benefactor."

"My poor child," I said, "I didn't do anything for you." And seeing that Zéphira's fury was ready to burst, I had the presence of mind to add while bowing in her direction, "It is Madame you must thank."

Then with ingratiating charm, Négra bowed before the dethroned dancer and expressed her gratitude so warmly and affectionately that Zéphira was touched and forced to be kind. "I'll see you at my party," she said to Négra. Then taking my arm, she dragged me off, far away from those deep eyes following me.

Close behind, Stella and her lover figured out how to rescue me. They reminded me that it was time for me to put on my disguise and took Zéphira off in their gondola.

CHAPTER XVII

COUNT LUIGI, Zéphira's official lover, lived in one of the most beautiful palaces on the Grand Canal. Around one in the morning, all the windows of that patrician dwelling blazed with such brilliant light that all the sculptures on the facade stood out. Two rows of liveried lackeys holding torches and flambeaux, were lined up from the threshold to the top of the main staircase. The quiet black waters of the lagoon reflected and doubled that illuminated palace. But soon the coming and going of gondolas bringing guests disturbed that tranquil mirror, and for an hour the bustle of guests, and the sounds of lapping oars and voices brought to mind the Venetian festivals of former days. Mingling in the stream of guests up the stairway which stood out like a ladder of fire, were heads covered with feathers, flowers, gems, and exotic coiffures. All faces wore identical black velvet masks. All figures blended together because of the hooded black capes, called dominos, which hid their luxurious historical or fantasy costumes. As the crowd reached the drawing rooms and galleries, some of the guests tossed aside their superfluous capes, even removed their masks, so that they could be recognized. The women especially enjoyed showing off the splendor of their becoming costumes. It was as if a sudden stroke of magic had made this monumental palace swarm with costumes of all epochs. The figures in the frescoes of the great masters seemed attentive. There was a procession of Jews in dalmatic garb. Greeks and Turks resplendent in embroideries and cashmere. Then came ancient Romans; Bohemians; Hindus; knights of the Middle Ages, completely armed; powdered marquis and mesdames de Pompadour; Mexicans in feathered tunics; Olympic goddesses; Tyrolean lasses; harlequins; pulcinellas. All permissible costumes were carried out ravishingly in rich variety. I say "permissible," for the Austrian police expressly forbade any kind of religious disguise.[1] So we were extremely surprised to see Count Luigi, who had taken off his mask to receive us, dressed like a Camaldolese Benedictine.

"That's a travesty that could cost you fifteen days in prison," said the French consul who had dropped by for a few moments to see the spectacle.

"It's one of silly Zéphira's whims," replied the count. "She claims that she has obtained police protection and that we're not running any risk. Here she comes now, dressed as a nun."

And, indeed, there she was in the robe of an abbess. A rosary of black Venetian pearls belted the ample garment around her slender waist. A large rosewood cross with a golden Christ and a death's head in black enamel and diamonds dangled at her left hip. Her white crepe veil had its precise folds and pleats secured to her head by a crown of white roses. The sparkle in her eyes was enhanced by the monastic headband, and her giddy expression made a provocative contrast with her modest habit.

Stella's lover, who was in the same group as the consul and

1. Napolean put an end to the Republic of Venice by conquering it and turning it over to the Austrians in 1797. Except for a brief period, March 22, 1848, through August 22, 1849, under revolutionary republicans in the risorgimento, Venice stayed under Austrian rule until 1866.

myself, said to us discreetly, "Zéphira's wearing another costume underneath that nun's costume which she's chosen, I feel sure, only to get Luigi to dress like a monk. She's planning to play some mean trick on him."

"I'll keep an eye on it," said the consul, "and I promise you faithfully that if Count Luigi is punished for his disguise, Zéphira will follow him to prison."

I don't know whether the lady realized we were talking about her, but she ran up laughing and wild. She entwined her arm in mine and said, "Let's see what's going on."

I let myself be led into the first drawing room where the dance was beginning to the music of invisible orchestras scattered through the palace. Soon she wanted to drag me into a deserted gallery, small and badly lit.

"*Carissimo,* come see the reflection of the lighted hothouse on the dark canal."

"Not yet," I said, "after supper, perhaps."

While we were sparring this way, I noticed around the middle of the passage where we had stopped, a masked woman standing in front of a Venetian glass. I was all the more struck since the apparition seemed to bring to life before my eyes Paris Bordone's "Coronation of Venus," one of my favorite paintings in Venice. The closer I got, the better I could appreciate all the costume details which Titian's follower had bestowed upon his Venus, who was, as everyone knows, simply the picture of some Venetian noblewoman. "Her hair, clustered over the forehead and threaded with pearls, falls upon her arms and shoulders in long, wavy locks. A pearl necklace centered on the chest with a gold clasp, outlines the perfect contours of her bare breast. Her gown of changeable rose and blue taffeta was raised at the knee by a ruby pin to reveal a leg as polished as marble. Her arms are adorned with lavish bracelets, and she rests her feet in scarlet mules with gold laces."

That excellent description was made by a contemporary poet. I wondered who that woman could be. She appeared to have chosen that raiment just to please me. I had so often looked at Bordone's Venus with love in my eyes. However, she remained motionless, her masked face turned away from me. As soon as she saw Zéphira following me, she suddenly bolted and disappeared into the depths of that narrow gallery. I rushed after her, but couldn't catch up with her. In my vain pursuit I reached a sitting room where a young Milan marquis, dressed up as Ludovico Sforza, sat by himself at a gaming table.[2] He proposed we play a game, and I sat down mechanically to get my breath. I was preoccupied by that woman who had just disappeared. So who was she? Négra? Impossible! How could that poor ignorant African have dreamt up that historical costume? Then, too, that woman appeared much taller than the dancer whose image had been haunting me since her triumph at the Fenice. She had brought all my senses to such a fever pitch that, I might as well confess, I was wild to see her again. I played with persistent good luck which exasperated the Milan marquis and pushed him to double his stakes. I felt goaded by a thirst of gain, a new passion for me and one I didn't know I was capable of feeling. Gold was stacking up in front of me, but as I was beginning a new game, a rustling of taffeta made me look up, and I saw over my opponent's shoulder Paris Bordone's Venus. She was keeping absolutely still, her eyes shining at me through her mask. I shifted my attention to her and played absent-mindedly. By the supple curve of the figure, I said, "It's Négra";

2. Ludovico Sforza (1451–1508), called Il Moro, was a patron of Leonardo da Vinci and regent of the Duchy of Milan.

however, the shoulders, neck, and arms were lily white, and Négra was copper brown. It's true that when I leaned over a little, I discovered that my apparition wore extremely high-heeled mules. In examining the hair, I realized some of the loose curls were blond, some black, the same for the little curls at the nape. What craft had been required to blend together these two heads of hair for my inspection!

That mystery redoubled my curiosity. I lost that hand. A masked woman tapped the Milanese on the shoulder and whispered in his ear. He said, "I'll come with you."

So I could get up without losing face. With one hand I swept up the gold belonging to me, and with the other I seized the arm of my Venus. I felt her quiver and hum, so to speak, like the string of a harp. I had put back my mask. At that moment the orchestra in a nearby room struck up a frenetic waltz which turned the dancers' excitement into frenzy. I enlaced the trembling woman who surrendered to me, and I carried her off in the whirlwind.

"Who are you?" I murmured in our flight.

"Signor, I am your slave."

"Oh, so it's you."

I recognized Négra's voice.

"But how did you guess, my poor girl, that I would like this Venus costume?"

"One day, Signor, I dared to follow you, and I came upon you ecstatic in front of the picture of Venus. Since that day I've been thinking I want to look like that woman."

"But the whiteness of your skin and the weaving in your hair?"

"My mother was a servant in the Constantinople seraglio. She taught me all the sultanas' beauty secrets."

While we were exchanging those words almost lip to lip, I felt her turning in my arms as if a gale was carrying us away. She was irresistibly guiding me in the nervous circles traced by her nimble little feet.

Little by little she had led me out of the ballroom. The orchestra, more distant, was still with us. We were in a gallery that was more dimly lit and almost deserted. I didn't realize that we had changed galleries. It seemed to me that my eyes were having trouble seeing and that the blood flowing into my ears was keeping me from hearing the music. I was no longer my own master. It was my turn to quiver and tremble in Négra's arms. She had me sit down on a divan.

Suddenly I felt someone else take my hand. I looked up and saw Count Luigi, now unmasked, in his Camaldolese garb. He was laughing, "Would the handsome Knight of Malta give his arm to Madame and come into the gallery where supper is served?"

"With all my heart," I replied, and I followed the count with poor Négra, expiring with happiness, on my arm.

At the door to the gallery where Count Luigi was leading us, we found Zéphira. She had removed her mask and the nun's veil. A bacchante wreath of golden vine leaves and grapes had replaced the coronet of white roses. Her floating cassock, half-opened, gave a glimpse of a fantastic Erigone costume comprised of a short tiger-skin tunic held tight at the ribs by a wide belt of Damascene gold. Her bare throat was covered by a bizarre and voluminous necklace made of tiny gold thyrsi.

Seeing me with Négra, she bounded over, "So you followed and found the mysterious lady," she shouted. Then grabbing Négra's arm she added, "My dear, you should know that you don't sit down at the table with your mask on." And her hand was already touching the trembling African's face.

"Stand back," I said to Zéphira angrily.

But Négra humbly bowed before the woman she called her mistress and said to her submissively, mask in hand, "It is I, Madame, your most unworthy servant."

"It's the new dancing star at La Fenice," people began exclaiming on all sides.

Several guests, who recognized her, began cheering and applauding like in the theater. Négra, bewildered, didn't dare approach. She remained bent in curtsy before Zéphira. Count Luigi, either to give his mistress a lesson or because he was giving in to some caprice which just struck him, gallantly held out his hand to the poor African and had her seated on his right, while having me sit next to her on the other side. To ward off the storm I saw brewing in Zéphira's eyes, I had offered her my arm with cocksure aplomb.

"I'm not letting you out of my sight again," she said, digging her nails into my ungloved hand, "and if you look at that woman, I'll get out my dagger."

I burst out laughing and sat down on the chair Count Luigi had indicated. Zéphira sat down on my other side, so I supped between two dancers. On one side the subterranean flame of a volcano; on the other, the crackling and noisy jet of fireworks. Zéphira kept my glass filled and provocatively entwined her leg around mine beneath the table. Négra enveloped me in the glow of her deep eyes, full of sorrowing love, quite indifferent to Signor Luigi's flirtatious compliments.

The ballroom orchestras kept playing symphonies. Wines bubbled in crystal goblets. Dishes steamed on silver platters. Heady flowers and fragrant fruits spread their perfumes from filigree baskets on the buffets. The gallery resounded with a steady hum of gala chatter, provocative overtures, and words uttered in that soft Italian idiom. As Byron says in "Beppo":

> I love the language, that soft bastard Latin,
> Which melts like kisses from a female mouth,

And sounds as if it should be writ on satin,
With syllables which breathe of the sweet South,

Who could have resisted the enervating atmosphere that closed in around us? All of us, men and women alike, were either tight or drunk. The nymphs and fauns painted on the ceiling in lascivious poses seemed to be coming out at us.

At dessert Zéphira gave the signal for all the orchestras to begin a deafening, throbbing waltz.

"You're coming with me now," she ordered imperiously, and winding her arms tightly around me, she dragged me into the dizzying speed of the dance. Since she had removed her nun's garb entirely, she was crushing me against her bare throat and her tiger-skin tunic which flopped in my face from time to time as we tumultuously heaved to the music. My brain was hallucinating. I could no longer tell whether Zéphira or Négra was carrying me off. A thousand and one turns of the waltz had gotten us to a conservatory which subdued lighting left in penumbra. Disoriented and breathless, we were about to collapse on an ottoman sheltered by flowering shrubs.

"Not here," Zéphira said, "but in a secret boudoir where no one will follow us." She grabbed my hand and led me to a door which opened on a stairway to a terrace. We were greeted by a chilling gust of air that cleared my head. I realized I was with Zéphira.

"But Count Luigi is the master here," I said. "He knows all the nooks and crannies of the palace. He could find us."

She burst our laughing, "Probably at this very moment Count Luigi is being led off to prison for having worn a monk's habit at a masked ball. *Carissimo*, we shall have two weeks free for fun." And she tried to force me down the stairs.

I was seized by an ungovernable wave of disgust. I pushed her out on the stairway landing and shut her out there, locking the door from the conservatory side. I didn't worry about her cries which were drowned by the orchestra anyway. As I passed from the conservatory to a Moorish room made up like something out of the Alhambra, I saw my Paris Bordone Venus standing on a big round ottoman, for lack of a pedestal, and holding out her arms with yearning.

"Come to me," she kept murmuring. Her magnetic eyes drew me closer. I felt her breath coursing over my face. "Thank you," she murmured still lower, "for having left her. Come to me! I want you!" I felt myself crushed against her heart, which pounded like the surf. She clutched me with all the gyrations of passion. Her dance had turned into the act of love. I was no longer conscious of reality, and I was blissful in the dream.

The room we were in was relatively dark, lit by a single suspension lamp. As I was returning her caresses, a sudden beam of light was projected on us, lighting up her face. She opened her eyes wide. I started with a cry. For she had Antonia's look in her eyes. At the same instant, the black-hooded figure holding the torch passed by us, laughing sardonically. Was it Zéphira? No, it wasn't. The dancer's voice didn't have that serious timbre. The voice I thought I recognized seemed to bring me an echo of Antonia's!

I wrenched myself free from the African, repulsing her furiously, violently detaching her hands which were clinging to my clothes. I threw her all the gold I had on me and shouted, "Get out of Venice and don't let me ever set eyes on you again!"

The person in the domino cloak, however, had fled to the next gallery. I put myself in pursuit but couldn't catch up. I saw the cloak trailing down the main palace staircase and disappear in a gondola.

Stella and her lover, who were just leaving, saw me. "Where are you running like that, bareheaded and without a cape?" the prima donna asked. "Climb in our gondola, and we'll take you home."

When I was seated next to them and the curtains closed, I put my head down on my knees and began to weep.

"What's the matter?" Stella was frightened.

I seized her hand and put it in her lover's. "If you're in love, don't ever leave each other. Don't make each other suffer. Death is better."

They didn't dare question me about my distress and being kind remained silent.

However, the approaching dawn sent white lines through the black hangings of the gondola.

I suddenly asked my friends, "Where are you planning to take me?"

"Why, we'll take you to your hotel, if you wish."

"No, please don't yet, later. Let me stay a few hours in your house.

"We'd be only too glad to," Stella replied, "You're in pain; your livid face would frighten your sweetheart. Come rest at our house."

Their house was on the Schiavoni Quay, near the palace where Petrarch used to live. When we got there, it was daybreak, but Venice was still sleeping. My friends took me to a room and urged me to lie down. I promised I would. But as soon as I was alone, I went over to the balcony to lean out. I stayed there a long time, motionless, overwhelmed, watching the mists ripple over the deserted lagoon and cover the silent palaces with a curtain. I thought of that description of Venice waking up, composed so faithfully by one of our great poets.

"The wind barely stirred the water. A few sailboats appeared in the distance from Fosca, bringing the former queen of the seas her daily provisions. Alone at the summit of the sleeping city, the angel of St. Mark's campanile gleamed through the dawn, and the first rays of the sun sparkled on its gilded wings.

"Then the countless churches of Venice began to toll the Angelus. Pigeons, as in the days of the Republic, alerted by the sound of the bells, which they counted by some marvelous instinct, crossed the Schiavoni Quay in flocks and at full speed to get the grain customarily fed them on the Piazza at that hour. The mists rose little by little. The sun came out. Some fishermen shook out their sails and began to clean their boats. One of them started singing the first couplet of a national song in a clear tenor voice. From inside a commercial vessel a bass voice replied. Another voice, further off, joined in at the refrain of the second couplet. Soon a choir emerged. Each sang his part while working, and a beautiful national song saluted the break of day."

The fresh morning tempered my feverish blood. The prolonged ringing of the church bells, the increasing movement of the city, and the song of workmen drew me out of the obsession of my delirous night. I shook off the memory like an impossible dream.

And I, too, had my task to accomplish. My work was waiting. Antonia gave me an example of courage and renunciation. Why hadn't I imitated her? She was right: rules are healthy. Discipline is indispensable for man, always wavering and dispersed, as Montaigne would say.

Feeling a new vigor in my spirit, resolved to make reparations and reconquer the woman I loved, I rushed to leave my friends' house. I left a pencilled note, requesting them not to seek me out for a week.

I was famished for absolute seclusion with Antonia. As much as I had sought out excitement, I now sought repose at her side.

I came back in furtively. Although it was broad day, Antonia was still sleeping. She was staying in bed much later than usual. I myself didn't even attempt to rest. I wrote in one sitting one of the most moving acts in one of my Italian dramas. I didn't even put down my pen until I thought I heard a slight rustle in Antonia's room. Then I waited and listened anxiously. I realized that she was getting dressed. I could imagine her gestures and movements on the other side of the partition. Finally she opened her door into the hall. I heard her give some orders to the maid. I thought she was going to come into my room. Her steps approached, but as if hesitant, she called out without coming in, "Albert, come have lunch."

"I'm working," I answered, hoping she would come in.

She made no answer. I was still waiting, when suddenly she pushed open the connecting door between our rooms and appeared smiling before me, "What a long time I slept this morning! Now I'm lazy, and you're industrious!"

"I'm madness, and you're wisdom," I replied. "You proceed at a firm, even pace. I run, stagger, and fall, and in the end I'll be swallowed up."

"Is that a speech from your play you're reciting for me?" she countered. "My poor Albert, put down your pen, and let's have lunch. You must be exhausted from last night."

I didn't dare look her in the eye. She wasn't questioning me, but I figured she could guess everything. Her apparent calm made me think of undermined terrains which conceal abysses. I presumed that she was hurt, contemptuous perhaps, and that her gentle manner could conceal some revenge.

"You look as dark as remorse or like a dungeon in the Wells of the ducal prisons," she continued. "Come now, Albert, look a little bit cheerful. Tomorrow I'm sending my manuscript to France, and we can begin to live again."

"Oh, how much I am going to love you," I cried, convulsively holding out my arms.

She looked at me with astonishment. Her eyes affected me like two cold blades going through my heart, and just like blood escaping, tears flooded my face.

"Why are you crying?" she asked. "You absolutely must go to bed. Your nerves are overwrought."

I looked at her amorously. I thought she was so beautiful, fresh, serene. I wanted her to rock me in her arms.

She resumed her affectionate, maternal manner, kept me from drinking coffee, led me back into my room, closed the window curtains, and forced me to get in bed. I let myself be led around like a child. Crying had made me calm down, and I was falling down from exhaustion. When she saw my eyes beginning to close, she tiptoed out. I fell asleep immediately, a heavy sleep, filled with nightmares. I didn't wake up until dark. I called out. Antonia didn't answer. The maid came to tell me that Madame had gone out to relax and hadn't wanted to wake me. At first I was terrified. Had she left me? Was she gone for good? I ran into her room and was reassured in finding all her belongings. Her manuscript which she had just finished was open on her worktable alongside a letter to her editor.

Then I had another idea. Perhaps she wanted to have a good time, too, and I was suddenly wild with jealousy. I was getting ready to dress and go out when I heard her coming up the stairs singing.

"I'm as happy as a schoolboy on a lark," she said. "I was eager to get out, to get some fresh air, to take a little ride on the open sea. Since you were asleep, I went by myself."

"Don't you want us to go out together?" I asked.

"Of course I do," she replied heartily. "Now that I've gotten that burden off my back, I'll wear you out with my female fantasies."

"Fine, what do you want to do?"

"Let's go eat supper on the Lido."

"Oh yes, let's do. I know a cabaret where the owner knew Byron."

We climbed in a gondola, and although the night was dark and cold, we reached our destination. The innkeeper, we discovered, had fallen asleep, but his desire to make money roused him in a hurry. He served us ham, an omelette, and his famous Samos wine. We were as gay as when we first fell in love. I remembered our room at the Fontainebleau gamekeeper's, our best hours in Genoa, our first days in Venice. The surf was beating on the shore, the wind blew through the window frame of the smoke-filled room where we were sheltered.

"What if we spent the night here?" I ventured.

"No," she replied, "it would be better out on the open sea in the gondola."

A few moments later the waves were rocking us like a hammock. The panes and curtains of the gondola were sealed tight. Antonia stretched out on the cushions of that floating alcove, and I knelt by her side, kissing her hands and forehead.

"I see you humble, my proud poet," she laughed. "Are you afraid of me? Have you forgotten how to make love?"

I covered her with the tenderest caresses mixed with tears. Finally I had found her again! Yes, she was still mine! She erased my disgraceful behavior! She reconciled me with happiness and life. She seemed more loving and passionate than before. There was something poignant and intense about her.

For the next eight days there was a resurgence of youth and passion that I had thought I could no longer feel and that I thought she could no longer inspire. Every morning we took a different excursion outside Venice, visiting the neighboring islands or wandering in the countryside along the Brenta.

We were always looking for a new setting for our renewed happiness. It seemed as if strange places revived our feelings and made them more pure and tender.

Sometimes at those moments of supreme ecstasy she would laugh and say, "I really think you've been unfaithful. But what difference does that make? You're young, handsome, inspired, and I love you."

When she said that, I wanted to break her bones. I wanted to shout, "You don't really love me. You're frigid by nature and passionate when it suits you; you don't care what you've made me suffer." But when I looked at her, her beautiful face disarmed me, and I would say to myself, "She's generous and kind. She's worth more than I am." At such times I wanted to throw myself at her feet and confess everything. But at the first word she would stop me.

"Don't say anything. I don't want to know. Rather, I already know everything. You are too weak to abstain, too weak to wait, too weak to love."

Oh, if she had only been jealous, impetuous, bursting with reproaches like an Italian or Greek woman! Then we could have quarreled, made up, and made love all the more passionately. But her sententious speeches and her assumed superiority in love forced me to remember at every hour how different we were.

CHAPTER XVIII

THOSE ALTERNATIONS of joy and pain, passion and labor, too many late nights and too many long excursions, repressed desires and sudden ecstasies—that life with neither peace nor certain happiness was rapidly destroying me. I felt my strength dwindling and my mind tottering. It seemed to me that my youth was getting away and my intelligence was going to die.

One warm autumn day as we were touring the Isle of Torcello, my legs gave out from under me. A tremor went through all my limbs. To get back my strength I had to lie down on the beach and cover up with the warm sand blowing in the sirocco.

My temples were throbbing violently. I felt a band of fire on my blinking eyes. My hair blowing in the wind seemed enormously heavy. My feet and legs, stuck in heaps of warm sand, were as cold as if buried in ice. All my blood was rushing to my head. My cheeks were getting redder and redder. Overcome by a burning fever, I had to tell Antonia that I felt sick. She had me carried to the gondola, stretched me out on the cushions and supported my head in the crook of her elbow.

"My poor Antonia," I said, "I think your instincts of a Sister of Charity will have an outlet. I am really sick, and if I don't die, I'll be a burden for some time."

"What a morbid thing to say! Die? What are you thinking about? Now that we could spend so many fine days making love!"

The voice in my heart was crying out, "You should have thought of this belated tenderness earlier! Your arm supporting my drooping head should have reached out to save me from harm!"

But all reproaches died on my lips. I thanked her and put myself in her care.

The crossing doubled my fever, and when we got back, Antonia was terrified to see that I could no longer stand up. She put me to bed and then dashed off a request to the consul to find us a doctor. The consul came over himself.

"I think you're just overtired," he said. "The sirocco, which Byron found so dreadful, gave me the same thing a year ago. A bleeding relieved me, but I didn't want it done by the most famous physician in Venice. He's an oldster whose trembling hand nearly cut the artery of a beautiful countess. I called on a young doctor who had recently arrived from Padua. His hand is sure. He has no great scientific pretensions. He doesn't ramble on like the old *dottissimi* but, what's more to the point, has been practicing with rather good results. I'm sure he can get you through this in a few days."

Antonia thanked him effusively and begged him to send us the doctor as fast as he could.

"How is Stella?" I asked the consul, who was ready to leave. "Please give her and her sweetheart my regrets. You can see that for a while I am going to be obliged to be a boor."

"They'll come to call, when you're up to it, and regale you with several good stories."

"What good stories? Oh, tell me quickly."

"Zéphira's in prison, keeping Count Luigi company."

"What? Both punished for their monk and nun costumes?"

"Austrian authorities don't permit joking on that subject," the consul replied. "And another adventure, much talked about also, was little Négra's departure, the very day after her triumph at the Fenice."

I started in spite of myself.

"Does anyone know why?" I murmured.

"There's no dearth of conjectures. She broke her engagement at the theater and forced the fat Arab who loved her to leave Venice."

Antonia began chuckling and accompanied the consul to the door.

The African girl's blind submission to my will ought to have touched me, but when love, as Chamfort puts it,[1] has only been

1. Nicolas-Sebastien Roche de Chamfort (1741–94) was a moralist who committed suicide during the Reign of Terror.

one epidermis in contact with another, only a fleeting trace is left behind, sometimes even an irritating and humiliating memory. It's quite the opposite when the soul is involved. Then the bond of love becomes so strong and puts such tentacles everywhere that only death can break its hold.

My fever was rising so fast that by the time the doctor came, I no longer had any real awareness of what was going on around me. Although my delirium was still in the mute stage, it was sending a thousand confused images whirling through my head. I thought I saw poor Négra standing weeping on the bridge of a ship. Her tears flowed so copiously that they soon inundated her entirely as waves would have. Then I saw her submerged in tears, blending in with the waves, and swallowed by the sea.

The young doctor skillfully bled me, clearing my brain instantly and putting it back under my control. I opened my eyes and saw Antonia thanking someone she was calling my savior. He was tall and young, his handsome features perfect, but rather common in Italy. You know Alfieri says that in Italy the human plant grows more robust and beautiful than anywhere else.[2] You have to see the Neapolitan lazzaroni sleeping in the sun or the Venetian sailors threading rope on the yard of the ships to understand the natural beauty of that favored race. Even in rags, says the poet, they are beggars you would mistake for gods.

The young doctor was tall. His physique was so vigorous and shapely that it looked elegant even in a badly tailored redingote. His features were regular, and his thick, curly hair was brown and silky. He had a low forehead like Apollo. His beautiful black eyes had a steady glow. His aquiline nose had quivering nostrils. His mouth was full and smiling, embellished further by white teeth. He personified health, happiness, and the carefree life. He took

2. Vittorio Alfieri (1749–1802) was an Italian dramatic poet.

my pulse with a hand that was on the large side. Antonia questioned him with an anxious glance.

"He still has fever," he said, shaking his head. "He could have a bad night. Don't leave his bedside."

He prescribed some kind of potion and then left, promising to return the next morning.

Antonia sat down at the foot of my bed. She looked pale in her black velvet dressing gown. From time to time she would get up and support my head while I drank. Soon I had the feeling that everything was turning around me and that the night-light had gone out. The band of fire was tightening around my head once more. I could no longer see. I could no longer hear. And in the end I no longer knew where I was. All night long I had terrifying hallucinations followed by relentless fever. I was unconscious, on the point of death for a week.

One cold morning, dark as our gloomiest fall days in Paris, I regained my sense of being alive. I heard the wind whistling in the corridors of the old palace we lived in, and it seemed to me that the distant Adriatic was whipping its waves clear up to my window. It was caused by a noisy squall in the Grand Canal.

When I opened my eyes, I saw Antonia seated in an armchair at the foot of my bed. She was sewing a flannel vest for me. I followed the movement of her delicate hands and the movement of her eyes which were not raised on me. Her expression had something so pensive and absorbed that I could tell her thoughts were far away.

I made an immense effort and managed to say, "Oh, my dearest, I'm not in pain anymore."

She got up, had me swallow a few spoonfuls of some cordial and then placing her fingers on my lips, forbade me to talk. I wanted to raise myself up to kiss her, but I fell back helpless on my bolster. Why didn't she bend over to me?

At that moment the door opened, and a young man entered. I recognized the doctor who had bled me. There were two changes in his appearance. His clothing was more studied, and his expression was more serious. I perceived all this clearly, but physically, so to speak, since my thinking was still as unstructured and unreflecting as a child's

Antonia said, "This is Dr. Tiberio Piacentini, who saved your life."

A terrible name like Tiberius made me smile because the doctor was transparently mild and amenable.[3]

He took my pulse, declared that I was on the way to recovery but that I must not take any chances.

"Do you hear?" Antonia was recommending silence to me again.

The doctor sat down opposite her, handed her some books and newspapers and told her the latest Venetian news. There was considerable talk about a famous male singer who had just made his debut at La Fenice and was playing to packed houses.[4]

"I'll go hear him when our invalid is better," she replied.

"Even today you could start getting out in the gondola for some fresh air," he said. "You haven't slept for ten days."

"Ten days," I murmured, "oh, my poor darling, how much trouble I've given you."

"You mustn't talk," they both said at once.

"She should take care of herself, get some rest," I added sadly, noticing that she had gotten pale and thin.

3. The Roman Emperor Tiberius, who lived from 42 B.C. to 37 A.D., was inscrutable and bloodthirsty.

4. Sand was interested in hearing tenor Domenico Donzelli (1790–1873) who sang in Venice during their stay. Alfred Tattet took her to hear Madame Pasta.

"Do you want to come now to take a turn on the Grand Canal?" the doctor asked.

"No, some other day when he can get up."

The doctor went out saying, "I'll see you this evening."

Antonia accompanied him out. I could hear them talking for a few moments in the hall. When she came back, she sat down near my bed and resumed her sewing.

I studied her tenderly. Then I drowsed off and fell asleep until nightfall.

When I woke up, the maid had me drink a little bouillon. I asked her where Antonia was.

"Madame is doing her hair and changing clothes. She'll be in shortly."

She reappeared a short time later. Her beautiful black hair was brushed smoothly over her inspired brow. She was wearing a violet damask gown with a fitted bodice. She seemed young and charming again.

"Are you going out?" I asked.

"No, not for several days," she replied.

"How can I thank you and bless you?"

"By getting well," she smiled kindly.

Then gesturing for me to rest, she sat down next to a lamp with a green shade and opened a book. My eyes were half-closed, but none of her movements escaped me. Her fingers weren't turning the pages, and I could tell she wasn't reading. What was on her mind? I was still too weak to make any effort at speech or gesture, but my sensations were waking up, and my thoughts were beginning to connect.

She remained pensive, keeping her book open. Suddenly she started and stood up. She came over to my bed, but since I was motionless, she thought I was asleep. My painful breathing and my wheezing chest added to the appearance of sleep. I heard walking in the hallway. She went to the door and let in the doctor.

"Let's speak quietly; he's asleep."

"That's a good sign," the doctor said. "He's out of danger."

Then they both sat down at the lamp table and began to look at books of prints. They opened one that was larger than the others and leafed through it together. When their fingers stretched out beneath the page, I imagined them touching; sometimes I thought I saw a fleeting pressure. Since they paid no attention to me, I kept my eyes wide open, giving them all of my attention.

Antonia had her back to me. I could only see it in outline. But Tiberio's handsome face was in full view. I fancied I could see it glow with an inner light. Once he fastened his sparkling eyes tenderly upon her.

"*Carissima,*" he said very softly, "you absolutely must spare yourself. Since he's sleeping so peacefully, come to bed, too."

The acute hearing of invalids is well known. I didn't miss a single whisper.

"I'd like to," she murmured almost inaudibly.

My bed faced somewhat at an angle the mantelpiece where a large Venetian glass was hung tipping outward, reflecting the door to Antonia's room. Since I had gotten ill, the door was always kept open. She had even had the swinging doors removed so that the noise of the hinges and locks wouldn't disturb me.

Antonia got up first. She quietly lit the night-light placed on the floor of my fireplace. Then she picked up the lamp with the green shade and went to her room. Tiberio followed her.

I don't know why, but some suspicion pierced me like a sword. With that kind of energizing will power that can keep a man mortally wounded standing in battle a few seconds before collapsing, I braced myself, and powerless as I was even to raise my arms, I convulsively seized a rod of my bedstead and raised myself on my tottering feet. Then I could see their reflection in the inclined mirror. They were still on the threshold of the door, but a little recessed in the other room. Antonia still had the lamp in one hand. Tiberio had grasped the other. They were both livid in the greenish light, their faces bending toward each other, and I saw their lips touch. I uttered a cry of fright and fell back on my bed like a corpse.

Only Antonia came running.

"What's the matter now?" she asked with that impassiveness which makes her so strong and invulnerable. And since I was shivering convulsively, thrashing about in my covers, and biting my sheet, she believed or pretended to believe that I had relapsed into delirium. She called the maid, "Go as fast as you can. Try to call back the doctor."

My voice was strangled in my throat. I couldn't manage to utter a single word, and I soon relapsed so completely into total prostration that I could scarcely make out the servant when she returned to say she hadn't been able to make the doctor hear. He had already climbed back into his gondola. He had undoubtedly divined the meaning of my cry and had no desire to show his face.

However, Antonia put my head on the bolster, put my arms back under the covers, and passed her hand gently over my burning brow. The maid offered to take her place at my bedside, but she refused, "He's suffering too much for me to leave him even for a minute."

She stayed bent over my bed until my more regular and calm breathing once more led her to think I was sleeping. Then she sat down in the armchair where I soon saw her lean back her head to rest. Her face in sleep was so secure and serene that it made me doubt what I had seen. Desertion is not devoted to this extent. Betrayal is not so radiant.

Sick as my poor brain was, had I been dreaming? Could I be sure of my experience when I wasn't even sure of myself? This awful, humiliating doubt inspired my willpower to new vigor which was to dominate my prostration and triumph over it. I vowed to come back to life, a new person, no longer a child or a madman who could be controlled and deceived. From that moment on I exercised a well-thought-out control over myself. I imposed a regime on myself and tolerated no backsliding. I prescribed sleep and I slept. When I woke up, I was imperious about my need to eat. Antonia wanted me to wait for the doctor before giving in, but she had to obey me. My ideas began to gradually stabilize. I began to understand my situation. When I was alone with the maid, I asked her to bring me the little mirror I used for trimming my beard. I looked at myself and shuddered with terror. I was looking at my own ghost. Death had come so close that it had left its mark upon me. Despite the resurgence of my strength, or, rather, my will, my efforts to get up were powerless. But at least I had my faculties to see and think. Memory returned to me the way objects submerged for a long time gradually float up to the surface. I thought about France, my family whom I had left in anguish and who must be dying of worry during this long silence. I thought of my friends who were expecting to be surprised and amused by the publication of my latest work. What had happened to my mind? Would I ever create another book? Another page? I felt as sad and humiliated as a sterile woman. What was left of me, dear God, from that crisis of love which had taken over my body and soul?

So I returned once more to loving and desiring my country, my parents, fame, everything that had been irrelevant to me a few months earlier. The renascence of these ideas made me extremely agitated. I wanted to seize it all, but everything was still beyond my grasp. If I could have managed, I would have left Venice that instant, taking Antonia with me, since the possibility of ever being separated from her never entered my mind. She was gentle, solicitous, cold, impenetrable. I wracked my brain trying to fathom the secret of this sphinx who glided around me like a living sacrifice. She took care of me like a mother, bore up under my snappish disposition, never talked back during my sudden tantrums. But never from her a caress or a word that would have melted both our hearts. How was I to win her back?

Tiberio had returned. She must have persuaded him that I didn't suspect anything, for nothing in his simple friendly manner showed embarrassment. He took care of me with temperate zeal. Such benevolent calm disoriented me. The scene of the kiss, constantly on my mind, could have been an effect of my hallucinating. And besides, if it had happened, what could I do about it? Alas, he was young, full of life and irresistible good looks, such a contrast with my withered, puny body. His steady kindness must gratify Antonia after the turmoil of our love affair. Tired of the tormented heart of the poet, she was trying out that placid nature. Then, she was undoubtedly vindictive and resented my attacks on her self-esteem. Had she been aware of my passing infatuation with Négra? Wasn't she the person in the domino cloak who had surprised us by torchlight in the Moorish den? She believed she had the right—and perhaps she did—to control her own body and use it as she saw fit. When I returned to her after Count Luigi's ball, I had brought that marble statue to life and had bestowed upon her every thrill the flesh can know.

The vibration of our renewed passion was still throbbing when I was struck down. Tiberio then appeared in all his beauty, novelty, and youth. How could I be surprised that she would love him? And love each other they did! And a kind of certainty took hold of my heart and squeezed it like a vice.

Between two persons living in intimacy there is always a horrible doubt, even in their most thrilling, culminating embrace. This is because neither can see through the mystery of the other's naked thought. Hence the secret cleavage in apparent union.

I spent my days and nights analyzing Antonia into little pieces. I spied on her every action. When Tiberio was there, I always pretended to be drowsy or distracted in order to discover some sign. But always in vain. Nothing incriminating happened.

One day Antonia announced the arrival of one of my friends from France.

"Oh, have him come in!" I cried, stretching out my arms to the fatherland. When I saw Albert Nattier step in, I shouted with happiness. It was my carefree youth on the threshold.

My own emotion kept me from seeing his, which was painful but controlled. He blinked back a few tears at the sight of my thin and livid face. Despite his life of dissipation, Albert Nattier had a warm heart.

"You must have been very sick, my poor friend," he said as he shook my hand. "But now at last you're out of danger."

"Yes, she saved me," I replied, gesturing toward Antonia.

Antonia replied that the doctor singlehandedly had cured me through skill and prudent prescriptions. Tiberio, who had just entered, said simply in his turn that nature, aided by Antonia's affection, had done everything.

Antonia then proceeded to heap praise on Tiberio. The latter, embarrassed, began to talk to Albert Nattier about Venice and offered to guide him around.

My friend eagerly accepted, saying he would be overjoyed to have the company of a man who saved my life, regarding himself henceforth as much obliged also.

I urged Antonia to go with them, but she refused, adding

kindly that she would rather stay with me. As soon as we were alone, I thanked her tenderly and tried to kiss her. She drew back saying, "Albert, don't get excited." And she picked up a piece of embroidery and went to sit by the window.

I looked at her in despair. It was clear she didn't love me anymore.

When Albert returned from his excursion with the doctor, he looked distraught. He took advantage of a moment when we were by ourselves to beg me to return to France immediately, either going the next day with him, if I felt up to it, or joining him in Milan in a few days so we could cross Mont Cenis together.

His insistence amazed me.

"But what about Antonia?" I asked.

"Think about your family," he answered. "Any bit of excitement will keep you from getting well. The Venetian atmosphere does nothing for you. You need your native air." He consulted Tiberio who came in the room at that moment. The latter agreed in principle, but thought an immediate departure impossible. I was still too weak to take the strains of travel.

Albert Nattier left the next day. We were both a bit surprised to cry when he left, for our friendship was usually clothed in raillery and a kind of skepticism. When I said good-bye, I had the feeling that I would never see him again, that death would strike me down in this foreign city, far from all those whose memory his visit has just rekindled. Alas, it was my heart that was to die. Venice has kept its ashes.

The following days I was able to get up. I was carried in a large armchair over to the window of our living room which opened on the Grand Canal. Any movement was still forbidden. I was like an old paralytic. Through the windowpanes I sadly watched the black gondolas file past. They looked like so many floating coffins to me. The sky was gray. The winter chill was inescapable, I was as numb and cold as a dying man. I demanded a big fire in my own room and didn't want to leave the corner of my fireplace. I was full of a convalescent's caprices. I demanded French dishes that were hard to prepare, rare wines to warm me up, flowers to cheer my eyes, furs to bed me down. Antonia gratified all my whims with maternal solicitude. Alert and active despite all the time these attentions took, she still found time to write, get dressed up, and go out each day. Sometimes she went out alone, sometimes with Tiberio, whom she would ask to accompany her in my presence. When they went off together with this appearance of good faith which reassured me, I suffered less than when I saw her leave furtively under some pretext of note-taking or a purchase. Then I would say to myself, "That's it! He's waiting for her. She's going to meet him. I'm being deceived so shabbily, since I can't even verify her betrayal."

How many times, as soon as she had disappeared, I would try to get up out of my chair, walk across my room, and start out on her trail. But my legs would buckle, and my extreme weakness made me dizzy. Then I would sit down, bursting with rage, cursing the vitality that wouldn't return. In that state of impotence, my torment redoubled in intensity. When she returned, carefree and relaxed, I would be brusque, sometimes insulting or so taciturn that she couldn't get a word out of me.

She had stopped sitting at my bedside at night a week earlier. As soon as I was tucked in, she would go rest and sleep herself. Poor woman, she had spent two weeks at my bedside like a heroic Sister of Charity. I realized that I was an ingrate vis-à-vis such kindness. But could I be grateful when I saw her love slipping away from me? When I couldn't hear any more noise from her room and her light went out, I would figure that she had gone out. Then I would get up and creep up to her bed. Sometimes I would find her sleeping. Sometimes she would rise on an elbow and say, "What's the matter? If you're in pain, you should call me."

I was ashamed to spy on her, but love has its desperate crises which ravage the heart and make it lose all dignity.

Since I constantly complained of the cold, she told me one day that she was going to have the swinging doors between our rooms put up again.

"No," I replied. "Portieres will do. I don't want to risk getting sick at night with you out of earshot."

She gave in, but I could tell from her smile that she had guessed my distrust.

Worries like this were holding up my recovery, and my strength was very slow returning. I ardently desired to leave and separate Antonia from Tiberio. Venice and everything about it had become hateful to me. I had refused to receive Stella's lover, and every time the consul came to inquire about my health, I wouldn't let them admit him. I didn't want to be an object of pity for anyone. I felt so changed and unhappy that I was well aware that no one could see me without feeling sorry for me.

One morning when I had placid Tiberio to myself, I informed him that I was determined to return to France. He gave a slight start and replied that I could leave safely. Antonia came in, and I told her the doctor's opinion and announced that we would be leaving shortly.

"I don't think we can," she responded, blushing. "I for one have started some work on Venice that I want to finish, and I'll need another month."

"Well, my dear," I retorted, "you'll finish it from memory because I've decided positively to leave by the end of the week."

"We'll see," she laughed enigmatically and left to go work.

At suppertime she reappeared, and I was very much surprised to see her in evening attire. She was wearing a black satin gown embroidered with jet with a lace Spanish mantilla fastened to her hair with a sprig of red roses.

"Where do you intend to go dressed up like that?" I asked.

"To the Opera to hear the famous tenor all Venice is talking about."

"With handsome Mr. Tiberio, no doubt," I snapped back, no longer able to contain myself.

"You're mistaken," she said disdainfully, "I thought I could go innocently enough with our landlady."

Why didn't she simply show then candor and free will?

"You shall not go," I ordered, since I suspected she was lying.

"You're tyrannical and absurd," she cried. "That's the finishing touch: becoming my jailer to repay me for the care I've taken of you. I surrender. I don't want to argue. But I declare to you that I consider myself absolutely in charge of my desires."

"Just try," I answered, more and more exasperated.

She said nothing but picked up a book. I watched her, furious at first but calming down gradually beneath the spell of her person. I should have liked to draw her over to me, caress her, hold her against my heart, as I did when she belonged to me.

The doctor entered for his evening visit. Antonia nodded without speaking. He came over and took my pulse to save his embarrassment.

"You're freezing," he said.

"Yes, I'm really cold!" And my teeth were chattering as if I had had an attack of fever.

Antonia put down her book and got up.

"Doctor Tiberio, would you be kind enough to hold the light for me. Our maid is out, and I'll have to get the wood myself."

"No, don't," I replied, "I've got enough fire. Please stay. I find the room suffocating."

I realized that she wanted to let Tiberio know that she couldn't go to the theater, and I was determined to keep them from speaking in secret. Stabbed by jealousy, I had decided that they would never see each other alone again.

She sat back down and shrugged her shoulders. Tiberio was embarrassed and left.

He had scarcely left before she withdrew to her own room, closing after her the thick portieres which replaced the door.

I heard her get in bed. I got back in bed myself, but I couldn't sleep. After an hour of silent insomnia, I thought I could tell she was writing. I got up noiselessly and materialized before her.

"What are you doing?" I asked.

"I'm working."

"You don't have a notebook on your bed," I countered, "and if you've written something, it was a letter you've just hidden."

I thought I had heard the rustle of a sheet of paper under her covers.

"Oh, go away, you're mean and nasty," she snapped and blew out her candle.

I got back in my bed, tottering and disconsolate. I was ashamed of myself, ashamed for her. Good God! What had we done to love?

It was futile trying to calm down and go to sleep. I stifled my crying under the covers. I felt an indefinable anguish. What could I say to her? How could I get the truth out of her?

Since she could hear no other sound except my difficult breathing, she must have imagined that I had gone back to sleep. I saw a thin sliver of light through the portieres and thought I heard the grating of a pen on paper.

This time I rushed in.

She only had time to crush the letter and put it in her mouth, covering her mouth with her handkerchief. I was taken back, uncertain, just as if I were watching a magician perform.

"I want to see that piece of paper," I ordered, not quite knowing where she had put it.

She didn't answer but darted from her bed to the basin where there was still water from her evening ablutions. She pretended to be overcome with vomiting.

I'm not inventing. This is exactly what happened.

Then she immediately opened the window over the alley and threw out the water in the basin.

Then I was sure she was hiding her crumpled letter from me. But what could I have said to her? When you're facing that much daring and dissimulation, you have to have proofs. What good would words have done?

I retreated, as mute and disembodied as a ghost. And until dawn I remained motionless in my armchair. At the first glimmer of daybreak, I wrapped up in my bathrobe and slipped into the hall and down to the alley.

It was still very dark in that damp, narrow street. But although I could hardly distinguish here and there pieces of crumpled white paper like so many white spots on the blackened pavement, I bent down and quickly scooped them up. While I was in that crouching position, I bumped my head against something living, stirring in the shadows. It was Antonia, who had had the same idea and had gotten up to get ahead of me, wanting to keep me from it. But it was too late. I held the incriminating paper in my clenched fist.

I still hadn't read anything, but her very presence made me certain of her betrayal.

"Get down on your knees," I seized her arm violently. "On your knees to beg my forgiveness. I want to kill you. I want to put an end to your duplicity."

I was so desperate I was oblivious to how ridiculous I was. She rose up under my quivering hand and said, "What gives you the right to speak to me like that? You who preferred all the street-walkers in Venice to me?"

"You know you're lying!" I shouted. "It was in your power to keep the breath of another woman from brushing my cheeks!"

She went on as if she hadn't understood me. "At least, I can love Tiberio without being ashamed of it. He's as beautiful as a Platonic ideal and so good that his kindness outweighs genius."

"So you confess you love him," my voice was broken by despair.

"Of course, I love him," she cried without a moment's hesitation. "But with a love so pure I can shout it to the heavens. You men are too gross to ever understand anything about our raptures and reticences. The mystery is too divine for you ever to penetrate it."

And with that mystical announcement, she went into the house. I followed, full of rage and hesitation. I had gone from accuser to accused.

However, as soon as I got back to my room, I lit a candle to read the fragments of the letter that I clutched in my hand.

She sat down opposite me and crossed her arms in a pose of calm disdain.

I managed to decipher the following: "Don't wait for me this evening, Tiberio dear, this mean madman is keeping me from going out, but tomorrow I'll join you at . . ." The rest was chewed or missing.

"But you have to confess," I cried. "You've given yourself to this man. You've even used the familiar 'you'."

"A fine proof that is!" she shot back. "You forget that I use the familiar 'you' with all my friends in Paris in front of you. It's a way I show my friendship. And besides who would force me to lie? Aren't I a free agent? I certainly don't have any tie to you! Exasperated yesterday evening by your tyrannical behavior, I wrote that note to the only person who loves me in this foreign city. That's my crime."

"But you're his," I protested. "I know it. I'm sure of it. One evening I saw your lips touching."

"I told you I loved him," she replied. "But out of pity for you, I struggled and resisted . . ."

"I don't want your pity," I answered. "Tomorrow I'm going back, leaving you to your new love affair."

When I said that, it seemed as if the walls of the room turned around me. I sank down in my chair, and my tears flowed silently over my cheeks like so much blood from the wound she had made.

I said nothing else to her. I no longer saw her. Everything around me had disappeared. I felt that my sorrow was incurable. Then something unaccountable happened. She knelt before me, put her head on my lap and drank the tears I was shedding.

"Albert, dear, you're suffering," she said gently. "Just say the word and I'll sacrifice for you the attraction I feel for Tiberio."

I pushed her away.

"I don't want sacrifice. And I don't want you anymore," I retorted, lying for love, for I still loved her with all my strength.

She stood up.

"You're making a mistake to talk to me this way," she continued affectionately. "I have the good sense and tenderness that you don't have anymore. I realize now that we need to separate and subject our hearts to the terrible trial by absence. One day we'll come back together more loving and less demanding."

"What are you trying to say?" I said. "Get to the point."

"I think it's wise for you to leave. Your family is expecting you. The air of France is vital for you. Constant contact has embittered both of us. Perhaps my feeling for Tiberio is only an illusion. When you're out of sight, perhaps I'll love you. Then when you see me again, I'll no longer be disturbed and hesitant but radiant and excited like the first day you loved me. Yes, Albert dear, something tells me I'll come back to you. But leave me my free will. Let's part the better to be reunited some day."

I didn't interrupt her, I just let her ramble on. In everything she said I sensed that truth and falsehood were doing battle.

"Well," she said after a rather long pause that made her uncomfortable, "what do you think you'll do?"

"I shall leave this very night."

What little strength had returned vanished in that supreme crisis. I sank down upon my bed, retaken by fever.

Antonia stayed by me, resuming her maternal care. Toward evening, feeling better, I told her I was determined to leave Venice the following day. She implored me to delay my departure for a day. I was still too weak, she maintained, to get on the road. She demanded this last proof of affection. She would accompany me to Padua and wouldn't leave me unless reassured on the state of my health.

I listened, dumbfounded. What an inexplicable mixture of solicitude and cruelty! Can the same person be both guardian angel and hangman to that extent? Only women are capable of such dual natures.

I didn't fight her wish. I had only one fixed idea: to get as far away as possible and escape from the torture of this inexplicable creature.

It was agreed that I would leave two days later. She spared me the anguish and humiliation of seeing Tiberio again. I was grateful to her for that. While I was waiting out those two days, she made me her exclusive concern. She showered me with those excessive attentions customarily granted to dying men during their last hours. She herself packed my trunk. She filled it with countless maternal indulgences. I remember in getting back to France I discovered charming pieces of jewelry she had bought me. She put in my wallet half the money her editor had sent her, had a warm overcoat tailored for me, and wore me out with zealous suggestions for travelling. When the hour came for me to leave, she got in the carriage with me.

"You can see I'm not abandoning you. These lagoons which we greeted together must see us united as you leave."

As she spoke, I watched Venice fade in the distance, veiled by a mist that made it as gloomy and lugubrious as a city in the North. It was no longer the smiling city we first saw a few months before crowned with sunlight. You would have thought the city was in somber mourning, grieving for a poet.

Antonia took me as far as Padua. There we separated. I no longer had the courage either to weep or complain.

She said in a firm voice that sounded sincere, "I'll write you the true story. If I give in, we'll never see each other again. If I keep myself for you, I'll rejoin you in a month."

I was no longer listening. The separation had already taken place. My heart was broken forever.

Antonia's expressive eyes were her best feature. Anyone cursed or caressed by those eyes, tender and terrible in turn, will remember them until he dies.

I recall that when I passed Mont Cenis, I exclaimed to the Alps in their eternal calm, "What sight will ever make me forget, will remove those eyes that I see ever before me?" I had the abyss at my feet, the avalanche at my brow. A black eagle hovered over the crests of the motionless trees. I walked forward pensively, continuing to see, like two flames advancing before me, those eyes, masters of my soul. Thus, during the Middle Ages, there was a superstition that inextinguishable fires preceded the march of the damned. The dark pines seemed to form my funeral cortège. Some were standing like phantoms. Others were laid out like corpses.

When I passed beneath their shade, I remembered that Byron said in the same spot that these trees made the forest look like a cemetery and reminded him of his dead friends. Oh Byron, when you crossed that immense wasteland and the dead branches of those thunderstruck tree trunks crackled beneath your feet, your heart, I am sure, heard their silence! They know more about heartbreak than we do perhaps, those mute old creatures chained to the earth.

CHAPTER XIX

WHEN I RETURNED TO PARIS, I was like a soldier back from the wars. I had left gay and impetuous, ardent and hopeful. I returned obscure, wounded, my brow disfigured and my heart revolted by those will-o'-the-wisps of glory. I was so changed that my family and friends couldn't hold back a start of fright when they saw me again. Their compassion would have been still greater if they could have seen the fearful ravages of my wounded soul. What could I give my allegiance to? What sentiments could I live by? I've never had much interest in fame since it can't bring us love. It's a truth, if not a truism, that fame arouses envy and criticism, turning away the very hearts it should attract. The power of the mind, even when incontestable and limitless, seems tyrannical to those who are compelled to recognize it. It does us no good to be naturally tender and devoted, to humble ourselves. We impress people as arrogant, supercilious, judgmental. We are threatening and hence are condemned to the ostracism of isolation.

Even Antonia herself who ought by affinity to be partial to poets, those eternal social exiles, didn't she tactlessly say in Tiberio's defense that "his kindness outweighs genius"?

Those who have no visible superiority are freely credited with hidden talents, while exceptional beings endowed with the rarest gifts are denied even the most ordinary attributes. Passivity arouses a kind of cult of submission which flatters the mediocre, while any mastery, even when exercised involuntarily, terrifies their insecure self-esteem.

Abandoned by Antonia, I was subjected to heart-rending humiliation by fate and fortune that would have made any elite mind long for inferiority. Alas, it is this longing which binds us to the world and brings about our downfall. We lose faith in ourselves when we are rejected and since we can't make those around us fly, too, we cut our wings and trudge in their ruts.

Live alone or submit bestially to the company of commoners. That is the definitive sentence that any poet who accepts life pronounces on himself.

Before being amazed that a lofty soul is deteriorating, you ought to find out what blows it has received, what bruises it has sustained, what it has suffered because of its very grandeur.

"Take me," I said to the life stirring in me once more, "make me your slave, since I couldn't bend you to my proud aspirations."

So I simply lacked the strength to live alone face to face with the ghost of my love affair. That's what brought about my degradation.

Those who held me dear, even those who bore me the most serious and saintly affection, advised me to circulate, to have a good time, in order to restore my health and weakened faculties.

So I plunged again into all those simulated passions which had disgusted me so quickly before I fell in love with Antonia. What would they be like for me now, after I had experienced sincere intoxication? Now they could only sting, making me feel my wound at every hour of the day.

I found Albert Nattier in Paris. He was overjoyed to see me again.

"Finally, free at last!" he cried jovially.

"Free and alone," I replied.

"That's why I'm congratulating you. Don't ever regret *her*."

"Can a person be so much in control that he deposits his sorrow somewhere and changes sentiments the way he changes clothes?" I asked, "I was created to love her."

"You're too proud and too critical to remain the dupe of an illusion," he retorted.

"But," I argued, "she was still the best and greatest of women. This is a fact. If I didn't know how to keep her love, that was my fault. I should have fought that pretty boy Tiberio for her. It was my false pride that prevented me. What did I have to reproach her? She was tender and sincere with me."

At "sincere" Albert Nattier burst out laughing.

"You're as sniveling as a Lamartine elegy," he hooted. "You're acting like a deceived husband who wallows in self-pity telling his tale of woe. Come now, call on irony. It's the best balm for wounds like that."

"I wonder what she's doing right this minute," I mused, paying no attention.

"Good God, she's having a good time with Tiberio, and when she's tired of him, she'll leave him the way she left you."

"No, she's fighting against it, and perhaps will come back to me without having surrendered." I remember that I uttered these words on the Place de la Concorde. It was evening. And at that instant a street lamp lit up Albert's face. His sardonic smile made me heartsick.

I grabbed his arm convulsively, "What do you know about her?"

"I know that if you ever see her again, I won't have anything more to do with you, much as I love you, because I don't want to see you led around like some comedy cuckold. You're young, elegant, famous. You have the right to leave and not to be left."

In matters of the heart Albert had a store of worldly maxims little concerned with life-and-death passion but dedicated above all to saving face. While chatting, he made a pirouette and since he wanted to avoid my questions, darted into a cabriolet which was passing by.

The next day I went to his place to demand an explanation. I was told that he had gone to England for three months.

I didn't have the fortitude to try to forget myself in work, but good old René, who was already an old friend, came to see me as soon as he heard of my return and urged me to publish what I had written in Italy. I read him a play, a short novel, and a few poems.

"You'll make Frémont a fortune with that," he said with that frank and friendly collegiality, typical of him alone in my experience. And that very day he got my editor excited about the treasures in my portfolio. Tantalized by René's prodigal praise, Frémont came over to make me some brilliant offers. I accepted them fast; I was in a hurry to send Antonia more than I owed her. The money a woman lends us is always scandalous in my opinion. I did not write to her. I was waiting for her to begin. Finally her first letter arrived. It was long and belabored, or so I felt later. It was composed of eloquent and ingenious sentences, as worked over as the best pages in her novels.

She described her sadness after my departure. She had wanted to see again all the places we had visited together. She went alone, wrapped in a black cloak as if wearing mourning for our love. In vain had Tiberio insisted on accompanying her during those commemorative excursions. She had refused for fear of profaning my memory with a new sensation, for she had to confess to me that she still felt attracted to Tiberio. Submissive as a son, tender as a younger brother, he provided her hours of serenity and quiet which she cherished all the more since they were never troubled by the demands of love and the outbursts of passion. The two of them were still at the stage of purity in tenderness and idealism in desire.

I received twenty letters written in that elegant pathos betraying the practiced pen of the novelist.

Finally her last letter narrated the peripeteia of her surrender, her "fall," as she called it. She had given herself to Tiberio, but she was mine too, for in his arms she still saw me. I was the dead beloved who still lived and moved within her and whom she hoped to find again in eternity. I remember that those studied expressions, presumptuous, even mystical, used to describe the simple and natural, but brutal and terrible, fact of infidelity horrified me. It was like a dagger decorated with flowers or a strangling by a golden silk shoelace. I tore that letter to shreds in my despair and answered with only these words: "I am grateful for your frankness, but you should realize that you have killed my youth."

My new works had come out. I had let my editor take care of it just as I left anything that concerned me to the unforeseen. Every morning I would rise with no fixed goal or purpose, determined only to give in to all passing sensations which came my way. When the heart doesn't have a steady inner direction—love, ambition, duty, or religion—it's just something moving back and forth.

I spent my days in stupid idleness or foolish and costly distractions. I strolled on the boulevards dressed like a dandy, I rode horseback, I dined in the most fashionable cafés, and every evening I went out in society.

The success of my books in conjunction with the notoriety of my affair with Antonia, made me for some time an object of Parisian curiosity. The salons of high society and literature sought me out like some exotic to be proudly shown to guests. That was the time, my dear Marquise, that I met you at the Arsenal one Sunday evening. I was struck by your youthful manner and candid expression. Oh, why didn't we fall in love then? I could still have been saved and beneath your guidance become again an energetic creature!

You were only a momentary mirage for me. During that troubled period I followed any glimmer of light. But I was too deeply lost in blind skepticism to persist in my search for the true light and bathe in it. I never dreamed of looking for your soul. I was not cured of my love affair.

When you're as wrenched and torn as that, you ought to be able to escape to some desert and hide your wound. Perhaps it would close and heal. But out in society shocks continually reopen it. You meet people who remind you of happier days. Friends who pity or deride, in refrain, "We told you so!" Women who carry on a flirtation while discussing our great betrayal. Even inanimate things are poignant and cruel. We were together the last time I looked at this monument, crossed this garden, or heard this music. Where is the woman who made every emotion twice as strong?

One evening after leaving a ball at the Spanish Embassy, I had wandered up and down the quays for a long time—reliving my nocturnal promenades there with Antonia. When I got home, I found a letter from my editor requesting my presence at a dinner the next day. There was to be, he said, a lively gathering of all kinds of celebrities, among whom I was sure to encounter an unexpected treat.

I paid little attention to the note, leaving to my mood the next day, whether to accept or refuse.

When I woke up, I had a visit from René, who used to surprise me like that in the morning either to recite some lines or hear some of mine.

"Are you going to Frémont's with me to dinner this evening?" I asked.

"No, and you shouldn't go either. We should not indulge our impresarios overmuch. They'll begin to think they're our collaborators."

"He can do whatever he likes where I'm concerned," I laughed. "Since he's given me hope of some distraction tonight, I'll eat his dinner."

"He's preparing a surprise for you which perhaps will be painful," René explained. "That's why I advise you to refuse."

"Get to the point, René."

"Well, Antonia is back, and Frémont thinks it would be amusing to have you to dinner together."

"She's back? Since when? Have you seen her? Where is she staying?"

"She lives in the same place she did when you met her. She got in three days ago with Tiberio. I met them yesterday in the Tuileries."

Every word in René's reply was like the smart of the iron tips of a scourge.

So she loved him enough to bring him back in triumph to the very city I lived in!

"I won't go to Frémont's," I said simply. Then I tried to hide my agitation by reciting some extremely beautiful stanzas of Leopardi whom I'd just been reading.

When I was alone, I surrendered to the truth of my emotion. It was a combination of rage and shame. The idea of seeing them together frightened me. To avoid even the possibility and the humiliation of such an encounter, I decided to shut myself in and work. I began to work on a project that very day and by the next morning I had already written several pages of a novel on Italy when Frémont came by.

"What a coincidence, my dear editor, I'm just making a copy for you."

"I'm delighted to see it," he replied, "and if it was inspiration which kept you from coming to my dinner yesterday, I forgive you."

"There's a certain kind of surprise I don't like," I said sharply, "and I ask you in the future not to plan on making a spectacle of me for your friends."

"My joke was well-intentioned. I thought you were over it," replied Frémont with that cunning and frank cordiality this Danube peasant of the bookdealers affects toward authors.

"I've been through with childhood diseases for a long time," I retorted, "but that still doesn't make me seek out cases of measles and chicken pox."

"Poor Antonia, you make her sound like a malady. However, she was exceptionally captivating last night, and she needed all the fire of her eyes and wit to make us put up with her Italian."

"Well?" I asked with a certain curiosity.

"Her handsome doctor was a complete fiasco," Frémont replied. "He's magnificent, I'll agree to that. But you shouldn't remove these native beauties from their natural setting. Tiberio's looks are almost shocking in Parisian society. It's as if you transplanted the arena of Verona into the midst of our boulevards. Tiberio's gaucheness cancelled out his prestige. He may be a good-looking lover in solitude, but he will embarrass Antonia in front of her friends."

"Who else was there?" I asked.

"Dormois, Sainte-Rive, Laubaumée, and the pianist Hess whom Antonia wanted to meet because the Marquise de Vernoult's infatuation with that handsome German makes him twice as famous at the moment.[1] Dormois, who puts into his conversation the wit and warmth you find in his paintings, engaged the Italian on Michelangelo, Titian, and Tintoretto. Tiberio showed such ignorance that Antonia was disconcerted. In his turn Sainte-Rive tried to make him talk poetry but shrugged his shoulders when he heard the Italian say he preferred Metastasio to Dante.[2] Hess pouted disdainfully at the insipid things he said on music. Antonia, to come to the poor boy's rescue and raise him in our opinion, pretended that he was quite strong in archaeology and that she thought one should specialize and not dissipate his intellect. In her pontification she didn't realize that Labaumée, who was listening, is a learned archaeologist who hides his knowledge behind his literary atticisms. He immediately began to embarrass Tiberio with a host of questions on Roman and Etruscan antiquities. The poor fellow, hounded on all sides by the vivacity and irony of the French *esprit*, managed to get out of it, I must confess to his honor, by candor.

"'Messieurs,' he said to my guests with noble dignity and touching simplicity, 'you are wrong to laugh at me. I am no savant, and I do not pretend to be. I am here solely as the *amico, servitor,* and *cavaliere* of the most cherished and illustrious Signora, and for this you should treat me with the courtesy due anyone in her company.' As he said this, he bowed to Antonia as a sign of servitude and extended his hand to seek her protection. But she didn't even look at him, but began to smoke and chat privately with the pianist. Then, suddenly, laughing, she asked why you hadn't come—this

1. These men are, respectively, Eugène Delacroix (1798–1863), historical painter; Charles Sainte-Beuve (1804–69), literary critic; Charles Magnin (1793–1862), newspaper literary critic; and Franz Liszt. The Marquise de Vernoult is novelist Marie d'Agoult, whose pen name was Daniel Stern.

2. Pietro Metastasio (1698–1782), celebrated librettist, was poet laureate for the Austrian court from 1730 until his death.

made the unhappy doctor shudder. She would have loved, she said, to compliment you on your successful new works.

"Sainte-Rive then launched into enthusiastic praise of your talent, and Dormois, sardonic as ever, seized the opportunity to murmur to Antonia, 'How could you have preferred this Antinous to him? Even physically, Albert is clearly superior because he has distinction, the only true beauty among civilized peoples.'

" 'You perfectly well know,' Antonia replied gaily, 'that your detractors have always claimed that you don't understand aesthetics.'

"Antonia left us almost as soon as dinner was over on the pretext of a visit she was expecting. It was plainly apparent to all of us that her Italian's poor showing humiliated her. So I regard Tiberio as condemned *in petto* and his expulsion tacitly decided. From now on it's just a matter of time. You know that Antonia goes into this sort of thing quickly and that she gets them over with without a qualm."

I let Frémont go on talking without interrupting him. I suffered from what he said about the woman I had loved so much, but he was parcelling out justice, and I didn't have the right to stop him.

Since I didn't show any reaction to his narrative, he changed the subject to what I was writing.

When he left, I covered my face with my hands, and felt them flooded with scalding tears.

In courting scandal to that point, Antonia wanted to carry out an act of feminine independence. She thought Tiberio's beauty and simplicity, not without their grandeur, would interest her friends back in France in her new passion. If I had been present at Frémont's dinner, perhaps everyone would have found it good fun to lionize him at my expense, but with me absent, they judged it better taste to sacrifice him to me.

What Frémont predicted came true. Antonia conceived for her handsome lover that sudden disgust that intelligence communicates to the senses. She came to find him vulgar and ugly. That was the clearest sign of her boredom, for Tiberio's looks had been the real attraction of the fleeting power he had held over her.

As soon as he ceased to give her pleasure, Antonia had no more use for that gentle and passive creature. Frémont on another visit told me that Tiberio had received his dismissal the night before.

"The execution was clean and swift," he reported. "On occasions like this, Antonia is a peer of Elizabeth of England and Catherine the Great of Russia. She had written me for an advance of one thousand francs on her new novel and asked me to bring them over when I went there for lunch. I arrived at the hour indicated. I found her with poor Tiberio, sad and distraught. He offered me his hand and implored me to intercede for him.

" 'The dearest lady wants to send me away on the pretext that I have nothing to do in Paris, that I have my career to pursue, and that she will never forgive herself if she is an obstacle to it. But what is she thinking about? What difference does it make whether I practice medicine in Venice? I want to live for her alone. I'm just a tiny worm she can crush. Oh, most beautiful lady, you know that I would rather be your slave than live in my native land,' he added turning to Antonia.

"She blew a smoke ring at the ceiling and replied gravely, 'My dear child, art imposes sacrifices on me. For me, you are a distraction incompatible with the work of the mind. I owe myself to my public, to my fame. And we must separate for me to accomplish the mission of my intellect. I abandon you only for the ideal. So don't be sad, my handsome Venetian.'

" 'Chaste lady,' cried Tiberio innocently, conquered by the euphony of her ethereal rhetoric. 'Oh most noble muse, I shall obey you, but I will die in the effort.'

" 'Bah,' Antonia laughed. 'I promise to come see you in Venice next autumn.'

"'Oh *grazie,* merciful lady,' replied the Italian, kissing her hands.

"'Let's go have lunch,' Antonia said. 'Let's be cheerful and chase away any evil omen.'

"We all three ate with a rather good appetite, but Tiberio began to cry at dessert.

"'Take heart, my brave fellow,' Antonia said. 'It's time now to part. Let's cut short our farewells and think only about our next meeting.' Then, pulling from her pocket the 1,000-franc note that I'd just given her, she slipped it into Tiberio's vest pocket. The poor fellow was so unstrung that he let her do it, so I really couldn't tell whether he lacked self-respect. After all, what else could the poor devil do? She had whisked him away from Venice, she had wrecked his career. He didn't have a private income, so perhaps he didn't have enough to pay for his return trip to his country, so joyously forsworn for her."

All the while Frémont chattered away, I was thinking: this is the third lover whose heart she has broken. When will she ever stop?

Frémont was still going on, "While pushing the Italian to the door, she held out her forehead to be kissed. 'Oh, most cruel creature,' he said, permitting himself a more intimate caress. I grabbed his arm to separate them, for I had been given the responsibility of getting him to the diligence. Antonia closed the door behind us, and a few minutes later, the hero of one of the episodes of her life was rolling down the road to Italy."

"Well," I sniffed, trying to affect indifference, "whom will she love now?"

"The pianist Hess is being mentioned," was Frémont's parting shot.

Poor Tiberio, I thought as soon as I was alone. He, too, although not a poet, is going to drag his grief upon the Venetian lagoons which have seen me weep also. But suddenly I burst out laughing, as if the mocking shade of Albert Nattier had appeared. "Really," an ironic voice said to me, "feeling sorry for him was all that you lacked."

Then I paused. So she's going to have an affair with that German pianist? Frémont's last words struck home.

"Well, let her love the devil himself," I raged as I paced up and down, furious with my own torment. There are times when you would pluck out your heart to get rid of the memory. Alas, no one has such control over that immortal part of himself.

What I dreaded the most was to find myself suddenly face to face with her, either in the street or at the theater. Nothing is so horrible as those chance encounters where a person whom we've loved above all else, passes by like a stranger. That indifferent head once rested on our breast. That cold, mute mouth once lavished kisses and terms of endearment. I felt that if she had suddenly appeared before me that way, I would have fallen lifeless at her feet or else I would have held out my arms and carried her off somewhere to make love to her still.

In order to avoid her and in order to repress her irritating image, I would work all day and go out every night, to some salon where I could be sure I wouldn't see her. But when I wrote, a specter with her eyes always stood in front of me. In society, whenever I spoke tenderly to a woman, what I was saying always seemed like a weak, jarring echo of what I had said to her so many times. Soon, desiring wrenching distractions, I turned again to the courtesans I'd met through Albert Nattier. I tried debauchery without a second thought.

My health, which had returned, increased the vehemence of my misery. What use was the strength of my youth? Sometimes desperately ashamed of those nights that sapped my energy, I would have liked to undertake some heroic action, to dedicate myself to some glorious cause and die like Byron. But Europe was at peace, and the ideas behind noble wars no longer fermented in human hearts.

One morning I read in a newspaper that the prince who had been my friend in school was going to lead our troops to fight in Africa. I paid a formal visit. He received me, as always, with heartwarming friendliness.

"Your Excellency, I come to ask a favor."

"For yourself, dear Albert? It will be the first time. I grant it in advance."

"I want to go on the African campaign with you."

"As historiographer?"

"No, as a soldier . . ."

His handsome face became jovial and gleeful. "Let me guess. Unlucky in love?"

"Does it matter, Your Excellency? Do you consent?" I replied gravely.

"No, I withdraw my promise. I refuse. France, my dear Albert, has thousands of brave soldiers, but she does not have three poets like you." He kissed me on both cheeks. "I am sparing you for the poetic glory of France which is as precious to me as its military glory."

Those who knew him will know how graciously he said that.

One evening, two weeks after Tiberio had been dispatched to Venice, as I was getting ready to go out, Sainte-Rive dropped by. He had been dining in the neighborhood and wanted to congratulate me on my last book.

"Do you know who came with me as far as your door?" he asked.

"No, who?"

"Antonia, whom I found strolling on the quay.

"What? I could have bumped into her also," I cried involuntarily.

"No doubt, and she would have been overjoyed, because she stopped me to talk about you, to ask me what you were doing and whom you were loving at the moment. I certainly realized from that amorous inquisition that you were still on her mind."

"Can't she even let me live in peace and go out for a breath of evening air? What is she doing prowling around my house? Rather than run the risk of seeing her, I would stop going out altogether."

"Well, that's proof enough that you still love her," Sainte-Rive observed, "and since she for her part can't do without you, you two will be reconciled in the end."

"You know that's impossible. Besides, she no more desires it than I do."

"Which means she's thinking about it, my dear Albert! Why did she kick out Tiberio? Why has she refused to see the German pianist for the past week, if not for you? For you whose pardon and peace she wants."

"I think I detect there one of her lines," I retorted. "Did she share her sentiments with you?"

"Yes, by Jove, with me and the rest of our friends. She loves you and doesn't want to love anyone else now."

"I didn't know you were so naive, my dear Sainte-Rive," I answered putting on a smile. "You know perfectly well that if she sent Tiberio away, it's because such a lover embarrassed her at Frémont's dinner, nor are you unaware that if she's shut her door to Hess, the pianist, it's because he prefers a certain blond marquise."

"You're mean and crafty," Sainte-Rive replied, "and outsmarting yourself, in my opinion, to reject a woman of Antonia's wit and charm, when she comes back to you, with fits like St. Anthony with the devil, for you are tempted, my good man, and if it weren't for your pride, you would shout, 'Come as fast as you can!'"

"You'll kindly not bring her up again," I said, somewhat brusquely, picking up my hat and gloves to make him realize I wanted to go out.

That night I got myself drunk in the worst way. I managed to kill her memory. The next night I started over again and so on several days running, so completely that I became inert flesh. I didn't work on anything, and I soon got such a fever that I thought my Venice illness was going to return.

When Frémont, to whom I had promised the last pages of a book, couldn't find out anything about me, he dropped by one morning and caught me in that splendid besotted state. He could figure out the cause.

"Your behavior is unpardonable. You are killing your genius to get rid of an obsessive memory. Believe me, it would be better to kill your passion by profaning it."

"What do you mean?"

"That Antonia still loves you and you would be wiser to take her back than to lead a life like this. I may be brutally frank, without any tact, but I'm speaking as a friend."

"You speak to me as an outsider because what you're advising is the most painful of all: the contempt I would have for myself if I renewed relations with her. Only an unhealthy and disturbed love affair could take place between us now. Hatred is better, active hatred, keen and inspiring. To mend a beautiful broken passion is as clumsy and impossible as putting an arm back on a classical statue."

Frémont didn't insist, but Saint-Rive who knew I was sick came by to see me.

"Antonia is very moving," he said, "when she talks about you.

She accuses herself and takes all the blame. Haughty as she is, she often weeps and tells us that she can't go on living if you don't forgive her."

"What I don't like," I responded, "is this drama of dolor. If the cry of her soul is sincere, she should utter it to me in secret and to me alone."

"But she's afraid of you. She fears your disdain."

"Well, I'm afraid of her. Don't talk to me about it anymore!" I exclaimed irritably.

I don't know whether Sainte-Rive reported my words to Antonia, but two days later, around midnight, as I was resting in a deep armchair, I heard the cord of my bell faintly stirred. Who would come at this hour? I had sent my servant to bed; I rushed to open the door, struck by the sudden idea that a serious emergency was imminent. Perhaps my mother was ill? Perhaps someone was coming to tell me that Antonia had killed herself? I was just at that last thought when I opened the door and saw Antonia before me, wrapped in a black cloak. I drew back, staggering, and dropped the candle I held in my hand. In the darkness, Antonia threw herself on my chest and clasped me so tightly that any resistance would have been futile. Besides, I didn't dream of doing so. I felt her tears wetting my cheeks, her hair permeating me with its familiar, heady fragrance. She joined her hands behind my neck and asked me for forgiveness. I found her this time at my mercy, she who so often had pushed me away with her cold contempt. Now she was as humble and passionate as the Oriental woman who pacifies her angry master with caresses. Her breath ran over me like an electric flame and she was saying,

"Remember! We were happy once. We can be happy again!"

How could I have freed myself? How could I have rejected the happiness I had so often regretted? It is true that such happiness was from that moment perverted, sickening, devoid of all prestige, but the gross part of the senses was content. Never during the most shining hours of my cult for her did I feel such quickening, energizing tremors. I returned her furious kissing but without deluding her soul.

"Don't ask me to forgive your impure acts," I told her, "because I am even more impure than you! I give you what is left over from debauchery. What you find now is a withered heart corrupted through sorrow. You wounded my heart, and it will make you suffer from that wound. From now on, our love, bitter as hatred, will be nothing more than the senses defying the conscience. You become a courtesan when you throw yourself into my arms, and I am only one more heartless debauchee returning your embrace!"

"What differences does that make?" she inhaled deliriously, accepting the sullied intoxication. All the sacred memories of our love, once so beautiful, were thus mingled in with the burning sensations of a degrading passion.

But what an impenetrable mystery the union of beings is! Despite the cruel words I had just uttered, I felt all the resentment in my heart melting in her arms. I became tender and affectionate again, and my eyes, brimming with tears, looked at her gratefully.

She knew what I was thinking, "You see, I was right to come."

"Yes, yes," I sighed, hiding my face on her breast, "I'll always love you."

The next day I had my old place in her life. The first days were almost happiness. Cut off from society, I was oblivious to everything but her, and in her I saw and rediscovered only what had made me happy. Her calm and gentle disposition restored peace to my heart. Her intelligence in all matters charmed me. What other woman would have been able to speak to me about the creations of my mind with the certainty of genius and the enthusiasm of love? I read her the works I had done recently, and in her praise and criticism I found a superiority which did my love proud. Who would ever have understood me as well as she did? Who would ever have sensed to that extent the poet in the lover?

Despite some jarring notes, wasn't she, after all, the only woman with whom I could live the double life of body and soul?

But storms were brewing. Blown by all the outside forces, they could not fail to find us.

Our reconciliation attracted a great deal of attention. My family despaired over it, foreseeing more distress ahead. My friends cracked jokes about it, and society treated me as a coward and fool.

I braved both advice and public opinion, as one almost always would in such a case.

Mine had been the stronger passion. So I had to glorify it or at least make everyone believe I wasn't ashamed of it. I reappeared with Antonia, out walking, at the theater. She often wore men's clothing which made everyone stare at us. She affected the greatest disdain for what she labelled prejudices and dragged me along in imitation. We led that unbridled, artist's life that has since been called Bohemian. After leaving some performance, a few people would come over to smoke and chat with us, more her friends than mine. Not that mine were better behaved, but they had, even informally, an aristocratic reserve that Antonia found exasperating. What is true is that in her presence they were mindful of her talent, and this impressed them, placing some restraint on their nonchalant behavior. They had kept in that respect the tradition of courtly manners which under the ancien régime always prevented Madame de Sévigné from being treated like a chorus girl, whether she had lovers or not.[3] Antonia's friends were not so restrained. They used the familiar "tu"; she had set

3. Madame de Sévigné (1626–96), who developed letter writing into an art form, is remembered also as a dedicated mother. Widowed at twenty-five when her blackguard husband was killed in a duel over a courtesan, she never remarried but devoted herself to her son and daughter, the principal recipients of her letters. Maxim writer La Rochefoucauld (1630–80) was a close friend, some-

the example herself. As for me, attached to her by the grosser side of passion, I let them get by with it, basically unconcerned by the respect due her dignity. At first I felt I was in an unwholesome atmosphere, but eventually I got used to the polluted air. Ironic, contemptuous, I treated her like a common mistress. Since the idol had voluntarily come down from her pedestal, I taunted myself when I was tempted to put her back up. With her, my manner was sometimes harsh, sometimes sarcastic, showing how unstrung my soul was. When she reproached me gently and simply, I felt bad, but as soon as she assumed her sermonizing pompousness, I broke out in offensive jokes. She could have made an appeal to what was still noble in me with a tear or a sincere word, and I would have fallen at her feet. But in these struggles she would use a language so patently in contradiction with all the acts of her life that I was revolted.

One evening I didn't get back until around midnight, having made her wait for me all day. I had gone off through the countryside to unburden my soul of its relentless weight. Near Bougival, I went bathing in the Seine, then rolled on the grass and went to sleep beneath the trees on that warm August night. When I arrived, she burst out in reproaches, told me she'd never be able to wean me from dissipation and debauchery and that her sacrifice had been a pure loss.

"What sacrifice?" I cried. "Surely not sending Tiberio away?"

"That sacrifice and ever so many others," she continued with a brash naiveté which exasperated me. "I have bestowed upon you a devotion that has reached to the extreme limits of abnegation, to the immolation of my proud instincts, and to the degradation of my chaste nature."

---

times linked to her, but all in all, Albert's aside seems curious for so discreet a woman as Madame de Sévigné.

I burst out laughing.

She kept on, "Your impious incredulousness can't hurt me. God knows that I had to transcend my disgust for things of the senses to save you from the abyss. I threw myself back into your arms only to snatch you from the sullied arms of others. And now you taunt me with my fall, treat me like the women I wanted to protect you from. You forget that I have been a sister and a mother to you . . ."

"Enough!" I shouted. These words awakened an echo of the similar rhetoric she had used at the very moment she was leaving me for Tiberio. "That's enough hypocrisy!" My rage was mounting. "You don't have to be a puritanical Madame de Warens.[4] You don't have to put adolescent Jean-Jacques in your bed and protest afterwards that it was for his greater good and by pure abnegation! Come on, admit that you found some pleasure in it, too!

"I don't like the mystical exclamations of Madame de Krüdener, when she cries out in the ecstasy of amorous spasms, 'Dear God, forgive me for being as happy as this!'[5] God and remorse have nothing to do with it. I find more honorable the refrain of beautiful Roman women who at such moments used to sigh in Greek, 'Zoe kai psyche, my life and soul!'

"Remember, my dear, that if the things of the senses disgust you, you weren't forced to indulge in them. When you present society what it calls a scandalous love affair, you should at least be honest in your passion. On this point the women of the eighteenth-century were better than you. They didn't distill love into metaphysics."

While I was speaking, Antonia's perennially calm face expressed pain and fury through the flush on her cheeks and the

4. Madame de Warens is Louise-Elénore de la Tour du Pil (1700–1762). She was Jean-Jacques Rousseau's protector.

5. Juliana de Krüdener (1764–1824) was a Russian mystic, cultist, and novelist.

sparks in her eyes. But suddenly her features relaxed. She grew pale, let her head drop back, and remained still.

When I had finished, she said to me in a steady voice, "You're the punishment for my pride. This had to happen."

I saw two large tears roll down her cheeks, and I loathed myself. What I had said could have been said by anyone else, but I should have kept quiet.

After such cruel scenes, however, I still tried to love her, to be happy, to bind her to me. I remembered the past, I made myself evoke cherished images. I spun such memories around her like a fantastic rondo and made myself a prisoner of the dance. But next to these smiling scenes arose others, insulting, tyrannical, which murmured to me irreparable words that death cannot efface. Always I saw at her side, like her shadow, the jeering phantom of Infidelity.

We were no longer working during those stormy days. But during gentle Tiberio's so brief and peaceful reign, she had written a novel which had just appeared and which soon aroused the liveliest of debates in the newspapers.[6] Some called it a philosophical work that summed up the suffering and aspirations of the times. Others found in it an empty and ambitious lucubration where any verisimilitude or moral code was violated by a style that was alternately charming and pompous. One journalist found it amusing to identify the author in the heroine and allowed himself to direct against Antonia attacks so very violent that I felt offended, too. Indeed, in the poignant wrath of my love I could see through her and pass judgment. But I forbade anyone else any kind of insult against a woman who belonged to me and who appeared in public on my arm.

I had just read the injurious article and was getting ready to go

6. The novel is probably *Jacques* (1834).

out to demand satisfaction, when I saw Albert Nattier coming in my room.

"I thought you were still in England," I said, kissing him on both cheeks, delighted and surprised to see him.

"I arrive like the *deus ex machina*."

"You speak more truly than you think," I replied. "You come just in time for the denouement, for tomorrow I am fighting a duel, and you will be my second."

"We'll see, we'll see," he laughed. "But first come to lunch with me at the Café Anglais."

"Gladly. But someone is expecting me. I have to write a note to let her know."

"Who is she?" he asked, pretending ignorance.

"You know perfectly well; we made up."

"That's what I was told, but I didn't believe it. You're going to fight for *her?*"

I gestured affirmatively while dashing off a few lines for Antonia. Albert Nattier was watching me carefully. On his face was a serious expression which I had never seen before. We went down the stairs without a word and climbed into his carriage which took us to the Café Anglais. He narrated several adventures in which he had been the hero. The conversation continued on this subject until the end of lunch. But as soon as the waiter had left and we had lit our cigars, he got up, stood in front of me and said, "All right, Albert. You've made up your mind on this duel. You're going to fight for this woman?"

"My decision is irrevocable," I replied. "My father himself, if I were still so fortunate as to have him, would not make me give it up."

"Well, in this case, I shall have more power than your father," he countered, "for I swear to you this duel will not take place."

"You're mad," I snapped impatiently.

"No, I'm not, but I'm going to do something vicious, if you do not immediately give me your word that you will not fight."

"What you demand is impossible."

"Well, then I will have to speak," he said, growing very pale.

I began to shiver, and I had a sudden premonition of something terrible. He seemed to be hesitating.

"So, speak," I shook his arm.

"You know," he began, "that Tiberio was Antonia's lover."

"Yes, since she told me herself, and I've already told you the story. How does that allow me to fail honor and, I might add, fail Antonia, who has only me to defend her? After all, she is more worthy than other women, for she was frank and great in her confession and as loyal as a mother to me during my long illness in Venice."

"Yes," he replied in a strange tone of voice, "that illness will be the outstanding page in her life story."

"But what are you trying to say," I choked. "Get on with it. Let's get this over with."

"I say that while you were dying, she was gaily giving herself to Tiberio."

"You lie!" I shouted, making a gesture of reprobation.

My anguish made him mute. He took fright, he told me later, when my face went to pieces.

I interrogated him in my turn. "What do you know about it? Who told you? I'd believe you only if you had proof."

He continued, "It was poor Tiberio himself. He was so embarrassed by the gratitude I expressed for the care he had given you that he confessed everything during our tour of Venice."

"Oh," I stammered, "that's why you were so upset when you came back that day. I remember . . . I remember it."

I couldn't say another word. I covered my face with my hands to hide the shame that overwhelmed me.

"It was she," he continued implacably, "who seduced Tiberio because he believed fidelity was owed to the dying, and I saw him seized with superstitious terror when he recalled that sinister coupling, carried out almost in view of the mortuary couch. He loved her . . ."

"Stop it! Stop it! I don't want to hear anything more. Take me where you wish." And I clutched his arm for support.

CHAPTER XX

NATTIER kept me with him for several days. He didn't try to distract me, advise me, or guide me. He left me complete freedom of thought and action, which is the best course for rebuilding resilience in the soul. Because one of two things will happen. Either the blow we've received will kill us, and then nothing can be done about it. Or if we are meant to live, solitude and reflection will re-establish us more effectively than incomplete and commonplace consolations.

He also avoided speaking contemptuously about Antonia. As for me, strongly resolved to give her up forever, I stopped accusing her and, to outward appearance, even stopped thinking about her at all. We hardly made any allusions to her when her letters were delivered to me in his presence.

On the first day of my unexpected disappearance, Antonia had written me three times to express anxiety, surprise, disappointment. She began all over again the next few days, and I must say that her first letters revealed only affectionate concern. But as I maintained a stubborn silence, she eventually broke out in reproaches and accused me in offensive language of leaving her only because I was afraid of defending her against the men insulting her. I must have gone white when I received that letter because Nattier, who was present, asked spontaneously, "What's the matter?"

"Here," I replied, handing it to him, "read this and answer it for me."

"I have your permission?"

"Absolutely. I had one lingering weakness. I wanted to hear her once more through her letters. Now I really feel that it is all over. She should learn it through you. You will be like one of those rough, cold walls separating prisoners in a jail."

While I was speaking, he dashed off the following note:

> I kept Albert from duelling over you because on a day when he might have died, you gave yourself to Tiberio in Venice. I learned that through Tiberio himself!
>
> Albert doesn't want to see you again and will not answer your letters.

"Fine, her pride will not forgive me for that, and my solitude is assured."

"What are you going to do to take your mind off her?" my friend asked.

"First, I'm going to travel, then I'll get to work."

"That's better than the mindless diversions which I would have plunged you into. I'm beginning to get disgusted with them myself. I'm thinking about going into politics for a little excitement."

"A little boredom is more likely," I laughed.

The thought of Nattier as a deputy or councillor of state struck me as hilarious. We made a few wild jokes on the subject and parted in rather high spirits at the end of the afternoon.

When I got back to my place, I noticed on the quay facing my house a hackney-cab with the blinds lowered. "Some society woman waiting for her lover," I thought. In any other frame of mind, I would undoubtedly have opened the window and watched the mystery cab. But I was hardly inside my deserted lodging, when I felt the specter of solitude clutching at my throat. I went over to my worktable where the sheets of the book I was working on were still scattered from that interruption a few days earlier. Near my writing desk in a Chinese vase there was still a bouquet of dried flowers that Antonia had given me, and in sitting down my foot struck a tapestry cushion she had made. Her portrait, placed in a corner of my room watched me with her large questioning eyes. I could imagine her picture saying, "Try as you will, I will always be with you." I was feeling what you feel at the hour the body of a beloved has just been taken off to the cemetery. You look on all the remaining effects with anguish. You shudder when you touch them, as if touching the cadaver itself. You close your eyes so you won't see anything, but your eyes fill with tears, and through these tears you still see the the person who is gone.

I was a prey of such funereal meditations when my servant, who had gone out to get a lamp, returned saying some woman asked to speak to me. I smiled because by some kind of quirk of the imagination I thought it could be the pretty Countess of Nerval. She had been seeking me out and giving me encouraging looks at several balls. It must be she who had come to watch for my return in the motionless cab.

I rose to go meet her when I saw it was Antonia. She prostrated herself at my feet like Mary Magdalene. She resembled the classic pose of that saint all the more since she held a skull in her outstretched hands.

"What the devil," I snorted. "What weird role are you playing and what are you trying to do with these theatrics?"

Her face was livid, and her eyes were as hollow and deep as the empty orbits of the cranium she was holding out to me. She didn't speak but walked on her knees to get to me. And soon she touched me with her sinister offering. My start of horror made the death's head roll at my feet. Immediately I saw spill out a thick black coil of hair as if this graveyard debris had held on to that earthly adornment. I looked at Antonia and saw that her pale forehead was bereft of her beautiful hair.

"What an act of dementia!" I cried.

"I am only a worthless sinner, no longer expecting your love," she said. "But I wanted to sacrifice to you what you liked best in me when you loved me."

"Are you going to act out all the plots of your novels?" I continued brutally. "Are you going to wear white like an abbess and shut yourself up in some Italian cloister like your heroine Lélia?"

"Oh," she moaned, "you are harsh indeed to rail at my repentance."

"I don't like these religious comedies," I shot back. "In my opinion, remorse has no role in stunts like this. Tomorrow when you want to be attractive again, you will sincerely regret these tresses which were so becoming."

Raising her with a resolute hand, I led her to the door. I felt her trembling beneath my convulsive pressure.

"Is this your last word?" she asked, as she prepared to step out.

"Yes, the last in this lifetime. Because I would blow out my brains before I would set eyes on you again."

My door closed upon her. I heard her going down the stairs. Then I went over to the window to watch her climb back into the cab waiting on the quay.

"She won't die from it," I was thinking. "Fatal sorrow doesn't carry on like this."

I pushed the skull away with my foot, but that lustrous hair, still seemed to emit sparks, that beautiful hair, caressed so often, still emanating her personal fragrance . . . I gathered the locks in my trembling hands and in a frenzy plunged my burning forehead into them. That was the final supreme spasm, the last embrace she received from me.

Alas, in removing myself from her life, I didn't remove her shadow from mine. I wasn't able to sleep in the days that followed. As another of our poets has put it so well, "I always seemed to see her head resting next to mine on my bolster. I could no longer love her; neither could I love anyone else nor do without loving. Love was forever poisoned in my heart, but I was too young to give up loving, and I kept coming back to it. I would say to myself, If passion leaves me, won't I die? If I try solitude, that will lead me to nature, and nature will lead me to love. Be coarse! Be corrupt! cries the voice of the crowd. And you will suffer no more! Soon debauchery became my companion and threw its corrosive poisons on the wound in my heart."

From then on I created only songs of despair, quickly composed from an inspiration sustained by the dolorous tension in my soul. But for longer works, my genius lacked the indispensable patience and energy. What was originally strong and upright in my talent seemed to have escaped with the blood spurting from my wound. Enervating nights of orgy completed my spiritual impoverishment. The world treated me as a spoiled child. It greeted my works with nearly unanimous admiration. But I feel myself that I haven't been able to give what I could have. People know the lively, graceful, joking, and passionate side of my talent. But of the vigorous and calm side, only presentiments. Only here and there is the print of the lion, who is forced to his flank by a mysterious hand and who will die without revealing his power.

What became of her heart, I didn't try to find out. I was told that she was consoled and calm, and I can believe it. The rips and tears of an eternal rupture would not lay waste her life as it did mine. She had abandoned others before me. But she was my first and only great love.

Through the fleeting years, through the shadows enshrouding almost half my days, she remained forever in the back of my mind. When she was mentioned, I shuddered. When she was attacked, I was ready to defend her. The praise her genius received sometimes made my face glow with pride. She seemed to have given up false and outrageous concepts, and every year produced more valuable works. It made me happy, and I followed her progress with the solicitude that a father feels for the intelligence of his son. Thus, little by little, my resentment sank into slumber, leaving only the forebearance of memory. I saw the happy days come to the fore again, lighting the dark days with their rays. Full of forgiveness, I would say, is it her fault if she couldn't love me better? In our overrefined civilization, complete love is impossible between two persons of equal intelligence but dissimilar constitutions and combative abilities. In order for such persons always to understand each other and to stay united in unchanging love, they would have to have had a similar education in childhood, the same beliefs, the same mental habits, even identical codes of behavior. That's what Bernardin de Saint-Pierre certainly understood when he wanted to depict ideal love.[1] He chose two children, born, he would have us believe, of a kindred breath, animated by their mothers with a single mind, growing, so to speak, on a single stalk, and growing up under the influence of the same atmosphere. But we are the tormented offshoots of a stormy and corrupted society, stepmother of its divided children and more cruel in its furious phases than in the savage state. So why should we be astonished after so many public struggles and bloody executions at the incessant divorce

1. Bernardin de Saint-Pierre (1737–1814) wrote *Paul et Virginie* (1788).

between hearts and the impossibility of intimate bonds? Love, like politics, is marked by incompatibility. The individuals are part of the masses. All ideas have been dismissed, reviled, thrown to the winds. How could they re-enter our minds in the orderliness of olden times or come out again with the old meanings? Morals, like laws, have been overturned, and the breath of revolution has even blown on love.

Was I justified in reproaching Antonia for her prejudices, racial instincts, or for the indelible imprint of her convent education? Didn't I, too, have my uncontrollable tendencies, which roared like a tornado, whirling away what was best in me?

One day Nattier dropped in while I was in the midst of these reflections which not only reminded me constantly of my ineffable memory of Antonia, but in my opinion, justified it. I shared these ideas with my skeptical friend.

"Very well," he replied cuttingly. "You poets are dreamers. You give in to subtle and slippery definitions of things, no matter how clear-cut. So much so that in the end you lose a clear sense of what the thing is. But your wounded heart, I feel sure, is a better logician, than your head, and since that heart still bleeds, I doubt that it grants absolution to Antonia for her betrayal in Venice, especially not for the sordid and novelistic manner of the deception, so hypocritically developed in the letters which followed. Among the refinements of your indulgent argumentation, have you found, my good man, an explanation for that gratuitous lying?"

"It's very simple," I replied. "Antonia merely succumbed to nature in giving herself to Tiberio, and she hid the truth from me in Venice to spare my feelings. Today I can make out her apprehensive kindness where formerly I saw only her overweening duplicity. It wasn't herself she feared humiliating!"

Nattier retorted, "You would be right if everything in her life and writings didn't formally belie that interpretation. Think it over and judge. She always clothes her heroines' weakness in arrogance. Natural love seems like something sullying or inferior to her. In the belief that it will be ennobling, she drapes herself in chastity and hides her precious little sins between the folds of a biblical garment. She had for Tiberio a passing fancy that Madame d'Epinay might have permitted herself, but she would certainly have confessed to it with a laugh, accepting as punishment an epigram or some other reprisal from Grimm.[2] But Antonia, for fear of being a fallen woman, has to hoist herself up on the clouds. From the heights of heaven where she can't be touched, she accuses you after having struck the first blow. In short, she was intent upon proving that she was faithful while cheating on you and narrated the tale of an Italian peccadillo in the ethereal rhetoric of Ossian. What I'm telling you now, you yourself noted in her letters just as her public notes it in her novels. Her heroines always preach sublimities unrealizable to begin with and in contradiction with their precise situation. *O santa semplicità!* as the Italians say, what became of you in her soul? If she paints rustic manners some day, you can be sure that she will have her peasant women discussing philosophy. And what really exasperates me is that she thinks she is natural and unaffected."

"Well, she really is," I replied. "That's what absolves her. Because what is false in her character and talent is not the result of a bias but of her sincere admiration for the conventionally beautiful, which seems like true beauty to her."

"But why didn't you—you have so decisive and clear-thinking a mind—show her the simple and geniune grandeur of genius, before, of course, your heart drowned in the fogs of that affair?"

"Because she thought herself the stronger, and she always re-

2. Separated from her husband, Madame d'Epinay had a lifelong relationship with Baron Grimm (1723–1807), man of letters and diplomat. They also collaborated on his correspondence.

treated to her moral infallibility in our discussions. Oh, if I could have made her more unbending, not from pride, but through tenderness, I would have bent her to my heart, I would have subjected her to my love!"

"Haven't we talked enough about her?" Nattier interrupted impatiently. "You've said nothing about her for several years, and I am quite grateful to you for your steadfast silence. Today I find you in a loquacious mood, morbid and vaporous. If I leave you alone, you will write some self-pitying elegy. Come with me instead to have dinner in the country where I'm expecting some jolly friends."

I followed him, as I'd been following for a long time any convenient distraction that came my way.

Nattier had a picturesque place in the environs of Fontainebleau. It bordered on the forest. But, I confess to my weakness, until that day I had never been able to force myself to return to those tall trees and see again those wild and magnificent bluffs we'd explored together so many times. The idea of going in the forest filled me with as the same terror as a child forced to enter by himself a dark woods filled with brigands and wild beasts. It seemed to me that all passions and memories would break loose and gnaw at my heart if I went into those places where I had been happy. That day, I don't know why, I had more courage.

The guests Nattier was expecting hadn't come yet when we arrived, so I suggested getting on horseback and taking an excursion into the forest.

"I'd be delighted," he replied, somewhat surprised by my new resolve.

We passed through a somewhat open crossroad. But soon, either by instinct or will, I headed us toward the densest section of the forest which had always attracted me when I was with her. Although it was a brilliant day, the light barely pierced the branches of the old trees. Around us there was a solitude and silence so absolute that it tempered the heat of the day. Where there is no movement and noise, you can feel peace descending. Our horses advanced slowly, and soon we were forced to go on foot to make our way through the interlaced thickets and fissures of the huge boulders. I walked without getting tired or sad, but Nattier, who feared something might call up a phantom, decided it would be prudent to divert me with some of his maddest episodes. I listened smiling, and from time to time I would crack some sharp and happy joke which would put him off the scent of what was really going on in my heart. As we proceeded and I recognized the stream, the clearing and the enormous boulder covered with black moss, something sweet and tender took hold of me. I experienced none of the heart-wrenching I had feared. It was a blessed and calming resurrection of beautiful scenes of youth and love. This appeasement which took place, without my knowledge, so to speak, filled me with serenity and brought a smile to my lips. This sensation, entirely internal, was not revealed by an utterance. I continued to respond in kind to Nattier's jokes.

When we reached the summit of the boulder, at the very spot where I had picked up Antonia in my arms and had clasped her in an embrace to carry her into eternity, I had an intense beam of sunlight on my face. Involuntarily I held out my arms to a shade from the past as if to a returning friend I hadn't hoped to see.

On returning to the house, I experienced the same apparent gaiety and the same secret working of my heart. I thought I would suffer, and I had been happy.

Two years later I wrote about that memory in the stanzas which have been much discussed, and which you, in your amiable partiality, say you prefer to Lamartine's "Le Lac."[3]

Now you know what that woman has made of me, what I have

3. These stanzas are the "night" poems: "La Nuit de mai" (1835), "La Nuit de décembre" (1835), "La Nuit d'août" (1836), and "La Nuit d'octobre" (1837).

remained after so many disappointments and fruitless attempts at deplorable consolations. You see, my dear Marquise, a devastated creature; you see also a heart still vibrating, the way an echo quivers and spreads life in a ruined monument. Since I've met you, Stéphanie dear, the pulsations of my youth have reawakened. I feel again the good, the beautiful, love itself! Let me be reborn, let me love you!"

As HE FINISHED SPEAKING, Albert, unstrung and exhausted by the emotion of his long narrative, rested his head on my knees and covered my hands with convulsive kisses. I didn't push him away. I was truly too touched to be worried. Something chaste and radiant gave the great poet an aura. I felt he was a brother to be consoled, and my involuntary tears fell on his hands in answer to his caresses.

"Oh, you can see that I love you," he murmured, "and that you could make another man of me."

"What you love, Albert," I told him, "is love. Your memories! Antonia herself! For when one has loved like that, one loves only once."

"No, no," he cut me short, "listen carefully, I still have two more things to tell you, two things I had forgotten and which will persuade you.

"I didn't set eyes on Antonia for many, many years. Chance was kind to me. It never let me find her on my path. I always saw her through my memories: young, irresistible in her terrible impassiveness and in the formidable power she exerted over me. But a year or so ago, one evening in the actors' foyer of the Théâtre Français, I was standing with my head raised to study a portrait of Mademoiselle Clairon.[4] I heard someone coming over to me and

4. Mademoiselle Clairon is Claire-Joseph Léris (1723–1803).

calling me by name. I lowered my gaze and saw a woman with common bearing and style. Only by the sparkle in the eyes could I recognize Antonia. Her complexion had changed for the worse; her cheeks and all her features showed the sagging of age. She was smoking a cigarette at the time and had another one in her fingers, and since I was smoking, too, she chuckled, 'Albert, give me a light.'

"I bowed without answering and handed her my cigar. Then I left the foyer.

"Only my heart had quivered, perhaps from astonishment. My senses had been unmoved, even repelled. It wasn't Antonia whom I had seen again, not even her shadow. It was her caricature! If her rekindled desire had impelled her toward me, my arms would not have opened. If she had cried, 'I love you still,' I would have replied with conviction, 'I am cured!'

"Oh, it wouldn't have been that way if we had gone loving through life, aging together, sharing our labors, joys, and pains. Then old age and decrepitude would have occurred imperceptibly. The beautiful memories of a happy youth would have hidden them, and the brilliance of inalterable feelings would have effaced them! But when love has made you enemies, when violent separation has caused antagonism, the physical eye is implacable. It proceeds as coldly in its dissection as a scalpel on a cadaver.

"So you see that I couldn't love her anymore. The charm and attraction are destroyed. I speak about it as I would something dead. If I have taken pains with the details of this narrative, if I have tried to take you into the infinite mysteries of a desperate psychology, I did it for you, not for her. For you, whom I want to love me, for you to whom I have just revealed, as if to God, all the contradictions in my heart, wretchedness and grandeur, tenderness and hatred.

"Others have heard this demoralizing story from me, but they have seen only the skeleton. For you alone I have brought it to life. You have reviewed the drama in action, followed its events, understood its sorrows, counted its sobs. To you alone, in short, have I shown the complete truth about myself. What greater proof of love can I give you? What more intimate communion could unite our two souls?

"That's what I still had to say to you, and now I feel relieved."

After uttering these last words, his head fell on my lap again, as if overcome by exhaustion, and I felt his mute lips drinking in my tears which still fell on his clasped hands.

I was overcome by immense pity for him. Forgetting my fears of previous days, which would have seemed puerile next to his pain, I wanted to keep him with me until evening. It was my duty as host to comfort him.

Hearing my son and Marguerite coming in the apartment, I said to Albert, "Let's hold back our tears. They would alarm the child."

He obeyed and moved away from my knees where his hands were still resting. He put his arms around my son and hugged him. We stayed that way until midnight, like a family, and even when the child was no longer present, Albert said nothing which could have troubled me and roused me from my fraternal mood. But before leaving, he clutched me poignantly to his heart and said, "Until tomorrow, Stéphanie darling; now that we love each other, life will be beautiful!"

Those parting words brought me back to myself, to the complete confession I owed him, and during my sleep, troubled by the shock of so many emotions, I thought I could hear Léonce's voice crying, "Well, are you going to love him?"

CHAPTER XXI

I COULDN'T get to sleep until daybreak, and at the hour my son usually got up, I was awakened from this brief, troubled sleep by Marguerite coming into my room. I shook off my malaise and began at once to write to Léonce. I didn't want to wait until evening to tell him the story Albert had confided in me. I was under the sway of blind love. That is why during the great poet's own lifetime I entrusted his painful and secret confessions to another heart. But that other heart no longer contains anything but dead ashes, colder than the dust in coffins. So I won't call on that heart to confirm the truth of my testimony. For all those who have lived by both heart and mind, its truth throbs sufficiently both in the overall outline and in the details I've just related.

If this narrative were a fiction meant for a book, perhaps the rules of what we call art would require ending it here. But in my opinion, real concern outweighs imaginary concern, and the unforeseeable attraction of a real action outweighs the contrived effect of a clever composition. Then, too, nothing which bears on a truly great person is trivial. Nothing is irrelevant if it was part of a life that was dear to us. So I will tell you Albert's last emotions, mixed in, as they are, with events of my own life.

I had written to Léonce without either restraint or uneasiness because secure as he was of having all my love, what I told him about Albert's enthusiastic feelings for me could indeed somewhat upset him, but never frighten or hurt him.

I waited calmly for his reply, while I was overwrought and hence preoccupied with what I could say to Albert. How could he be brought down from his keyed-up state of the night before by the pointblank confession of my love for Léonce? This love affair, which he refused to believe, how could I insist on its reality and make that cruel conviction penetrate his wounded and loving heart? To reject him as a lover was to lose him as a friend, to forgo forever our heartfelt camaraderie, our fellowship of kindred minds which meant so much to me. I was well aware that he wouldn't want my friendship. From the moment love strikes, all other feelings disappear, consumed, so to speak. It's the spark that sets the flame ablaze. And still I felt hesitating would show bad faith on my part. To say nothing was to deceive both Albert and Léonce, for leaving one of them room for hope meant removing the other's sense of security.

I was in the grips of this nagging dilemma when the doorbell rang. It had to be Albert. I thought I was going to faint, but I felt immediately relieved to see his servant instead. He came to tell me that his master was indisposed and wouldn't be able to come to see me either during the day or in the evening.

"Is he seriously ill," I asked, "since he didn't write? If this is the case, I'll go to see him."

His servant dissuaded me, informing me that during such nervous attacks which his master suffered once or twice a month, he insisted on keeping completely to himself. "He keeps completely still and doesn't talk," he added, "taking what he calls his 'bath of silence and repose,' and in twenty-four hours he's over it."

"Tell him anyway that if he wants to see me, I'll run over," I repeated as the man went off.

As soon as I was alone I realized that my message, when quoted, would make Albert think I loved him.

I spent the rest of the day inexpressibly agitated. I didn't know what course to take or what form to give my confession. If I wrote Albert about my passion for Léonce, it would be like sending him a cold-blooded dismissal. For the written word always has something fixed and unpardonable about it, while what comes from the voice, no matter how grievous the meaning, responds to the feelings of the listener. So I finally decided to wait until Albert visited and let the moment be my guide.

The next morning, I heard from Léonce.

There had never been a novel, he said, which interested him so much as the story of Antonia and Albert's romance. That man had put into his passion the grandeur, intensity, and duration which made it truly beautiful. But it was doubtful that after so many painful incidents and so many repeated and deleterious attempts at consolation in debauchery, Albert could still love as he once had. This second love he was offering me would be only a pale and grimacing simulacrum of the first. I deserved something better than the vestiges of a damaged heart and dormant genius. Albert was famous and he himself was unknown, but he, at least, was giving me his entire soul where no image obscured my own. I would always be the only woman, the inspiration of his solitude, the beloved bond of his youth, the gentle light hovering over his decline, like Mohammed's first wife. She was the prophet's destined mate, loved to very last days, old and whitehaired, preferred to the fresh young brides who never had his heart.

He was too proud, he continued, to add anything more, but he waited for the decision of my love with an impatience which was disturbing his work and solitude. In closing, he begged me to continue unreservedly to give him reports on Albert. Albert was, he said, a living case study of unparalleled interest, and in satisfying his curiosity, I would give him genuine proof of my love!

I crumpled that letter convulsively. Nowhere did I find a cry from the heart. Oh, my God, I thought, what held him back? Why didn't he show spontaneous feeling? How could he leave me alone when my soul was in such a state of distress? The last sentence affected me like a scalpel which would have cut into living flesh. He wanted to know everything about Albert, whose noble genius had become an object of analysis for his cold, reclusive intellect. Well, no! I thought, I would not continue with the dissection of that great wounded heart. That would be like treason. I would stop. On the first day I ought to have refused to expose Albert's drama. And yet could I have done anything else? To conceal part of my life from Léonce was to love him only halfway and consequently not to love him, because according to the profound injunction of the *Imitation,* "Let my love know no bounds." He whose love has limits, doesn't love at all.[1]

But did he have an unlimited love for me? Alas, I didn't see any sign of it in that letter. But other letters were more tender. They had made my heart expand and filled it with contentment. It wasn't a dream. I really was loved. I was convinced in his arms and reassured in his letters. Suddenly I was seized by a violent desire to reread them. I pulled out several at random from the strongbox I kept them in, and as their calm, measured tenderness took hold of me, I felt my serenity return. He loves me! I repeated with sweet tears, and in that confidence I found the strength to tell Albert everything. I was ready to confess my love the way the first Christians confessed their faith.

At that moment I heard Albert's voice. Marguerite had met him on the staircase and was going to let him in my study. My first impulse was to hide Léonce's letters. But that was followed at once by another idea, and I left the letters scattered over my worktable.

Albert came in. He was a little wan, but his very studied manner of dress gave him an appearance of health.

"So, you wanted to come see me," he said with a kiss. "Sending that kind thought cured me, and I have come to see you and

1. *Imitatio Christi* was written between 1390 and 1440 and is ascribed to Thomas à Kempis (1380–1471). It is alleged to be the most influential book in Christendom, aside from the Bible.

thank you. But, my dear, are you ill yourself?" he added, studying me carefully. "You're as white and cold as a marble bust. And you have tears in your eyes. Why are you crying? I want to know."

"You shall," I exclaimed, "you shall know everything. Albert, listen to me without getting angry and don't take away your friendship. Several times already I've wanted to tell you, and you haven't wanted to hear me out. Albert, I can't love you as a lover, because I love someone else, someone who loves me, and from whom nothing could separate me!"

He staggered and became so ghastly pale that I was afraid of the injury I might have done.

"Oh," he murmured slowly, "You're worth no more than *she* was. You, too; I give you love, and you make me suffer."

"Is it my fault," I asked, pressing his hands in mine, "if before meeting you I had given away my heart? Are you going to resent me for telling the truth the way you resented Antonia for telling lies? Was I supposed to deceive you? . . ."

"Yes, rather than snatch away that dream that was going to let me live again. So good-bye forever. I don't want to know anything more."

"You are harsh," I told him. "And you ill repay my loyalty. Was I supposed to treat you like a child who can't bear to have anyone step in between his desires and their impossibility? Oh, my dearest Albert, if the confidence of a strong, sincere mind frightens you, why were you surprised when Antonia lied to you? She must have realized in the depths of her genius that men will always deny us women freedom in love and dignity in frankness."

"Oh, be quiet!" he shouted, losing his composure. "I really don't care what you say. I prefer to look at you so pale and dejected. Your looks at least lead me to believe that you suffer from the pain you're inflicting."

"Oh yes," I agreed, kissing him as I would have kissed my son,

"I suffer to see you unhappy. I would so much rather change it into happiness."

"You have the persuasiveness of kindness," he replied. "And you make me see that I wasn't rational. It is true, I can't keep you from loving someone else, but what I could have done, what I certainly would have done when I was younger and better looking is take his place. Let's see. This isn't possible. This lover is not a husband. He is not even an assiduous lover, since he lets you languish like this."

His voice had suddenly taken on considerable detachment. He seemed to be smiling with lust.

"How about it, my dear? Shall we try a bit of love-making? Afterwards, you may prefer me to this terrible absentee."

"No!" I cried, hurt but fortified by his change in tone. "He alone attracts me. He alone is my type."

"Ah, well, I understand," he said, looking at himself in the mirror. "I have the same effect on you that Antonia had on me at our last meeting. But if that's the way it is, why don't you avoid me? Why, on the contrary, do you keep after me? And why do you weep over me?"

"Because in your genius there is something eternally young and handsome, which, distinct from romantic love, exerts a powerful seduction, an ideal attraction. I would not want to betray him, but I would not want to lose you; you are my beloved poet. You hold my trembling soul in your hands. Don't you realize that?"

"You're a kind creature," he said. "I'll try to forget my egoistic desires and hear you out. Come now, tell me whom you love. Does he at least deserve his good fortune?"

"What I would say wouldn't let you know him very well," I answered. "I have all the bias and blindness of love. But read these letters. Be for me the judicious heart receiving the confidence of a friend."

He took himself in hand and picked up a letter at random, motivated somewhat, I suspect, by curiosity.

It was painful watching him read. My head bent towards him, I tried to figure out the impressions he was getting from his eyes, his lips, alternately smiling or pursed, the fleeting wrinkles on his forehead. He read twenty or so of them without a pause, without a word. But I saw on his face, like in a mirror, all the reactions in his soul. I saw from one moment to the next his impatience with familiarity that was too coarse; his genius' contempt of those tedious disquisitions on art and fame tactlessly mixed in with expressions of love; his mocking pity of Léonce's monstrous personality which increased continually in his isolation the way pyramids in the desert keep growing beneath the layers of sterile sand covering and compressing them. Sometimes I saw bitterness and scorn, betrayed by a cutting ironic glance that seemed to whiplash certain racial vices which Léonce's letters exposed. He had read everything, and not once did I detect a sign of involuntary sympathy for the truth of that love which had taken over my life.

"Well?" I ventured, undone by his silence, questioning him since I could see he wasn't going to speak.

"Stéphanie, my dear," he replied, studying me sadly, "you are loved by that man's brain, but not by his heart."

"Don't speak badly of him," I cried. "You would be suspect."

"Don't go suspecting me of being jealous of that Léonce," he retorted, raising his head proudly. "No, I am reassured, because I'm worth more than he is, worth more by the sincerity of my emotions. In my old, damaged heart there is more warmth and enthusiasm than in that cold, inert thirty-year-old heart. I am reassured, I repeat, and I am no longer jealous because I am certain that one day you will love me and no longer love him. There are too many differences between you. Even while your feelings try to blend, too much shocks and grates. Sooner or later you will become enemies. And then, dead or alive, you will love me. If dead, it will be a happiness to make me quiver in my casket, feeling you are all mine!"

"Albert," I implored, "you have a place in my heart, but show some mercy. Don't kill the poor love affair which has kept me alive for ten years. For ten years others besides yourself have hurled themselves against its strength and have drawn back at its steadfastness. It's an inaccessible rock where no one may tread. You can torment me with your doubts and afflict me with your predictions, but I feel within the will to love forever and the certainty of being loved. The love which you don't find in these letters, for me quivers and burns on every line. You have the diffident eye of defiance, and defiance makes you an atheist. I am confident, I believe, and I sense the hidden god!"

While I was speaking, I had seized the open letters in my hands and held them out like witnesses.

"If I explicated them in front of you," Albert continued, "you would say I am cruel. The hour hasn't struck for you to hear the truth."

"I fear nothing," I replied, "for nothing can undermine my love."

"All right, then, you will hear me out. The fight is on between that man and me, and I will not show bad sportsmanship, fighting with the arms he has furnished. He is not only odious to me because I love you but because I sense in him also the antagonist of my spirit and all my instincts. Look at this one," he said, picking up a letter and glancing through it. "Here the young man positively on fire with love regales you with a four-page apologia on solitude. You are his life, he says, and he willingly lives apart from you in order to bury himself in frenetic labor. He suppresses his heart's affections in hopes of being inspired. It's absolutely as if we suppressed a lamp's oil in hopes of making it burn brighter. Think back over the lives of all our great men. They tamed their genius by loving! What do these petty Origens of art for art's sake want?[2] Do they imagine that self-mutilation will help them procreate?

"Here I find," he continued, taking up another letter, "that he presumes to surpass us all in the correctness of style. Naive arrogance! As if writing was a matter of symmetry, marquetery, and floor polish. If the idea does not make the word throb, what importance will it have anyway? If perfect pleats of material shudder on a mannequin, will I be moved?" And Albert broke into the sneering laugh that the fresh young girl slings at contrived beauty of a painted coquette.

He went on. "This man has been working for four years on a long novel which he tells you about, day in, day out. Each day he adds a painfully worked out page, and there where inspired writers experience the energizing of spiritual exhilaration, he confesses that he experiences only the agonies of the craft. He's the pedagogue who at the hour of creation feels as torpid as a bump on a log, while any schoolboy can fantasize like Cherubim.[3] I know another pedant of the same species as your Léonce, who cloistered himself for two years to imitate one of my poems, the liveliest in manner and the least didactic. In our times we have

2. It is hard to find Albert's comparison especially apt. He is extremely unlikely to have read this early Egyptian defender of Christianity against paganism. Perhaps Albert considers the devotees of art for art's sake belaboring the obvious also. If Albert were aware of the unverifiable account of Origen's self-castration, he would see an analogy with Léonce, presumably immolating himself by seclusion.

3. Cherubim is a page in Beaumarchais' *Le Mariage de Figaro*.

slow, sure, mathematical procedures for these imitations of Romantic literature, just as there used to be for counterfeit Classical literature. For example, Campistron aped Racine.[4] A sculptor in my set who has turned out more fine phrases than fine statues, has called my patient imitator a pawn in the Romantic chess game.[5] You may be sure that the book your lover has been gestating for forty-eight months will be a flagrant, heavy-handed compilation of Balzac!"

"Does one bestow genius upon oneself?" I cried. "Not everyone can have a creative spirit. Wishing won't make it so. But it's an effort of the intelligence having its own grandeur to pursue beauty without respite and approach it. You cannot deny that despite his lack of genius he possesses this powerful will to beauty. It's not his fault, if it's not greater."

"Well, who would dream of humiliating him," replied Albert, "if he didn't display his monstrous arrogance himself? In the letters you had me read, he's always hovering overhead like a condor, who with all his weight, imagines he's superior to an eagle! How loftily he passes judgment on all contemporary writers. He is kind enough to make an exception for Chateaubriand, Hugo, and myself, which makes little difference to me, my dear Marquise. But what disdain he heaps on great writers whom he will never equal. Sainte-Rive, for example, what a tone he takes to despise Sainte-Rive's marvelous psychological novel on love, one of the most impressive books of our times—without understanding it, of course.[6] None of this will probably hinder this presumptuous upstart, if he ever publishes his book, from going to beg Sainte-Rive for a few laudatory comments."

4. Jean Galbert de Campistron (1656–1723) was a derivative dramatist.

5. Albert may be referring to Antonie Auguste Préault (1809–79) who was called Aristophanes by his friends.

6. This novel is Sainte-Beuve's *Volupté* (1834).

And Albert crumpled the letter where Léonce made fun of this famous critic.

"But none of this implicates his heart and has little to do with my love," I kept protesting.

"Are you claiming that you can cut a person in two?" Albert jeered. "No indeed, nature is more logical than your love. Everything in an organism is either a coordinate or a complement. Your Léonce's heart is the manifest and palpable corollary of his brain. His heart is an indefinably dilated organ, but it is insensitive. It's an empty gibbosity where everything goes in and nothing comes out, like Harlequin's humpback," he added, laughing harder.

"Oh, you won't dislodge my idol with jokes like that!" I told him.

"Oh, you're right," he replied, bitter and ironic, "this gentleman deserves being taken seriously. By all means. I agree, and you are going to see, my dear, how he will profit!" And at this he picked up two letters which he had put to one side. "Two proofs, two attestations that he furnishes himself, on the tenderness and generosity in his heart." Albert paused. "One day the two of you were passing by the statue of Corneille. He was pontificating on this simplehearted great man, and you, in the touching effusion of your love, replied, 'I'd rather be loved by you than have the fame of Corneille'. Oh, if Antonia had said something like that to me about Michaelanglo or Dante when we were in Italy, I would have thanked her, blessed her, and clasped her all the more passionately in my arms. But what does this man feel? He reminds you of that ineffable exclamation in a letter. He censures it in no uncertain terms. He has the nerve to say that this loving exclamation has lowered you in his esteem, in spite of himself, because he will never understand putting feeling ahead of fame. Oh, Marquise, people who are truly inspired and who have written sublime things haven't uttered such sublimities in cold blood. A calculated obsession with fame as ruthless as this couldn't invade a heart happily in love. In reading the maxims he spouts off on art and renown, you'd think you were reading pompous aphorisms pronounced by some educated bourgeois!"

"Bourgeois? You can't call him bourgeois!" I interrupted with the naiveté that true love keeps forever, long after the age for naiveté. "It's obvious you don't know him. No one makes more fun of that flock of Philistines, as your friend Heinrich Heine used to say, than he does."

"Exactly," retorted Albert, "the way upstart nobles make fun of commoners while feeling the shoe pinch."

"This example, after all," he continued, "is just idle talk, the distant voice of a god who wants to dazzle you. Some Brahman incarnation scolding a slave believer. But here is a postscript wherein lies his whole heart. He wanted to confirm the popular opinion that the real motive appears at the end of the letter. Here I can say like Pilate: *Ecce homo!* But I'm not the blackguard in this case . . ."

"Stop it! This is enough!" I cried. "What did you find that was so monstrous? Get to the point!"

"Oh, this is more than betrayal," he kept on, waving the letter, "more than a skulking act. It's the insensitivity of stone vis-à-vis a heart that dares not cry out but bleeds in secret. Marquise, the least of your friends in such a circumstance would have figured out something ingenious and tactful. Duchemin himself would have thought of something, yes, this makes Duchemin rise in my estimation, because in his lust, Duchemin ceases to be avaricious, while this other creature in his sentimentality remains a Harpagon!"[7]

"I don't follow you. What are trying to say? I won't permit

7. Harpagon is Molière's miser in *L'Avare* (1668).

anyone to insult him," I was trembling with anger and emotion.

"But he's branded himself with his own hand," Albert insisted. "Listen, my poor dear soul, and judge for yourself. I see, I infer that sometime back in the straitened circumstances to which your lawsuit reduced you, to combat your poverty with a valiant smile, you thought about selling that big, beautiful album where all the geniuses of our time have inscribed their homage.[8] Chateaubriand begins the list, followed by Hugo, Rossini, Meyerbeer, Manzoni. That's where you keep that eloquent page of Humboldt you mentioned. This book, made for you, was truly dear to you, you were attached to it by every scruple of heart and mind, but less so than to your native pride. So, one day of distress, you sent it to England to the bookdealer of her Majesty the Queen, and you waited anxiously for some millionaire lord to buy this jewel of genius for a bit of gold. You wept when you sent it away, but what else could you have done? Selling it would be fortunate, for your dignity is worth more than this treasure. So you thought, and you waited every day for the happy news! But it didn't come. Well, I read here," once more he waved the letter, "that since this man was going to England, you asked him to see the Queen's bookdealer and tell you whether the album had been sold. How easy it would have been to lie. The lie of affection, the tactful, inspired lie which lets us oblige a friend mysteriously through subterfuge. This man is rich, he travels, he spares nothing to keep his ego resting on a bed of roses. He has written you many a time, in bursts of fantasy generosity, that he suffers over the privation you live in, that he would like to be a magician and put you in a white marble palace trimmed in gold. He knew well enough the nullity

8. Flaubert took Colet's album to London in September 1851. It does not appear to have preyed on his mind. The facts of this imbroglio will never be known, but depending upon one's point of view Colet was generous or prodigal, while Flaubert was frugal or stingy.

of such a wish. But when he discerned your extreme want, he never dreamed of saying to you, the sole love of his life, you whose pride he knows so well, 'The album is sold!' You would have believed him, and if a doubt had crossed your mind, his affection would have set it to rest. And he himself would have become the blessed owner of something which had belonged to you and where all the geniuses of our time have left their mark. A fragrance of love, intelligence, and kindness would have escaped from that secret act and perfumed his solitude!

"Ah, ah," Albert continued his harsh jeering, "you can imagine whether the man you prefer to me cares about all that! When it comes to the news you are so anxiously awaiting from London, he describes only the studies he is making of British manners. Then, bringing his letter to a close, he suddenly remembers your request and in the form of a final critical observation on the English, he tosses it into a postscript: 'By the way, the album hasn't been sold. It was a delusion to suppose that in this horde of lords and merchants who didn't understand Byron, there would be someone to buy these pages of genius.' That's all, but you must agree, Marquise, that these lines are luminous and that they make his character as bright as day. Oh, really," he pitched the letter contemptuously, "it would be more to that man's credit if he had struck you in an hour of jealousy and rage than to be the imperturbable Norman and play this cunning bourgeois trick! How did the blood of the ancestors that your mother transmitted to you, the blood mixed with the energy and sincerity of your grandfather of the Convention, how did this generous proud blood not boil in your veins when your lover was this base?"

While Albert was speaking, I was experiencing a kind of agony that only a woman, only a mother could ever understand. It was something like the mortal terrors of miscarriage when the dead weight which yesterday still we could feel twitch and jerk, pulls away from our living womb. All our maternal instincts revolt. We should like to keep and carry forever the burden that is tearing us apart. But the deed is done. The stillborn tortures us as it escapes.

That's how I felt beneath Albert's lashing tongue. I thought I could feel my love plummet and dissolve.

I was too gloomy to say anything. Albert looked at me and saw the tears streaming down my face.

"What have I done?" he asked. "Oh, if you could love me, I would console you, but since you don't, all I've been, I can tell, is an instrument of torture."

He covered his face with his hands, for some time neither of us said anything.

I was still weeping, staring wildly at those letters, now desecrated where Albert had told my miserable fortune.

He stood up abruptly and took my hand.

"Let's not prolong this agony. It's good-bye, since you cannot love me. This morning I wanted to rebuild my life. And you've brought in the pick and axe, and my dismantled ship sails rudderless again. Well, we can't do anything more for each other."

He was on the point of leaving.

"Oh, no, please don't say that," I said, joining my hands as in prayer, "I implore you: let us stay friends. Don't hold it against me that I love him. He has been the only great love of my life, as Antonia was for you. Don't punish me for having been honest with you. Don't abandon me in my anguish. Don't leave me alone with the terrifying suspicion that I am not loved."

"Since it is not by me you wish to be," he replied, "what are you asking of me? Seeing each other to make ourselves suffer every hour is stupid and morbid. Let's part on a lovely dream. I shall not see you again, but I shall keep the memory of you as long as my heart beats."

"No, no," I cried. "I don't want to lose you. Promise me you will come again."

"I shall come back only at your call, because I am going to fall again into mire where there can be no reflection of the stars."

He went out, and when I heard him shut my door decisively, it seemed that an insurmountable barrier would separate us from that point on.

CHAPTER XXII

I DIDN'T WRITE to Léonce for several days. That surprised and worried him. My letters were one of the liveliest distractions of his solitude. Less for the love they contained—I realized that quite well later—than for the breath of Paris they carried. I was the daily gazette bringing him news from the social whirl and the world of letters. Since I met Albert, he found these daily letters even more interesting. My sudden silence disturbed him, jarred him from his complacency. He implored me with words which I thought were truly tender to put an end to this torture which kept him from working and living. If I were suffering, if something was upsetting me, I had only to let him know, and he would join me within three days.

So, why doesn't he come in person? I asked myself whether I would always be the one who felt desire, who called and waited?

However, in my state of mind it would have been painful to see him. I needed some time to re-establish some calm and confidence in my heart. His letters helped do that. They became more and more soothing. It seemed as if he guessed what storm was raging in me and wanted to pacify me with gentle words. I replied without any embittered remarks but without mentioning our next meeting which I had so passionately desired. For the first time I almost lied to him. I explained my silence by a demanding assignment which I had to finish and put off his questions about Albert, saying I wasn't seeing him anymore and thought he was out of town.

And, in fact, Albert had not reappeared. The days slipped by. Every morning I was hopeful, and every evening I said to myself, "It's really over now. He's not going to come back." In my anxiety I sent Marguerite over several times to see how he was. His porter always replied that Monsieur de Lincel wasn't receiving visitors, he was spending his nights out and shutting himself in to sleep during the day. His absence preoccupied me entirely. I heard echoing all around me everything charming and passionate he had said. I was living, you might say, in the vibration of his spirit and love. His absence made me feel my solitude. My son missed him also, for he had gotten very fond of him. He asked me repeatedly, "Why doesn't Albert come back to see us?"

July was as rainy and dreary as November that year. I spent the hours shivering, looking out at the rain which streamed across the windowpanes and fell upon the leaves of the treetops in a steady monotone. The stormy frustrations brought on by the nice weather were being tranquilized. I was no longer affected by the perilous effluvia of a searing atmosphere which permeated and burned me as I breathed it in. I submitted as if to a foretaste of sudden old age where the heart and blood are pacified with only a placid sympathy remaining for those who were once tempestuously loved. My melancholy was pleasant; I felt free from indignation against Léonce and free from fear of Albert. I thought about the hour when death would bear all three of us to that mysterious city which brings souls together. I said to myself, "Unhappy are those having loved in life, who cannot love in death." Then I would have such ideas of mercy that I would have liked to give the kiss of peace, the soul's embrace, to all who were dear to me here below. One morning when I was lost in one of these charitable reveries, watching the rain that wouldn't let up, my son got my attention by pulling my sleeve.

"Mama, let's go see Albert. I saw him last night in my dreams. He was pale as could be, stretched out on his bed. He held out his arms and called me by name."

"We'll go, darling," I answered, "but I'd rather wait till the sun came out."

"No," the child argued, "because then he'd go out, and in bad weather like this, we'll find him at home."

We left around two o'clock. The rain had stopped, but large clouds were still racing across the gray sky.

"Let's hurry," my son urged, "we can take advantage of the lull in the storm and get there before it breaks out and soaks us."

We crossed the Place de la Concorde and the Tuileries quickly. When we reached Rue Castiglione, we saw in the arcades a delivery boy with a backpack full of flowers.

"It would be nice," my son said, "to give Albert a pretty pot of camellias like the ones that man is carrying. If he's sick, he'll enjoy looking at them."

"It's all right with me," I replied. "This is the day for the flower market at the Madeleine. Do you feel like walking all the way there?"

"Oh, I'd go farther than that to make Albert happy," he answered.

Once we were in the midst of all the fragrant potted plants and bouquets, I said to him, "Choose one you like for our friend."

He decided on a beautiful camellia with pink petals. A little delivery boy shouldered the pot we bought, and we resumed our walk to Albert's.

As we were approaching the main entry, my son cautioned, "I

think it's best just to pass through without asking the porter anything. He could very well tell us Albert's not in, while upstairs we'll see for ourselves." As he spoke, he took the pot from the delivery boy, and we slipped by to the stairway. I was a little apprehensive about going on up, but my son's company gave me courage.

He put the camellias on the threshold and then rang the bell with aplomb.

The servant, who recognized us, looked glad to see us.

"Please tell Monsieur de Lincel," the child said, "that someone who loves him has come to call."

It was not the servant who came back to let us in. It was Albert. He ran up crying, "Why, it's you!" Then bending over, he began kissing my son so passionately that I knew those kisses were meant for me.

"Oh, my dear Stéphanie, so you've stayed a good friend after all? What a charming thing you've done! If I'd known you were coming, I would have filled my apartment with flowers to receive you." He clutched the potted plant. He pressed his haggard cheeks and burning forehead against the cool blossoms. Then he turned to the child and kissed him again. He was wearing a white wool dressing gown which floated on his frail frame. His neck, without a cravat, stood out stringy and fleshless, while his cheekbones poked out his sallow face.

"You've been ill," I said.

"Yes, but only for twenty-four hours. The worst is over. It was inevitable," he added, "considering what I did to forget you. But you come in one of my better moments. I'm not strong enough to do anything rash, and I feel good enough to savor the sweetness of seeing you. Since you've been so gracious as to pay a call, Marquise, you must take a tour of my apartment. I have over here on this side the charming portrait of a woman whom I greet sadly every morning when I awake. She looks at me with a smile that is almost affectionate, but her eyes are so haughty that I must lower my own."

As he said this, he pushed open the large French doors between the living room and his bedroom, and I could see at the foot of his bed a little charcoal sketch he'd asked for one day while going through my album.

My son who was right behind us said, "Why, that's mama! Now that proves you like us, so why don't you come see us anymore?"

"You're too curious, young man, and it's not for me to tell you."

"Come on, don't be mean now," my son said, "Come out this very day for some fresh air and have dinner with us."

"Your mother won't like that," Albert told him.

I held out my hand, "You know that's not true."

"Well, well, life still has blessed hours in store. I'd be a fool indeed not to seize them on the wing."

He led us back into the living room, then went back into his bedroom where he quickly got dressed.

Ten minutes later we were in a carriage going down the Champs-Elysées, as we had so many times before. But now it wasn't a silent, torrid night. It was the hour when people swarm into the Bois de Boulogne on horseback or in a calèche. The sky had cleared, and a soothing light smiled through the white clouds.

My son, who was sitting on Albert's lap, was asking him one question after another, forcing him to look at everything that caught his own eye and leaving Albert little possibility of paying attention to me.

I watched and listened. At that moment Albert seemed to me like a beloved brother showing affection to his sister's child. I felt no uneasiness at all. I was completely given over to the joy of being with Albert again.

"Where do you want to go, my little despot?" he asked my son.

"To the Hippodrome," the child replied without a second's hesitation.

My son's glee was great, seeing the horseback numbers and the acrobatic acts. With Albert's incredibly mobile mind, he could go from the most sublime or heartrending ideas to the most comic and juvenile fantasies and share my son's high spirits. You'd have thought them two schoolboys on a holiday.

I was very comfortable to be on the outside, isolated by my son's babble and Albert's verve. They both chattered constantly. I was enjoying one of those hours when the soul rests, putting down for a moment its burden of passion and pain.

As we were coming back down the Champs-Elysées to go to my apartment, there was an even heavier flow of people out for a ride. We saw Duchemin preening himself in an ambassador's carriage. He smiled like a Cheshire cat to see me with Albert.

"I'll never forgive that grotesque cynic for the mean trick he played on you with Frémont," Albert said.

And forthwith, to puncture Duchemin with the arrows of his wit, he improvised a cuttingly comic quatrain at the pedant's expense. It had a lively quick beat, like those aerial taps from the paws of Charles Nodier's Trilby.[1]

"Well, we seemed destined to meet the mean and foolish today," Albert observed. "Look, over there are Sansonnet and Daunis in the same coupe. While the former was a peer of France, he strove ardently, but vainly, to alienate me from my friend the prince. He has never forgiven me for having told some dull journalist who compared him to La Fontaine, that he was hardly even Florian's ape. As for Daunis, he has kept me from being performed at a

1. Nodier was the host at the Arsenal in Chapter II.

theater where he used to be director because, ten years ago, I refused to let him make a five-act play out of one of my comedies.[2] Without undue pride, I think you will agree, Marquise, that would have been like crushing a flower with a paving stone. They deserve their quatrain, too," he added, and forthwith another epigram, sharp and wild, hit the coupe carrying Sansonnet and Daunis like a handful of mud.

I was enthralled with these witticisms, so concise, so clean, that came to Albert when he played with words.

"Come, my dear Marquise, try your hand. I've taught you to compose French verse. You've promised to try. Take your turn. It's now or never."

"And who is to be the target of my rapier?" I asked.

"Use me," he laughed. "There are days when I am a fair target for irony. I permit you to try your beautiful teeth on me."

A spark of his burning wit must have set me on fire because without hesitation, I did a quatrain with the same beat. It was teasing set of lines on the loose ends in his life. He laughed heartily at the grotesque note of my parting shot which just came to me.

He, in turn shot back the same number of lines railing me rather crudely for being too idealistic, so that his thought and his words made a sharp comic contrast. I caught the ricochet of the epigram and sent it against an actress passing at that moment in the imposing carriage of a Russian prince.

Albert shot back again. He aimed four satiric lines against a chubby-cheeked critic, who was powerless to create and tireless to destroy.[3] Then four more against the old novelist Sidonville whom

2. Sansonnet is possibly Gustave Planche (1808–57), a Musset enemy for many years. Claris de Florian (1755–94) was a fabulist. Daunis fits F. A. Harel, director at the Odéon when plans were first made to produce *Un Caprice*, eventually a success at the Comédie Français.

3. This could be Charles Magnin, a dinner guest in Chapter XIX. Sainte-

he spotted in a tilbury.[4] "There's a 64-year-old fool who still thinks he's irresistible," Albert cried. "One day at one of my cousin's, he said something really memorable. Seeing my cousin's daughter, a beautiful fourteen-year-old, looking a little sad, he leaned over toward the mother and murmured mysteriously, 'I hope I'm not making her starry-eyed'."

We got so much fun out of this rhyming game that we kept it up during dinner and part of the evening. All literature was touched. Even Victor and René themselves were not spared some good-natured sarcasm.

When we separated, Albert bantered, "You know, Marquise, it's a pity you don't have a slightly darker complexion and a slightly thinner figure. If you did, you could have put on men's clothing—which would have helped with the illusion—and we would have stayed the best of friends for life."

CHAPTER XXIII

I DIDN'T ANALYZE my impressions of those hours with Albert. But I did know I felt less depressed, more lighthearted, better disposed to work and live.

We didn't say "au revoir," when he left. Still, I hoped that by

---

Beuve fits this chubby-cheeked description in a 1856 picture. He is, however, sympathetically portrayed here as Sainte-Rive. Another strong possibility is Jules Janin (1804–74), theater critic who held forth at the *Journal des Débats* for forty years.

4. In 1852 this would have to be a writer born in 1788. Villemain, already vilified as Duchemin, would have been the right age. Such a remark would have been quite in character also for Ulric Guttinguer (1785–1866), minor Romantic novelist much given to post-adolescent escapades.

avoiding certain emotions, we would both settle into a cheerful brother-sister relationship.

As for Léonce, I felt that the awful interpretation Albert had given to his letters was receding in my mind. However, I hadn't risked rereading them for fear of finding the cruel confirmation myself. Fortunately those I was now receiving from him daily were so tender that my shaken confidence was steadily growing stronger.

One morning Albert wrote to propose going to the Théâtre Français to see Voltaire's *Oedipe*. He had promised himself a hilarious evening watching all the long-winded Alexandrines drag past. He added, that if I were agreeable, he would offer a seat to an old gentleman of our acquaintance.

The gentleman was an old dandy of the Empire. He took Voltaire's tragedies seriously, spoke respectfully of De Jouy's *Scylla*, and never questioned the sublimity of Pichat's *Leonidas*.[1]

I accepted Albert's invitation, and as the hour of the performance approached, he came to pick me up in a carriage. The weather had become scorching again, and the evening promised to be so suffocating that I put on a gown of white mousseline to make tolerable the double oppressiveness of the atmosphere and the tragedy. The lines of my shoulders and bosom were visible beneath the light fabric, and my arms were almost completely bare. I wore a hat of very light rice straw, decorated with a spray of pink magnolias. Albert complimented me on the elegance of

1. Voltaire's *Oedipe* dates from 1718. The other playwrights are even more derivative Neoclassicists. Victor-Joseph Etienne de Jouy (1764–1846) had *Scylla* first performed in 1822; he was also a librettist. Michel Pichat (1790–1828), contemporary of Villemain and Cousin, had *Leonidas* first performed in 1825. There are too few clues to know who the "dandy" was, nor is it certain that Colet and Musset would have considered that they needed a chaperone. His companion-housekeeper, a woman, often accompanied them.

my ensemble, but immediately his sweeping glance stopped, fixed embarrassingly on the bodice of my gown.

I tried to divert his attention by chatting about the actor who was going to play Oedipus, "What courage an actor must have to recite a role like that!"

"Still, if Jocasta had your arms," he responded, moving closer.

"But you're crushing my dress," I cautioned, "and I want your old friend to find me charming!"

"Don't act coquettish; you know perfectly well that you disturb me," he snapped.

At that moment the carriage reached the theater entrance, so I was spared worrying about what could come next.

The curtain had just gone up, when we entered the box where the old dévoté of tragedies was waiting for us. Finger on lips, he warned us with an imperious "Shhhh!"

"Shush the play instead," Albert burst out laughing. And he proceeded to scandalize the Voltaire admirers present by parodying each line. He was so funny that I was overcome with irrepressible giggling. The old dévoté was so indignant that he threatened to leave us. Menacing murmurs rose all around us from the white-haired spectators whose enthusiasm was offended. And when you think that these same hotheads, so zealous to defend this bad tragedy, would have repudiated Voltaire's philosophical writings, banned his masterpiece *Candide*, and found his marvelous letters boring! Oh human stupidity! . . .

At each intermission, Albert left the box for a few minutes, and I was surprised to notice that the usual pallor of his cheeks was giving way to a growing flush. Once, leaning toward the house, he rested his ungloved hand on my nearly bare shoulder. His hand positively burned me.

"Do you feel bad?" I asked.

"Feel bad? What a question! I've never felt better." And he

began to relate sotto voce the wildest anecdotes about the actress playing Jocasta. His volubility, his gestures—all his movements—struck me as signs of nervous overexcitement which made me a little alarmed.

Meanwhile, the symmetrical tragedy had rolled bombastically to its final act. The bravos of the aged amateurs resounded. Our own dévoté advertised his extravagant ecstasy by leading the curtain calls for the actor playing Oedipus!

Albert seized that moment to bow perfunctorily to his other guest. Then grabbing my arm rather roughly, he hissed, "Let's get out quickly." We found our coupe waiting near the theater. But scarcely had I gotten seated next to Albert than his strange appearance set me trembling. His eyes glittered like carbuncles. His face was crimson. Without a word, he grabbed my arms with his bony hands, gripping me like vise.

"Albert, my dear, what's wrong?" I murmured, getting really terrified.

"What's wrong," he answered, leaden and sinister, "is you. You've tortured me long enough. You wore this dress just to tempt me." And with this, he began butting me with his head, trying to tear the mousseline of my bodice with his teeth.

"Please leave me alone. You're scaring me to death."

"So, be scared, what difference does that make? I've suffered enough. I don't want to suffer any more. You shouldn't dress like women who try to be provocative. Such women show more honesty and decency with loose manners than you do with your reticence. Come here, my beauty. The lion has roared. You must submit!"

I wondered whether he was mad or drunk. "Albert," I cried imperiously, "I swear that if you don't take yourself in hand, I'm going to jump out of the carriage this very instant, at the risk of my life."

"Ah," he snorted defiantly, "you wouldn't have the courage, and besides, I've got you in my grip."

I made a superhuman effort and managed to free myself from his clenched hands.

At that moment the carriage was speeding forbiddingly through the Place du Carrousel. I didn't even think of the danger. I opened the carriage door with a violent jerk and following the impulse of my southern blood—that Greek and Roman mixture that makes heroes, martyrs, and maniacs—I jumped. I was thrown about twenty feet on a heap of rubble from the houses then being demolished at the Doyenne Impasse. If my head had hit the ground, I would have been killed. But I landed on my knees, and since the rain of the preceding days had softened the broken plaster and lathes, I got only some skin burns. Inwardly, however, I felt such intense distress that I thought I was going to die without seeing my poor son again. With that thought came the memory of Léonce, and my limp arms made a gesture of farewell.

Dragging myself painfully through the wreckage, I reached a wall that had some large beams stacked against it. I lay down on the stack as if it were a bed and turned my face to the sky to take deep breaths of the revivifying night air.

I heard footsteps approaching, and I shuddered to recognize Albert's voice. He was calling my name, begging me to answer if I was there. I held my breath. The idea of seeing him again was more than I could bear. The wall I was backed against hid me from his view. He walked all around it without seeing me.

As he conducted his fruitless search, I heard him saying, "Oh God, has she died like the poor prince I loved so much?"

And giving up hope of finding me, he went back to the carriage waiting for him on the other side of the square.

Convinced by this that he could neither see me nor follow me, I crossed through the entry arch of the Louvre and rushed through the Pont des Arts. And I kept on running down the quays. Anyone who saw me pass at that hour of the night in my white dress, would have thought he saw a ghost.

I arrived home without stopping to get my breath and by the sheer speed of my flight proved that I hadn't broken anything in my sore, bruised body.

I found poor Marguerite sick with fright. "What happened to you?" she shrieked. Albert in a hair-raising state of agitation had just been by asking for me a few minutes earlier. Since I wasn't there, he wouldn't stop for questions. He kept repeating, "She's dead, she's dead . . . I'll go back to look for her again."

I reassured Marguerite and gave her emphatic orders not to let Albert see me. If he returned, she was to tell him that I was asleep and had forbidden him to come in. Then I ran to shut myself in my room where I threw myself on my knees at the head of my little boy's bed. I asked God's forgiveness for having forgotten this cherished, irreplaceable treasure for a single moment and swore that henceforth he would be the guiding influence in my life.

I looked at him with deep love. His expressive face was turned toward me, resting on the ripples of his curly hair. He was sleeping so peacefully that I didn't want to risk waking him with a kiss, but my look was a passionate caress. I stayed there, engrossed, still weeping at the thought I might never have seen him again. Finally, I rose after having placed my lips on the tips of his little toes, playing between his sheet and coverlet.

I was getting ready to get into bed when I heard Albert's voice. He was insisting on speaking to me. But abruptly he must have given in to Marguerite, for I heard nothing more but his footsteps moving off in the distance.

The next day Marguerite told me he really made her feel sorry for him. He was as pale as a corpse. He was weeping and trying to give her all the money he had on him if she would let him see me.

Not being able to go to sleep, I wrote to Léonce during the night.[2] I hid nothing of that terrifying adventure from him. I assured him—and it was true at the time—that his calm, even-tempered love seemed like happiness itself compared to such excessive, delirious passion.

I waited impatiently for his reply, rather, I waited for him. He didn't come. But in the letter I received I detected his anxiety of losing me through his emotional language. I shouldn't see Albert again, he said, because I could be touched by his repentance and he didn't deserve my forgiveness after the demented act which nearly cost me my life. "Oh, keep me, keep me," he implored in closing, "I'm better than he is."

In my first reading I was elated, but in thinking it over, I was indignant. He ought to have been at my side, not sent that cold piece of paper. Was it really the time to perfect some cold pages of his novel, when the tremors of the living drama of his heart should have taken all his attention?

As for Albert, at least he was trying to make reparations for a moment of madness by touching and untiring demonstrations of remorse. He had come three times during the day, and as I still refused to see him, he wrote me a letter of supplication the next morning. Great poet that he was, he still had no fear of wasting his time in futile errands, of giving himself over entirely to all-consuming cares, and thus of stealing a page or two from posterity! He felt instinctively that the palpitations of the heart are the essence of genius and that sap cannot be drained from a dead tree. Although already very ill, he climbed the steep stairway to

2. To judge from Flaubert's reaction in his letter of July 7–8, 1852, this chapter records the events of July 6. He told Colet it was good enough for a novel but chided her for not simply shouting to the coachman to stop and rescue her.

my fifth floor apartment twice a day without complaining or getting discouraged. Oh you great storm-tossed heart, how could one stay angry with you? Even if you had killed me, I feel that I would have forgiven you as I died.

I admit that I was tempted to see him again, but it seemed to me that the resolution I had made brought dignity and safety back into my life. I wasn't thinking of myself. I was thinking of my precious child, and, to some extent, of Léonce.

One day when Albert had arrived sad and suffering and was vainly insisting as usual to speak to me, my son heard him. He ran in to see him despite my prohibition.

"If Mama doesn't love you any more," he was saying, "I do, and I'll go out with you."

"Oh, yes, do come," Albert replied, "then your mother will have to show herself if she wants to get you away from me."

I rang for Marguerite and told her to bring my son back. He came in stamping with rage. For the first time in his life he was insubordinate. I've never seen a stronger sympathy than that child's for Albert. To calm him down I had to promise that I would receive his friend in a few days. He went gleefully back to report the good news, and I heard him laughing to Albert, "I made Mama obey!"

The next day as I was getting up, I received this charming note from Albert:

> Don't prolong my torture. And since, God be praised, you were not injured, please forgive my involuntary misconduct. I have never committed a premeditated bad action. Please, let me see you this very day. I have written a ballad for you, and like Oronte I want to read it it to you. A word from you, and I shall come running![3]

3. Oronte is the would-be poet in Molière's *The Misanthrope* (1666).

I couldn't bring myself to say "Come!" But I found a middle ground between the heart which says "yes" and the mind which says "no." I had his servant informed that I wouldn't be going out during the day.

When he arrived toward the end of the afternoon, I was alone. Without a word, he took both my hands in his and pressed them for a few minutes. He looked deep into my eyes.

"It's really true," he said finally, "You're not suffering. Isn't there even a small part of you which remembers my madness?"

"Shhh," I replied, smiling, "let's not talk about it ever."

"But will you ever forget that dreadful moment? And if you ask me not to mention it, is that really a complete pardon?"

"Do you doubt me? I'm not a person who hides things. I love and hate openly. If I leave my hands in yours, that's a reconciliation pact that I sign with you for life."

"How can I not love you?" he continued. "But while loving you I am still capable of some act of madness. Who will keep me within the impossible bounds of tranquil tenderness?"

"I myself," I said, "in not giving in again, my dear Albert, to the sweet temptation of accompanying you on an outing, paying you a call, accepting attractive diversions which can end in catastrophe."

"Oh, I knew it," he cried out, "you're going to forgive me and avoid me. Is that your idea of kindness?"

"You're not following me. You will come to visit me. You have seen how my son adores you, and I, . . . well, I would not be able to forgo seeing you without being supremely sad. Now, my dear poet, won't you recite the ballad you mentioned."

"Here it is," he said, holding out a sheet of paper, "but as for reading it to you, what would be the point? What it says, you don't want to hear. It's a firm decision?" he continued, "I shall see you henceforth only here with your son or with other third parties?"

"That's the vow I made when I got back alive to my sleeping son."

He seemed to be thinking it over.

"It would be unpardonable to fight you on this," he said. "You're a stout heart. But before my dream dies forever, indulge me one last time. You know how it is when a friend is leaving on a long trip, you listen to him, give in to him, happily let him have his way during those last few hours."

"But why such an analogy? We're not taking leave of each other. You'll come back. We'll see each other again, won't we?" I added, feeling in my turn a kind of panic.

"Come now, my dear Marquise, no equivocation. Let at least the frankness of our farewell shed its beams on our memories. We'll see each other again, but as friends, never again as lovers in waiting."

"You're right. That's the way it has to be. You feel it yourself," I murmured.

"Oh, don't make me a party to your decision! You came to it without thinking of me! If you hadn't had another love in your heart, a voice would have come to my defense. But there was no voice. I can hope for nothing better than second place. That's not the place you want when you love. Second place is humiliating; it drives you wild, when it doesn't make you ridiculous. That's why we have all those jokes at the husband's expense."

"But never at the expense of a brother or friend," I interjected quickly.

He was silent a few moments, then resumed more quietly, "You're right. Your loyal sincerity has removed my resentment. And when I think of you, it will be gently and sweetly. I am resigned to your wishes, but won't you in turn, grant a heartsick child's wish without apprehension? Your son must often say to you, 'promise me something before I tell you what.' And you promise, having confidence in his innocence. Well, have confidence also in my respect."

I held out my hand. "Speak, Albert dear, I am ready to do what you wish."

"I wish to return with you this very evening to see for the last time that path in the Bois du Boulogne where you loved me for one minute! I wish, when we return tonight, for you to read my poem and respond in the same immortal tongue I've taught you. I wish, finally, for you to bring, some dark day, the lines you have composed for me. You will sit in my chair, if I'm not there, and when I return, I shall find your shadow. Because," he added in a tone of conviction, "you don't know what visions I have!"

While he was speaking his haggard eyes and livid face would have made anyone believe in ghosts! It was some ineffable, fantastic quality he had.

"Well, shall we leave?" he asked, almost lightheartedly, picking up his hat.

I had promised, and I didn't dare go back on my word, but I was terrified in spite of myself at the idea of being alone in a carriage with him.

But I made up my mind without thinking anymore about it. The stormy afternoon had brought the night on early. The sky was starless, and the wind, howling in the trees like autumn, twisted their upper branches and sent their leaves whirling.

As soon as we were in the carriage, he said to me calmly, very clearly, and with no change in tone, "I always see again those I've loved, whether death or absence separates us. They obstinately intrude upon my solitude where I am never alone."

He didn't look at me while he was saying this. He seemed to be staring into space. His face had the expression of a sleepwalker.

"For years now I've seen visions and heard voices. How can I doubt what all my senses confirm? How many times when night falls, have I seen and heard the young prince who was so dear to me and whom another friend struck down in a duel in front of me? But it's especially women who appear to me and call, those who have stirred my heart or whom I've clasped in my arms. They don't frighten me at all, but they arouse a singular sensation which is apparently unknown to other living persons. When that communication is taking place, it seems as if my mind is detached from my body to answer the voice of the spirits speaking to me. It's not always the dead who come to say 'Remember!' Sometimes the living, those far away and those nearby but abandoned, knock on my heart where they once had their place. Their passing breath blows away the oblivion hiding them. They are reanimated. They rear up the way phantoms would rear up from tombs whose stone had been removed. I see them again in their youth and beauty. Decomposition has not touche them. They do not change or alter or frighten me unless I stubbornly dash after them to uncover their mysterious fate.

"I remember meeting on a rather unfrequented beach in Brittany a sixteen-year-old English girl. She was so thin and tottering that she bent like a willow whenever the strong ocean winds would rise, catching her off guard on the strand. The effort she made to walk made her pale face red and blotchy. Her hair, swirling in the violent wind, beat against her frail body like unfolding wings. The hurricane seemed to be trying to carry her off. One day when I had followed her over the dunes, and she seemed to be trembling, ready to break under the threatening storm, I approached and without a word offered her my arm for support.

"She grabbed my hand and said without any self-consciousness, like a child who takes everything for granted, including death and its unknown terrors, 'See, I'm walking. I bend and straighten up without any pain, and I shall live two more years. Two years is a long time, so why feel bad?'

" 'I don't understand,' I murmured, very low, figuring that a too firm a tone of voice would knock her over.

" 'My mother is dead, and I'll die, too. The doctor said so to my aunt yesterday evening. I was hiding so I could hear. But he promised me two more years, and I want to spend them travelling, to see the whole earth, and to keep on singing.'

"While she was speaking, her mouth was smiling but her eyes, I thought, were weeping. I wondered whether she were mad or whether in her childish glee she wanted to scare me.

" 'And so, you're still singing,' I said, not quite knowing what to ask or answer.

" 'Yes, I am,' she replied with her unchanging smile, confiding and pure. 'You will come to my aunt's this evening to hear me.' And as we were a little farther from the beach so that the winds were less strong, she began to scamper up to the rock where someone was waiting for her. As she disappeared, she warbled a few clear, pearly notes, positively angelic.

"I went to her aunt's that very evening. When I arrived, she was at the piano singing. The instrument blended its voice with hers, or rather, it let her voice soar and held back its own vibrations. During that month I heard her sing every evening, and I came to adore her when she sang. By some kind of intuition that borders on the uncanny, that childlike soul could pour into her song passions she couldn't even have known the name of. She sent forth flames which never burnt her, sublime cries whose echo remained mute in her innocent heart. She had the power of those ancient sybils, possessed by a god unawares.

"One evening she blithely said to me, 'Tomorrow we're leaving for Palermo. But in two years, in the fall, when I am to die, you will see me again. I'll be in Paris at the Hotel Meurice. Don't forget. Instead of a white marble tomb, I want to be buried in a beautiful song of yours. I will shine forever in your lines, and I will be happy!'

"When she saw my eyes filling with tears, she said with her eternal smile, 'Don't feel sorry for me. I assure you that I will die singing.' And running her delicate fingers across her harp, she began to sing Mozart's *Requiem*.

"I listened, but I didn't dare look at her for fear I'd have second sight of her, dead. Completely upset, I left before she had finished singing, convinced that she would fly away in the last chord of the funereal hymn.

"Two years went by. I had forgotten her in the dissipation of my unbridled life. One evening at the Vaudeville as I was laughing at Odry's slapstick,[4] I felt on my ungloved right hand (the same hand which had touched hers that day on the beach) a chilling breath three times in succession. It was a shock that pulled me to attention. Immediately I heard a very low voice at my ear, 'So, why have you forgotten me?' The frail, smiling face of the girl who always sang, rose before me. She was walking, turning her head around, her neck bent down, beckoning me to follow her. I left the theater, following on her footsteps from street to street. We reached the Rue de Rivoli. We glided along the garden grill. The autumn wind blew the leaves from the trees, whirling them around our feet. We entered a wide gateway with its carriage doors wide open. Leaving at that very moment was the equipage of a famous doctor whom I recognized. I was still following the impalpable shade. She went up to the second floor, crossed the antechamber and a sitting room, raised a dark portiere and vanished from sight. I was alone in a dimly lit room. I heard someone

4. J. C. Odry (1781–1853), was a comic performer with legendary stage presence; his mere appearance on stage would incite hilarity.

sobbing near a white bed in the shadow of an alcove. The girl herself was stretched out, stiff, her hands joined in death, her smile lingering on her face. Her old aunt, the person kneeling at the mortuary couch, heard me and rose. She said without a trace of surprise, 'Oh, it's you. I was expecting you. She has just died, saying, "There he is! He's coming in now!"' "

Albert paused a few seconds and then resumed, "Don't get tired, Stéphanie dear. I still have other visions to tell you."

"One evening I was at a ball at the Austrian Embassy. A Russian princess waltzed passed me. Her tightly curled hair with its gold highlights, her bacchantian torso, and her heaving breast—for she was wearing a very revealing gown—reminded me suddenly of a poor streetwalker who had tempted me one evening. For a while I watched the lady caught up in the whirlwind of the waltz. But soon the thought went out of my mind, and I went into another drawing room. I was there staring at an enormous floral arrangement around a fountain when I felt on my hand some pearly drops falling in cadence. So I stepped back, but the drops still reached me, regular and insistent, keeping a kind of beat which seemed to come from some invisible hand. I saw my gloves getting wet, and by some strange effect of light, the drops of water seemed to have a bloody tinge. The longer I looked at them, the darker they got. I was distracted from this weird sight by a distant voice, which I alone could hear, but which I heard very distinctly.

" 'I want a tomb, I want a tomb,' the voice kept repeating. 'I was touched and sullied enough by flesh and bones while I was alive. I want to be alone in the grave. I want a tomb, I tell you, I want a tomb!'

"The voice saying all this came from a woman who looked like the Russian princess. But instead of wearing costly evening regalia, the woman who had come up and latched on to my arm, was wearing a faded black cloak and an equally faded and shapeless pink flowered hat. I recognized the prostitute, and I was ashamed in such a gathering. But she held fast and repeated without letting up, 'I want a tomb, I want a tomb.'

"Obsessed by this persistent vision, I left the ball and went back home. The voice would not cease. In the carriage taking me home, in my bed, in my dreams, she repeated all night long, 'I want a tomb, I want a tomb.'

"I rose at daybreak, exhausted and having such a mask of fright on my face you'd have thought I'd spent the night in the cemetery. I went out, hoping to get away from my vision and get a grip on myself in ordinary life and movement.

"It was very cold. I bounded down the quays. Feeling restored by my exercise, I kept walking. I found I had reached the grill of the Jardin des Plantes. I felt like going in, but some stronger will than mine made me turn away and put it into my head to go to see one of my old school friends, now resident at Salpêtrière. I entered this enormous hospital with its cheerful facade. Both the old women and the mad women were still asleep, so their decrepitude and wretchedness didn't clutter up the spacious, tree-planted courtyards. I got someone to take me to the resident's apartment. I found him busy at his daily task of dissection.

" 'You arrived just in time, my dear poet,' he laughed. 'Yesterday evening I received one of the most beautiful human subjects my scalpel has ever touched. Here, see for yourself.' And without further ado, he led me over to a mutilated body whose flanks he had just slit. The head and arms were missing, but the beauty of the breasts and torso made me cry out in fright. I had seen only two women with figures like that. It couldn't be the Russian princess. It had to be the poor streetwalker!

" 'Do you have that woman's head?' I asked.

" 'Yes, there in the basket.'

"I bent over. The head with its open eyes looked threateningly at me. Waves of her golden-glinted hair overflowed the basket.

"'You're afraid to touch it,' my friend smiled, and casually pulled out the livid head by its hair!

"My God, it was the very girl! That mouth, now so drawn, was the same which had called to me one evening and kissed me. And so I found her again, that wreckage of our barbarity and lust. An encounter like that makes a man feel the full horror of the selfishness he invests in debauchery.

"But I'm frightening you, my dear Marquise, and tonight you're going to dream of severed heads."

While Albert was talking, the carriage rolled into the Avenue de Neuilly and approached Port Maillot. He continued, "Here is a less sinister vision:

"It was the Twelfth Day of Christmas. I was eating with my family. All the guests were festive, and the table was groaning. As I bore to my lips a piece of excellent pheasant Albert Nattier had sent us from Fontainebleau, I received a jolt to my right arm which made me drop my fork. It was as if someone passing by had given me a shove, and yet no one had touched me. At the same instant I heard a distinct plaintive voice at my ear, 'I'm hungry, very, very hungry.'

"I knew this voice, and it made me shudder. It seemed to me that I could see standing behind my chair a thin little woman who kept repeating, 'I'm hungry, very, very hungry.'

"It was the shopworn shade of a fresh, laughing grisette whom I'd once loved for a few days. I did her portrait in both poetry and prose. I'd lost sight of her for years. No doubt she's died, I thought, and I fell into a reverie which made me forget entirely that I was celebrating a holiday at a family dinner. One of my relatives who was sitting next to me reproached me goodnaturedly for my distraction. I jumped as if I had come out of a trance, and I tried to eat. But the fork fell out of my hand again, removed by some electric force, and the voice murmured more lugubriously, 'I'm hungry, very, very hungry.'

"I rose from the table on the pretext of a sudden malaise. I went to my room and asked that I be left to rest by myself for a few hours. The shade and its voice pursued me, and since I couldn't get rid of this obsession, I decided to go try to find this poor grisette who was sending me this cry of distress. I climbed in a carriage and went looking for her at the house where I last knew her. She didn't live there anymore. But after gleaning bits of information from porters and old gossips, I learned where she had moved. While I was looking for her throughout the Latin Quarter, the shade and its voice kept me company. Impatient and worried, I told the driver to hurry over to the Quai de l'Ecole where my little shopgirl lived, but suddenly the shade left me and the voice hushed. This phenomenon indicated some change in fortunes or destiny of the grisette. When I reached the Quai de l'Ecole, I confronted a tall house, black and dilapidated. I was walking in the dark. It was after ten at night, and the Quarter was then very badly lighted. The only house which sent out a few beams in these shadows was the ground-floor shop of a rotisserie where the flaming fireplace lit up the street like a smithy's. Chickens, turkeys, and fried fish were heaped up in the open display case. Such a neighbor must have been a constant insult to my poor grisette's starvation.

"'How many times,' I said to myself, 'her mouth must have watered for these overloaded platters as she passed by. How often their nauseating smell must have seemed delicious to her!'

"I entered the shop and ordered the shopkeeper to send his best piece of poultry, some fried gudgeon, and some good wine and bread to Mademoiselle Suzette.

"'I know where it is,' he said, 'on the left, two houses from here, sixth floor, the door at the end of the hall.'

"His answer reassured me. It was obvious that my grisette didn't die from hunger every day since the rotisserie man knew her so well. I climbed contentedly up the steep dark stairway leading to the poor girl's mansard, and as I drew near, I heard her singing the happy refrain of a song she used to sing when I knew her. This time, I was thinking, the shade that appeared was not from a corpse, and without knocking, I gave a carefree push to the half-opened door.

" 'You're here already,' a fresh voice cooed. 'Come in, come in, I'm almost finished.'

"I saw the grisette standing, her head and neck craning toward a little mirror. She was wearing a Pierrette costume and at the moment was putting rouge and beauty patches on her cheeks.

"Next to her pitiful bed, nothing but a pallet, was a little table where I saw the remains of a roast chicken and some fried potatoes.

"I burst out laughing as I went in. The grisette turned around and recognized me.

" 'Why, it's you, Monsieur Albert,' she cried, throwing her arms around my neck. 'What a marvelous idea! If you wish, we will go to the Opera ball together. It will be ever so much nicer than going with that other man, whom I didn't even know until an hour ago.'

" 'What kind of a tale are you telling me' I asked.

" 'Well, it's like this. I should have guessed that you would come,' she added, 'I thought about you all day long . . . Because, didn't you know . . . I'll tell you everything right away, now that I'm cheerful and smart, it won't be so sad for you to hear. I've really and truly suffered. I've been nearly dead from hunger for a week. Every day I went out to ask for piece work from a clothing trimmer. Every day she told me people were out of work. Finally, a little while ago, as night fell, I was coming back discouraged, hardly able to stand up. I had had only a little water during the day. I thought about writing to you, then killing myself with coal smoke, when I suddenly realized that a gentleman was following me. I don't know if he was handsome or homely. He said he liked my looks. I told him he had to be joking. "By no means," he answered. "Do you want to go to the Opera ball?" "In my raggedy dress and dying from hunger?" I said sadly, "Oh, if that's all that's the matter, here take twenty francs, sweetheart, go get back your strength. I'll send you a pretty Pierrette costume, and I'll be at your place in an hour."

"'What should I have answered? My God, it was better than dying. I accepted, I gave him my address, I ordered a good supper at the rotisserie as I went past. I'm at your disposition, Monsieur Albert. This chicken is very tender. I'd scarcely eaten half of it when my pretty costume came. I put it on at once, overjoyed and thanking the good Lord. Doesn't it look good on me, and aren't I as pretty as I used to be, if a little on the thin side? Well, have you made up your mind? Take the place of my unknown admirer whom I don't love at all, and let's go the ball!'

"'No, my little Suzette,' I replied. 'You must keep your word, above all. Don't disappoint this lover's hopes, whoever he is. Here are some louis to use for a better place and some nicer clothing. A voice told me you were in trouble, and so I came.'

"She kissed me with tears in her eyes.

"'Come now, Mimi Pinson, no tears. Take up your tune and let me leave.'[5]

"'Will you come back at least?' she asked.

"'Maybe,' I answered and went back down.

"Crossing the corridor, I bumped into the rotisserie owner who was bearing in triumph the hearty supper I had ordered."

"Oh, you've got a good heart," I said to Albert when he finished this last tale where affection and high spirits went hand in hand.

5. Mimi Pinson is the name Musset gave this grisette in fiction and poetry. Best known is his novella "Mimi Pinson" (1846).

At that moment we were in the very lane where Albert had held me to his heart one evening.

"Stéphanie dear," he resumed, "you gave me my most recent vision. When I was frantically looking for you in the rubble of the Place du Carrousel, I thought I saw your shade, or rather I did see it, I'm sure, rising up behind me, pursuing me, crying, 'You've killed me! You've killed me!' For two nights I saw you dead. You were even more beautiful and looked transfigured. And you loved me despite my crime. Because death let you read in the depths of my heart, and by some miracle, which, alas, hasn't come true, you didn't love the other man any more. He, not I, was ruining himself like some beast in shameful, hidden acts. But he was not reaping that mortal gloom and pallor, which signify a great man's suffering in his fall. On the contrary, he was thriving in the mire: robust, ruddy-cheeked, smug and famous! He made women of easy virtue into goddesses so he could go on believing he was a god! And you, Stéphanie dear, dead and bewitching, saintly and white, you wound your arms tenderly around me, saying, 'You're the one I love. Carry me away. Your love doesn't frighten me now. In death souls know their mates. Yours was created for me!'

"That's the vision I had of you. I know it will fade. But for me it will drift into infinity where nothing is lost. I shall find it again one day, I am absolutely certain, and then I will be happy!"

He said nothing more. His eyes were closed as if to make sure he wouldn't see me, and he didn't take the hand I held out to him. He was still lost in his reverie. Suddenly a jolt of the carriage shook him. He opened his eyes and saw where we were. We had just reached the stone cross where on another evening he had spoken to me of the stars and galaxies scattered through the firmament. He kissed me without a word, with that solemn tenderness you put into your last kiss to a dying loved one.

"Thank you, my dearly beloved," he said, "for this last indulgence. Never again will you see me frightening, tyrannical, or mean. From this day forward it is as a devoted brother I put my hand in yours."

I took his hand and held it motionless in mine while, too moved to speak, we returned to Paris.

CHAPTER XXIV

WE PARTED without a word but with that inner tenderness that seems to grow and intensify the more it's contained. From that moment on he had taken a special place in my heart, a place for him alone. Sometimes I even thought it might be the first place. He became warmth and light for me, while Léonce was fading into the opaque and chilling shadows of the solitude he preferred to me.

The next evening in coming in I found on my work table a poem from Albert and a letter from Léonce. First I read Albert's poem. I was touched by these lines, so lilting and sweet, bringing back our stroll in the Jardin des Plantes:

Beneath those trees where I went in,
To pluck in turn a sprig of vervain,
Beneath those trees, where your sweet breath,
Vied with all the perfumes of spring,

The children were out, frolicking 'round
Me and my sorrow, as I thought of you,
And if my pain doesn't sound true,
At least you know my love's profound.

But who will know of my distress?
The woodland flowers perhaps can guess.
Tell me, Antelope, what's her name?

Ah, lion, you know, my fettered beast,
You saw me blanch when first she reached
To pat and stroke your tawny mane.[1]

Léonce's letter contained only one line which caught my attention. He announced that he would be coming to Paris in a week. The joy of such anticipation was not unmixed. The peace and certainty of that long love affair were beginning to dissipate.

I didn't answer that evening.

But, rereading Albert's quatorzain reminded me of my promise. So I composed the following lines to echo his:

Dear poet of mine,
Whenever you're sad
Think of me
Thinking of you.

Think of me rushing
To let you in
My son at my side
For the fun to begin.

Our place, our pace,
Our hearts, our home,
A special place,
That's yours alone.

1. This poem, which refers back to Chapter VI, was written by Musset after the near-tragedy at the Jardin des Plantes. See Maurice Allem, ed., Alfred de Musset, *Poésies complètes* (Paris: Gallimard Pléiade, 1939), pp. 549, 894–95.

So when you're sad,
Think of me
Rereading each line,
Dear poet of mine.

For three days I looked for him in vain. I knew through René that he was getting ready to take a trip. I wanted to see him one more time, for I was convinced that Léonce, once he came, would get the upper hand again. You can't break the chains you've worn for years in a single day. Love is like despotism: it imposes through its demands on a trusting woman's heart the way tyranny imposes through its presumption on a blind populace. The hour of insight comes sooner or later, and then rupture occurs between the deceiver and the deceived. For me that hour of illumination was about to blaze, but, alas, with the force of lightning.

I had promised Albert to deliver my poem in person. I knew that he went out every evening and that if I went around nine o'clock, I would find his apartment empty but still filled with his presence. What ineffable happiness it would be to sit down in his little reception room, leaf through his books, write my name at his desk to tell him "I came!" so that in coming back in he would find me there in spirit as I had found him. In imagining that sensation so warm, so pure, I couldn't resist my desire to experience it in fact. I went out by myself. The weather was cold, autumn showing its first inclemencies.

At Albert's door I rang with no hesitation. Since I knew he would be out, I would avoid any ambivalence in seeing him.

I told his servant I wanted to leave him a note. The man invited me in.

"Monsieur has just gone out, and everything is still where he left it," he added.

He was right. I saw the clothes Albert had just taken off scattered on a small sofa near the fireplace in the little reception room. The fire was crackling in the hearth. One lamp lit the mirror over the mantel; another through its shade projected a veiled glow on the desk. Some of the pages he had been writing, some opened letters, and a few blank sheets of paper were heaped in disarray. The pen he had used was still plunged in the inkstand. I seized it. I would have liked to steal the pen which had written such great and rare things! Perhaps it would communicate to me some spark of his genius, I mused, as I turned it around in my fingers. And sitting down in his chair, I let my mind wander.

First I took a clean envelope and enclosed the ballad I'd written the night before. Then, just as if the poet's dwelling contained some of his creative spirit, I felt the following lines mount from my heart to my mind. I wrote them down as rapidly as I could:

A VISIT TO SOMEONE ABSENT

It's cold; your fire's bright.
You dress; and then you leave.
And that's when I rush in,
Sit in your chair, seize your pen.

I will not write you much,
But enough to let you know
The love that makes you reel
Is one I'd like to feel.

But can you read this note?
My weeping may erase
What my hand can trace.

Yet why should I rewrite?
When to your eyes and soul
A tear will speak my role.

I didn't reread these lines. I hurried to put them in the envelope with the others. If I had reread them while I was there, perhaps I wouldn't have left them. There's always something exalted in poetic rhetoric which says something more than we meant. This is due the rhyme which sometimes forces us to use more affectionate words, and it is due also to the use of the familiar "you."

When I got back home, I was shivering with cold. All my blood had gone to my heart.

My son was struck by my pallor. My emotion had been stronger than I had expected.

CHAPTER XXV

I REALIZED how imprudent I had been when Albert came by the next day. He was beaming, "Stéphanie, what delightful poems!"

"Don't overdo it, Albert," I said with a smile, "and don't act like a father of a backward child. Without you, Albert, I would never have written a line of poetry in my life. My poor little lyrics derive from you, but they're not worthy of you."

"Let me at least take heart in the sentiment they reveal. That at least comes from you!"

"René told me you were going out of town, so I wanted to send you a somewhat affectionate adieu."

"I want to believe it was heartfelt," he continued. "Somewhere a poet has said that an adieu makes the return more dear. How happy I'm going to be when I get back from my little trip!"

"So where are you going?" I asked.

"To preside at the dedication of two statues.[1] It's a ludicrous idea which came to the mind, or rather the hundred or so minds, of a scholarly body to send someone like me, caprice and irony personified, to pronounce the citations and receive the official congratulations. It's true that Amelot is being sent along with me, and I shall leave to him all the serious—or rather the comic—part of the ceremony.[2]

"There is something serious for me in all this because it is public homage that is going to be paid Bernardin de Saint-Pierre by placing his statue opposite the storm-tossed ocean he described so well. You know, Marquise, that I don't feel pride on account of my works, but I do in my aspirations. They have always reached for the beautiful and ideal in art and have made me experience the creations of genius with delight. That is why even as a child, I was fired by the exquisite idyl in *Paul et Virginie*. My cult for the author meant that I couldn't refuse this assignment I've been given, although it is contrary to all my usual behavior. As for the other statue, it will be inaugurated by Amelot, by the natural successor of negative talent to whom homage equal to that given a man of genius will be paid. I see now the bewildered glances eternally cast upon that secluded seacoast with its figure of the true poet and that of the rhymester called the advocate of bourgeois poetry.[3] Such a contradiction in terms is like saying materialistic idealism! But good old Amelot won't countenance such mocking of the reputation of one of his forefathers in metermania. He is indeed the most committed exemplar of that puerile, pontifical, and banal literature of common sense which claims to have revived not the literature of the

1. This dedication took place in Le Havre, on August 9, 1852.

2. Amelot is Jacques Ancelot (1794–1854), one of the Académie Française judges, when Colet won the Académie poetry prize in 1843.

3. Casimir Delavigne (1793–1843) was a late Neoclassic dramatist.

Greeks, as I said to him once, but of the lesser Neoclassicists like Pradon."[4]

"You're going to have a fight, perhaps even on the way," I warned.

"No, no, have no fear," he reassured me. "Poetry means too much to me, for me ever to discuss it with Amelot. He's a *bon vivant* and knowing gourmet. I discuss only cuisine with him. But, Marquise, in coming over here, I made some wonderful plans."

"Tell me, Albert dear. What, for example?"

"You will come with us on the pretext of attending the inaugural festivities for the two statues, but actually to spend a few days alone with me on that beautiful ocean beach where we would enjoy our love so much."

"Don't tempt me in my poverty and solitude," I told him. "Until that day when I win my property suit, I have vowed to live like a recluse."

"Oh, but if you loved me just ever so little, that vow wouldn't stand up against the vow of my heart. But I'm talking like a Dorat romance.[5] Make up your mind quickly, my tyrannical Marquise, what you want to do with me. If I leave without you, I'm going to be bored. If I stay—and I'm really tempted—will you love me?"

"Go ahead with your trip," I said breezily, "and we'll see."

"You're an impenetrable sphinx. At least, I bear away your lyrics, and I can interrogate them."

"Will you be back soon?" I asked.

"Oh, of course, if I leave. And I will come running to take you by surprise when I return. So, watch out!"

He went off laughing, and I had some doubts as to whether he would really leave Paris.

4. Racine competitor Nicolas Pradon (1632–98) wrote a *Phèdre* also.

5. Claude-Joseph Dorat (1734–80) was a popular writer.

A View of Him

CHAPTER XXVI

I WAITED TWO DAYS before sending Marguerite over to his apartment. She was told he had left and would be gone at least a week.

As if Léonce had guessed that Albert had offered me an attractive seaside excursion, he wrote that he was moving up his arrival and that he proposed going to visit the beautiful Renaissance châteaux along the Loire, the ruins at Chantilly, and that shaded solitude at Rosny where a princess spent the only happy, peaceful days of her life.[1]

I was overwhelmed by the idea. It seduced me, lured me as a temptation to relax and be happy. For so long all distraction had been out of the question in the austere life I led. A few days of carefree travel were as alluring to me as the first ball for a girl. To enjoy this pause in my life of labor with the man I had loved so much and loved still and who must love me since he had thought up this delightful diversion—oh, it was a feast for the soul hard to resist! I didn't feel the same reluctance with Léonce as with Albert. I had belonged to Léonce. I belonged to him still, and despite some doubts and heartaches, my love was still intact. I just needed hope and illusion to rebuild it in my heart.

As the hour to bring us together grew near, something took hold of me, setting me on fire, making me dizzy.

Libertines claim that possession brings detachment. But for those who are loved by the soul as well, the contrary is true. A union of the senses, which has merely been the confirmation of a spiritual union, seems to bind two lovers eternally. That's why marriage consecrating true love is so beautiful and pure.

How could I forget those delights, I might even say those inti-

1. Mary Queen of Scots (1542–87), who lived at Rosny, was first married to François II of France.

mate familiarities? Is a child lewd if he has a happy memory of falling asleep on his nurse's breast?

What purpose is served by an artificial morality that tries, like Solomon's false mother, to cut the human being in two? The soul and body complete each other. They mutually reverberate their various emotions. Just as the memory of a betrayal or sorrow fills the eyes with tears, the memory of a joy brings a smile to the face and that of a noble action makes the brow beam. Even the mere image, suddenly recalled, of a dangerous fall or the anguishing pangs of childbirth, depresses and terrifies us. So, too, the pleasant image of a delectable caress or a voluptuous quiver revives and thrills the mind, communicating, so to speak, the exciting counterpart of what presumably the body alone would have felt!

Let's not separate what nature and God have so closely intertwined. The casuists, who have made a virtue out of complete chastity, have only managed to produce deceptive appearances in a hypocritical society. It is high time to dare to glorify the sacred harmony of the indivisible bond between the emotions of body and soul!

I had understood all of that instinctively before being convinced of it by reflection. Sincere and complete love teaches more on the subject than any philosophical argument.

Just the thought of seeing Léonce again, and I felt reawakening all the ecstasy he had brought me in the past. It was an involuntary recall. A magnetic influence, so to speak. His approach had me in its spell. He was still far away, and yet his breath surrounded me, hovered around me.

However, I did not write him how enchanted I was by his proposed trip. I didn't even know if I would take him up on it. But I certainly savored my longing. It became the dream of my nights and the reverie of my days. So much so that one morning, verses expressing all the details of this dream of love and liberation suddenly escaped from my heart, like a bird, singing and frolicking in the sunshine:

WHERE ROYAL LOVE RESIDES

With their long avenues,
And their silent statues,
Reflected in basin and pool,
Their large parks, shaded and deep,
Their hothouses of tropical flowers,
Their moats bridged by rustic bowers,
These châteaux have a room for us.
Let's go in and make it ours!

Arm in arm, our souls entranced,
Let's spend our blissful hours in strolls
Beneath the trellised garden arbors,
And into woods where swift deer roam;
Let's cross currents of rushing foam
On a skiff slumbering on the banks.
These châteaux have a room for us.
Let's go in and give our thanks!

Let's go visit the galleries past
The portraits in their oval frames,
With heaving breasts, the noble dames,
Their cavaliers in haughty pose,
Radiant in death, alive in art,
Exuding a hint of amber and rose.
These châteaux have a room for us.
Let's go in and take our part!

On the bench in the orangeries,
In the stable of the métairies,
Where queens played dairy maid,
In the gazebos or in the chalets,
Or on the terraces of the galleries,

We can talk to our hearts' content.
These châteaux have a room for us.
Let's go in; it's heaven sent!

Beneath the pink jasper portal
Where love still smiles and sleeps,
Let us seek the mystic bath,
The bath adored by god and mortal.
Diana and her startled nymphs
Still run across the marble frieze.
These châteaux have a room for us.
Let's go in and take our ease!

In the wary woods let's read
Poets fêting love's happiness.
The murmur of the verdant boughs
Will blend with music in the verse
That pour out words of love to bless
With mellow notes and harmonies.
These châteaux have a room for us.
Let's go in for these ecstasies!

In sweet ravines with slopes inviting,
The banks of periwinkle and moss,
Will make soft beds veiled from the day.
Moans of love mount to our lips,
The shade exciting, the air igniting
As into one God melts two souls.
These châteaux have a room for us.
Let's go in and play our roles!

Above our gaze the sky unfurls,
Beyond our gaze the lake expands.
We see happy pairs of swans
Furrow blue circles in the waves.
Shores, hills, and valleys frame

A perfect setting for our delight.
These châteaux have a room for us.
Let's go in and spend the night!

Chantilly sleeps beneath its oaks.
No queens rule Rosny or Chambord.
For lovers are the masters now,
And savor each new magic hour.
Where royalty has disappeared,
Laughing loves come back to life.
These châteaux have a room for us.
Let me go with you and be your wife!

I would hardly dare claim that something of Albert's soul and memory had made its way into that song! But would I have written it if I hadn't known him? No, because without him I would never have known the language of poetry, which his genius had taught me. Léonce did not know it at all, and I doubt whether his nature, devoid of inspiration and flexibility was even susceptible of penetrating such refined delicacy and exquisite sensitivity.

When I finished these stanzas, I kept on repeating them, even humming them to an old tune that came back to me.

Finally, one evening I received a letter from Léonce announcing his arrival for the next day. I sent my son to visit one of his uncles who lived in the country near Paris. The child was thrilled to leave. Any new distraction delighted him. I knew he didn't like Léonce, and I would have suffered if I disturbed his guileless heart and seen a notion of struggle beginning to form.

The next day came. I decorated my poor apartment with flowers as soon as it was day. I adorned myself with his favorite colors. I made everything look festive—as I always did when he was to come.

I was expecting him at dinnertime. I was so agitated that I

couldn't do anything. Sometimes the hours seemed too slow, sometimes too fast. I would pick up a book and try to read, but it was futile. I could only reread my own poem which contained a prelude to my happiness. Then I put it on the table and sat by it, my head propped up on my elbows. I watched the clock. I said to myself, "He'll be here soon," but in spite of myself, Albert's image overlaid his. "He will sit there, where Albert sat, on that cushion where he wept and told me he loved me." And that seemed like a sacrilege to me. I paled and shuddered at the least noise. It seemed to me that I was going to be taken by surprise, condemned by someone who had rights over my life. I had an intuition I should run away, as if some dreadful danger or great sorrow was in store for me. Then I would smile away that childish terror. I would think again on the happiness bound to return. I would put my thoughts together again like a composition and repulse the phantom that had just darkened my happiness.

My clock struck five. "He'll be at my side in one hour," I was breathless. I looked at myself in the mirror, pleased that I looked gorgeous. The bell rang. I gasped, "He's here! He wanted to surprise me by coming an hour early!"

I went running in, meeting Marguerite who was just opening the door. I let out a shriek of surprise, almost of fright. It was Albert instead!

He must have believed that I had shrieked from delight because his face lost nothing of its happy expression. He looked healthier. His complexion was a better color, and his beautiful eyes were sparkling. In one hand he held a little gilded cage with a pretty pair of darling parakeets, the kind called "inseparable," and in the other a silvered filigree cage with two fluttering hummingbirds.

"Where is your dear child?" he asked. "I'd like for him to take these birds off my hands. They'll distract him, so I'll have my hands free to clasp yours and kiss you."

"The little fellow wanted to go to the country," I replied blushing.

"But what about you?" he continued. "Are you going out? You're so dressed up."

"Yes," I stammered. "I'm dining out."

While we were exchanging these remarks, we crossed the dining room. He placed the two elegant cages on the buffet where the tropical birds began their amorous cavorting. Then he held out his arms to me, "I can't restrain myself another minute, dearest. I had to return to see you and hear you. Come on. Say something. What did you do during my absence? Why are you going out and why didn't you save today for me as I was expecting you to."

He was kissing my hands, my forehead. He couldn't take his eyes off me.

I've never seen your face so expressive, so much soul is visible," he continued when we sat down in my study. "Is your beauty due my return? You didn't forget me? Do you love me just a little?" And he got down in a cajoling pose on the cushion where he had so often sat.

I was stunned speechless. How could I be so cruel as to disillusion him? How could I tell him who was coming? Was I going to have to resign myself to lying?

"Why don't you answer me, Stéphanie dear?" he resumed, still studying me kindly.

"I'm still overwhelmed by this sweet surprise, and so very sorry, believe me, not to be free to fête your return. But I'm expected. A family affair. I simply have to go out. I'll see you tomorrow, Albert dear."

I said all this very fast, almost staccato. The clock was ticking away, and in a sense I was shivering to its rhythm. Léonce was going to arrive.

"What kind of Marais rentier are you eating with?"[2] Albert laughed, "Leaving for dinner at 5:15! Don't leave me so soon. Let's talk a little while longer, or I'm going to imagine that you're unfaithful to me. Is it really true," he persisted tenderly, "that you made yourself so beautiful for some aged relative? No, I want it to be for me. Come, be your usual kindhearted self and write some excuse and let me finish this day with you. You won't be bored, I can promise you that. Amelot gave me quite a repertory! As soon as we got in the compartment, the massive creature said, 'I feel full of verve. My spirit's soaring. Just watch it run!' 'Well, my good man,' I replied, 'let it run. I won't try to catch it.' Come now, Marquise, I feel like beginning my recitative immediately and keeping you enthralled by curiosity like the sultan in *A Thousand and One Nights*. I've some poems to read you, because I dreamed up some for you along the sea shore. And you, my dear, haven't you made for me one of those lyrics you do so well?"

While talking, his hand was playing with the papers on the table. He espied my stanzas for "Where Royal Love Resides" and seized them. I wanted to keep him from reading them, but he clutched them tightly in his hand, crying gleefully, "Ah ha, the schoolgirl already dares to run from her master? She has no use for his criticism?"

I made no more effort to avert anything. I didn't know what to say or what to do. I didn't even dare look at him while he was reading.

"I like these lines," he said quickly when he had finished skimming them. "I am proud of you for composing them, but, Stéphanie, are they really for me?"

2. Marais was a section of town houses in the third and fourth arrondissements occupied chiefly by individuals on fixed incomes. Albert is implying that Stéphanie is going to see rigid persons of somewhat advanced years.

"Without you I could never have written them," I replied, trembling and ashamed of my jesuitical subterfuge.

"But are they for me? Are they for me?" he repeated, increasingly dubious. "Oh, Stéphanie, if these lines are for someone else, you know, don't you, that you are like the child who kills his father with the weapons the latter taught him how to use! You don't want to deceive me, you who've never lied. Come on, tell me, who are these for?"

I got up. I was pale and distraught as if I'd committed a crime. Seizing his hand, I said, "Albert dear, don't ask me about it until tomorrow. Tomorrow I will be sure what my heart wants, but today I must leave you. I must go this very instant. Good-bye."

He didn't say a word. His eyes had rested on the large bouquets on the mantel. He looked at them, smiling ironically. He bowed in farewell without taking my hand, and then he left. I went with him saying, "We'll talk tomorrow."

When we crossed the dining room, by one of fatal coincidences of petty details that almost always jolt and wound our feelings, Marguerite was beginning to set the table. She had just put a cherry dessert between the two pretty American bird cages on the buffet. Albert had seen everything and realized I was expecting someone for dinner.

"And so farewell," he said when he reached the threshold of the outer door.

I knew I couldn't say now, "We'll talk tomorrow."

A carriage had just stopped in front of the house. A man was rushing into the courtyard. Almost immediately I heard steps on the stairway, and while Albert was beginning to go down, I saw, as I leaned over the top of the banister, Léonce who was coming up![3]

3. Flaubert came to Paris on August 10, 1852. Musset would have still been in Le Havre for the dedication ceremonies on August 9, 1852. This poignant

I drew back, terrified by that encounter. I rushed back in, closing the door behind me. I tore to the window overlooking the courtyard to see Albert pass one last time.

I shall never forget the dark, heartsick look he threw in my direction as he raised his head. I don't know whether he saw me, but a bitter smile passed across his face. I was tempted to call him back. My voice seemed strangled. A sob was choking me.

At that moment Léonce rang. And I fled to my room to hide my tears.

CHAPTER XXVII

MORE THAN TWO YEARS had passed since that day which I cannot erase from my memory. What I suffered during that time I will never reveal. I want to cover those two years with a black crepe like those used by patrician families in Venice to cover portraits of relatives condemned to death.

Of that love which had seized my entire soul by surprise and sortilege, of that love to which I sacrificed Albert, nothing re-

---

encounter could not have occurred in real life. Nor did Flaubert and Colet tour the châteaux country at that time.

On the other hand, Joseph F. Jackson's careful collating of Colet's verifiable activities two years later (1854) indicates that Colet's relationship with Cousin, Flaubert, and Vigny could have led to a "scène de surprise" (p. 218). Her relationship with Alfred de Vigny (1797–1863), in Jackson's opinion, might have been partly a misguided attempt to make Flaubert jealous. But with Flaubert's closest male friend Louis Bouilhet (1821–69), as her chief go-between, no happy ending was ever possible. Bouilhet was as much as an exploiter as Flaubert.

mained. You would have said that struck by Albert's fateful prediction, that love had decomposed day by day.

I had seen the proud and arrogant recluse deny all his doctrines on art and love one by one and sell his opinions for small change—and for his least lofty lusts.

When conscience no longer guides our actions, when self-interest and vanity become the spirit's sole motives, then any notion of honor and idealism disappears. Life then has no other constraint than the prudence of escaping punishment from the law. From thence, unrecognized traitors, cruel voluptuaries who hide their murderous instincts behind a smile, agitators of human affairs, ready for any crime, are decorated in public with the title of statesmen.

In seeing the man I had placed so high fall like this, I received the counter-blow of his fall. A mysterious malady took hold of me. I was wasting away in my prime. And soon I realized from the sadness of my friends and the hesitancy of my doctors that I was lost.

Albert had never tried to see me again, and I hadn't dared call him back. Several times he met my son out walking. He would stop the boy to ask him not to forget his old friend, and without mentioning me, would kiss him tenderly.

I knew through René that Albert was dying and looking increasingly to forget his pain in corrosive and fatal distractions. I felt an unconquerable desire to see him again, to speak to him, to feel again his hand in mine.

One April day when the sky was blue and the temperature almost mild, I climbed into a carriage to go to the Tuileries. I sat down on the terrace along the water and feeling that the air had given me strength, I wanted to try to return home on foot. As I was slowly crossing the bridge at the Place de la Concorde, I espied Albert standing against the parapet on the right. He was leaning against the balustrade to watch a boat coming down the Seine from Saint-Cloud. He didn't see me approaching, and I was almost touching him before he saw me. I pulled away the veil from my face and placed my hand on his. He raised his head and looked at me without appearing to recognize me at first. His eyes were dull, and his lips so white, you might have wondered whether he were really alive.

"Ah, it's you," he said, shuddering, coming to himself. "It's really you. What they told me was true: you really have been sick."

I shook his hand without answering. We walked painfully side by side to the end of the bridge. There he stopped.

"Albert," I asked, trembling. "Won't you come as far as my house? Oh, please, do come."

"What would be the point? I'm completing life, and you're commencing death. We would be sad just looking at each other, without being able to say anything consoling. Oh, my poor Marquise, there is no time left for us to love each other."

"Albert, love is not bound to life and time. You told me that yourself once, and now I feel and believe it."

"No reflection, no regret," he retorted, forcing a laugh. "Let's keep up our courage for *leaving*." He stressed the word, then, turning back on the bridge, "Farewell, my dear, the first one who gets well will go see the other."

I wanted to keep him a moment longer by taking his hand, but he had dropped it to his side.

We parted like two shades, meeting for a moment, then fading, destined never to meet again.

I took a few hesitant, tottering steps. Then I stopped. As I rested against the grill of the Palais Bourbon, I saw through my tears Albert slowing moving to the other end of the bridge.

CHAPTER XXVIII

HE DIED on a beautiful night in May when all nature was beginning to come to life again.[1] He passed away in his sleep, without a struggle.

When I learned the sinister news, I had been in bed for a week. I made an effort to get up. I wanted to see him again before he was put in his shroud and press my lips on his cold brow. I was seized with a coughing fit so long and violent that I fainted. I had to go back to bed and weep for him from afar.

I sent my son and Marguerite to the interment. For the first time I decided to explain death to my child. He listened, attentive and thoughtful, then said gravely, "My father left us. Albert has just left us, and now you want to leave me, too, for I can certainly see that you are sick and pale like them. And I will be left all by myself."

"Oh, no, my dear child," I cried, clasping him in my thin arms. "I will live for you!"

"You said, 'I will!' " he replied smiling angelically, "But don't go playing with death the way you often play with me when I am stubborn and you give in."

"No, no," I said, hugging him more tightly. "I will obey you alone."

He and Marguerite returned from Albert's funeral, aggrieved and amazed. "There were only a few friends and a few weeping women in mourning at the church," he reported.

He and Marguerite had sat apart in a chapel, and he had said a prayer for Albert. After leaving the church, they watched the procession. Several people around them expressed surprise that state

1. Alfred de Musset died on May 2, 1857.

honors were not paid and that the princes of the hour had not sent their carriages to accompany the coffin.

"I was really heartsick to see him go away to the cemetery like that almost all by himself, like a pauper. Please, Mama, try to get well soon, so we can put some nice flowers on his tomb!"

Alas, I didn't get well, and my poor child was so terrified seeing me fail that I decided to send him to boarding school to remove him from the sight of my suffering and pain. But he languished away from me, refused to play, and paid attention only to his studies. When vacation time approached, I remember that the day he was to be brought home, I made a violent effort to stand up. I drank a little wine—thinking of Albert—and dragged myself into the garden. At the very place where we are now, I sat down in a deep armchair. My pale head rested back on the cushions, and, shivering, I warmed myself in the burning August sun.

Albert had been dead only three months. A few more months, I thought, and I would join him. As for the *other*, I didn't want to think about him. But that love affair in ruins still weighed upon my soul, smothering it, you might say, beneath its debris. I had been crushed by an arm of inert stone, brutal and unconcerned about my feelings. The ponderous Egyptian colossi which time has eventually uprooted in the ruins of Thebes have no consciousness when they crush the Nubian who has sat down in their shade.

My son arrived around noon. On a table near me I had set out a nice watch and an album where I had mounted a sketch of Albert and inscribed passages from his most pure and beautiful works. The child ran towards me, holding in his arms the school prize crowns and books he had received. I pulled him on my lap and held him in my arms a long time without speaking. I couldn't contain my tears. And so he wouldn't see them, I placed his crowns on his head and playfully pulled them down over his eyes. Then, pointing to the watch and album, I said, "See if there's something you like . . ."

He to took off his crowns impatiently and pushed away my presents also, and clasping his hands behind my neck, he exploded with anxiety, "That's not all I want."

"And what do you want, darling?"

"I want you to stay alive for me. I want you to become beautiful and strong again, the way you were three years ago, when I was little. Now I understand everything," he added, glaring, revealing his inflexible adolescent pride. "I have figured out who's been killing you, and if you die, understand, well, one day I will kill him."

"Be still, be still," I cried, pressing him to my breast.

I was ashamed of my sorrow, and in front of my son I blushed for my love.

Love is great and holy when it completes life, but if it leads to annihilation of our self-esteem, it degrades us.

I raised my head to confront the proud expression of my noble child, and I said, "Do not worry. I will get well. Let's not spoil this fine day with tears. Look at this picture of Albert."

I have lived for my son. As the wound of my ignoble and blind love closed, the image of Albert shone ever more brightly in my heart. I saw him again young, handsome, passionate, and in death I loved him.

FINIS